"Golden Wings" by **Boris Vallejo**
FROM THE BOOKS OF

THE CHRONICLES OF AMBER

VOLUME I

The Chronicles of Amber

VOLUME I

Nine Princes in Amber
The Guns of Avalon

ROGER ZELAZNY

NELSON DOUBLEDAY, INC.
Garden City, New York

NINE PRINCES IN AMBER
Copyright © 1970 by Roger Zelazny

THE GUNS OF AVALON
Copyright © 1972 by Roger Zelazny

Published by arrangement with
Doubleday & Company, Inc.
245 Park Avenue
New York, New York 10017

Printed in the United States of America

CONTENTS

THE CHRONICLES OF AMBER

VOLUME I

NINE PRINCES IN AMBER

I

It was starting to end, after what seemed most of eternity to me.

I attempted to wriggle my toes, succeeded. I was sprawled there in a hospital bed and my legs were done up in plaster casts, but they were still mine.

I squeezed my eyes shut, and opened them, three times.

The room grew steady.

Where the hell was I?

Then the fogs were slowly broken, and some of that which is called memory returned to me. I recalled nights and nurses and needles. Every time things would begin to clear a bit, someone would come in and jab me with something. That's how it had been. Yes. Now, though, I was feeling halfway decent. They'd have to stop.

Wouldn't they?

The thought came to assail me: *Maybe not.*

Some natural skepticism as to the purity of all human motives came and sat upon my chest. I'd been over-narcotized, I suddenly knew. No real reason for it, from the way I felt, and no reason for them to stop now, if they'd been paid to keep it up. So play it cool and stay dopey, said a voice which was my worst, if wiser, self.

So I did.

A nurse poked her head in the door about ten minutes later, and I was, of course, still stacking Z's. She went away.

By then, I reconstructed a bit of what had occurred.

I had been in some sort of accident, I remembered vaguely. What had happened after that was still a blur; and as to what had happened before, I had no inkling whatsoever. But I had first been in a hospital and then brought to this place, I remembered. Why? I didn't know.

However, my legs felt pretty good. Good enough to hold me up, though I didn't know how much time had lapsed since their breaking —and I knew they'd been broken.

So I sat up. It took me a real effort, as my muscles were very tired. It was dark outside and a handful of stars were standing naked beyond the window. I winked back at them and threw my legs over the edge of the bed.

I was dizzy, but after a while it subsided and I got up, gripping the rail at the head of the bed, and I took my first step.

Okay. My legs held me.

So, theoretically, I was in good enough shape to walk out.

I made it back to bed, stretched out and thought. I was sweating and shaking. Visions of sugar plums, etc.

In the State of Denmark there was the odor of decay. . . .

It had been an accident involving an auto, I recalled. One helluva one. . . .

Then the door opened, letting in light, and through slits beneath my eyelashes I saw a nurse with a hypo in her hand.

She approached my bedside, a hippy broad with dark hair and big arms.

Just as she neared, I sat up.

"Good evening," I said.

"Why—good evening," she replied.

"When do I check out?" I asked.

"I'll have to ask Doctor."

"Do so," I said.

"Please roll up your sleeve."

"No thanks."

"I have to give you an injection."

"No you don't. I don't need it."

"I'm afraid that's for Doctor to say."

"Then send him around and let him say it. But in the meantime, I will not permit it."

"I'm afraid I have my orders."

"So did Eichmann, and look what happened to him," and I shook my head slowly.

"Very well," she said. "I'll have to report this. . . ."

"Please do," I said, "and while you're at it, tell him I've decided to check out in the morning."

"That's impossible. You can't even walk—and there were internal injuries. . . ."

"We'll see," said I. "Good night."

She swished out of sight without answering.

So I lay there and mulled. It seemed I was in some sort of private place—so somebody was footing the bill. Whom did I know? No visions of relatives appeared behind my eyes. Friends either. What did that leave? Enemies?

I thought a while.

Nothing.

Nobody to benefact me thus.

I'd gone over a cliff in my car, and into a lake, I suddenly remembered. And that was all I remembered.

I was . . .

I strained and began to sweat again.

I didn't know *who* I was.

But to occupy myself, I sat up and stripped away all my bandages. I seemed all right underneath them, and it seemed the right thing to do. I broke the cast on my right leg, using a metal strut I'd removed from the head of the bed. I had a sudden feeling that I had to get out in a hurry, that there was something I had to do.

I tested my right leg. It was okay.

I shattered the cast on my left leg, got up, went to the closet.

No clothes there.

Then I heard the footsteps. I returned to my bed and covered over the broken casts and the discarded bandages.

The door swung inward once again.

Then there was light all around me, and there was a beefy guy in a white jacket standing with his hand on the wall switch.

"What's this I hear about you giving the nurse a hard time?" he asked, and there was no more feigning sleep.

"I don't know," I said. "What is it?"

That troubled him for a second or two, said the frown, then, "It's time for your shot."

"Are you an M.D.?" I asked.

"No, but I'm authorized to give you a shot."

"And I refuse it," I said, "as I've a legal right to do. What's it to you?"

"You'll have your shot," he said, and he moved around to the left side of the bed. He had a hypo in one hand, which had been out of sight till then.

It was a very foul blow, about four inches below the belt buckle, I'd say, and it left him on his knees.

"—— ——!" he said, after a time.

"Come within spitting distance again," I said, "and see what happens."

"We've got ways to deal with patients like you," he gasped.

So I knew the time had come to act.

"Where are my clothes?" I said.

"___ ___!" he repeated.

"Then I guess I'll have to take yours. Give them to me."

It became boring with the third repetition, so I threw the bedclothes over his head and clobbered him with the metal strut.

Within two minutes, I'd say, I was garbed all in white, the color of Moby Dick and vanilla ice cream. Ugly.

I shoved him into the closet and looked out the latticed window. I saw the Old Moon with the New Moon in her arms, hovering above a row of poplars. The grass was silvery and sparkled. The night was bargaining weakly with the sun. Nothing to show, for me, where this place was located. I seemed to be on the third floor of the building though, and there was a cast square of light off to my left and low, seeming to indicate a first floor window with someone awake behind it.

So I left the room and considered the hallway. Off to the left, it ended against a wall with a latticed window, and there were four more doors, two on either side. Probably they let upon more rooms like my own. I went and looked out the window and saw more grounds, more trees, more night, nothing new. Turning, I headed in the other direction.

Doors, doors, doors, no lights from under any of them, the only sounds my footsteps from the too big borrowed shoes.

Laughing Boy's wristwatch told me it was five forty-four. The metal strut was inside my belt, under the white orderly jacket, and it rubbed against my hip bone as I walked. There was a ceiling fixture about every twenty feet, casting about forty watts of light.

I came to a stairway, off to the right, leading down. I took it. It was carpeted and quiet.

The second floor looked like my own, rows of rooms, so I continued on.

When I reached the first floor I turned right, looking for the door with light leaking out from beneath it.

I found it, way up near the end of the corridor, and I didn't bother to knock.

The guy was sitting there in a garish bathrobe, at a big shiny desk, going over some sort of ledger. This was no ward room. He looked up at me with burning eyes all wide and lips swelling toward a yell they didn't reach, perhaps because of my determined expression. He stood, quickly.

I shut the door behind me, advanced, and said:

"Good morning. You're in trouble."

People must always be curious as to trouble, because after the three seconds it took me to cross the room, his words were:

"What do you mean?"

"I mean," I said, "that you're about to suffer a lawsuit for holding me incommunicado, and another one for malpractice, for your indiscriminate use of narcotics. I'm already suffering withdrawal symptoms and might do something violent. . . ."

He stood up.

"Get out of here," he said.

I saw a pack of cigarettes on his desk. I helped myself and said, "Sit down and shut up. We've got things to talk about."

He sat down, but he didn't shut up:

"You're breaking several regulations," he said.

"So we'll let a court decide who's liable," I replied. "I want my clothes and my personal effects. I'm checking out."

"You're in no condition—"

"Nobody asked you. Pony up this minute, or answer to the law."

He reached toward a button on his desk, but I slapped his hand away.

"Now!" I repeated. "You should have pressed that when I came in. It's too late now."

"Mr. Corey, you're being most difficult. . . ."

Corey?

"I didn't check in here," I said, "but I damn well have a right to check me out. And now's the time. So let's get about it."

"Obviously, you're in no condition to leave this institution," he replied. "I cannot permit it. I am going to call for someone to escort you back to your room and put you to bed."

"Don't try it," I said, "or you'll find out what condition I'm in. Now, I've several questions. The first one's Who checked me in, and who's footing my bill at this place?"

"Very well," he sighed, and his tiny, sandy mustaches sagged as low as they could.

He opened a drawer, put his hand inside, and I was wary.

I knocked it down before he had the safety catch off: a .32 automatic, very neat; Colt. I snapped the catch myself when I retrieved it from the desk top; and I pointed it and said: "You will answer my questions. Obviously you consider me dangerous. You may be right."

He smiled weakly, lit a cigarette himself, which was a mistake, if he intended to indicate aplomb. His hands shook.

"All right, Corey—if it will make you happy," he said, "your sister checked you in."

"?" thought I.

"Which sister?" I asked.

"Evelyn," he said.

No bells. So, "That's ridiculous. I haven't seen Evelyn in years," I said. "She didn't even know I was in this part of the country."

He shrugged.

"Nevertheless . . ."

"Where's she staying now? I want to call her," I said.

"I don't have her address handy."

"Get it."

He rose, crossed to a filing cabinet, opened it, riffled, withdrew a card.

I studied it. *Mrs. Evelyn Flaumel.* . . . The New York address was not familiar either, but I committed it to memory. As the card said, my first name was Carl. Good. More data.

I stuck the gun in my belt beside the strut then, safety back on, of course.

"Okay," I told him. "Where are my clothes, and what're you going to pay me?"

"Your clothes were destroyed in the accident," he said, "and I must tell you that your legs were definitely broken—the left one in two places. Frankly, I can't see how you're managing to stay on your feet. It's only been two weeks—"

"I always heal fast," I said. "Now, about the money. . . ."

"What money?"

"The out-of-court settlement for my malpractice complaint, and the other one."

"Don't be ridiculous!"

"Who's being ridiculous? I'll settle for a thousand, cash, right now."

"I won't even discuss such a thing."

"Well, you'd better consider it—and win or lose, think about the name it will give this place if I manage enough pretrial publicity. I'll certainly get in touch with the AMA, the newspapers, the—"

"Blackmail," he said, "and I'll have nothing to do with it."

"Pay now, or pay later, after a court order," I said. "I don't care. But it'll be cheaper this way."

If he came across, I'd know my guesses were right and there was something crooked involved.

He glared at me, I don't know how long.

Finally, "I haven't got a thousand here," he said.

"Name a compromise figure," I said.

After another pause, "It's larceny."

"Not if it's cash-and-carry, Charlie. So, call it."

"I might have five hundred in my safe."

"Get it."

He told me, after inspecting the contents of a small wall safe, there was four-thirty, and I didn't want to leave fingerprints on the safe, just to check him out. So I accepted and stuffed the bills into my side pocket.

"Now what's the nearest cab company that serves this place?"

He named it, and I checked in the phone book, which told me I was upstate.

I made him dial it and call me a cab, because I didn't know the name of the place and didn't want him to know the condition of my memory. One of the bandages I had removed *had* been around my head.

While he was making the arrangement I heard him name the place: it was called Greenwood Private Hospital.

I snubbed out my cigarette, picked up another, and removed perhaps two hundred pounds from my feet by resting in a brown upholstered chair beside his bookcase.

"We wait here and you'll see me to the door," I said.

I never heard another word out of him.

II

It was about eight o'clock when the cab deposited me on a random corner in the nearest town. I paid off the driver and walked for around twenty minutes. Then I stopped in a diner, found a booth and had juice, a couple of eggs, toast, bacon, and three cups of coffee. The bacon was too greasy.

After giving breakfast a good hour, I started walking, found a clothing store, and waited till its nine-thirty opening.

I bought a pair of slacks, three sport shirts, a belt, some underwear, and a pair of shoes that fit. I also picked up a handkerchief, a wallet, and pocket comb.

Then I found a Greyhound station and boarded a bus for New York. No one tried to stop me. No one seemed to be looking for me.

Sitting there, watching the countryside all autumn-colored and tickled by brisk winds beneath a bright, cold sky, I reviewed everything I knew about myself and my circumstances.

I had been registered at Greenwood as Carl Corey by my sister Evelyn Flaumel. This had been subsequent to an auto accident some fifteen or so days past, in which I had suffered broken bones which no longer troubled me. I didn't remember Sister Evelyn. The Greenwood people had been instructed to keep me passive, were afraid of the law when I got loose and threatened them with it. Okay. Someone was afraid of me, for some reason. I'd play it for all it was worth.

I forced my mind back to the accident, dwelled upon it till my head hurt. It was no accident. I had that impression, though I didn't know why. I would find out, and someone would pay. Very, very much would they pay. An anger, a terrible one, flared within the middle of my body. Anyone who tried to hurt me, to use me, did so at his own peril and now he would receive his due, whoever he was, this one. I felt a strong desire to kill, to destroy whoever had been responsible, and I knew that it was not the first time in my life that I had felt this thing, and I knew, too, that I followed through on it in the past. More than once.

I stared out the window, watching the dead leaves fall.

When I hit the Big City, the first thing I did was to get a shave and haircut in the nearest clip joint, and the second was to change my shirt and undershirt in the men's room, because I can't stand hair down my back. The .32 automatic, belonging to the nameless individual at Greenwood, was in my right-hand jacket pocket. I suppose that if Greenwood or my sister wanted me picked up in a hurry, a Sullivan violation would come in handy. But I decided to hang onto it. They'd have to find me first, and I wanted a reason. I ate a quick lunch, rode subways and buses for an hour, then got a cab to take me out to the Westchester address of Evelyn, my nominal sister and hopeful jogger of memories.

Before I arrived, I'd already decided on the tack I'd take.

So, when the door to the huge old place opened in response to my knock, after about a thirty-second wait, I knew what I was going to say. I had thought about it as I'd walked up the long, winding, white gravel driveway, between the dark oaks and the bright maples, leaves crunching beneath my feet, and the wind cold on my fresh-scraped neck within the raised collar of my jacket. The smell of my hair tonic mingled with a musty odor from the ropes of ivy that crowded all over the walls of that old, brick place. There was no sense of familiarity. I didn't think I had ever been here before.

I had knocked, and there had come an echo.

Then I'd jammed my hands into my pockets and waited.

When the door opened, I had smiled and nodded toward the mole-flecked maid with a swarthy complexion and a Puerto Rican accent.

"Yes?" she said.

"I'd like to see Mrs. Evelyn Flaumel, please."

"Who shall I say is calling?"

"Her brother Carl."

"Oh come in please," she told me.

I entered a hallway, the floor a mosaic of tiny salmon and turquoise tiles, the walls mahogany, a trough of big-leafed green things occupying a room divider to my left. From overhead, a cube of glass and enamel threw down a yellow light.

The gal departed, and I sought around me for something familiar.

Nothing.

So I waited.

Presently, the maid returned, smiled, nodded, and said, "Please follow me. She will see you in the library."

I followed, up three stairs and down a corridor past two closed doors. The third one to my left was open, and the maid indicated I should enter it. I did so, then paused on the threshold.

Like all libraries, it was full of books. It also held three paintings, two indicating quiet landscapes and one a peaceful seascape. The floor was heavily carpeted in green. There was a big globe beside the big desk with Africa facing me and a wall-to-wall window behind it, eight stepladders of glass. But none of these was the reason I'd paused.

The woman behind the desk wore a wide-collared, V-necked dress of blue-green, had long hair and low bangs, all of a cross between sunset clouds and the outer edge of a candle flame in an otherwise dark room, and natural I somehow knew, and her eyes behind glasses I didn't think she needed were as blue as Lake Erie at three o'clock on a cloudless summer afternoon; and the color of her compressed smile matched her hair. But none of these was the reason I'd paused.

I knew her, from somewhere, though I couldn't say where.

I advanced, holding my own smile.

"Hello," I said.

"Sit down," said she, "please," indicating a high-backed, big-armed chair that bulged and was orange, of the kind just tilted at the angle in which I loved to loaf.

I did so, and she studied me.

"Glad to see you're up and around again."

"Me, too. How've you been?"

"Fine, thank you. I must say I didn't expect to see you here."

"I know," I fibbed, "but here I am, to thank you for your sisterly kindness and care." I let a slight note of irony sound within that sentence just to observe her response.

At that point an enormous dog entered the room—an Irish wolfhound—and it curled up in front of the desk. Another followed and circled the globe twice before lying down.

"Well," said she, returning the irony, "it was the least I could do for you. You should drive more carefully."

"In the future," I said, "I'll take greater precautions, I promise." I didn't know what sort of game I was playing, but since she didn't know that I didn't know, I'd decided to take her for all the information I could. "I figured you would be curious as to the shape I was in, so I came to let you see."

"I was, am," she replied. "Have you eaten?"

"A light lunch, several hours ago," I said.

So she rang up the maid and ordered food. Then, "I thought you might take it upon yourself to leave Greenwood," she said, "when you were able. I didn't think it would be so soon, though, and I didn't think you'd come here."

"I know," I said, "that's why I did."

She offered me a cigarette and I took it, lit hers, lit mine. "You always were unpredictable," she finally told me. "While this has helped you often in the past, however, I wouldn't count on it now."

"What do you mean?" I asked.

"The stakes are far too high for a bluff, and I think that's what you're trying, walking in here like this. I've always admired your courage, Corwin, but don't be a fool. You know the score."

Corwin? File it away, under "Corey."

"Maybe I don't," I said. "I've been asleep for a while, remember?"

"You mean you haven't been in touch?"

"Haven't had a chance, since I woke up."

She leaned her head to one side and narrowed her wonderful eyes.

"Rash," she said, "but possible. Just possible. You might mean it. *You* might. I'll pretend that you do, for now. In that case, you may have done a smart, safe thing. Let me think about it."

I drew on my cigarette, hoping she'd say something more. But she didn't, so I decided to seize what seemed the advantage I'd obtained in this game I didn't understand with players I didn't know for stakes I had no inkling of.

"The fact that I'm here indicates something," I said.

"Yes," she replied, "I know. But you're smart, so it could indicate more than one thing. We'll wait and see."

Wait for what? See what? Thing?

Steaks then arrived and a pitcher of beer, so I was temporarily freed from the necessity of making cryptic and general statements for her to ponder as subtle or cagey. Mine was a good steak, pink inside and full of juice, and I tore at the fresh tough-crusted bread with my teeth and gulped the beer with a great hunger and a thirst. She laughed as she watched me, while cutting off tiny pieces of her own.

"I love the gusto with which you assail life, Corwin. It's one of the reasons I'd hate to see you part company with it."

"Me, too," I muttered.

And while I ate, I pondered her. I saw her in a low-cut gown, green as the green of the sea, with full skirts. There was music, dancing, voices behind us. I wore black and silver and . . . The vision faded. But it was a true piece of my memory, I knew; and inwardly I cursed that I lacked it in its entirety. What had she been saying, in her green, to me in my black and silver, that night, behind the music, the dancing and the voices?

I poured us more beer from the pitcher and decided to test the vision.

"I remember one night," I said, "when you were all in green and I in my colors. How lovely things seemed—and the music . . ."

Her face grew slightly wistful, the cheeks smoothing.

"Yes," she said. "Were not those the days? . . . You really have not been in touch?"

"Word of honor," I said, for whatever that was worth.

"Things have grown far worse," she said, "and the Shadows contain more horrors than any had thought. . . ."

"And . . . ?" I inquired.

"He still has his troubles," she finished.

"Oh."

"Yes," she went on, "and he'll want to know where you stand."

"Right here," I said.

"You mean . . . ?"

"For now," I told her, perhaps too quickly, for her eyes had widened too much, "since I still don't know the full state of affairs," whatever that meant.

"Oh."

And we finished our steaks and the beer, giving the two bones to the dogs.

We sipped some coffee afterward, and I came to feel a bit brotherly but suppressed it. I asked, "What of the others?" which could mean anything, but sounded safe.

I was afraid for a moment that she was going to ask me what I meant. Instead, though, she leaned back in her chair, stared at the ceiling, and said, "As always, no one new has been heard from. Perhaps yours was the wisest way. I'm enjoying it myself. But how can one forget—the glory?" I lowered my eyes, because I wasn't sure what they should contain. "One can't," I said. "One never can."

There followed a long, uncomfortable silence, after which she said: "Do you hate me?"

"Of course not," I replied. "How could I—all things considered?"

This seemed to please her, and she showed her teeth, which were very white.

"Good, and thank you," she said. "Whatever else, you're a gentleman."

I bowed and smirked.

"You'll turn my head."

"Hardly," she said, "all things considered."

And I felt uncomfortable.

My anger was there, and I wondered whether she knew who it was that I needed to stay it. I felt that she did. I fought with the desire to ask it outright, suppressed it.

"Well, what do you propose doing?" she finally asked, and being on the spot I replied, "Of course, you don't trust me. . . ."

"How could we?"

I determined to remember that *we*.

"Well, then. For the time being, I'm willing to place myself under your surveillance. I'll be glad to stay right here, where you can keep an eye on me."

"And afterward?"

"Afterward? We'll see."

"Clever," she said, "very clever. And you place me in an awkward position." (I had said it because I didn't have any place else to go, and my blackmail money wouldn't last me too long. "Yes, of course you may stay. But let me warn you"—and here she fingered what I had thought to be some sort of pendant on a chain about her neck—"this is an ultrasonic dog whistle. Donner and Blitzen here have four brothers, and they're all trained to take care of nasty people and they all respond to my whistle. So don't start to walk toward any place where you won't be desired. A toot or two and even you will go down before them. Their kind is the reason there are no wolves left in Ireland, you know."

"I know," I said, realizing that I did.

"Yes," she continued, "Eric will like it that you are my guest. It should cause him to leave you alone, which is what you want, *n'est-ce pas?*"

"*Oui,*" I said.

Eric! It meant something! I *had* known an Eric, and it had been very important, somehow, that I did. Not recently. But the Eric I had known was still around, and that was important.

Why?

I hated him, that was one reason. Hated him enough to have contemplated killing him. Perhaps I'd even tried.

Also, there was some bond between us, I knew.

Kinship?

Yes, that was it. Neither of us liked it being—brothers. . . . I remembered, I remembered. . . .

Big, powerful Eric, with his wet curly beard, and his eyes—just like Evelyn's!

I was racked with a new surge of memory, as my temples began to throb and the back of my neck was suddenly warm.

I didn't let any of it show on my face, but forced myself to take another drag on my cigarette, another sip of beer, as I realized that Evelyn was indeed my sister! Only Evelyn wasn't her name. I couldn't think of what it was, but it wasn't Evelyn. I'd be careful, I resolved. I'd not use any name at all when addressing her, until I remembered.

And what of me? And what was it that was going on around me?

Eric, I suddenly felt, had had some connection with my accident. It should have been a fatal one, only I'd pulled through. *He* was the one, wasn't he? Yes, my feelings replied. It had to be Eric. And Evelyn was working with him, paying Greenwood to keep me in a coma. Better than being dead, but . . .

I realized that I had just somehow delivered myself into Eric's hands by coming to Evelyn, and I would be his prisoner, would be open to new attack, if I stayed.

But she had suggested that my being her guest would cause him to leave me alone. I wondered. I couldn't take anything at face value. I'd have to be constantly on my guard. Perhaps it would be better if I just went away, let my memories return gradually.

But there was this terrible sense of urgency. I had to find out the full story as soon as possible and act as soon as I knew it. It lay like a compulsion upon me. If danger was the price of memory and risk the cost of opportunity, then so be it. I'd stay.

"And I remember," Evelyn said, and I realized that she had been talking for a while and I hadn't even been listening. Perhaps it was because of the reflective quality of her words, not really requiring any sort of responses—and because of the urgency of my thoughts.

"And I remember the day you beat Julian at his favorite game and he threw a glass of wine at you and cursed you. But you took the prize. And he was suddenly afraid he had gone too far. But you laughed then, though, and drank a glass with him. I think he felt badly over that show of temper, normally being so cool, and I think he was envious of you that day. Do you recall? I think he has, to a certain extent, imitated many of your ways since then. But I still hate him and hope that he goes down shortly. I feel he will. . . ."

Julian, Julian, Julian. Yes and no. Something about a game and my baiting a man and shattering an almost legendary self-control. Yes, there was a feeling of familiarity; and no, I couldn't really say for certain what all had been involved.

"And Caine, how you gulled *him!* He hates you yet, you know. . . ."

I gathered I wasn't very well liked. Somehow, the feeling pleased me.

And Caine, too, sounded familiar. Very.

Eric, Julian, Caine, Corwin. The names swam around in my head, and in a way, it was too much to hold within me.

"It's been so long. . . ." I said almost involuntarily, and it seemed to be true.

"Corwin," she said, "let's not fence. You want more than security, I know that. And you're still strong enough to get something out of this, if you play your hand just right. I can't guess what you have in mind, but maybe we can make a deal with Eric." The *we* had obviously shifted. She had come to some sort of conclusion as to my worth in whatever was going on. She saw a chance to gain something for herself, I could tell. I smiled, just a little. "Is that why you came here?" she continued. "Do you have a proposal for Eric, something which might require a go-between?"

"I may," I replied, "after I've thought about it some more. I've still so recently recovered that I have much pondering to do. I wanted to be in the best place, though, where I could act quickly, if I decided my best interests lay with Eric."

"Take care," she said. "You know I'll report every word."

"Of course," I said, not knowing that at all and groping for a quick hedge, "unless your best interests were conjoined with my own."

Her eyebrows moved closer together, and tiny wrinkles appeared between them.

"I'm not sure what you're proposing."

"I'm not proposing anything, yet," I said. "I'm just being completely open and honest with you and telling you I don't know. I'm not positive I want to make a deal with Eric. After all . . ." I let the words trail off on purpose, for I had nothing to follow them with, though I felt I should.

"You've been offered an alternative?" She stood up suddenly, seizing her whistle. "Bleys! Of course!"

"Sit down," I said, "and don't be ridiculous. Would I place myself in your hands this calmly, this readily, just to be dog meat because you happen to think of Bleys?"

She relaxed, maybe even sagged a little, then reseated herself.

"Possibly not," she finally said, "but I know you're a gambler, and I know you're treacherous. If you came here to dispose of a partisan, don't even bother trying. I'm not that important. You should know that by now. Besides, I always thought you rather liked me."

"I did, and I do," I said, "and you have nothing to worry about, so don't. It's interesting, though, that you should mention Bleys."

Bait, bait, bait! there was so much I wanted to know!

"Why? *Has* he approached you?"

"I'd rather not say," I replied, hoping it would give me an edge of some kind, and now that I knew Bleys' gender: "If he had, I'd have answered him the same as I would Eric—'I'll think about it.'"

"Bleys," she repeated, and *Bleys,* I said to myself inside my head, *Bleys. I like you. I forget why, and I know there are reasons why I shouldn't—but I like you. I know it.*

We sat awhile, and I felt fatigue but didn't want to show it. I should be strong. I knew I had to be strong.

I sat there and smiled and said, "Nice library you've got here," and she said, "Thank you.

"Bleys," she repeated after a time. "Do you really think he has a chance?"

I shrugged.

"Who knows? Not I, for certain. Maybe he does. Maybe not, too."

Then she stared at me, her eyes slightly wide, and her mouth opening.

"Not you?" she said. "You're not going to try yourself, are you?"

I laughed then, solely for purposes of countering her emotion.

"Don't be silly," I said when I'd finished. "Me?"

But as she said it, I knew she'd struck some chord, some deep-buried thing which replied with a powerful "Why not?"

I was suddenly afraid.

She seemed relieved, though, at my disavowal of whatever it was I was disavowing. She smiled then, and indicated a built-in bar off to my left.

"I'd like a little Irish Mist," she said.

"So would I, for that matter," I replied, and I rose and fetched two.

"You know," I said, after I'd reseated myself, "it's pleasant to be together with you this way, even if it is only for a short time. It brings back memories."

And she smiled and was lovely.

"You're right," she said, sipping her drink. "I almost feel in Amber with you around," and I almost dropped my drink.

Amber! The word had sent a bolt of lightning down my spine!

Then she began to cry, and I rose and put my arm around her shoulders to comfort her.

"Don't cry, little girl. Please don't. It makes me unhappy, too."
Amber! There was something there, something electrical and potent!
"There will be good days once again," I said, softly.

"Do you really believe that?" she asked.

"Yes," I said loudly. "Yes, I do!"

"You're crazy," she said. "Maybe that's why you were always my favorite brother too. I can almost believe anything you say, even though I know you're crazy."

Then she cried a little more and stopped.

"Corwin," she said, "if you do make it—if by some wild and freakish chance out of Shadow you should make it—will you remember your little sister Florimel?"

"Yes," I said, knowing it to be her name. "Yes, I will remember you."

"Thank you. I will tell Eric only the essentials, and mention Bleys not at all, nor my latest suspicions."

"Thank you, Flora."

"But I don't trust you worth a damn," she added. "Remember that, too."

"That goes without saying."

Then she summoned her maid to show me to a room, and I managed to undress, collapsed into the bed, and slept for eleven hours.

III

In the morning she was gone, and there was no message. Her maid served me breakfast in the kitchen and went away to do maid-things. I'd disregarded the notion of trying to pump information of the woman, as she either wouldn't know or wouldn't tell me the things I wanted to know and would no doubt also report my attempt to Flora. So, since it seemed I had the run of the house, I decided I'd return to the library and see what I could learn there. Besides, I like libraries. It makes me feel comfortable and secure to have walls of words, beautiful and wise, all around me. I always feel better when I can see that there is something to hold back the shadows.

Donner or Blitzen, or one of their relatives, appeared from somewhere and followed me up the hallway, walking stiff-legged and sniffing after my spoor. I tried to make friends with him, but it was like exchanging pleasantries with the state trooper who signaled you to pull off the road. I looked into some of the other rooms as I went along, and they were just places, innocuous-looking ones.

So I entered the library, and Africa still faced me. I closed the door behind me to keep the dogs out, and I strolled around the room, reading the titles on the shelves.

There were lots of history books. In fact, they seemed to dominate her collection. There were also many art books, of the big and expensive variety, and I leafed through a few of these. I usually do my best real thinking when I'm thinking about something else.

I wondered at the sources of Flora's obvious wealth. If we were related, did that mean that perhaps I enjoyed somewhat of opulence, also? I thought about my economic and social status, my profession, my origins. I had the feeling that I'd never worried much about money, and that there'd always been enough or ways of getting it, to keep me satisfied. Did I own a big house like this? I couldn't remember.

What did I do?

I sat behind her desk and examined my mind for any special caches of knowledge I might possess. It is difficult to examine yourself this way, as a stranger. Maybe that's why I couldn't come up with anything. What's yours is yours and a part of you and it just seems to belong there, inside. That's all.

A doctor? That came to mind as I was viewing some of Da Vinci's anatomical drawings. Almost by reflex, in my mind, I had begun going through the steps of various surgical operations. I realized then that I had operated on people in the past.

But that wasn't it. While I realized that I had a medical background, I knew that it was a part of something else. I knew, somehow, that I was not a practicing surgeon. What then? What else was involved?

Something caught my eye.

Seated there at the desk, I commanded a view of the far wall, on which, among other things, hung an antique cavalry saber, which I had overlooked the first time around the room. I rose and crossed over to it, took it down from its pegs.

In my mind, I *tsked* at the shape it was in. I wanted an oily rag and a whetstone, to make it the way it should be once again. I knew something about antique arms, edged weapons in particular.

The saber felt light and useful in my hand, and I felt capable with it. I struck an *en garde*. I parried and cut a few times. Yes, I could use the thing.

So what sort of background was that? I looked around for new memory joggers.

Nothing else occurred to me, so I replaced the blade and returned to the desk. Sitting there, I decided to go through the thing.

I started with the middle one and worked my way up the left side and down the right, drawer by drawer.

Stationery, envelopes, postage stamps, paper clips, pencil stubs, rubber bands—all the usual items.

I had pulled each drawer all the way out though, and held it in my lap as I'd inspected its contents. It wasn't just an idea. It was part of some sort of training I'd once received, which told me I should inspect the sides and bottoms as well.

One thing almost slipped by me, but caught my attention at the last instant: the back of the lower right-hand drawer did not rise as high as the backs of the other drawers.

This indicated something, and when I knelt and looked inside the drawer space I saw a little box-like affair affixed to the upper side.

It was a small drawer itself, way in the back, and it was locked.

It took me about a minute of fooling around with paper clips, safety pins, and finally a metal shoehorn I'd seen in another drawer. The shoehorn did the trick.

The drawer contained a packet of playing cards.

And the packet bore a device which caused me to stiffen where I knelt, perspiration suddenly wetting my brow and my breath coming rapidly.

It bore a white unicorn on a green field, rampant, facing to the dexter.

And I knew that device and it hurt me that I could not name it.

I opened the packet and extracted the cards. They were on the order of tarots, with their wands, pentacles, cups, and swords, but the Greater Trumps were quite different.

I replaced both drawers, being careful not to lock the smaller one, before I continued my inspection.

They were almost lifelike in appearance, the Greater Trumps ready to step right out through those glistening surfaces. The cards seemed quite cold to my touch, and it gave me a distinct pleasure to handle them. I had once had a packet like this myself, I suddenly knew.

I began spreading them on the blotter before me.

The one bore a wily-looking little man, with a sharp nose and a laughing mouth and a shock of straw-colored hair. He was dressed in something like a Renaissance costume of orange, red, and brown. He wore long hose and a tight-fitting embroidered doublet. And I knew him. His name was Random.

Next, there was the passive countenance of Julian, dark hair hanging long, blue eyes containing neither passion nor compassion. He was dressed completely in scaled white armor, not silver or metallic-colored, but looking as if it had been enameled. I knew, though, that it was terribly tough and shock-resistant, despite its decorative and festive appearance. He was the man I had beaten at his favorite game, for which he had thrown a glass of wine at me. I knew him and I hated him.

Then came the swarthly, dark-eyed countenance of Caine, dressed all in satin that was black and green, wearing a dark three-cornered hat set at a rakish angle, a green plume of feathers trailing down the back. He was standing in profile, one arm akimbo, and the toes of his boots curled upwards, and he wore an emerald-studded dagger at his belt. There was ambivalence in my heart.

Then there was Eric. Handsome by anyone's standards, his hair was so dark as to be almost blue. His beard curled around the mouth that always smiled, and he was dressed simply in a leather jacket and leggings, a plain cloak, high black boots, and he wore a red sword belt bearing a long silvery saber and clasped with a ruby, and his high cloak collar round his head was lined with red and the trimmings of his sleeves matched it. His hands, thumbs hooked behind his belt, were terribly strong and prominent. A pair of black gloves jutted from the belt near his right hip. He it was, I was certain, that had tried to kill me on that day I had almost died. I studied him and I feared him somewhat.

Then there was Benedict, tall and dour, thin; thin of body, thin of face, wide of mind. He wore orange and yellow and brown and reminded me of haystacks and pumpkins and scarecrows and the *Legend of Sleepy Hollow*. He had a long, strong jaw and hazel eyes and brown hair that never curled. He stood beside a tan horse and leaned upon a lance about which was twined a rope of flowers. He seldom laughed. I liked him.

I paused when I uncovered the next card, and my heart leaped forward and banged against my sternum and asked to be let out.

It was me.

I knew the me I shaved and this was the guy behind the mirror. Green eyes, black hair, dressed in black and silver, yes. I had on a cloak and it was slightly furled as by a wind. I had on black boots, like Eric's, and I too wore a blade, only mine was heavier, though not quite as long as his. I had my gloves on and they were silver and scaled. The clasp at my neck was cast in the form of a silver rose.

Me, Corwin.

And a big, powerful man regarded me from the next card. He resembled me quite strongly, save that his jaw was heavier, and I knew he was bigger than I, though slower. His strength was a thing out of legend. He wore a dressing gown of blue and gray clasped about the middle with a wide, black belt, and he stood laughing. About his neck, on a heavy cord, there hung a silver hunting horn. He wore a fringe beard and a light mustache. In his right hand he held a goblet of wine. I felt a sudden affection for him. His name then occurred to me. He was Gérard.

Then came a fiery bearded, flame-crowned man, dressed all in red and orange, mainly of silk stuff, and he held a sword in his right hand and a glass of wine in his left, and the devil himself danced behind his eyes, as blue as Flora's, or Eric's. His chin was slight, but the beard covered it. His sword was inlaid with an elaborate filigree of a golden color. He wore two huge rings on his right hand and one on his left: an emerald, a ruby, and a sapphire, respectively. This, I knew, was Bleys.

Then there was a figure both like Bleys and myself. My features, though smaller, my eyes, Bleys' hair, beardless. He wore a riding suit of green and sat atop a white horse, heading toward the dexter side of the card. There was a quality of both strength and weakness, questing and abandonment about him. I both approved and disapproved, liked and was repelled by, this one. His name was Brand, I knew. As soon as I laid eyes upon him, I knew.

In fact, I realized that I knew them all well, remembered them all, with their strengths, their weaknesses, their victories, their defeats.

For they were my brothers.

I lit a cigarette I'd filched from Flora's desk box, and I leaned back and considered the things I had recalled.

They were my brothers, those eight strange men garbed in their strange costumes. And I knew that it was right and fitting that they should dress in whatever manner they chose, just as it was right for me to wear the black and the silver. Then I chuckled, as I realized what I was wearing, what I had purchased in the little clothing store of that little town I had stopped in after my departure from Greenwood.

I had on black slacks, and all three of the shirts I had purchased had been of a grayish, silvery color. And my jacket, too, was black.

I returned to the cards, and there was Flora in a gown green as the sea, just as I'd remembered her the previous evening; and then there was a black-haired girl with the same blue eyes, and her hair hung long and she was dressed all in black, with a girdle of silver about her waist. My eyes filled with tears, why I don't know. Her name was Deirdre. Then there was Fiona, with hair like Bleys or Brand, my eyes, and a complexion like mother of pearl. I hated her the second I turned over the card. Next was Llewella, whose hair matched her jade-colored eyes, dressed in shimmering gray and green with a lavender belt, and looking moist and sad. For some reason, I knew she was not like the rest of us. But she, too, was my sister.

I felt a terrible sense of distance and removal from all these people. Yet somehow they seemed physically close.

The cards were so very cold on my fingertips that I put them down again, though with a certain sense of reluctance at having to relinquish their touch.

There were no more, though. All the rest were minor cards. And I knew, somehow, that *somehow*, again—ah, somehow!—that several were missing.

For the life of me, however, I did not know what the missing Trumps represented.

I was strangely saddened by this, and I picked up my cigarette and mused.

Why did all these things rush back so easily when I viewed the cards—rush back without dragging their contexts along with them? I knew more now than I'd known before, in the way of names and faces. But that was about all.

I couldn't figure the significance of the fact that we were all done up on cards this way. I had a terribly strong desire to own a pack of them, however. If I picked up Flora's, though, I knew she'd spot in a hurry that they were missing, and I'd be in trouble. Therefore, I put them back in the little drawer behind the big drawer and locked them in again. Then, God, how I racked my brains! But to little avail.

Until I recalled a magical word.

Amber.

I had been greatly upset by the word on the previous evening. I had been sufficiently upset so that I had avoided thinking of it since then. But now I courted it. Now I rolled it around my mind and examined all the associations that sprang up when it struck.

The word was charged with a mighty longing and a massive nostalgia. It had, wrapped up inside it, a sense of forsaken beauty, grand achievement, and a feeling of power that was terrible and almost ultimate. Somehow, the word belonged in my vocabulary. Somehow, I was part of it and it was a part of me. It was a place name, I knew then. It was the name of a place I once had known. There came no pictures, though, only emotions.

How long I sat so, I do not know. Time had somehow divorced itself from my reveries.

I realized then, from the center of my thoughts, that there had come a gentle rapping upon the door. Then the handle slowly turned and the maid, whose name was Carmella, entered and asked me if I was interested in lunch.

It seemed like a good idea, so I followed her back to the kitchen and ate half a chicken and drank a quart of milk.

I took a pot of coffee back to the library with me, avoiding the dogs as I went. I was into the second cup when the telephone rang.

I longed to pick it up, but I figured there must be extensions all over the house and Carmella would probably get it from somewhere.

I was wrong. It kept ringing.

Finally, I couldn't resist it any longer.

"Hello," I said, "this is the Flaumel residence."

"May I speak with Mrs. Flaumel please?"

It was a man's voice, rapid and slightly nervous. He sounded out of breath and his words were masked and surrounded by the faint ringing and the ghost voices that indicate long distance.

"I'm sorry," I told him. "She's not here right now. May I take a message or have her call you back?"

"Who am I talking to?" he demanded.

I hesitated, then, "Corwin's the name," I told him.

"My God!" he said, and a long silence followed.

I was beginning to think he'd hung up. I said, "Hello?" again, just as he started talking.

"Is she still alive?" he asked.

"Of course she's still alive! Who the hell am I talking to?"

"Don't you recognize the voice, Corwin? This is Random. Listen, I'm in California and I'm in trouble. I was calling to ask Flora for sanctuary. Are you in with her?"

"Temporarily," I said.

"I see. Will you give me your protection, Corwin?" Pause, then, "Please?"

"As much as I can," I said, "but I can't commit Flora to anything without consulting her."

"Will you protect me against her?"

"Yes."

"Then you're good enough for me, man. I'm going to try to make it to New York now. I'll be coming by a rather circuitous route, so I don't know how long it will take me. If I can avoid the wrong shadows, I'll be seeing you whenever. Wish me luck."

"Luck," I said.

Then there was a click and I was listening to a distant ringing and the voices of the ghosts.

So cocky little Random was in trouble! I had a feeling it shouldn't have bothered me especially. But now, he was one of the keys to my past, and quite possibly my future also. So I would try to help him, in any way I could, until I'd learned all I wanted from him. I knew that there wasn't much brotherly love lost between the two of us. But I knew that on the one hand he was nobody's fool; he was resourceful, shrewd, strangely sentimental over the damnedest things; and on the other hand, his word wasn't worth the spit behind it, and he'd probably sell my corpse to the medical school of his choice if he could get much for it. I remembered the little fink all right, with only a touch of affection, perhaps for a few pleasant times it seemed we had spent together. But trust him? Never. I decided I wouldn't tell Flora he was coming until the last possible moment. He might be made to serve as an ace, or at least a knave, in the hole.

So I added some hot coffee to what remained in my cup and sipped it slowly.

Who was he running from?

Not Eric, certainly, or he wouldn't have been calling here. I wondered then concerning his question as to whether Flora was dead, just because I happened to be present here. Was she really that strongly allied with the brother I knew I hated that it was common knowledge in the family that I'd do her in, too, given the chance? It seemed strange, but then he'd asked the question.

And what was it in which they were allied? What was the source of this tension, this opposition? Why was it that Random was running?

Amber.

That was the answer.

Amber. Somehow, the key to everything lay in Amber, I knew. The secret of the entire mess was in Amber, in some event that had transpired in that place, and fairly recently, I'd judge. I'd have to be on my toes. I'd have to pretend to the knowledge I didn't possess, while piece by piece I mined if from those who had it. I felt confident that I could do it. There was enough distrust circulating for everyone to be cagey. I'd play on that. I'd get what I needed and take what I wanted, and I'd remember those who helped me and step on the rest. For this, I knew, was the law by which our family lived, and I was a true son of my father. . . .

My headache came on again suddenly, throbbing to crack my skull.

Something about my father I thought, guessed, felt—was what had served to set it off. But I wasn't sure why or how.

After a time, it subsided and I slept, there in the chair. After a much longer time, the door opened and Flora entered. It was night outside, once more.

She was dressed in a green silk blouse and a long woolen skirt that was gray. She had on walking shoes and heavy stockings. Her hair was pulled back behind her head and she looked slightly pale. She still wore her hound whistle.

"Good evening," I said, rising.

But she did not reply. Instead, she walked across the room to the bar, poured herself a shot of Jack Daniels, and tossed it off like a man. Then she poured another and took it with her to the big chair.

I lit a cigarette and handed it to her.

She nodded, then said, "The Road to Amber—is difficult."

"Why?"

She gave me a very puzzled look.

"When is the last time you tried it?"

I shrugged.

"I don't remember."

"Be that way then," she said. "I just wondered how much of it was your doing."

I didn't reply because I didn't know what she was talking about. But then I recalled that there was an easier way than the Road to get to the place called Amber. Obviously, she lacked it.

"You're missing some Trumps," I said then suddenly, in a voice which was almost mine.

She sprang to her feet, half her drink spilling over the back of her hand.

"Give them back!" she cried, reaching for the whistle. I moved forward and seized her shoulders.

"I don't have them," I said. "I was just making an observation."

She relaxed a bit, then began to cry, and I pushed her back down, gently, into the chair.

"I thought you meant you'd taken the ones I had left," she said. "Rather than just making a nasty and obvious comment."

I didn't apologize. It didn't seem right that I should have to.

"How far did you get?"

"Not far at all." Then she laughed and regarded me with a new light in her eyes.

"I see what you've done now, Corwin," she said, and I lit a cigarette in order to cover any sort of need for a reply.

"Some of those things were yours, weren't they? You blocked my way to Amber before you came here, didn't you? You knew I'd go to Eric. But I can't now. I'll have to wait till he comes to me. Clever. You want to draw him here, don't you? He'll send a messenger, though. He won't come himself."

There was a strange tone of admiration in the voice of this woman who was admitting she'd just tried to sell me out to my enemy, and still would—given half a chance—as she talked about something she thought I'd done which had thrown a monkey wrench into her plans. How could anyone be so admittedly Machiavellian in the presence of a proposed victim? The answer rang back immediately from the depths of my mind: it is the way of our kind. We don't have to be subtle with each other. Though I thought she lacked somewhat the finesse of a true professional.

"Do you think I'm stupid, Flora?" I asked. "Do you think I came here just for purposes of waiting around for you to hand me over to Eric? Whatever you ran into, it served you right."

"All right, I don't play in your league! But you're in exile, too! That shows you weren't so smart!"

Somehow her words burned and I knew they were wrong.

"Like hell I am!" I said.

She laughed again.

"I knew that would get a rise out of you," she said. "All right, you walk in the Shadows on purpose then. You're crazy."

I shrugged.

She said, "What do you want? Why did you really come here?"

"I was curious what you were up to," I said. "That's all. You can't keep me here if I don't want to stay. Even Eric couldn't do that. Maybe I really did just want to visit with you. Maybe I'm getting sentimental in my old age. Whatever, I'm going to stay a little longer now, and then probably go away for good. If you hadn't been so quick to see what you could get for me, you might have profited a lot more, lady. You asked me to remember you one day, if a certain thing occurred. . . ."

It took several seconds for what I thought I was implying in sink in.

Then she said, "You're going to try! You're really going to try!"

"You're goddamn right I'm going to try," I said, knowing that I would, whatever it was, "and you can tell that to Eric if you want, but remember that I might make it. Bear in mind that if I do, it might be nice to be my friend."

I sure wished I knew what the hell I was talking about, but I'd picked up enough terms and felt the importance attached to them, so that I could use them properly without knowing what they meant. But they *felt* right, so very right. . . .

Suddenly, she was kissing me.

"I won't tell him. Really, I won't, Corwin! I think you can do it. Bleys will be difficult, but Gérard would probably help you, and maybe Benedict. Then Caine would swing over, when he saw what was happening—"

"I can do my own planning," I said.

Then she drew away. She poured two glasses of wine and handed one to me.

"To the future," she said.

"I'll always drink to that."

And we did.

Then she refilled mine and studied me.

"It had to be Eric, Bleys, or you," she said. "You're the only ones with any guts or brains. But you'd removed yourself from the picture for so long that I'd counted you out of the running."

"It just goes to show: you never can tell."

I sipped my drink and hoped she'd shut up for just a minute. It seemed to me she was being a bit too obvious in trying to play on every side available. There was something bothering me, and I wanted to think about it.

How old was I?

That question, I knew, was a part of the answer to the terrible sense of distance and removal that I felt from all the persons depicted on the playing cards. I was older than I appeared to be. (Thirtyish, I'd seemed when I looked at me in the mirror—but now I knew that it was because the Shadows would lie for me.) I was far, far older, and it had been a very long time since I had seen my brothers and my sisters, all together and friendly, existing side by side as they did on the cards, with no tension, no friction among them.

We heard the sound of the bell, and Carmella moving to answer the door.

"That would be brother Random," I said, knowing I was right. "He's under my protection."

Her eyes widened, then she smiled, as though she appreciated some clever thing I had done.

I hadn't, of course, but I was glad to let her think so.

It made me feel safer.

IV

I felt safe for perhaps all of three minutes.

I beat Carmella to the door and flung it open.

He staggered in and immediately pushed the door shut behind himself and shot the bolt. There were lines under those light eyes and he wasn't wearing a bright doublet and long hose. He needed a shave and he had on a brown wool suit. He carried a gabardine overcoat over one arm and wore dark suede shoes. But he was Random, all right—the Random I had seen on the card—only the laughing mouth looked tired and there was dirt beneath his fingernails.

"Corwin!" he said, and embraced me.

I squeezed his shoulder. "You look as if you could use a drink," I said.

"Yes. Yes. Yes. . . ." he agreed, and I steered him toward the library.

About three minutes later, after he had seated himself, with a drink in one hand and a cigarette in the other, he said to me, "They're after me. They'll be here soon."

Flora let out a little shriek, which we both ignored.

"Who?" I asked.

"People out of the Shadows," he said. "I don't know who they are, or who sent them. There are four or five though, maybe even six. They were on the plane with me. I took a jet. They occurred around Denver. I moved the plane several times to subtract them, but it didn't work—and I didn't want to get too far off the track. I shook them in Manhattan, but it's only a matter of time. I think they'll be here soon."

"And you've no idea at all who sent them?"

He smiled for an instant.

"Well, I guess we'd be safe in limiting it to the family. Maybe Bleys, maybe Julian, maybe Caine. Maybe even you, to get me here. Hope not, though. You didn't, did you?"

" 'Fraid not," I said. "How tough do they look?"

He shrugged. "If it were only two or three, I'd have tried to pull an ambush. But not with that whole crowd."

He was a little guy, maybe five-six in height, weighing perhaps one thirty-five. But he sounded as if he were talking dead serious talk. I felt reasonably sure that he meant it when he said he'd take on two or three bruisers, singlehanded. I wondered suddenly about my own physical strength, being his brother. I felt comfortably strong. I knew I'd be willing to take on any one man in a fair fight without any special fears. How strong was I?

Suddenly, I knew I would have a chance to find out.

There came a knocking at the front door.

"What shall we do?" asked Flora.

Random laughed, undid his necktie, tossed it atop his coat on the desk. He stripped off his suit jacket then and looked about the room. His eyes fell upon the saber and he was across the room in an instant and had it in his hand. I felt the weight of the .32 within my jacket pocket and thumbed off the safety catch.

"Do?" Random asked. "There exists a probability that they will gain entrance," he said. "Therefore, they will enter. When is the last time you stood to battle, sister?"

"It has been too long," she replied.

"Then you had better start remembering fast," he told her, "because it is only a matter of small time. They are guided, I can tell you. But there are three of us and at most only twice as many of them. Why worry?"

"We don't know what they are," she said.

The knocking came again.

"What does it matter?"

"Nothing," I said. "Shall I go and let them in?"

They both blanched slightly.

"We might as well wait. . . ."

"I might call the cops," I said.

They both laughed, almost hysterically.

"Or Eric," I said, suddenly looking at her.

But she shook her head.

"We just don't have the time. We have the Trump, but by the time he could respond—if he chose—it would be too late."

"And this might even be his doing, eh?" said Random.

"I doubt it," she replied, "very much. It's not his style."

"True," I replied, just for the hell of it, and to let them know I was with things.

The sound of knocking came once again, and much more loudly.

"What about Carmella?" I asked, upon a sudden thought.

Flora shook her head.

"I have decided that it is improbable that she will answer the door."

"But you don't know what you're up against," Random cried, and he was suddenly gone from the room.

I followed him, along the hallway and into the foyer, in time to stop Carmella from opening the door.

We sent her back to her own quarters with instructions to lock herself in, and Random observed, "That shows the strength of the opposition. Where are we, Corwin?"

I shrugged.

"If I knew, I'd tell you. For the moment at least, we're in this together. Step back!"

And I opened the door.

The first man tried to push me aside, and I stiff-armed him back.

There were six, I could see that.

"What do you want?" I asked them.

But never a word was spoken, and I saw guns.

I kicked out and slammed the door again and shot the bolt.

"Okay, they're really there," I said. "But how do I know you're not pulling something?"

"You don't," he said, "but I really wish I were. They look wild."

I had to agree. The guys on the porch were heavily built and had hats pulled down to cover their eyes. Their faces had all been covered with shadows.

"I wish I knew where we are," said Random.

I felt a hackle-raising vibration, in the vicinity of my eardrums. I knew, in that moment, that Flora had blown her whistle.

When I heard a window break, somewhere off to my right, I was not surprised to hear a growled rumbling and some baying, somewhere off to my left.

"She's called her dogs," I said, "six mean and vicious brutes, which could under other circumstances be after us."

Random nodded, and we both headed off in the direction of the shattering.

When we reached the living room, two men were already inside and both had guns.

I dropped the first and hit the floor, firing at the second. Random leaped above me, brandishing his blade, and I saw the second man's head depart his shoulders.

By then, two more were through the window. I emptied the automatic at them, and I heard the snarling of Flora's hounds mixed with gunfire that was not my own.

I saw three of the men upon the floor and the same number of Flora's dogs. It made me feel good to think we had gotten half them, and as the rest came through the window I killed another in a manner which surprised me.

Suddenly, and without thinking, I picked up a huge overstuffed chair and hurled it perhaps thirty feet across the room. It broke the back of the man it struck.

I leaped toward the remaining two, but before I crossed the room, Random had pierced one of them with the saber, leaving him for the dogs to finish off, and was turning toward the other.

The other was pulled down before he could act, however. He killed another of the dogs before we could stop him, but he never killed anything again after that. Random strangled him.

It turned out that two of the dogs were dead and one was badly hurt. Random killed the injured one with a quick thrust, and we turned our attention to the men.

There was something unusual about their appearance.

Flora entered and helped us to decide what.

For one thing, all six had uniformly bloodshot eyes. Very, very bloodshot eyes. With them, though, the condition seemed normal.

For another, all had an extra joint to each finger and thumb, and sharp, forward-curving spurs on the backs of their hands.

All of them had prominent jaws, and when I forced one open, I counted forty-five teeth, most of them longer than human teeth, and several looking to be much sharper. Their flesh was grayish and hard and shiny.

There were undoubtedly other differences also, but those were sufficient to prove a point of some sort.

We took their weapons, and I hung onto three small, flat pistols.

"They crawled out of the Shadows, all right," said Random, and I nodded. "And I was lucky, too. It doesn't seem they suspected I'd turn up with the reinforcements I did—a militant brother and around half a ton of dogs." He went and peered out the broken window, and I decided to let him do it himself. "Nothing," he said, after a time. "I'm sure we got them all," and he drew the heavy orange drapes closed and pushed a lot of high-backed furniture in front of them. While he was doing that, I went through all their pockets.

I wasn't really surprised that I turned up nothing in the way of identification.

"Let's go back to the library," he said, "so I can finish my drink."

He cleaned off the blade, carefully, before he seated himself, however, and he replaced it on the pegs. I fetched Flora a drink while he did this.

"So it would seem I'm temporarily safe," he said, "now that there are three of us sharing the picture."

"So it would seem," Flora agreed.

"God, I haven't eaten since yesterday!" he announced.

So Flora went to tell Carmella it was safe to come out now, so long as she stayed clear of the living room, and to bring a lot of food to the library.

As soon as she left the room, Random turned to me and asked, "Like, what's it between you?"

"Don't turn your back on her."

"She's still Eric's?"

"So far as I can tell."

"Then what are you doing here?"

"I was trying to sucker Eric into coming around after me himself. He knows it's the only way he'll really get me, and I wanted to see how badly he wanted to."

Random shook his head.

"I don't think he'll do it. No percentage. So long as you're here and he's there, why bother sticking his neck out? He's still got the stronger position. If you want him, you'll have to go after him."

"I've just about come to the same conclusion."

His eyes gleamed then, and his old smile appeared. He ran one hand through his straw-colored hair and wouldn't let go of my eyes.

"Are you going to do it?" he asked.

"Maybe," I said.

"Don't 'maybe' me, baby. It's written all over you. I'd almost be willing to go along, you know. Of all my relations, I like sex the best and Eric the least."

I lit a cigarette, while I considered.

"You're thinking," he said while I thought, " 'How far can I trust Random this time? He is sneaky and mean and just like his name, and he will doubtless sell me out if someone offers him a better deal.' True?"

I nodded.

"However, brother Corwin, remember that while I've never done you much good, I've never done you any especial harm either. Oh, a few pranks, I'll admit. But, all in all, you might say we've gotten along best of all in the family—that is, we've stayed out of each other's ways. Think it over. I believe I hear Flora or her woman coming now, so let's change the subject. . . . But quick! I don't suppose you have a deck of the family's favorite playing cards around, do you?"

I shook my head.

Flora entered the room and said, "Carmella will bring some food shortly."

We drank to that, and he winked at me behind her back.

The following morning, the bodies were gone from the living room, there were no stains upon the carpet, the window appeared to have been repaired, and Random explained that he had "taken care of things." I did not see fit to question him further.

We borrowed Flora's Mercedes and went for a drive. The countryside seemed strangely altered. I couldn't quite put my finger on what it was that was missing or new, but somehow things felt different. This, too, gave me a headache when I attempted to consider it, so I decided to suspend such thinking for the nonce.

I was at the wheel, Random at my side. I observed that I would like to be back in Amber again—just to see what sort of response would obtain.

"I have been wondering," he repleid, "whether you were out for vengeance, pure and simple, or something more," thereby shifting the ball back to me, to answer or not to answer, as I saw fit.

I saw fit. I used the stock phrase:

"I've been thinking about that, too," I said, "trying to figure my chances. You know, I just might 'try.' "

He turned toward me then (he had been staring out of the side window) and said:

"I suppose we've all had that ambition, or at least that thought—I know I have, though I dismissed me early in the game—and the way I feel about it, it's worth the attempt. You're asking me, I know, whether I'll help you. The answer is 'yes.' I'll do it just to screw up the others." Then, "What do you think of Flora? Would she be of any help?"

"I doubt it very much," I said. "She'd throw in if things were certain. But then, what's certain at this point?"

"Or any," he added.

"Or any," I repeated, so he'd think I knew what sort of response I would obtain.

I was afraid to confide in him as to the condition of my memory. I was also afraid to trust him, so I didn't. There were so very many things I wanted to know, but I had no one to turn to. I thought about it a bit as we drove along.

"Well, when do you want to start?" I asked.

"Whenever you're ready."

And there it was, right in my lap, and I didn't know what to do with it.

"What about now?" I said.

He was silent. He lit a cigarette, I think to buy time. I did the same.

"Okay," he finally said. "When's the last time you've been back?"

"It's been so damn long," I told him, "that I'm not even sure I remember the way."

"All right," he said, "then we're going to have to go away before we can come back. How much gas have you got?"

"Three-quarters of a tank."

"Then turn left at the next corner, and we'll see what happens."

I did this thing, and as we drove along all the sidewalks began to sparkle.

"Damn!" he said. "It's been around twenty years since I've taken the walk. I'm remembering the right things too soon."

We kept driving, and I kept wondering what the hell was happening. The sky had grown a bit greenish, then shaded over into pink.

I bit my lip against the asking of questions.

We passed beneath a bridge and when we emerged on the other side the sky was a normal color again, but there were windmills all over the place, big yellow ones.

"Don't worry," he said quickly, "it could be worse."

I noticed that the people we passed were dressed rather strangely, and the roadway was of brick.

"Turn right."

I did.

Purple clouds covered over the sun, and it began to rain. Lightning stalked the heavens and the skies grumbled above us. I had the windshield wipers going full speed, but they weren't doing a whole big lot of good. I turned on the headlights and slowed even more.

I would have sworn I'd passed a horseman, racing in the other direction, dressed all in gray, collar turned high and head lowered against the rain.

Then the clouds broke themselves apart and we were riding along a seashore. The waves splashed high and enormous gulls swept low above them. The rain had stopped and I killed the lights and the wipers. Now the road was of macadam, but I didn't recognize the place at all. In the rear-view mirror there was no sign of the town we had just departed. My grip tightened upon the wheel as we passed by a sudden gallows where a skeleton was suspended by the neck, pushed from side to side by the wind.

Random just kept smoking and staring out of the window as our road turned away from the shore and curved around a hill. A grassy treeless plain swept away to our right and a row of hills climbed higher on our left. The sky by now was a dark but brilliant blue, like a deep, clear pool, sheltered and shaded. I did not recall having ever seen a sky like that before.

Random opened his window to throw away the butt, and an icy breeze came in and swirled around inside the car until he closed the window again. The breeze had a sea scent to it, salty and sharp.

"All roads lead to Amber," he said, as though it were an axiom.

Then I recalled what Flora had said the day before. I didn't want to sound like a dunce or a withholder of crucial information, but I had to tell him, for my sake as well as his own, when I realized what her statements implied.

"You know," I began, "when you called the other day and I answered the phone because Flora was out, I've a strong feeling she was trying to make it to Amber, and that she found the way blocked."

At this, he laughed.

"The woman has very little imagination," he replied. "Of course it would be blocked at a time like this. Ultimately, we'll be reduced to walking, I'm sure, and it will doubtless take all of our strength and ingenuity to make it, if we make it at all. Did she think she could walk back like a princess in state, treading on flowers the whole way?

She's a dumb bitch. She doesn't really deserve to live, but that's not for me to say, yet.

"Turn right at the crossroads," he decided.

What was happening? I knew he was in some way responsible for the exotic changes going on about us, but I couldn't determine how he was doing it, where he was getting us to. I knew I had to learn his secret, but I couldn't just ask him or he'd know I didn't know. Then I'd be at his mercy. He seemed to do nothing but smoke and stare, but coming up out of a dip in the road we entered a blue desert and the sun was now pink above our heads within the shimmering sky. In the rear-view mirror, miles and miles of desert stretched out behind us, for as I could see. Neat trick, that.

Then the engine coughed, sputtered, steadied itself, repeated the performance.

The steering wheel changed shape beneath my hands.

It became a crescent; and the seat seemed further back, the car seemed closer to the road, and the windshield had more of a slant to it.

I said nothing, though, not even when the lavender sandstorm struck us.

But when it cleared away, I gasped.

There was a godawful line of cars all jammed up, about half a mile before us. They were all standing still and I could hear their horns.

"Slow down," he said. "It's the first obstacle."

I did, and another gust of sand swept over us.

Before I could switch on the lights, it was gone, and I blinked my eyes several times.

All the cars were gone and silent their horns. But the roadway sparkled now as the sidewalks had for a time, and I heard Random damning someone or something under his breath.

"I'm sure I shifted just the way he wanted us to, whoever set up that block," he said, "and it pisses me off that I did what he expected —the obvious."

"Eric?" I asked.

"Probably. What do you think we should do? Stop and try it the hard way for a while, or go on and see if there are more blocks?"

"Let's go on a bit. After all, that was the only the first."

"Okay," he said, but added, "who knows what the second will be?"

The second was a thing—I don't know how else to describe it.

It was a thing that looked like a smelter with arms, squatting in the middle of the road, reaching down and picking up cars, eating them.

I hit the brakes.

"What's the matter?" Random asked. "Keep going. How else can we get past them?"

"It shook me a bit," I said, and he gave me a strange, sidelong look as another dust storm came up.

It had been the wrong thing to say, I knew.

When the dust cleared away, we were racing along an empty road once more. And there were towers in the distance.

"I think I've screwed him up," said Random. "I combined several into one, and I think it may be one he hasn't anticipated. After all, no one can cover all roads to Amber."

"True," I said, hoping to redeem myself from whatever faux pas had drawn that strange look.

I considered Random. A little, weak-looking guy who could have died as easily as I on the previous evening. What was his power? And what was all this talk of Shadows? Something told me that whatever Shadows were, we moved among them even now. How? It was something Random was doing, and since he seemed at rest physically, his hands in plain sight, I decided it was something he did with his mind. Again, how?

Well, I'd heard him speak of "adding" and "subtracting" as though the universe in which he moved were a big equation.

I decided—with a sudden certainty—that he was somehow adding and subtracting items to and from the world that was visible about us to bring us into closer and closer alignment with that strange place Amber, for which he was solving.

It was something I'd once known how to do. And the key to it, I knew in a flash, was remembering Amber.

But I couldn't.

The road curved abruptly, the desert ended, to give way to fields of tall, blue, sharp-looking grass. After a while, the terrain became a bit hilly, and at the foot of the third hill the pavement ended and we entered upon a narrow dirt road. It was hard-packed, and it wound its way among greater hills upon which small shrubs and bayonet-like thistle bushes now began to appear.

After about half an hour of this, the hills went away, and we entered a forest of squat, big-boled trees with diamond-shaped leaves of autumn orange and purple.

A light rain began to fall, and there were many shadows. Pale mists arose from mats of soggy leaves. Off to right somewhere, I heard a howl.

The steering wheel changed shape three more times, its latest version being an octagonal wooden affair. The car was quite tall now, and we had somewhere acquired a hood ornament in the shape of a flamingo. I refrained from commenting on these things, but accommodated myself to whatever positions the seat assumed and new operating requirements the vehicle obtained. Random, however, glanced at the steering wheel just as another howl occurred, shook his head, and suddenly the trees were much higher, though festooned with hanging vines and something like a blue veiling of Spanish Moss, and the car was almost normal again. I glanced at the fuel gauge and saw that we had half a tank.

"We're making headway," my brother remarked, and I nodded.

The road widened abruptly and acquired a concrete surface. There were canals on both sides, full of muddy water. Leaves, small branches, and colored feathers glided along their surfaces.

I suddenly became lightheaded and a bit dizzy, but "Breathe slowly and deeply," said Random, before I could remark on it. "We're taking a short cut, and the atmosphere and the gravitation will be a bit different for a time. I think we've been pretty lucky so far, and I want to push it for all it's worth—get as close as we can, as quickly as we can."

"Good idea," I said.

"Maybe, maybe not," he replied, "but I think it's worth the gam— Look out!"

We were climbing a hill and a truck topped it and came barreling down toward us. It was on the wrong side of the road. I swerved to avoid it, but it swerved, too. At the very last instant, I had to go off the road, onto the soft shoulder to my left, and head close to the edge of the canal in order to avoid a collision.

To my right, the truck screeched to a halt. I tried to pull off the shoulder and back onto the road, but we were stuck in the soft soil.

Then I heard a door slam, and saw that the driver had climbed down from the right side of the cab—which meant that he probably was driving on the proper side of the road after all, and we were in the wrong. I was sure that nowhere in the States did traffic flow in a British manner, but I was certain by this time that we had long ago left the Earth that I knew.

The truck was a tanker. It said ZUÑOCO on the side in big, blood-red letters, and beneath this was the motto "Wee covir the werld." The driver covered me with abuse, as I stepped out, rounded the car, and began apologizing. He was as big as I was, and built like a beer barrel, and he carried a jack handle in one hand.

"Look, I said I'm sorry," I told him. "What do you want me to do? Nobody got hurt and there was no damage."

"They shouldn't turn goddamn drivers like you loose on the road!" he yelled. "You're a friggin' menace!"

Random got out of the car then and said, "Mister, you'd better move along!" and he had a gun in his hand.

"Put that away," I told him, but he flipped the safety catch off and pointed.

The guy turned around and started to run, a look of fear widening his eyes and loosening his jaw.

Random raised his pistol and took careful aim at the man's back, and I managed to knock his arm to the side just as he pulled the trigger.

It scored the pavement and ricocheted away.

Random turned toward me and his face was almost white.

"You bloody fool!" he said. "That shot could have hit the tank!"

"It could also have hit the guy you were aiming at."

"So who the hell cares? We'll never pass this way again, in this generation. That bastard dared to insult a Prince of Amber! It was *your* honor I was thinking about."

"I can take care of my own honor," I told him, and something cold and powerful suddenly gripped me and answered, "for he was mine to kill, not yours, had I chosen," and a sense of outrage filled me.

He bowed his head then, as the cab door slammed and the truck took off down the road.

"I'm sorry, brother," he said. "I did not mean to presume. But it offended me to hear one of them speak to you in such a manner. I know I should have waited to let you dispose of him as you saw fit, or at least have consulted with you."

"Well, whatever," I told him, "Let's get back onto the road and get moving, if we can."

The rear wheels were sunken up to their hubcaps, and as I stared at them, trying to decide the best way to go about things, Random called out, "Okay, I've got the front bumper. You take the rear and we'll carry it back to the road—and we'd better deposit it in the left lane."

He wasn't kidding.

He'd said something about lesser gravitation, but *I* didn't feel that light. I knew I was strong, but I had my doubts about being able to raise the rear end of a Mercedes.

But on the other hand, I had to try, since he seemed to expect it of me, and I couldn't tip him off as to any gaps in my memory.

So I stooped, squatted, grasped, and started to straighten my legs. With a sucking sound, the rear wheels freed themselves from the moist earth. I was holding my end of the car about two feet above the ground! It was heavy—damn! it was heavy!—but I could do it!

With each step that I took, I sank about six inches into the ground. But I was carrying it! And Random was doing the same with his end.

We set it down on the roadway, with a slight jouncing of springs. Then I took off my shoes and emptied them, cleaned them with swatches of grass, wrung out my socks, brushed off the cuffs of my trousers, threw my footgear into the rear seat and climbed back into the front, barefooted.

Random jumped in, on the passenger's side, and said, "Look, I want to apologize again—"

"Forget it," I said. "It's over and done with."

"Yes, but I don't want you to hold it against me."

"I won't," I told him. "Just curb your impetuosity in the future, when it involves life-taking in my presence."

"I will," he promised.

"Then let's get rolling," and we did.

We moved through a canyon of rocks, then passed through a city which seemed to be made entirely of glass, or glass-like substance, of tall buildings, thin and fragile-appearing, and of people through whom the pink sun shone, revealing their internal organs and the remains of their last meals. They stared at us as we drove by. They mobbed the corners of their streets, but no one attempted to halt us or pass in front of us.

"The Charles Forts of this place will doubtless quote this happening for many years," said my brother.

I nodded.

Then there was no roadway whatsoever, and we were driving across what seemed an eternal sheet of silicon. After a while it narrowed and became our road, and after another while there were marshes to our left and our right, low, brown, and stinking. And I saw what I'd swear to be a Diplodocus raise its head and stare down upon us. Then, overhead, an enormous bat-winged shape passed by. The sky was now a royal blue, and the sun was of fallow gold.

"We've now got less than a quarter tank of gas," I commented.

"Okay," said Random, "stop the car."

I did this and waited.

For a long time—like maybe six minutes—he was silent, then, "Drive on," he said.

After about three miles we came to a barricade of logs and I began driving around it. A gate occurred on one side, and Random told me, "Stop and blow your horn."

I did so, and after a time the wooden gate creaked upon its huge iron hinges and swung inward.

"Go on in," he said. "It's safe."

I drove in, and off to my left were three bubble-headed Esso pumps, the small building behind them being one of the kind I had seen countless times before, under more ordinary circumstances. I pulled up before one of the pumps and waited.

The guy who emerged from the building was about five feet tall, of enormous girth, with a strawberry-like nose, and his shoulders maybe a yard across.

"What'll it be?" he asked, "Fill 'er up?"

I nodded. "With regular," I said.

"Pull it up a bit," he directed.

I did, and asked Random, "Is my money any good here?"

"Look at it," he told me, and I did.

My wallet was stuffed with orange and yellow bills, Roman numerals in their corners, followed by the letters "D.R."

He grinned at me as I examined the sheaf.

"See, I've taken care of everything," he said.

"Great. By the way, I'm getting hungry."

We looked around us, and we saw a picture of a gent who sells Kentucky Fried Chicken in another place, staring down at us from a big sign.

Strawberry Nose sloshed a little on the ground to make it come out even, hung up the hose, approached, and said, "Eight Drachae Regums."

I found an orange note with a "V D.R." on it and three more with "I D.R." and passed them to him.

"Thanks," he said, and stuffed them in his pocket. "Check your oil and water."

"Yeah."

He added a little water, told me the oil level was okay, and smeared the windshield a bit with a dirty rag. Then he waved and walked back into shack.

We drove over to Kenni Roi's and got us a bucket full of Kentucki Fried Lizzard Partes and another bucket of weak, salty-tasting beer.

Then we washed up in the outbuilding, beeped the horn at the gate, and waited till a man with a halberd hanging over his right shoulder came and opened it for us.

Then we hit the road again.

A tyrannosaurus leaped before us, hesitated for a moment, then went on his way, off to the left. Three more pterodactyls passed overhead.

"I am loath to relinquish Amber's sky," said Random, whatever that meant, and I grunted back at him.

"I'm afraid to try it all at once, though," he continued. "We might be torn to bits."

"Agreed," I agreed.

"But on the other hand, I don't like this place."

I nodded, so we drove on, till the silicon plain ended and bare rock lay all about us.

"What are you doing now?" I ventured.

"Now that I've got the sky, I'm going to try for the terrain," he said.

And the rock sheet became rocks, as we drove along. There was bare, black earth between. After a while, there was more earth and fewer rocks. Finally, I saw splotches of green. First a bit of grass here and there. But it was a very, very bright green, of a kind like yet unlike that common on Earth as I knew it.

Soon there was much of it.

After a time there were trees, spotted occasionally along our way.

Then there was a forest.

And what a forest!

I had never seen trees such as this—mighty and majestic, of a deep, rich green, slightly tinged with gold. They towered, they soared. They were enormous pines, oaks, maples, and many others which I could not distinguish. Through them crept a breeze of fantastic and lovely fragrance, when I cracked the window a bit. I decided to open it all the way and leave it like that after I'd had a few whiffs.

"The Forest of Arden," said the man who was my brother, and I knew he was right, and somehow I both loved and envied him for his wisdom, his knowledge.

"Brother," said I, "you're doing all right. Better than I'd expected. Thank you."

This seemed to take him somewhat aback. It was as if he'd never received a good word from a relative before.

"I'm doing my best," he said, "and I'll do it all the way, I promise. Look at it! We've got the sky, and we've got the forest! It's almost too good to be true! We've passed the halfway point, and nothing's bugged us especially. I think we're very fortunate. Will you give me a Regency."

"Yes," I said, not knowing what it meant, but willing to grant it, if lay within my powers.

He nodded then and said, "You're okay."

He was a homicidal little fink, who I recalled had always been sort of a rebel. Our parents had tried to discipline him in the past, I knew, never very successfully. And I realized, with that, that we had shared common parents, which I suddenly knew was not the case with me and Eric, me and Flora, me and Caine and Bleys and Fiona. And probably others, but these I'd recalled, I knew for sure.

We were driving on a hard, dirt roadway through a cathedral of enormous trees. It seemed to go on forever and ever. I felt safe in the place. Occasionally, startled a deer, surprised a fox crossing or standing near the road. In places, the way was marked with hoofprints. The sunlight was sometimes filtered through leaves, angling like tight golden strings on some Hindu musical instrument. The breeze was moist and spoke of living things. It came to me that I knew this place, that I had ridden this road often in the past. I had ridden through the Forest of Arden on horseback, walked through it, hunted in it, lay on my back beneath some of those great boughs, my arms beneath my head, staring upward. I had climbed among the branches of some of those giants and looked down upon a green world, constantly shifting.

"I love this place," I said, only half realizing I had said it aloud, and Random replied, "You always did," and there might have been a trace of amusement in his voice. I couldn't be sure.

Then off in the distance I heard a note which I knew to be the voice of a hunting horn.

"Drive faster," said Random suddenly. "That sounds to be Julian's horn."

I obeyed.

The horn sounded again, nearer.

"Those damn hounds of his will tear this car to pieces, and his birds will feed on our eyes!" he said. "I'd hate to meet him when he's this well prepared. Whatever he hunts, I know he'd willingly relinquish it for quarry such as two of his brothers."

" 'Live and let live' is my philosophy these days," I remarked.

Random chuckled.

"What a quaint notion. I'll bet it will last all of five minutes."

Then the horn sounded again, even nearer, and he remarked, "Damn!"

The speedometer said seventy-five, in quaint, runic numerals, and I was afraid to go any faster on that road.

And the horn sounded again, much nearer now, three long notes, and I could hear the baying of hounds, off to the left.

"We are now very near to the real Earth, though still far from Amber," said my brother. "It will be futile to run through adjacent Shadows, for if it is truly us that he follows, he will pursue us. Or his shadow will."

"What shall we do!"

"Speed, and hope it is not us that he follows."

And the horn sounded once again, almost next to us this time.

"What the hell is he riding, a locomotive?" I asked.

"I'd say he is riding the mighty Morgenstern, the fastest horse he has ever created."

I let that last word roll around in my head for a while, wondering at it and wondering at it. Yes, it was true, some inner voice told me. He did create Morgenstern, out of Shadows, fusing into the beast the strength and speed of a hurricane and a pile driver.

I remembered that I had call to fear that animal, and then I saw him.

Morgenstern was six hands higher than any other horse I'd ever seen, and his eyes were the dead color of Weimaraner dog's and his coat was all gray and his hooves looked like polished steel. He raced along like the wind, pacing the car, and Julian was crouched in his saddle—the Julian of the playing card, long black hair and bright blue eyes, and he had on his scaled white armor.

Julian smiled at us and waved, and Morgenstern tossed his head and his magnificent mane rippled in the wind, like a flag. His legs were a blur.

I recalled that Julian had once had a man wear my castoff garments and torment the beast. This was why it had tried to trample me on the day of a hunt, when I'd dismounted to skin a buck before it.

I'd rolled the window shut once more, so I didn't think it could tell by scent that I was inside the car. But Julian had spotted me, and I thought I knew what that meant. All about him ran the Storm Hounds, with their tough, tough bodies and their teeth like steel. They too had come out of Shadow, for no normal dog could run like that. But I knew, for a certainty, that the word "normal" did not really apply to anything in this place.

Julian signaled us to stop then, and I glanced at Random and he nodded. "If we don't, he'll just run us down," he said. So I hit the brakes, slowed, stopped.

Morgenstern reared, pawed the air, struck the earth with all four hooves and cantered over. The dogs milled about, their tongues hanging out, their sides heaving. The horse was covered with a glistening sheen that I knew to be perspiration.

I rolled down the window.

"What a surprise!" said Julian, in his slow, almost impeded way of speaking; and a great hawk that was black and green circled and settled upon his left shoulder.

"Yes, isn't it," I replied. "How have you been?"

"Oh, capital," he decided, "as always. What of yourself and brother Random?"

"I'm in good shape," I said, and Random nodded and remarked, "I thought you'd be indulging in other sports at a time like this."

Julian tipped his head and regarded him crookedly, through the windshield.

"I enjoy slaughtering beasts," he said, "and I think of my relatives constantly."

A slight coldness worked its way down my back.

"I was distracted from my hunt by the sound of your motor vehicle," he said. "At the time, I did not expect it to contain two such as you. I'd assume you are not simply riding for pleasure, but have a destination in mind, such as Amber. True?"

"True," I agreed. "May I inquire why you are here, rather than there?"

"Eric set me to watching this road," he replied, and my hand came to rest upon one of the pistols in my belt as he spoke. I had a feeling a bullet couldn't breach that armor, though. I considered shooting Morgenstern.

"Well, brothers," he said, smiling, "I welcome you back and I wish you a good journey. I'll doubtless see you shortly in Amber. Good afternoon," and with that he turned and rode towards the woods.

"Let's get the hell out of here," said Random. "He's probably planning an ambush or a chase," and with this he drew a pistol from his belt and held it in his lap.

I drove on at a decent speed.

After about five minutes, when I was just beginning to breathe a bit easily, I heard the horn. I pushed down on the gas pedal, knowing that he'd catch us anyhow, but trying to buy as much time and gain as much distance as I could. We skidded around corners and roared up hills and through dales. I almost hit a deer at one point, but we made it around the beast without cracking up or slowing.

The horn sounded nearer now, and Random was muttering obscenities.

I had the feeling that we still had quite a distance to go within the forest, and this didn't hearten me a bit.

We hit one long straight stretch, where I was able to floor it for almost a minute. Julian's horn notes grew more distant at that time. But we then entered a section where the road wound and twisted and I had to slow down. He began to gain on us once again.

After about six minutes, he appeared in the rear-view mirror, thundering along the road, his pack all around him, baying and slavering.

Random rolled down his window, and after a minute he leaned out and began to fire.

"Damn that armor!" he said. "I'm sure I hit him twice and nothing's happened."

"I hate the thought of killing that beast," I said, "but try for the horse."

"I already have, several times," he said, tossing his empty pistol to the floor and drawing the other, "and either I'm a lousier shot than I thought, or it's true what they say: that it will take a silver bullet to kill Morgenstern."

He picked off six of the dogs with his remaining rounds, but there were still about two dozen left.

I had passed him one of my pistols, and he accounted for five more of the beasts.

"I'll save the last round," he said, "for Julian's head, if he gets close enough!"

They were perhaps fifty feet behind me at that point, and gaining, so I slammed on the brakes. Some of the dogs couldn't halt in time, but Julian was suddenly gone and a dark shadow passed overhead.

Morgenstern had leaped over the car! He wheeled then, and as horse and rider turned to face us I gunned the engine and the car sped forward.

With a magnificent leap, Morgenstern got them out of the way. In the rear-view mirror, I saw two dogs drop a fender they'd torn loose and renew the pursuit. Some were lying in the road, and there were about fifteen or sixteen giving chase.

"Good show," said Random, "but you're lucky they didn't go for the tires. They've probably never hunted a car before."

I passed him my remaining pistol, and "Get more dogs," I said.

He fired deliberately and with perfect accuracy, accounting for six.

And Julian was beside the car now, a sword in his right hand.

I blew the horn, hoping to spook Morgenstern, but it didn't work. I swerved toward them, but the horse danced away. Random crouched low in his seat and aimed past me, his right hand holding the pistol and resting upon his left forearm.

"Don't fire yet," I said. "I'm going to try to take him."

"You're crazy," he told me, as I hit the brakes again.

He lowered his weapon, though.

As soon as we came to a halt, I flung open my door and leaped out—barefooted yet! Damn it!

I ducked beneath his blade, seized his arm, and hurled him from the saddle. He struck me once on the head with his mailed left fist, and there were Roman candles going off all around me and a terrible pain.

He lay where he had fallen, being groggy, and there were dogs all round me, biting me, and Random kicking them. I snatched up Julian's blade from where it lay and touched his throat with its point.

"Call them off!" I cried. "Or I'll nail you to the ground!"

He screamed orders at the dogs and they drew back. Random was holding Morgenstern's bridle and struggling with the horse.

"Now, dear brother, what do you have to say for yourself?" I asked.

There was a cold blue fire within his eyes, and his face was without expression.

"If you're going to kill me, be about it," he said.

"In my own good time," I told him, somehow enjoying the sight of dirt on his impeccable armor. "In the meantime, what is your life worth to you?"

"Anything I've got, of course."

I stepped back.

"Get up and get into the back seat of the car," I told him.

He did this thing, and I took away his dagger before he got in. Random resumed his own seat, and kept his pistol with the single remaining round aimed at Julian's head.

"Why not just kill him?" he asked.

"I think he'll be useful," I said. "There is much that I wish to know. And there is still a long way to travel."

I began to drive. I could see the dogs milling around. Morgenstern began cantering along after the car.

"I'm afraid I won't be worth much to you as a prisoner," Julian observed. "Although you will torture me, I can only tell you what I know, and that isn't much."

"Start with that then," I said.

"Eric looks to have the strongest position," he told us, "having been right there in Amber when the whole thing broke loose. At least this is the way I saw it, so I offered him my support. Had it been one of you, I'd probably have done the same thing. Eric charged me with keeping guard in Arden, since it's the one of the main routes. Gérard controls the southern seaways, and Caine is off in the northern waters."

"What of Benedict?" Random asked.

"I don't know. I haven't heard anything. He might be with Bleys. He might be off somewhere else in Shadow and not even have heard of this thing yet. He might even be dead. It's been years since we've heard from him.

"How many men have you got in Arden," asked Random.

"Over a thousand," he said. "Some are probably watching you right now."

"And if they want you to go on living, that's all they'll do," said Random.

"You are doubtless correct," he replied. "I have to admit, Corwin did a shrewd thing in taking me prisoner rather than killing me. You just might make it through the forest this way."

"You're just saying that because you want to live," said Random.

"Of course I want to live. May I?"

"Why?"

"In payment for the information I've given you."

Random laughed.

"You've given us very little, and I'm sure more can be torn from you. We'll see, as soon as we get a chance to stop. Eh, Corwin?"

"We'll see," I said. "Where's Fiona?"

"Somewhere to the south, I think," Julian replied.

"How about Deirdre?"

"I don't know."

"Llewella?"

"In Rebma."

"Okay," I said, "I think you've told me everything you know."

"I have."

We drove on in silence, and finally the forest began to thin. I'd lost sight of Morgenstern long ago, though I sometimes saw Julian's falcon pacing us. The road took a turn upward, and we were heading toward a pass between two purple mountains. The gas tank was a little better than a quarter full. Within an hour, we were passing between high shoulders of stone.

"This would be a good place to set up a road block," said Random.

"That sounds likely," I said. "What about it, Julian?"

He sighed.

"Yes," he agreed, "you should be coming upon one very soon. You know how to get by it."

We did. When we came to the gate, and the guard in green and brown leather, sword unsheathed, advanced upon us, I jerked my thumb toward the back seat and said, "Get the picture?"

He did, and he recognized us, also.

He hastened to raise the gate, and he saluted as we passed by.

There were two more gates before we made it through the pass—and somewhere along the way it appeared we had lost the hawk. We had gained several thousand feet in elevation now, and I braked the car on a road that crawled along the face of a cliff. To our right hand, there was nothing other than a long way down.

"Get out," I said. "You're going to take a walk."

Julian paled.

"I won't grovel," he said. "I won't beg you for my life." And he got out.

"Hell," I said, "I haven't had a good grovel in weeks! Well . . . go stand by the edge there. A little closer, please." And Random kept his pistol aimed at his head. "A while back," I told him, "you said that you would probably have supported anyone who occupied Eric's position."

"That's right."

"Look down."

He did. It was a long way.

"Okay," I said, "remember that, should things undergo a sudden change. And remember who it was who gave you your life where another would have taken it.

"Come on, Random. Let's get moving."

We left him standing there, breathing heavily, his brows woven together.

We reached the top and were almost out of gas. I put it in neutral, killed the engine, and began the long roll down.

"I've been thinking," said Random; "you've lost none of your old guile. I'd probably have killed him, myself, for what he tried. But I think you did the right thing. I think he will throw us his support, if we can get an edge on Eric. In the meantime, of course, he'll report what happened *to* Eric."

"Of course," I said.

"And you have more reason to want him dead than any of us."

I smiled.

"Personal feelings don't make for good politics, legal decisions, or business deals."

Random lit two cigarettes and handed me one.

Staring downward through the smoke, I caught my first glimpse of that sea. Beneath the deep blue, almost night-time sky, with that golden sun hanging up there in it, the sea was so rich—thick as paint, textured like a piece of cloth, of royal blue, almost purple—that it troubled me to look upon it. I found myself speaking in a language that I hadn't realized I knew. I was reciting "The Ballad of the Water-Crossers," and Random listened until I had finished and asked me, "It has often been said that you composed that. Is it true?"

"It's been so long," I told him, "that I don't really remember any more."

And as the cliff curved further and further to the left, and as we swung downward across its face, heading toward a wooded valley, more and more of the sea came within our range of vision.

"The Lighthouse of Carba," said Random, gesturing toward an enormous gray tower that rose from the waters, miles out to sea. "I had all but forgotten it."

"And I," I replied. "It is a very strange feeling—coming back," and I realized then that we were no longer speaking English, but the language called Thari.

After almost half an hour, we reached the bottom. I kept coasting for as far as I could, then turned on the engine. At its sound, a flock of dark birds beat its way into the air from the shrubbery off to the left. Something gray and wolfish-looking broke from cover and dashed toward a nearby thicket; the deer it had been stalking, invisible till then, bounded away. We were in a lush valley, though not so thickly or massively wooded as the Forest of Arden, which sloped gently but steadily toward the distant sea.

High, and climbing higher on the left, the mountains reared. The further we advanced into the valley, the better came our view of the nature and full extent of that massive height of rock down one of whose lesser slopes we had coasted. The mountains continued their march to the sea, growing larger as they did so, and taking upon their shoulders a shifting mantle tinged with green, mauve, purple, gold and indigo. The face they turned to the sea was invisible to us from the valley, but about the back of that final, highest peak swirled the faintest veil of ghost clouds, and occasionally the golden sun touched it with fire. I judged we were about thirty-five miles from the place of light, and the fuel gauge read near empty. I knew that the final peak was our destination, and an eagerness began to grow up within me. Random was staring in the same direction.

"It's still there," I remarked.

"I'd almost forgotten. . . ." he said.

And as I shifted gears, I noticed that my trousers had taken on a certain sheen which they had not possessed before. Also, they were tapered considerably as they reached toward my ankles, and I noted that my cuffs had vanished. Then I noticed my shirt.

It was more like a jacket, and it was black and trimmed with silver; and my belt had widened considerably.

On closer inspection, I saw that there was a silver line down the outer seams of my pants legs.

"I find myself garbed effectively," I observed, to see what that wrought.

Random chuckled, and I saw then that he had somewhere acquired brown trousers streaked with red and a shirt of orange and brown. A brown cap with a yellow border rested on the seat beside him.

"I was wondering when you'd notice," he said. "How do you feel?"

"Quite good," I told him, "and by the way, we're almost out of gas."

"Too late to do much about that," he said. "We are now in the real world, and it would be a horrible effort to play with Shadows. Also, it would not go unnoticed. I'm afraid we'll have to hoof it when this gives out."

It gave out two and a half miles later. I coasted off to the side of the road and stopped. The sun by now was westering farewell, and the shadows had grown long indeed.

I reached into the back seat, where my shoes had become black boots, and something rattled as my hand groped after them.

I drew forth a moderately heavy silver sword and scabbard. The scabbard fit my belt perfectly. There was also a black cloak, with a clasp like a silver rose.

"Had you thought them lost forever?" asked Random.

"Damn near," said I.

We climbed out of the car and began walking. The evening was cool and briskly fragrant. There were stars in the east already, and the sun was diving toward its bed.

We trudged along the road, and Random said:

"I don't feel right about this."

"What do you mean?"

"Things have gone too easily, thus far," he told me. "I don't like it. We made it all the way through to the Forest of Arden with barely a hitch. True, Julian tried to take care of us there—but I don't know. . . . We've made it so very far so readily that I'd almost suspect we were permitted to do it."

"This thought has also crossed my mind," I lied. "What do you think it portends?"

"I fear," said he, "that we are walking into a trap."

We walked on for several minutes in silence.

Then, "Ambush?" said I. "These woods seem strangely still."

"I don't know."

We made maybe two miles, and then the sun was gone. The night was black and studded with brilliant stars.

"This is no way for two such as we to move," Random said.

"True."

"Yet I fear to fetch us steeds."

"And I, also."

"What is your assessment of the situation?" Random asked.

"Death and *dreck*," said I. "I feel they may be upon us soon."

"Do you think we should abandon the roadway?"

"I've been thinking about it," I lied again, "and I don't see that it would hurt any for us to walk off to the side a bit."

So we did.

We passed among trees, we moved past the dark shapes of rocks and bushes. And the moon slowly rose, big, of silver, and lighting up the night.

"I am taken by this feeling that we cannot do it," Random told me.

"And what reliance can we give this feeling?" I asked.

"Much."

"Why?"

"Too far and too fast," he responded. "I don't like it at all. Now we're in the real world, it is too late to turn back. We cannot play with Shadows, but must rely on our blades." (He wore a short, burnished one himself.) "I feel, therefore, that it is perhaps Eric's will that we have advanced to this point. There is nothing much to do about it now, but now we're here, I wish we'd had to battle for every inch of the way."

We continued for another mile and paused for cigarettes, which we held cupped in our hands.

"It's a lovely night," I said, to Random and the cool breeze.

"I suppose. . . . What was that?"

There was a soft rustling of shrubbery a bit of a way behind us.

"Some animal, maybe."

His blade was in his hand.

We waited, several minutes, but nothing more was heard.

So he sheathed it and we started walking again.

There were no more sounds from behind us, but after a time I heard something from up ahead.

He nodded when I glanced at him, and we began to move more cautiously.

There was a soft glow, as from a campfire, away, far, in the distance.

We heard no more sounds, but his shrug showed acquiescence to my gesture as I headed toward it, into the woods, to the right.

It was the better part of an hour before we struck the camp. There were four men seated about the fire and two sleeping off in the shadows. The girl who was bound to a stake had her head turned away from us, but I felt my heart quicken as I looked upon her form.

"Could that be . . . ?" I whispered.

"Yes," he replied, "I think it may."

Then she turned her head and I knew it was.

"Deirdre!"

"I wonder what the bitch has been up to?" Random said. "From those guys' colors, I'd venture they're taking her back to Amber."

I saw that they wore black, red, and silver, which I remembered from the Trumps and from somewhere else to be the colors of Eric.

"Since Eric wants her, he can't have her," I said.

"I never much cared for Deirdre," Random said, "but I know you do, so . . ." and he unsheathed his blade.

I did the same.

"Get ready," I told him, rising into a crouch.

And we rushed them.

Maybe two minutes, that's about what it took.

She was watching us by then, the firelight making her face into a twisted mask. She cried and laughed and said our names, in a loud and frightened voice, and I slashed her bonds and helped her to her feet.

"Greetings, sister. Will you join us on the Road to Amber?"

"No," she said. "Thanks for my life, but I want to keep it. Why do you walk to Amber, as if I didn't know."

"There is a throne to be won," said Random, which was news to me, "and we are interested parties."

"If you're smart, you'll stay away and live longer," she said, and God! she was lovely, though a bit tired-looking and dirty.

I took her into my arms because I wanted to, and squeezed her. Random found a skin of wine and we all had a drink.

"Eric is the only prince in Amber," she said, "and the troops are loyal to him."

"I'm not afraid of Eric," I replied, and I knew I wasn't certain about that statement.

"He'll never let you into Amber," she said. "I was prisoner myself, till I made it out one of the secret ways two days ago. I thought I could walk in Shadows till all things were done, but it is not easy to begin this close to the real place. So his troops found me this morning. They were taking me back. I think he might have killed me, had I been returned—though I'm not sure. At any rate, I'd have remained a puppet in the city. I think Eric may be mad—but again, I'm not sure."

"What of Bleys?" Random inquired.

"He sends things out of the Shadows, and Eric is greatly disturbed. But he has never attacked with his real force, and so Eric is troubled, and the disposition of the Crown and Scepter remains uncertain, though Eric holds the one in his right hand."

"I see. Has he ever spoken of us?"

"Not of you, Random. But of Corwin, yes. He still fears the return of Corwin to Amber. There is relative safety for perhaps five more miles—but beyond that, every step of the way is studded with peril. Every tree and rock is a booby trap and an ambush. Because of Bleys and because of Corwin. He wanted you to get at least this far, so that you could not work with Shadows nor easily escape his power. It is absolutely impossible for either of you to enter into Amber without falling into one of his traps."

"Yet you escaped. . . ."

"That was different. I was trying to get out, not in. Perhaps he did not guard me so carefully as he would one of you, because of my sex and my lack of ambition. And nevertheless, as you can see, I did not succeed."

"You have now, sister," I said, "so long as my blade is free to swing on your behalf," and she kissed my brow and squeezed my hand. I was always a sucker for that.

"I'm sure we're being followed," said Random, and with a gesture the three of us faded into the darkness.

We lay still beneath a bush, keeping watch on our trail.

After a time, our whispers indicated that there was a decision for me to make. The question was really quite simple: What next?

The question was too basic, and I couldn't stall any more. I knew I couldn't trust them, even dear Deirdre, but if I had to level with anybody, Random was at least in this thing with me, up to his neck, and Deirdre was my favorite.

"Beloved relatives," I told them, "I've a confession to make," and Random's hand was already on the hilt of his blade. That's how far we could trust one another. I could already hear his mind clicking: *Corwin brought me here to betray me,* he was saying to himself.

"If you brought me here to betray me," he said, "you won't take me back alive."

"Are you kidding?" I asked. "I want your help, not your head. What I have to say is just this: I don't know what the hell's going on. I've made some guesses, but I don't really know where the devil we are, what Amber is, what Eric is doing, who Eric is, or why we're crouched here in the bushes hiding from his troopers," I told him, "or for that matter, who I am, really."

There was an awfully long silence, and then Random whispered, "What do you mean?"

"Yes," said Deirdre.

"I mean," I said, "that I managed to fool you, Random. Didn't you think it strange that all I did on this trip was drive the car?"

"You were the boss," he told me, "and I figured you were planning. You did some pretty shrewd things along the way. I know that you're Corwin."

"Which is a thing I only found out a couple of days ago, myself," I said. "I know that I am the one you call Corwin, but I was in an accident a while back. I had head injuries—I'll show you the scars when we've got more light—and I am suffering from amnesia. I don't dig all this talk about Shadows. I don't even remember much about Amber. All I remember is my relatives, and the fact that I can't trust them much. That's my story. What's to be done about it?"

"Christ!" said Random. "Yes, I can see it now! I understand all the little things that puzzled me along the way. . . . How did you take Flora in so completely?"

"Luck," I said, "and subconscious sneakiness, I guess. No! That's not it! She was stupid. Now I really need you, though."

"Do you think we can make it into the Shadows," said Deirdre, and she was not speaking to me.

"Yes," said Random, "but I'm not for it. I'd like to see Corwin in Amber, and I'd like to see Eric's head on a pole. I'm willing to take a few chances to see these things, so I'm not turning back to the Shadows. You can if you want. You all think I'm a weakling and a bluff. Now you're going to find out. I'm going to see this through."

"Thanks, brother," I said.

"Ill-met by moonlight," said Deirdre.

"You could still be tied to a stake," said Random, and she did not reply.

We lay there a while longer and three men entered the campsite and looked about. Then two of them bent down and sniffed at the ground.

Then they looked in our direction.

"*Weir*," whispered Random, as they moved in our direction.

I saw it happen, though only in shadow. They dropped to all fours and the moonlight played tricks with their gray garments. Then there were the six blazing eyes of our stalkers.

I impaled the first wolf on my silver blade and there was a human howl. Random beheaded one with a single blow, and to my amazement, I saw Deirdre raise one in the air and break its back across her knee with a brittle, snapping sound.

"Quick, your blade!" said Random, and I ran his victim through, and hers, and there were more cries.

"We'd better move fast," said Random. "This way!" and we followed.

"Where are we going?" asked Deirdre, after perhaps an hour of furtive movement through the undergrowth.

"To the sea," he replied.

"Why?"

"It holds Corwin's memory."

"Where? How?"

"Rebma, of course."

"They'd kill you there and feed your brains to the fishes."

"I'm not going the full distance. You'll have to take over at the shore and talk with your sister's sister."

"You mean for him to take the Pattern again?"

"Yes."

"It's risky."

"I know. . . . Listen, Corwin," he said, "you've been decent enough with me recently. If by some chance you're not really Cor-

win, you're dead. You've got to be, though. You can't be someone
else. Not from the way you've operated, without memory even. No,
I'll bet your life on it. Take a chance and try the thing called the Pattern. Odds are, it'll restore your memory. Are you game?"

"Probably," I said, "but what is the Pattern?"

"Rebma is the ghost city," he told me. "It is the reflection of
Amber within the sea. In it, everything in Amber is duplicated, as in
a mirror. Llewella's people live there, and dwell as though in Amber.
They hate me for a few past peccadilloes, so I cannot venture there
with you, but if you would speak them fair and perhaps hint at your
mission, I feel they will let you walk the Pattern of Rebma, which,
while it is the reverse of that in Amber, should have the same effect.
That is, it gives to a son of our father the power to walk among
Shadows."

"How will this power help me?"

"It should make you to know what you are."

"Then I'm game," I said.

"Good man. In this case, we'll keep heading south. It will take several days to reach the stairway. . . . You will go with him,
Deirdre?"

"I will go with my brother Corwin."

I knew she would say that, and I was glad. I was afraid, but I was
glad.

We walked all that night. We avoided three parties of armed
troops, and in the morning we slept in a cave.

V

We spent two evenings making our way to the pink and sable sands of the great sea. It was on the morning of the third day that we arrived at the beach, having successfully avoided a small party the sundown before. We were loath to step out into the open until we had located the precise spot, Faiella-bionin, the Stairway to Rebma, and could cross quickly to it.

The rising sun cast billions of bright shards into the foaming swell of the waters, and our eyes were dazzled by their dance so that we could not see beneath the surface. We had lived on fruit and water for two days and I was ravenously hungry, but I forgot this as I regarded the wide, sloping tiger beach with its sudden twists and rises of coral, orange, pink, and red, and its abrupt caches of shells, driftwood, and small polished stones; and the sea beyond: rising and falling, splashing softly, all gold and blue and royal purple, and casting forth its life-song breezes like benedictions beneath dawn's violet skies.

The mountain that faces the dawn, Kolvir, which has held Amber like a mother her child for all of time, stood perhaps twenty miles to our left, the north, and the sun covered her with gold and made rainbow the veil above the city. Random looked upon it and gnashed his teeth, then looked away. Maybe I did, too.

Deirdre touched my hand, gestured with her head, and began to walk toward the north, parallel to the shore. Random and I followed. She had apparently spotted some landmark.

We'd advanced perhaps a quarter of a mile, when it seemed that the earth shook lightly.

"Hoofbeats!" hissed Random.

"Look!" said Deirdre, and her head was tilted back and she was pointing upward.

My eyes followed the gesture.

Overhead a hawk circled.

"How much farther is it?" I asked.

"That cairn of stones," she said, and I saw it perhaps a hundred yards away, about eight feet in height, builded of head-sized, gray stones, worn by the wind, the sand, the water, standing in the shape of a truncated pyramid.

The hoofbeats came louder and then there were the notes of a horn, not Julian's call, though.

"Run!" said Random, and we did.

After perhaps twenty-five paces, the hawk descended. It swooped at Random, but he had his blade out and took a cut at it. Then it turned its attention to Deirdre.

I snatched my own blade from its sheath and tried a cut. Feathers flew. It rose and dropped again, and this time my blade hit something hard—and I think it fell, but I couldn't tell for sure, because I wasn't about to stop and look back. The sound of hoofbeats was quite steady now, and loud, and the horn notes were near at hand.

We reached the cairn and Deirdre turned at right angles to it and headed straight toward the sea.

I was not about to argue with someone who seemed to know what she was doing. I followed, and from the corner of my eye I saw the horsemen.

They were still off in the distance, but they were thundering along the beach, dogs barking and horns blowing, and Random and I ran like hell and waded out into the surf after our sister.

We were up to our waists when Random said, "It's death if I stay and death if I go on."

"One is imminent," I said, "and the other may be open to negotiation. Let's move!"

We did. We were on some sort of rocky surface which descended into the sea. I didn't know how we would breathe while we walked it, but Deirdre didn't seem worried about it, so I tried not to be.

But I was.

When the water swirled and swished about our heads, I was very worried. Deirdre walked straight ahead, though, descending, and I followed, and Random followed.

Each few feet there was a drop. We were descending an enormous staircase, and it was named Faiella-bionin, I knew.

One more step would bring the water above my head, but Deirdre had already dropped below the water line.

So I drew a deep breath and took the plunge.

There were more steps and I kept following them. I wondered why my body was not naturally buoyed above them, for I continued to remain erect and each step bore me downward as though on a natural staircase, though my movements were somewhat slowed. I began wondering what I'd do when I could hold my breath no longer.

There were bubbles about Random's head, and Deirdre's. I tried to observe what they were doing, but I couldn't figure it. Their breasts seemed to be rising and falling in a normal manner.

When we were about ten feet beneath the surface, Random glanced at me from where he moved at my left side, and I heard his voice. It was as though I had my ear pressed against the bottom of a bathtub and each of his words came as the sound of someone kicking upon the side.

They were clear, though:

"I don't think they'll persuade the dogs to follow, even if the horses do," he said.

"How are you managing to breathe?" I tried saying, and I heard my own words distantly.

"Relax," he said quickly. "If you're holding your breath, let it out and don't worry. You'll be able to breathe so long as you don't venture off the stairway."

"How can that be?" I asked.

"If we make it, you'll know," he said, and his voice had a ringing quality to it, through the cold and passing green.

We were about twenty feet beneath the surface by then, and I exhaled a small amount of air and tried inhaling for perhaps a second.

There was nothing disturbing about the sensation, so I protracted it. There were more bubbles, but beyond that I felt nothing uncomfortable in the transition.

There was no sense of increasing pressure during the next ten feet or so, and I could see the staircase on which we moved as though through a greenish fog. Down, down, down it led. Straight. Direct. And there was some kind of light coming from below us.

"If we can make it through the archway, we'll be safe," said my sister.

"*You'll* be safe," Random corrected, and I wondered what he had done to be despised in the place called Rebma.

"If they ride horses which have never made the journey before, then they'll have to follow on foot," said Random. "In that case, we'll make it."

"So they might not follow—if that is the case," said Deirdre.

We hurried.

By the time we were perhaps fifty feet below the surface, the waters grew quite dark and chill, but the glow before us and below us increased, and after another ten steps, I could make out the source:

There was a pillar rising to the right. At its top was something globe-like and glowing. Perhaps fifteen steps lower, another such formation occurred to the left. Beyond that, it seemed there was another one on the right, and so on.

When we entered the vicinity of the thing, the waters grew warmer and the stairway itself became clear: it was white, shot through with pink and green, and resembled marble but was not slippery despite the water. It was perhaps fifty feet in width, and there was a wide banister of the same substance on either side.

Fishes swam past us as we walked it. When I looked back over my shoulder, there seemed to be no sign of pursuit.

It became brighter. We entered the vicinity of the first light, and it wasn't a globe on the top of a pillar. My mind must have added that touch to the phenomenon, to try to rationalize it at least a bit. It appeared to be a flame, about two feet in height, dancing there, as atop a huge torch. I decided to ask about it later, and saved my—if you'll excuse the expression—breath, for the rapid descent we were making.

After we had entered the alley of light and had passd six more of the torches, Random said, "They're after us," and I looked back again and saw distant figures descending, four of them on horseback.

It is a strange feeling to laugh under water and hear yourself.

"Let them," I said, and I touched the hilt of my blade, "for now we have made it this far, I feel a power upon me!"

We hurried though, and off to our left and to our right the water grew black as ink. Only the stairway was illuminated, in our mad flight down it, and distantly I saw what appeared to be a mighty arch.

Deirdre was leaping down the stairs two at a time, and there came a vibration now, from the staccato beat of the horses' hooves behind us.

The band of armed men—filling the way from banister to banister

—was far behind and above. But the four horsemen had gained on us. We followed Deirdre as she rushed downward, and my hand stayed upon my blade.

Three, four, five. We passed that many lights before I looked back again and saw that the horsemen were perhaps fifty feet above us. The footmen were now almost out of sight. The archway loomed ahead, perhaps two hundred feet distant. Big, shining like alabaster, and carved with Tritons, sea nymphs, mermaids, and dolphins, it was. And there seemed to be people on the other side of it.

"They must wonder why we have come here," said Random.

"It will be an academic point if we don't make it," I replied, hurrying, as another glance revealed that the horsemen had gained ten feet on us.

I drew my blade then, and it flashed in the torchlight. Random followed suit.

After another twenty steps or so, the vibrations were terrible within the green and we turned, so as not to be cut down as we ran.

They were almost upon us. The gates lay a hundred feet to our back, and it might have been a hundred miles, unless we could take the four horsemen.

I crouched, as the man who was headed toward me swung his blade. There was another rider to his right and slightly to his rear, so naturally I moved to his left, near to the rail. This required that he strike cross-body, as he held his blade in his right hand.

When he struck, I parried in *quarte* and riposted.

He was leaning far forward in the saddle, and the point of my blade entered his neck on the right side.

A great billow of blood, like crimson smoke, arose and swirled within the greenish light. Crazily, I wished Van Gogh were there to see it.

The horse continued past, and I leaped at the second rider from the rear.

He turned to parry the stroke, succeeded. But the force of his speed through the water and the strength of my blow removed him from the saddle. As he fell, I kicked, and he drifted. I struck at him, hovering there above me, and he parried again, but this carried him beyond the rail. I heard him scream as the pressure of the waters came upon him. Then he was silent.

I turned my attention then to Random, who had slain both a horse and a man and was dueling with a second man on foot. By the time I reached them, he had slain the man and was laughing. The blood billowed above them, and I suddenly realized that I *had* known mad, sad, bad Vincent Van Gogh, and it was really too bad that he couldn't have painted this.

The footmen were perhaps a hundred feet behind us, and we turned and headed toward the arches. Deirdre had already passed through them.

We ran and we made it. There were many swords at out sides, and the footmen turned back. Then we sheathed our blades, and Random said, "I've had it," and we moved to join with the band of people who had stood to defend us.

Random was immediately ordered to surrender his blade, and he shrugged and handed it over. Then two men came and stood on either side of him and a third at his back, and we continued on down the stair.

I lost all sense of time in that watery place, but I feel that we walked for somewhere between a quarter of an hour and half an hour before we reached our destination.

The golden gates of Rebma stood before us. We passed through them. We entered the city.

Everything was to be seen through a green haze. There were buildings, all of them fragile and most of them high, grouped in patterns and standing in colors that entered my eyes and tore through my mind, seeking after remembrance. They failed, the sole result of their digging being the new familiar ache that accompanies the half recalled, the unrecalled. I had walked these streets before, however, that I knew, or ones very much like them.

Random had not said a single word since he had been taken into custody. Deirdre's only conversation had been to inquire after our sister Llewella. She had been informed that Llewella was in Rebma.

I examined our escort. They were men with green hair, purple hair, and black hair, and all of them had eyes of green, save for one fellow whose were of a hazel color. All wore only scaled trunks and cloaks, cross-braces on their breasts, and short swords depending from sea-shell belts. All were pretty much lacking in body hair. None of them spoke to me, though some stared and some glared. I was allowed to keep my weapon.

Inside the city, we were conducted up a wide avenue, lighted by pillar flames set at even closer intervals than on Faiella-bionin, and people stared out at us from behind octagonal, tinted windows, and bright-bellied fishes swam by. There came a cool current, like a breeze, as we turned a corner; and after a few steps, a warm one, like a wind.

We were taken to the palace in the center of the city, and I knew it as my hand knew the glove in my belt. It was an image of the palace of Amber, obscured only by the green and confused by the many strangely placed mirrors which had been set within its walls, inside and out. A woman sat upon the throne in the glassite room I almost recalled, and her hair was green, though streaked with silver, and her eyes were round as moons of jade and her brows rose like the wings of olive gulls. Her mouth was small, her chin was small; her cheeks were high and wide and rounded. A circlet of white gold crossed her brow and there was a crystal necklace about her neck. At its tip there flashed a sapphire between her sweet bare breasts, whose nipples were also a pale green. She wore scaled trunks of blue and a silver belt, and she held a scepter of pink coral in her right hand and had a ring upon every finger, and each ring had a stone of a different blue within it. She did not smile as she spoke:

"What seek you here, outcasts of Amber?" she asked, and her voice was a lisping, soft, flowing thing.

Deirdre spoke in reply, saying: "We flee the wrath of the prince who sits in the true city—Eric! To be frank, we wish to work his downfall. If he is loved here, we are lost, and we have delivered ourselves into the hands of our enemies. But I feel he is not loved here. So we come asking aid, gentle Moire—"

"I will not give you troops to assault Amber," she replied. "As you know, the chaos would be reflected within my own realm."

"That is not what we would have of you, dear Moire," Deirdre continued, "but only a small thing, to be achieved at no pain or cost to yourself or your subjects."

"Name it! For as you know, Eric is almost as disliked here as this recreant who stands at your left hand," and with this she gestured at my brother, who stared at her in frank and insolent appraisal, a small smile playing about the corners of his lips.

If he was going to pay—whatever the price—for whatever he had done, I could see that he would pay it like a true prince of Amber— as our three dead brothers had done ages ago, I suddenly recalled. He would pay it, mocking them the while, laughing though his mouth was filled with the blood of his body, and as he died he would pronounce an irrevocable curse which would come to pass. I, too, had this power, I suddenly knew, and I would use it if circumstances required its use.

"The thing I would ask," she said, "is for my brother Corwin, who is also brother to the Lady Llewella, who dwells here with you. I believe that he has never given you offense. . . ."

"That is true. But why does he not speak for himself?"

"That is a part of the problem, Lady. He cannot, for he does not know what to ask. Much of his memory has departed, from an accident which occurred when he dwelled among Shadows. It is to restore his remembrance that we have come here, to bring back his recollection of the old days, that he might oppose Eric in Amber."

"Continue," said the woman on the throne, regarding me through the shadows of her lashes on her eyes.

"In a place in this building," she said, "there is a room where few would go. In that room," she continued, "upon the floor, traced in fiery outline, there lies a duplicate of the thing we call the Pattern. Only a son or daughter of Amber's late liege may walk this Pattern and live; and it gives to such a person a power over Shadow." Here Moire blinked several times, and I speculated as to the number of her subjects she had sent upon that path, to gain some control of this power for Rebma. Of course, she had failed. "To walk the Pattern," Deirdre went on, "should, we feel, restore to Corwin his memory of himself as a prince of Amber. He cannot go to Amber to do it, and this is the only place I know where it is duplicated, other than Tir-na Nog'th, where of course we may not go at this time."

Moire turned her gaze upon my sister, swept it over Random, returned it to me.

"Is Corwin willing to essay this thing?" she asked.

I bowed.

"Willing, m'lady," I said, and she smiled then.

"Very well, you have my permission. I can guarantee you no guarantees of safety beyond my realm, however."

"As to that, your majesty," said Deirdre, "we expect no boons, but will take care of it ourselves upon our departure."

"Save for Random," she said, "who will be quite safe."

"What mean you?" asked Deirdre, for Random would not, of course, speak for himself under the circumstances.

"Surely you recall," she said, "that one time Prince Random came into my realm as a friend, and did thereafter depart in haste with my daughter Morganthë."

"I have heard this said, Lady Moire, but I am not aware of the truth or the baseness of the tale."

"It is true," said Moire, "and a month thereafter was she returned to me. Her suicide came some months after the birth of her son Martin. What have you to say to that, Prince Random?"

"Nothing," said Random.

"When Martin came of age," said Moire, "because he was of the blood of Amber, he determined to walk the Pattern. He is the only of my people to have succeeded. Thereafter, he walked in Shadow and I have not seen him since. What have you to say to that, Lord Random?"

"Nothing," Random replied.

"Therefore, I will punish thee," Moire continued. "You shall marry the woman of my choice and remain with her in my realm for a year's time, or you will forfeit your life. What say you to that, Random?"

Random said nothing, but he nodded abruptly.

She struck her scepter upon the arm of her turquoise throne.

"Very well," she said. "So be it."

And so it was.

We repaired to the chambers she had granted us, there to refresh ourselves. Subsequently she appeared at the door of my own.

"Hail, Moire," I said.

"Lord Corwin of Amber," she told me, "often have I wished to meet thee."

"And I thee," I lied.

"Your exploits are legend."

"Thank you, but I barely recall the high points."

"May I enter here?"

"Certainly," and I stepped aside.

She moved into the well-appointed suite she had granted me. She seated herself upon the edge of the orange couch.

"When would you like to essay the Pattern?"

"As soon as possible," I told her.

She considered this, then said, "Where have you been, among Shadows?"

"Very far from here," I said, "in a place that I learned to love."

"It is strange that a lord of Amber should possess this capacity."

"What capacity?"

"To love," she replied.

"Perhaps I chose the wrong word."

"I doubt it," she said, "for the ballads of Corwin do touch upon the strings of the heart."

"The lady is kind."

"But not wrong," she replied.

"I'll give you a ballad one day."

"What did you do when you dwelled in Shadow?"

"It occurs to me that I was a professional soldier, madam. I fought for whoever would pay me. Also, I composed the words and music to many popular songs."

"Both these things occur to me as logical and natural."

"Pray tell me, what of my brother Random?"

"He will marry with a girl among my subjects who is named Vialle. She is blind and has no wooers among our kind."

"Are you certain," said I, "that you do the best thing for her?"

"She will obtain good status in this manner," said Moire, "though he depart after a year and never return. For whatever else may be said of him, he *is* a prince of Amber."

"What if she comes to love him?"

"Could anyone really do this thing?"

"In my way, I love him, as a brother."

"Then this is the first time a son of Amber has ever said such a thing, and I attribute it to your poetic temperament."

"Whatever," said I, "be very sure that it is the best thing for the girl."

"I have considered it," she told me, "and I am certain. She will recover from whatever pain he inflicts, and after his departure she will be a great lady of my court."

"So may it be," I said, and looked away, feeling a sadness come over me—for the girl, of course.

"What may I say to you?" I said. "Perhaps you do a good thing. I hope so." And I took her hand and kissed it.

"You, Lord Corwin, are the only prince of Amber I might support," she told me, "save possibly for Benedict. He is gone these twelve years and ten, however, and Lir knows where his bones may lie. Pity."

"I did not know this," I said. "My memory is so screwed up. Please bear with me. I shall miss Benedict, an' he be dead. He was my Master of Arms and taught me of all weapons. But he was gentle."

"As are you, Corwin," she told me, taking my hand and drawing me toward her.

"No, not really," I replied, as I seated myself on the couch at her side. Then she said, "We've much time till we dine." Then she leaned against me with the front of her shoulder which was soft.

"When do we eat?" I asked.

"Whenever I declare it," she said, and she faced me more fully.

So I drew her upon me and found the catch to the buckle which covered the softness of her belly. There was more softness beneath, and her hair was green.

Upon the couch, I gave her her ballad. Her lips replied without words.

After we had eaten—and I had learned the trick of eating under water, which I might detail later on if circumstances really warrant—we rose from our places within the marble high hall, decorated with nets and ropes of red and brown, and we made our way back along a narrow corridor, and down, down, beneath the floor of the sea itself, first by means of a spiral staircase that screwed its way through absolute darkness and glowed. After about twenty paces, my brother said, "Screw!" and stepped off the staircase and began swimming downward alongside it.

"It *is* faster that way," said Moire.

"And it is a long way down," said Deirdre, knowing the distance of the one in Amber.

So we all stepped off and swam downward through darkness, beside the glowing, twisting thing.

It took perhaps ten minutes to reach the bottom, but when our feet touched the floor, we stood, with no tendency to drift. There was light about us then, from a few feeble flames set within niches in the wall.

"Why is this part of the ocean, within the double of Amber, so different from waters elsewhere?" I asked.

"Because that is the way it is," said Deirdre, which irritated me.

We were in an enormous cavern, and tunnels shot off from it in all directions. We moved toward one.

After walking along it for an awfully long while, we began to encounter side passages, some of which had doors or grills before them and some of which did not.

At the seventh of these we stopped. It was a huge gray door of some slate-like substance, bound in metal, towering to twice my height. I remembered something about the size of Tritons as I regarded that doorway. Then Moire smiled, just at me, and produced a large key from a ring upon her belt and set it within the lock.

She couldn't turn it, though. Perhaps the thing had been unused for too long.

Random growled and his hand shot forward, knocking hers aside.

He seized the key in his right hand and twisted.

There came a click.

Then he pushed the door open with his foot and we stared within.

In a room the size of a ballroom the Pattern was laid. The floor was black and looked smooth as glass. And on the floor was the Pattern.

It shimmered like the cold fire that it was, quivered, made the whole room seem somehow unsubstantial. It was an elaborate tracery of bright power, composed mainly of curves, though there were a few straight lines near its middle. It reminded me of a fantastically intricate, life-scale version of one of those maze things you do with a pencil (or ballpoint, as the case may be), to get you into or out of something. Like, I could almost see the words "Start Here," somewhere way to the back. It was perhaps a hundred yards across at its narrow middle, and maybe a hundred and fifty long.

It made bells ring within my head, and then came the throbbing. My mind recoiled from the touch of it. But if I were a prince of Amber, then somewhere within my blood, my nervous system, my genes, this pattern was recorded somehow, so that I would respond properly, so that I could walk the bloody thing.

"Sure wish I could have a cigarette," I said, and the girls giggled, though rather a little too rapidly and perhaps with a bit of a twist on the treble control.

Random took my arm and said, "It's an ordeal, but it's not impossible or we wouldn't be here. Take it very slowly and don't let yourself be distracted. Don't be alarmed by the shower of sparks that will arise with each step. They can't hurt you. You'll feel a mild current passing through you the whole time, and after a while you'll start feeling high. But keep concentrating, and don't forget—keep walking! Don't stop, whatever you do, and don't stray from the path, or it'll probably kill you," and as he spoke, we walked. We walked close to the right-hand wall and rounded the Pattern, heading toward its far end. The girls trailed behind us.

I whispered to him.

"I tried to talk her out of this thing she's planned for you. No luck."

"I figured you would," he said. "Don't worry about it. I can do a year standing on my head, and they might even let me go sooner—if I'm obnoxious enough."

"The girl she has lined up for you is named Vialle. She's blind."

"Great," he said. "Great joke."

"Remember that regency we spoke of?"

"Yeah."

"Be kind to her then, stay the full year, and I will be generous."

Nothing.

Then he squeezed my arm.

"Friend of yours, huh?" he chuckled. "What's she like?"

"Is it a deal?" I said, slowly.

"It's a deal."

Then we stood at the place where the Pattern began, near to the corner of the room.

I moved forward and regarded the line of inlaid fires that started near to the spot where I had placed my right foot. The Pattern constituted the only illumination within the room. The waters were chill about me.

I strode forward, setting my left foot upon the path. It was outlined by blue-white sparks. Then I set my right foot upon it, and I felt the current Random had mentioned. I took another step.

There was a crackle and I felt my hair beginning to rise. I took another step.

Then the thing began to curve, abruptly, back upon itself. I took ten more paces, and a certain resistance seemed to arise. It was as if a black barrier had grown up before me, of some substance which pushed back upon me with each effort that I made to pass forward.

I fought it. It was the First Veil, I suddenly knew.

To get beyond it would be an Achievement, a good sign, showing that I was indeed part of the Pattern. Each raising and lowering of my foot suddenly required a terrible effort, and sparks shot from my hair.

I concentrated on the fiery line. I walked it breathing heavily.

Suddenly the pressure was eased. The Veil had parted before me, as abruptly as it had occurred. I had passed beyond it and acquired something.

I had gained a piece of myself.

I saw the paper skins and the knobby, stick-like bones of the dead of Auschwitz. I had been present at Nuremberg, I knew. I heard the voice of Stephen Spender reciting "Vienna," and I saw Mother Courage cross the stage on the night of a Brecht premiere. I saw the rockets leap up from the stained hard places, Peenemunde, Vandenberg, Kennedy, Kyzyl Kum in Kazakhstan, and I touched with my hands the Wall of China. We were drinking beer and wine, and Shaxpur said he was drunk and went off to puke. I entered the green forests of the Western Reserve and took three scalps one day. I hummed a tune as we marched along and it caught on. It became "*Auprès de ma Blonde.*" I remembered, I remembered . . . my life within the Shadow place its inhabitants had called the Earth. Three more steps, and I held a bloody blade and saw three dead men and my horse, on which I had fled the revolution in France. And more, so much more, back to—

I took another step.

Back to—

The dead. They were all about me. There was a horrible stink—the smell of decaying flesh—and I heard the howls of a dog who was being beaten to death. Billows of black smoke filled the sky, and an icy wind swept around me bearing a few small drops of rain. My throat was parched and my hands shook and my head was on fire. I staggered alone, seeing everything through the haze of the fever that burned me. The gutters were filled with garbage and dead cats and the emptyings of chamber pots. With a rattle and the ringing of a bell, the death wagon thundered by, splashing me with mud and cold water.

How long I wandered, I do not know, before a woman seized my arm and I saw a Death's Head ring upon her finger. She led me to her rooms, but discovered there that I had no money and was incoherent. A look of fear crossed her painted face, erasing the smile on her bright lips, and she fled and I collapsed upon her bed.

Later—again, how much later I do not know—a big man, the girl's Black Davy, came and slapped me across the face and dragged me to my feet. I seized his right biceps and hung on. He half carried, half pulled me toward the door.

When I realized that he was going to cast me out into the cold, I tightened my grip to protest it. I squeezed with all my remaining strength, mumbling half-coherent pleas.

Then through sweat and tear-filled eyes, I saw his face break open and heard a scream come forth from between his stained teeth.

The bone in his arm had broken where I'd squeezed it.

He pushed me away with his left hand and fell to his knees, weeping. I sat upon the floor, and my head cleared for a moment.

"I . . . am . . . staying here," I said, "until I feel better. Get out. If you come back—I'll kill you."

"You've got the plague!" he cried. "They'll come for your bones tomorrow!" and he spat then, got to his feet, and staggered out.

I made it to the door and barred it. Then I crawled back to the bed and slept.

If they came for my bones the next day, they were disappointed. For, perhaps ten hours later, in the middle of the night, I awoke in a cold sweat and realized my fever had broken. I was weak, but rational once more.

I realized I had lived through the plague.

I took a man's cloak I found in the wardrobe and took some money I found in a drawer.

Then I went forth into London and the Night, in a year of the plague, looking for something. . . .

I had no recollection of who I was or what I was doing there.

That was how it had started.

I was well into the Pattern now, and the sparks flashed continually about my feet, reaching to the height of my knees. I no longer knew which direction I faced, or where Random and Deirdre and Moire stood. The currents swept through me, and it seemed my eyeballs were vibrating. Then came a pins-and-needles feeling in my cheeks and a coldness on the back of my neck. I clenched my teeth to keep them from chattering.

The auto accident had not given me my amnesia. I had been without full memory since the reign of Elizabeth I. Flora must have concluded that the recent accident had restored me. She had known of my condition. I was suddenly struck by the thought that she was on that Shadow Earth mainly to keep tabs on me.

Since the sixteenth century, then?

That I couldn't say. I'd find out, though.

I took six more rapid steps, reaching the end of an arc and coming to the beginning place of a straight line.

I set my foot upon it, and with each step that I took, another barrier began to rise against me. It was the Second Veil.

There was a right-angle turn, then another, then another.

I was a prince of Amber. It was true. There had been fifteen brothers and six were dead. There had been eight sisters, and two were dead, possibly four. We had spent much of our time in wandering in Shadow, or in our own universes. It is an academic, though valid philosophical question, as to whether one with power over Shadow could create his own universe. Whatever the ultimate answer, from a practical point we could.

Another curve began, and it was though I were walking in glue as I moved slowly along it.

One, two, three, four . . . I raised my fiery boots and let them down again.

My head throbbed and my heart felt as though it were fibrillating to pieces.

Amber!

The going was suddenly easy once more, as I remembered Amber.

Amber was the greatest city which had ever existed or ever would exist. Amber had always been and always would be, and every other city, everywhere, every other city that existed was but a reflection of a shadow of some phase of Amber. Amber, Amber, Amber . . . I remember thee. I shall never forget thee again. I guess, deep inside me, I never really did, through all those centuries I wandered the Shadow Earth, for often at night my dreams were troubled by images of thy green and golden spires and thy sweeping terraces. I remember thy wide promenades and the decks of flowers, golden and red. I recall the sweetness of thy airs, and the temples, palaces, and pleasances thou containest, contained, will always contain. Amber, immortal city from which every other city has taken its shape, I cannot forget thee, even now, nor forget that day on the Pattern of Rebma when I remembered thee within thy reflected walls, fresh from a meal after starvation and the loving of Moire, but nothing could compare with the pleasure and the love of remembering thee; and even now, as I stand contemplating the Courts of Chaos, telling this story to the only one present to hear, that perhaps he may repeat it, that it will not die after I have died within; even now, I remember thee with love, city that I was born to rule. . . .

Ten paces, then a swirling filigree of fire confronted me. I essayed it, my sweat vanishing into the waters as fast as it sprang forth.

It was tricky, so devilish tricky, and it seemed that the waters of the room suddenly moved in great currents which threatened to sweep me from the Pattern. I struggled on, resisting them. Instinctively, I knew that to leave the Pattern before I'd completed it would mean my death. I dared not raise my eyes from the places of light that lay before me, to see how far I had come, how far I had yet to go.

The currents subsided and more of my memories returned, memories of my life as a prince of Amber. . . . No, they are not yours for the asking; they are mine, some vicious and cruel, others perhaps noble—memories going back to my childhood in the great palace of Amber, with the green banner of my father Oberon flaring above it, white unicorn rampant, facing to the dexter.

Random had made it through the Pattern. Even Deirdre had made it. Therefore I, Corwin, would make it, no matter what the resistance.

I emerged from the filigree and marched along the Grand Curve. The forces that shape the universe fell upon me and beat me into their image.

I had an advantage over any other person who attempted the walk, however. I knew that I had done it before, so I knew that I could do it. This helped me against the unnatural fears which rose like black clouds and were gone again, only to return, their strength redoubled. I walked the Pattern and I remembered all, I remembered all the days before my centuries on the Shadow Earth and I remembered other places of Shadow, many of them special and dear to me, and one which I loved above all, save for Amber.

I walked three more curves, a straight line, and a series of sharp arcs, and I held within me once again a consciousness of the thing which I had never really lost: mine was the power over Shadows.

Ten turns which left me dizzy, another short arc, a straight line, and the Final Veil.

It was agony to move. Everything tried to beat me aside. The waters were cold, then boiling. It seemed that they constantly pushed against me. I struggled, putting one foot before the other. The sparks reached as high as my waist at this point, then my breast, my shoulders. They were into my eyes. They were all about me. I could barely see the Pattern itself.

Then a short arc, ending in blackness.

One, two. . . . And to take the last step was like trying to push through a concrete wall.

I did it.

Then I turned slowly and looked back over the course I had come. I would not permit myself the luxury of sagging to my knees. I was a prince of Amber, and by God! nothing could humble me in the presence of my peers. Not even the Pattern!

I waved jauntily in what I thought to be the right direction. Whether or not I could be made out very clearly was another matter.

Then I stood there a moment and thought.

I knew the power of the Pattern now. Going back along it would be no trick at all.

But why bother?

I lacked my deck of cards, but the power of the Pattern could serve me just as well. . . .

They were waiting for me, my brother and sister and Moire with her thighs like marble pillars.

Deirdre could take care of herself from here on out—after all, we'd saved her life. I didn't feel obligated to go on protecting her on a day-by-day basis. Random was stuck in Rebma for a year, unless he had guts enough to leap forward and take the Pattern to this still center of power and perhaps escape. And as for Moire, it had been nice knowing her, and maybe I'd see her again some day, and like that. I closed my eyes and bowed my head.

Before I did so, though, I saw a fleeting shadow.

Random? Trying it? Whatever, he wouldn't know where I was headed. No one would.

I opened my eyes and I stood in the middle of the same Pattern, in reverse.

I was cold, and I was damn tired, but I was in Amber—in the real room, of which the one I had departed was but an image. From the Pattern, I could transfer myself to any point I wished within Amber.

Getting back would be a problem, however.

So I stood there and dripped and considered.

If Eric had taken the royal suite, then I might find him there. Or perhaps in the throne room. But then, I'd have to walk the Pattern again, in order to reach the escape point.

I transferred myself to a hiding place I knew of within the palace. It was a windowless cubicle into which some light trickled from observation slits high over head. I bolted its one sliding panel from the inside, dusted off a wooden bench set beside the wall, spread my cloak upon it and stretched out for a nap. If anyone came groping his way down from above, I'd hear him long before he reached me.

I slept.

After a while, I awakened. So I arose, dusted off my cloak and donned it once more. Then I began to negotiate the series of pegs which laddered their way up into the palace.

I knew where it was, the third floor, by the markings on the walls.

I swung myself over to a small landing and searched for the peephole. I found it and gazed through. Nothing. The library was empty. So I slid back the panel and entered.

Within, I was stricken by the multitudes of books. They always do that to me. I considered everything, including the display cases, and finally moved toward the place where a crystal case contained everything that led up to a family banquet—private joke. It held four decks of the family cards, and I sought about for a means of obtaining one without setting off an alarm which might keep me from using it.

After maybe ten minutes, I succeeded in gimmicking the proper case. It was tricky. Then, pack in hands, I found a comfortable seat for the consideration thereof.

The cards were just like Flora's and they held us all under glass and were cold to the touch. Now, too, I knew why.

So I shuffled and spread them all out before me in the proper manner. Then I read them, and I saw that bad things were in store for the entire family; and I gathered them all together then.

Save for one.

It was the card depicting my brother Bleys.

I replaced the others in their case and tucked it into my belt. Then I considered Bleys.

At about that time there came a scratching in the lock of the great door to the library. What could I do? I loosened my blade in its scabbard and waited. I ducked low behind the desk, though.

Peering out, I saw that it was a guy named Dik, who had obviously come to clean the place, as he set out emptying the ashtrays and wastebaskets and dusting the shelves.

Since it would be demeaning to be discovered, I exposed myself.

I rose and said, "Hello, Dik. Remember me?"

He turned three kinds of pale, half bolted, and said:

"Of course, Lord. How could I forget?"

"I suppose it would be possible, after all this time."

"Never, Lord Corwin," he replied.

"I suppose I'm here without official sanction, and engaged in a bit of illicit research," I said, "but if Eric doesn't like it when you tell him that you saw me, please explain that I was simply exercising my rights, and he will be seeing me personally—soon."

"I'll do that, m'lord," he said, bowing.

"Come sit with me a moment, friend Dik, and I'll tell you more."

And he did, so I did.

"There was a time," I said, addressing this ancient visage, "when I was considered gone for good and abandoned forever. Since I still live, however, and since I maintain all my faculties, I fear that I must dispute Eric's claim to the throne of Amber. Though it's not a thing to be settled simply, as he is not the first-born, nor do I feel he would enjoy popular support if another were in sight. For these, among other reasons—most of them personal—I am about to oppose him. I have not yet decided how, nor upon what grounds, but by God! he deserves opposition! Tell him that. If he wishes to seek me, tell him that I dwell among Shadows, but different ones than before. He may know what I mean by that. I will not be easily destroyed, for I will guard myself at least as well as he does here. I will oppose him from hell to eternity, and I will not cease until one of us is dead. What say you to this, old retainer?"

And he took my hand and kissed it.

"Hail to thee, Corwin, Lord of Amber," he said, and there was a tear in his eye.

Then the door cracked a crack behind him and swung open.

Eric entered.

"Hello," said I, rising and putting a most obnoxious twang to my voice. "I didn't expect to meet with you this early in the game. How go things in Amber?"

And his eyes were wide with amaze and his voice heavy with that which men call sarcasm, and I can't think of a better word, as he replied:

"Well, when it comes to things, Corwin. Poorly, on other counts, however."

"Pity," said I, "and how shall we put things aright?"

"I know a way," he said, and then he glared at Dik, who promptly departed and closed the door behind him. I heard it *snick* shut.

Eric loosened his blade in its scabbard.

"You want the throne," he said.

"Don't we all?" I told him.

"I guess so," he said, with a sigh. "It's true, that uneasy-lies-the-head bit. I don't know why we are driven to strive so for this ridiculous position. But you must recall that I've defeated you twice, mercifully granting your life on a Shadow world the last occasion."

"It wasn't that merciful," I said. "You know where you left me, to die of the plague. The first time, as I remember, it was pretty much a draw."

"Then it is between the two of us now, Corwin," he said. "I am your elder and your better. If you wish to try me at arms, I find myself suitably attired. Slay me, and the throne will probably be yours. Try it. I don't think you can succeed, however. And I'd like to quit your claim right now. So come at me. Let's see what you learned on the Shadow Earth."

And his blade was in his hand and mine in mine.

I moved around the desk.

"What an enormous *chutzpah* you possess," I told him. "What makes you better than the rest of us, and more fit to rule?"

"The fact that I was able to occupy the throne," he replied. "Try and take it."

And I did.

I tried a head-cut, which he parried; and I parried his riposte to my heart and cut at his wrist.

He parried this and kicked a small stool between us. I set it aside, hopefully in the direction of his face, with my right toe, but it missed and he had at me again.

I parried his attack, and he mine. Then I lunged, was parried, was attacked, and parried again myself.

I tried a very fancy attack I'd learned in France, which involved a beat, a feint in *quarte,* a feint in *sixte,* and a lunge veering off into an attack on his wrist.

I nicked him and the blood flowed.

"Oh, damnable brother!" he said, retreating. "Report has it Random accompanies thee."

"This is true," said I. "More than one of us are assembled against you."

And he lunged then and beat me back, and I felt suddenly that for all my work he was still my master. He was perhaps one of the greatest swordsmen I had ever faced. I suddenly had the feeling that I couldn't take him, and I parried like mad and retreated in the same fashion as he beat me back, step by step. We'd both had centuries under the greatest masters of the blade in business. The greatest alive, I knew, was brother Benedict, and he wasn't around to help, one way or the other. So I snatched things off the desk with my left hand and threw them at Eric. But he dodged everything and came on strong, and I circled to his left and all like that, but I couldn't draw the point of his blade from my left eye. And I was afraid. The man was magnificent. If I didn't hate him so, I would have applauded his performance.

I kept backing away, and the fear and the knowledge came upon me: I knew I still couldn't take him. He was a better man than I was, when it came to the blade. I cursed this, but I couldn't get around it. I tried three more elaborate attacks and was defeated on each occasion. He parried me and made me retreat before his own attacks.

Now don't get the wrong idea. I'm damn good. It's just that he seemed better.

Then there were some alarms and excursions in the hall outside. Eric's retainers were coming, and if he didn't kill me before they arrived, then I was confident that they'd do the job—probably with a bolt from a crossbow.

There was blood dripping from his right wrist. His hand was still steady but I had the feeling then that under other circumstances, by fighting a defensive fight, I just might be able to wear him down with that wrist injury going against him, and perhaps I could get through his guard at the proper moment when he began to slow.

I cursed softly and he laughed.

"You're a fool to have come here," he said.

He didn't realize what I was doing until it was too late. (I'd been retreating until the door was at my back. It was risky, leaving myself with no room for retreat, but it was better than sure death.)

With my left hand, I managed to drop the bar. It was a big, heavy door and they'd have to knock it down now to get in. That gave me a few more minutes. It also gave me a shoulder wound, from an attack I could only partly parry as I dropped the bar. But it was my left shoulder. My sword arm remained intact.

I smiled, to put up a good front.

"Perhaps *you* were a fool, to enter *here*," I said. "You're slowing, you know," and I tried a hard, fast, vicious attack.

He parried it, but he fell back two paces in doing so.

"That wound's getting to you," I added. "Your arm's weakening. You can feel the strength leaving it—"

"Shut up!" he said, and I realized I'd gotten through to him. This increased my chances by several percent, I decided, and I pressed him as hard as I could, realizing I couldn't keep that pace up very long.

But Eric didn't realize it.

I'd planted the seeds of fear, and he fell back before my sudden onslaught.

There was a banging on the door but I didn't have to worry about that for a while anyway.

"I'm going to take you, Eric," I said. "I'm tougher than I used to be, and you've had it, brother."

I saw the fear begin in his eyes, and it spread over his face, and his style shifted to follow suit. He began fighting a completely defensive battle, backing away from my attack. I'm sure he wasn't faking either. I felt I had bluffed him, for he had always been better than I. But what if it had been partly psychological on my part too? What if I had almost beaten myself with this attitude, which Eric had helped to foster? What if I had bluffed myself all along? Maybe I was as good. With a strange sense of confidence, I tried the same attack I had used before and I scored, leaving another trail of red on his forearm.

"That was rather stupid, Eric," I said, "to fall for the same trick twice," and he backed around a wide chair. We fought across it for a time.

The banging on the door stopped, and the voices which had been shouting inquiries through it fell silent.

"They've gone for axes," Eric panted. "They'll be in here in no time."

I wouldn't drop my smile. I held it and said: "It'll take a few minutes—which is more time than I'll need to finish this. You can hardly keep your guard now, and the blood keeps running—look at it!"

"Shut up!"

"By the time they get through, there will be only one prince in Amber, and it won't be you!"

Then, with his left arm, he swept a row of books from a shelf and they struck me and fell about me.

He didn't seize the opportunity to attack, however. He dashed across the room, picking up a small chair, which he held in his left hand.

He wedged himself into a corner and held the chair and his blade before him.

There were rapid footsteps in the hall outside, and then axes began to ring upon the door.

"Come on!" he said. "Try and take me now!"

"You're scared," I said.

He laughed.

"Academic," he replied. "You can't take me before that door falls, and then it will be all over for you."

I had to agree. He could hold off any blade with that setup, at least for quite a few minutes.

I crossed the room quickly, to the opposite wall.

With my left hand, I opened the panel through which I had entered.

"Okay," I said, "it looks like you're going to live—for a time. You're lucky. Next time we meet, there won't be anyone to help you."

He spat and called me a few traditional vile names, even putting down the chair to add an obscene gesture, as I ducked through the panel and closed it behind me.

There came a *thunk,* and eight inches of steel gleamed on my side of the panel as I was fastening it. He had thrown his blade. Risky, if I chose to return. But he knew I wouldn't, for the door sounded about ready to fall.

I descended the pegs as rapidly as I could, to the place where I had slept earlier. As I did, I considered my increased skill with the blade. At first, in the battle, I had been awed by the man who had beaten me before. Now, though, I wondered. Perhaps those centuries on the Shadow Earth were not a waste. Maybe I had actually gotten better during that time. Now I felt that I might be Eric's equal with the weapon. This made me feel good. If we met again, as I was sure we would, and there was no outside interference—who knew? I would court the chance, however. Today's encounter had scared him. I was certain. That might serve to slow his hand, to cause the necessary hesitation on the next occasion.

I let go and dropped the final fifteen feet, bending my knees as I landed. I was the proverbial five minutes ahead of the posse, but I was sure I could take advantage of it and escape.

For I had the cards in my belt.

I drew the card that was Bleys and stared at it. My shoulder hurt, but I forgot it, as the coldness came upon me.

There were two ways to depart directly from Amber into Shadow. . . .

One was the Pattern, seldom used for this purpose.

Another was the Trumps, if you could trust a brother.

I considered Bleys. I could almost trust him. He *was* my brother, but he was in trouble and could use my help.

I stared at him, flame-crowned, dressed all in red and orange, with a sword in his right hand and a glass of wine in his left. The devil danced in his blue eyes, his beard blazed, and the tracery on his blade, I suddenly realized, flared with a portion of the Pattern. His rings flashed. He seemed to move.

The contact came like an icy wind.

The figure on the card seemed life-sized now and changed position into whatever stance he presently held. His eyes did not quite focus upon me, and his lips moved.

"Who is it?" they said, and I heard the words.

"Corwin," said I, and he held forth his left hand, which no longer bore the goblet.

"Then come to me, if you would."

I reached forth and our fingers met. I took a step.

I was still holding the card in my left hand, but Bleys and I stood together on a cliff and there was a chasm to our side and a high fortress to our other side. The sky above us was the color of flame.

"Hello, Bleys," I said, tucking the card into my belt with the others. "Thanks for the assistance."

I suddenly felt weak and realized the blood was still flowing from my left shoulder.

"You're wounded!" he said, throwing an arm about my shoulder, and I started to nod but fainted instead.

Later that night, I sprawled in a big chair within the fortress and drank whisky. We smoked and passed the bottle and talked.

"So you were actually in Amber?"

"Yes, that's right."

"And you wounded Eric in your duel?"

"Yes."

"Damn! I wish you'd killed him!" Then he reflected. "Well, maybe not. Then you'd have held the throne. I might have a better chance against Eric than I'd have had against you. I don't know. What are your plans?"

I decided upon complete honesty.

"We all want the throne," I said, "so there's no reason to lie to one another. I'm not about to try killing you for it—that would be foolish—but on the other hand, I'm not about to renounce my claim because I'm enjoying your hospitality. Random would like it, but he's pretty much out of the picture. No one has heard from Benedict for some time now. Gérard and Caine seem to be supporting Eric, rather than promoting their own claims. The same goes for Julian. That leaves Brand and our sisters. I don't know what the hell Brand is up to these days, but I do know that Deirdre is without power, unless she and Llewella can raise something in Rebma, and Flora is Eric's creature. I don't know what Fiona is up too."

"And so that leaves us," said Bleys, pouring us each another drink. "Yes, you're right. I don't know what's going on in everyone's head right now, but I can assess our relative strengths and I think I'm in the best position. You made a wise choice in coming to me. Support me, and I'll give you a regency."

"Bless your heart," I said. "We'll see."

We sipped our whiskies.

"What else is there to do?" he asked, and I realized that the question was important.

"I might raise an army of my own, to lay siege to Amber," I told him.

"Where among Shadows lies your army?" he inquired.

"That, of course, is my affair," I said. "I don't think I'd oppose you. When it comes to monarchs, I'd like to see either you, me, Gérard, or Benedict—if he still lives—upon the throne."

"Preferably you, of course."

"Of course."

"Then we understand one another. So I think we can work together, for the time being."

"And I," I agreed, "else I would not have delivered myself into your hands."

He smiled within his beard.

"You needed someone," he said, "and I was the lesser evil."

"True," I agreed.

"I wish Benedict were here. I wish Gérard had not sold out."

"Wishes, wishes," I told him. "Wish in one hand and do something else in the other, and squeeze them both and see which comes true."

"Well taken," he said.

We smoked a while in silence.

"How far can I trust you?" he asked.

"As far as I can trust you."

"Then let's make a deal. Frankly, I had thought you dead for many years. I hadn't foreseen your showing up at a crucial time and pressing your own claim. But you're here, and that's that. Let's form an alliance—combine our forces and lay siege to Amber. Whichever of us lives through it winds up on top. If we both do, well—hell!—we can always fight a duel!"

I thought about it. It sounded like the best deal I'd get anywhere.

So I said, "I'd like to sleep on it. Tell you in the morning, okay?"

"Okay."

We finished our drinks then and fell to reminiscing. My shoulder throbbed a bit, but the whisky helped, and the salve which Bleys had supplied. After a time, we were almost maudlin.

It is strange, I guess, to have kin and to be without kinship, for as long as our lives had led us along our separate paths. Lord! We talked the moon out of the heavens before either of us grew tired. Then he clapped me upon my good shoulder and told me that he was beginning to feel his load and that a servant would be by in the morning to bring me breakfast. I nodded, we embraced, and he retired.

Then I moved to the window, and from that vantage I could see down far into the chasm.

The campfires below burned like stars. There were thousands of them. I could tell that Bleys had assembled a mighty force, and I was envious. But, on the other hand, it was a good thing. If anyone could take Eric, it was probably Bleys. He wouldn't be a bad thing in Amber; it was just that I preferred me.

Then I watched a while longer, and I saw that strange shapes moved among the lights. I wondered then as to the nature of his army.

Whatever, it was more than I possessed.

I made my way back to the table and poured me a final drink.

Before I quaffed it, however, I lighted a taper. In its light, I withdrew the pack of cards I had stolen.

I spread them before me and I came across the one depicting Eric. I laid it in the center of the table and put the rest away.

After a time, it came to life; and I saw Eric in his sleeping garments and I heard the words, "Who is it?" His arm was bound.

"Me," I said, "Corwin. How are you?"

He cursed then, and I laughed. This was a dangerous game and maybe the whisky had contributed to it, but I continued: "I just felt like telling you that all goes well with me. I also wanted to advise you that you were right when you spoke of the uneasy head. You won't be wearing it long, though. So cheerio! Brother! The day I come again to Amber is the day you die! Just thought I'd tell you— since that day is not too far off."

"Come ahead," he told me, "and I'll not want for grace in the matter of your own passing."

His eyes focused on me then and we were close.

I thumbed my nose at him and passed my palm over the card.

It was like hanging up a telephone, and I shuffled Eric in with all the rest.

I wondered though, as I approached sleep, concerning those troops of Bleys which occupied the defile below, and I thought upon Eric's defenses.

It would not be easy.

VI

The land was known as Avernus, and the assembled troops were not quite men. I reviewed them the following morning, walking behind Bleys. They were all of them around seven feet in height, had very red skins and little hair, cat-like eyes, and six-digited hands and feet. They wore garments that looked as light as silk, but were woven of something else and were mainly gray or blue in color. Each bore two short blades, hooked at the end. Their ears were pointed and their many fingers clawed.

The climate was warm and the colors bewildering, and everyone thought we were gods.

Bleys had found a place where the religion involved brother-gods who looked like us and had their troubles. Invariably, in the terms of this *mythos,* an evil brother would seize power and seek to oppress the good brothers. And of course there was the legend of an Apocalypse where they themselves would be called upon to stand on the side of the surviving good brothers.

I wore my left arm in a black sling and considered those who were about to die.

I stood before a trooper and looked up at him. I asked him, "Do you know who Eric is?"

"The Lord of Evil," he replied.

I nodded and said, "Very good," and passed on.

Bleys had custom-made cannon fodder.

"How large is your army?" I asked him.

"Around fifty thousand," he replied.

"I salute those who are about to Give Their All," I told him. "You can't take Amber with fifty thousand men, even providing you can get them all to the foot of Kolvir intact—and you can't. It's silly even to consider using these poor bastards against the immortal city, with their toy swords and all."

"I know," he said, "but they're not all I've got."

"You'll need a lot more."

"Then how do three navies sound—half again the size of Caines and Gérard's fleets put together?

"I've a way."

"Not yet enough," said I, "and barely a beginning."

"I know. I'm still building," he said.

"Well, we'd better build a lot more. Eric will sit in Amber and kill us as we march through Shadows. When the remaining forces finally reach the foot of Kolvir, he'll decimate them there. Then there will be the climb to Amber. How many hundred do you think will remain when we reach the city? Enough to be dispatched in five minutes, at almost no cost to Eric. If this is the best you've got, brother Bleys, I have misgivings concerning this expedition."

"Eric has announced his coronation in three months' time," he said. "I can triple my forces by then—at least. Perhaps I can even have a quarter of a million Shadow troops to lead against Amber. There are other worlds like this one, and I will penetrate them. I will raise me such a force of holy crusaders as has never been sent against Amber before."

"And Eric will have had the same time to intensify his defenses. I don't know, Bleys . . . it's almost a suicide run. I didn't know the full situation when I came here—"

"And what have you brought with you?" he asked. "Nothing! It is rumored that you once commanded troops. Where are they?"

I turned away from him.

"They are no more," I said. "I am certain."

"Could you not find a Shadow of your Shadow?"

"I don't want to try," I said. "I'm sorry."

"Then what real good are you to me?"

"I'll go," I told him, "if that's all you had in mind, if that's all you really wanted me around for—more bodies."

"Wait!" he cried out. "I spoke hastily. I don't want to lose your counsel, if nothing else. Stay with me, please. I will even apologize."

"That is not necessary," I said, knowing what this thing means to a prince of Amber. "I'll stay. I think I can help you."

"Good!" and he clapped me upon my good shoulder.

"And I'll get you more troops," I added. "Never fear."

And I did.

I walked among Shadows, and found a race of furry creatures, dark and clawed and fanged, reasonably man-like, and about as intelligent as a freshman in the high school of your choice—sorry, kids, but what I mean is they were loyal, devoted, honest, and too easily screwed by bastards like me and my brother. I felt like the dee-jay of your choice.

Around a hundred thousand worshiped us to the extent of taking up arms.

Bleys was impressed and shut up. After a week my shoulder was healed. After two months we had our quarter million and more.

"Corwin, Corwin! You're still Corwin!" he said, and we took another drink.

But I was feeling kind of funny. Most of these troops were destined to die. I was the agent responsible for much of this. I felt some remorse, though I knew the difference between Shadow and Substance. Each death would be a real death; however, I knew that also.

And some nights I dwelled upon the playing cards. The missing Trumps had been restored to the pack I held. One of them was a portrait of Amber itself, and I knew it could bear me back into the city. The others were those of our dead or missing relatives. And one was Dad's, and I skipped it over quickly. He was gone.

I stared at each face for a long while to consider what might be gained from each. I cast the cards several times, and the same thing came up on each occasion.

His name was Caine.

He wore satin that was green and black, and a dark three-cornered hat with a green plume of feathers trailing down behind. At his belt there was an emerald-studded dagger. He was dark.

"Caine," I said.

After a time, there came a reply.

"Who?" he asked.

"Corwin," said I.

"Corwin! Is this a joke?"

"No."

"What do you want?"

"What've you got?"

"You know that," and his eyes shifted and lay upon me, but I watched his hand, which was near to his dagger.

"Where are you?"

"With Bleys."

"There was a rumor you'd shown up in Amber recently—and I wondered at the bandages on Eric's arm."

"You're looking at the reason," I said. "What's your price?"

"What do you mean?"

"Let us be frank and to the point. Do you think Bleys and I can take Eric?"

"No, that's why I'm with Eric. And I won't sell out my armada either, if that's what you're after—and I'd imagine you are."

I smiled.

"Perceptive brother," I replied. "Well, it's been nice talking to you. See you in Amber—maybe."

I moved my hand, and he cried out.

"Wait!"

"Why?"

"I don't even know your offer."

"Yes, you do," I said. "You've guessed it, and you're not interested."

"I didn't say that. It's just that I know where the equities lie."

"You mean the power."

"Okay, the power. What've you got to offer?"

We talked for maybe an hour, after which time the northern seaways were open to the three phantom fleets of Bleys, which might enter expecting reinforcements.

"If you fail, there'll be three beheadings in Amber," said he.

"But you don't really expect that, do you?" I asked.

"No, I think either you or Bleys will sit upon the throne before too very long. I'll be satisfied to serve the winner. That regency should be nice. I'd still like Random's head as part of the price, though."

"No deal," I said. "Take it as you've heard it or forget it."

"I'll take it."

I smiled and placed my palm upon the card and he was gone.

Gérard was a matter I'd leave for the morrow. Caine had exhausted me.

I rolled into bed and slept.

Gérard, when he learned the score, agreed to lay off us. Mainly because it was I who was asking, as he had considered Eric a lesser of potent evils.

I concluded the deal quickly, promising him everything he asked, as no heads were involved.

Then I reviewed the troops again and told them more of Amber.

Strangely, they got along like brothers, the big red guys and the little hairy ones.

It was sad and it was true.

We were their gods, and that was that.

I saw the fleet, sailing on a great ocean the color of blood. I wondered. In the Shadow worlds through which they sailed, many of them would be lost.

I considered the troops of Avernus, and my recruits from the place called Ri'ik. Theirs was the task of marching to Earth and Amber.

I shuffled my cards and cast them. I picked up the one called Benedict. For a long while I searched it, but there was nothing but the cold.

Then I seized upon Brand's. For another long while there was nothing but the cold.

Then there came a scream. It was a horrible, tormented thing.

"Help me!" came the cry.

"How can I?" I asked.

"Who is that?" he asked, and I saw his body writhe.

"Corwin."

"Deliver me from this place, brother Corwin! Anything you name shall be yours in return!"

"Where are you?"

"I—"

And there came a swirling of things my mind refused to conceive of, and another scream, torn forth as though in agony and ending in silence.

Then the coldness came in again.

I found that I was shaking. From what, I did not know.

I lit a cigarette and moved to the window to consider the night, leaving the cards where they had fallen upon the tabletop of my room within the garrison.

The stars were tiny and misted over. There were no constellations that I could recognize. A small blue moon dropped quickly through the darkness. The night had come on with a sudden, icy chill and I wrapped my cloak close about me. I thought back to the winter of our disastrous campaign in Russia. Gods! I'd almost frozen to death! And where did it all lead?

To the throne of Amber, of course.

For that was sufficient justification for anything.

But what of Brand? Where was he? What was happening about him, and who had done this thing to him?

Answers? None.

I wondered, though, as I stared up and out, tracing the path of that blue disk in its descent. Was there something I was missing in the whole picture, some factor I didn't quite dig?

No answer.

I seated myself at the table once more, a small drink at my hand.

I fingered my way through the pack and found Dad's card.

Oberon, Lord of Amber, stood before me in his green and his gold. High, wide, and thick, his beard black and shot with silver, his hair the same. Green rings in gold settings and a blade of golden color. It had once seemed to me that nothing could ever displace the immortal liege of Amber from his throne. What had happened? I still didn't know. But he was gone. How had my father met with his end?

I stared and concentrated.

Nothing, nothing—

Something?

Something.

There came a responding movement, though ever so weak, and the figure on the card turned in upon itself and shriveled to a shadow of the man he had been.

"Father?" I asked.

Nothing.

"Father?"

"Yes . . ." Very faint and distant, as though through a seashell, immersed in its monotone humming.

"Where are you? What has happened?"

"I . . ." Long pause.

"Yes? This is Corwin, your son. What came to pass in Amber, that you are gone?"

"My time," he said, sounding even further away.

"Do you mean that you abdicated? None of my brothers has given me the tale, and I do not trust them sufficiently to ask them. I only know that the throne seems open to all grabbers. Eric now holds the city and Julian guards the Forest of Arden. Caine and Gérard maintain the seas. Bleys would oppose all and I am allied with him. What are your wishes in this matter?"

"You are the only one—who—has asked," he gasped. "Yes . . ."

" 'Yes' what?"

"Yes, oppose—them. . . ."

"What of you? How can I help you?"

"I am—beyond help. Take the throne. . . ."

"I? Or Bleys and I?"

"You!" he said.

"Yes?"

"You have my blessing. . . . Take the throne—and be quick—about it!"

"Why, Father?"

"I lack the breath— Take it!"

Then he, too was gone.

So Dad lived. That was interesting. What to do now?

I sipped my drink and thought about it.

He still lived, somewhere, and he was king in Amber. Why had he left? Where had he gone? What kind of, which, and how many? Like that.

Who knew? Not I. So there was no more to say, for now.

However . . .

I couldn't put the thing down. I want you to know that Dad and I never got along very well. I didn't hate him, like Random or some of the others. But I, sure as hell, had no reason to be especially fond of him. He had been big, he had been powerful, and he had been there. That was about it. He was also most of the history of Amber, as we knew it, and the history of Amber stretches back for so many millennia that you may as well stop counting. So what do you do?

As for me, I finished my drink and went to bed.

The following morning I attended a meeting of Bleys' general staff. He had four admirals, each in charge of roughly a quarter of his fleet, and a whole mess of army officers. Altogether there were about thirty of the high-ranking brass at the meeting, big and red or small and hairy, as the case might be.

The meeting lasted perhaps four hours, and then we all broke for lunch. It was decided that we would move three days hence. Since it would require one of the blood to open the way to Amber, I was to lead the fleet aboard the flagship, and Bleys would take his infantry through lands of Shadow.

I was troubled by this, and I asked him what would have happened had I not shown up to give this assistance. I was told two things in reply: one, if he had had to go it alone, he would have led the fleet through and left them at a great distance from shore, returned in a single vessel to Avernus and led his foot soldiers forward to a rendezvous at a given time; and two, he had purposely sought for a Shadow in which a brother would appear to give him aid.

I had some misgivings when I heard about the latter, though I knew I was really me. The former smacked of being a bit unworkable, since the fleet would be too far out to sea to receive any signals from the shore, and the chance of missing the date—allowing for mishaps when it came to a body that large—was too great, as I saw it, to encourage a whole big lot of faith in his general plan.

But as a tactician, I had always thought him brilliant; and when he laid out the maps of Amber and the outlying country which he himself had drawn, and when he had explained the tactics to be employed therein, I knew that he was a prince of Amber, almost matchless in his guile.

The only thing was, we were up against another prince of Amber, one who occupied what was definitely a stronger position. I was worried, but with the impending coronation, it seemed about the only course available to us, and I decided to go along for the whole ride. If we lost, we were creamed, but he held the biggest threat available and had a workable time schedule, which I didn't.

So I walked the land called Avernus and considered its foggy valleys and chasms, its smoking craters, its bright, bright sun against its crazy sky, its icy nights and too hot days, its many rocks and carloads of dark sand, its tiny, though vicious and poisonous beasts, and its big purple plants, like spineless cacti; and on the afternoon of the second day, as I stood on a cliff overlooking the sea, beneath a tower of massed vermilion clouds, I decided that I rather liked the place for all that, and if its sons would perish in the wars of the gods, I would immortalize them one day in song if I were able.

This mild balm in mind for what I feared, I joined the fleet and took command. If we made it, they would be feted forever in the halls of the immortals.

I was guide and opener of the way. I rejoiced.

So we set sail the following day, and I directed things from the lead ship. I led us into a storm, and we emerged that much nearer our destination. I led us past an enormous whirlpool, and we were so much to the good. I led us through a shallow rocky place, and the shade of the waters deepened afterward. Their colors began to approximate those of Amber. So I still knew how to do it. I could influence our fate in time and place. I could take us home. Home for me, that is.

I led us past strange islands where green birds cawed and green apes hung like fruit in the trees, swung, sometimes gibbered, and threw rocks into the sea, aimed, doubtless, at us.

I took us far out to sea, and then nosed the fleet around back in the direction of shore.

Bleys by now was marching across the plains of the worlds. Somehow, I knew he would make it, past whatever defenses Eric had set up. I kept in touch with him by means of the cards, and I learned of his encounters along the way. Like, ten thousand men dead in a plains battle with centaurs, five thousand lost in an earthquake of frightening proportions, fifteen hundred dead of a whirlwind plague that swept the camps, nineteen thousand dead or missing in action as they passed through the jungles of a place I didn't recognize, when the napalm fell upon them from the strange buzzing things that passed overhead, six thousand deserting in a place that looked like the heaven they had been promised, five hundred unaccounted for as they crossed a sand flat where a mushroom cloud burned and towered beside them, eighty-six hundred gone as they moved through a valley of suddenly militant machines that rolled forward on treads and fired fires, eight hundred sick and abandoned, two hundred dead from flash floods, fifty-four dying of duels among themselves, three hundred dead from eating poisonous native fruits, a thousand slain in a massive stampede of buffalo-like creatures, seventy-three gone when their tents caught fire, fifteen hundred carried away by the floods, two thousand slain by the winds that came down from the blue hills.

I was pleased that I'd lost only a hundred and eighty-six ships in that time.

To sleep, perchance to dream. . . . Yeah, there's a thing that rubs. Eric was killing us by inches and hours. His proposed coronation was only a few weeks away, and he obviously knew we were coming against him, because we died and we died.

Now, it is written that only a prince of Amber may walk among Shadows, though of course he may lead or direct as many as he chooses along such courses. We led our troops and saw them die, but of Shadow I have this to say: there is Shadow and there is Substance, and this is the root of all things. Of Substance, there is only Amber, the real city, upon the real Earth, which contains everything. Of

Shadow, there is an infinitude of things. Every possibility exists somewhere as a Shadow of the real. Amber, by its very existence, has cast such in all directions. And what may one say of it beyond? Shadow extends from Amber to Chaos, and all things are possible within it. There are only three ways of traversing it, and each of them is difficult.

If one is a prince or princess of the blood, then one may walk, crossing through Shadows, forcing one's environment to change as one passes, until it is finally in precisely the shape one desires it, and there stop. That Shadow world is then one's own, save for family intrusions, to do with as one would. In such a place had I dwelled for centuries.

The second means is the cards, cast by Dworkin, Master of the Line, who had created them in our image, to facilitate communications between members of the royal family. He was the ancient artist to whom space and perspective meant nothing. He had made up the family Trumps, which permitted the willer to touch his brethren wherever they might be. I had a feeling that these had not been used in full accord with their author's intention.

The third was the Pattern, also drawn by Dworkin, which could only be walked by a member of our family. It initiated the walker into the system of the cards, as it were, and at its ending gave its walker the power to stride across Shadows.

The cards and the Pattern made for instant transport from Substance through Shadow. The other way, walking, was harder.

I knew what Random had done in delivering me into the true world. As we had driven, he kept adding, from memory, that which he recalled of Amber, and subtracting that which did not agree. When everything corresponded, he knew we had arrived. It was no real trick, for had he the knowledge, any man could reach his own Amber. Even now, Bleys and I could find Shadow Ambers where each of us ruled, and spend all of time and eternity ruling there. But this would not be the same, for us. For none would be the true Amber, the city into which we were born, the city from which all others take their shapes.

So we were taking the hardest route, the walk through Shadow, for our invasion of Amber itself. Anyone knowing this and possessing the power could interpose obstacles. Eric had done so, and now we faced them as we died. What would come of this? No one knew.

But if Eric were crowned king, it would be reflected and shadowed everywhere.

All the surviving brothers, we princes of Amber, I am sure, felt it much better, each in his own simple way, personally to achieve this status and thereafter let the Shadows fall where they might.

We passed ghost fleets, the ships of Gérard, as we sailed—the Flying Dutchmen of this world/that world, and we knew we were coming near. I used them as reference points.

On the eighth day of our voyaging we were near to Amber. That is when the storm broke.

The sea turned dark, the clouds collected overhead, and the sails grew slack within the still that followed. The sun hid its face—an enormous blue one—and I felt that Eric had found us at last.

The the winds arose, and—if you'll excuse the expression—broke —upon the vessel I rode.

We were tempest-tossed and storm-torn, as the poets say, or said. My guts felt loose and watery as the first billows hit us. We were hurled from side to side like dice in a giant's hand. We were swept over the waters of the sea and the waters from the sky. The sky turned black, and there was sleet mixed in with the glassy bell ropes that pulled the thunder. Everyone, I'm sure, cried out. I know I did. I pulled my way along the shifting deck to seize the abandoned wheel. I strapped myself in place and held it. Eric had cut loose in Amber, that was for damn sure.

One, two, three, four, and there was no letup. Five hours, then. How many men had we lost? I dunno.

Then I felt and heard a tingling and a tinkling, and I saw Bleys as through a long gray tunnel.

"What's the matter?" he asked. "I've been trying to reach you."

"Life is full of vicissitudes," I replied. "We're riding out one of them."

"Storm?" he said.

"You bet your sweet ass. Its the granddaddy of them all. I think I see a monster off to port. If he has any brains, he'll aim for the bottom. . . . He just did."

"We just had one ourselves," Bleys told me.

"Monster or storm?"

"Storm," he replied. "Two hundred dead."

"Keep the faith," I said, "hold the fort, and talk to me later. Okay?"

He nodded, and there were lightnings at his back.

"Eric's got our number," he added, before he cut off.

I had to agree.

It was three more hours before things let up, and many more later I learned that we had lost half of the fleet (and on my vessel—the flagship—we had lost forty of the crew of one hundred and twenty). It was a hard rain that fell.

Somehow, to the sea over Rebma, we made it.

I drew forth my cards and held Random's before me.

When he realized who was talking, the first thing he said was "Turn back," and I asked him why.

" 'Cause, according to Llewella, Eric can cream you now. She says wait a while, till he relaxes, and hit him then—like a year from now, maybe."

I shook my head.

"Sorry," said I. "Can't. Too many losses involved in getting us this far. It's a now-or-never situation."

He shrugged, wearing a "Like, I warned you" expression.

"Why, though?" I asked him.

"Mainly because I just learned he can control the weather around here," he said.

"We'll still have to chance it."

He shrugged again.

"Don't say I didn't tell you."

"He definitely knows we're coming?"

"What do you think? Is he a cretin?"

"No."

"Then he knows. If I could guess it in Rebma, then he knows in Amber—and I *did* guess, from a wavering of Shadow."

"Unfortunately," I said, "I have some misgivings about this expedition, but it's Bleys' show."

"You cop out and let him get axed."

"Sorry, but I can't take the chance. He might win. I'm bringing in the fleet."

"You've spoken with Caine, with Gérard?"

"Yes."

"Then you must think you have a chance upon the waters. But listen, Eric has figured a way to control the Jewel of Judgment, I gather, from court gossip about its double. He *can* use it to control the weather here. That's definite. God knows what else he might be able to do with it."

"Pity," I said "We'll have to suffer it. Can't let a few storms demoralize us."

"Corwin, I'll confess. I spoke with Eric himself three days ago."

"Why?"

"He asked me. I spoke with him out of boredom. He went into great detail concerning his defenses."

"That's because he learned from Julian that we came in together. He's sure it'll get back to me."

"Probably," he said. "But that doesn't change what he said."

"No," I agreed.

"Then let Bleys fight his own war," he told me. "You can hit Eric later."

"He's about to be crowned in Amber."

"I know, I know. It's as easy to attack a king, though, as a prince, isn't it? What difference does it make what he calls himself at the time, so long as you take him? It'll still be Eric."

"True," I said, "but I've committed myself."

"Then uncommit yourself," he said.

" 'Fraid I can't do that."

"Then you're crazy, Charlie."

"Probably."

"Well, good luck, anyhow."

"Thanks."

"See you around."

And that was that, and it troubled me.

Was I heading into a trap?

Eric was no fool. Perhaps he had a real death-gig lined up. Finally, I shrugged and leaned out over the rail, the cards once again behind my belt.

It is a proud and lonely thing to be a prince of Amber, incapable of trust. I wasn't real fond of it just then, but there I was.

Eric, of course, had controlled the storm we'd just passed through, and it seemed in line with his being weather master in Amber, as Random had told me.

So I tried something myself.

I headed us toward an Amber lousy with snow. It was the most horrible blizzard I could conjure up.

The big flakes began to fall, out there on the ocean.

Let him stop them a normal enough Shadow offering, if he could.

And he did.

Within a half hour's time the blizzard had died. Amber was virtually impervious—and it was really the only city. I didn't want to go off course, so I let things be. Eric *was* master of the weather in Amber.

What to do?

We sailed on, of course. Into the jaws of death.

What can one say?

The second storm was worse than the first, but I held the wheel. It was electrified, and focused only on the fleet. It drove us apart. It cost us forty vessels more.

I was afraid to call Bleys to see what had been done to him.

"Around two hundred thousand troops are left," he said. "Flash flood," and I told him what Random had told me.

"I'll buy it," he said. "But let's not dwell on it. Weather or no, we'll beat him."

"I hope so."

I lit a cigarette and leaned across the bow.

Amber should be coming into sight soon. I knew the ways of Shadow now, and I know how to get there by walking.

But everyone had misgivings.

There would never be a perfect day, though. . . .

So we sailed on, and the darkness came upon us like a sudden wave, and the worst storm of them all struck.

We managed to ride out its black lashings, but I was scared. It was all true, and we were in northern waters. If Caine had kept his word, all well and good. If he was getting us out, he was in an excellent position.

So I assumed he had sold us out. Why not? I prepared the fleet—seventy-three vessels remaining—for battle, when I saw him approach. The cards had lied—or else been very correct—when they'd pointed to him as the key figure.

The lead vessel headed toward my own, and I moved forward to meet it. We hove to, and side by side regarded one another. We could have communicated via the Trumps, but Caine didn't choose to; and he was in the stronger position. Therefore, family etiquette required that he choose his own means. He obviously wanted to be on record as he called out, through an amplifier:

"Corwin! Kindly surrender command of your fleet! I've got you outnumbered! You can't make it through!"

I regarded him across the waves and raised my own amplifier to my lips.

"What of our arrangement?" I asked.

"Null and void," he said. "Your force is far too weak to hurt Amber, so save lives and surrender it now."

I looked over my left shoulder and regarded the sun.

"Pray hear me, brother Caine," said I, "and grant me this then: give me your leave to confer with my captains till the sun stands in high heaven."

"Very well," he replied, without hesitation. "They appreciate their positions, I'm sure."

I turned away then and ordered that the ship be turned about and headed back in the direction of the main body of vessels.

If I tried to flee, Caine would pursue me through the Shadows and destroy the ships, one by one. Gunpowder did not ignite on the real Earth, but if we moved very far away, it too would be employed to our undoing. Caine would find some, for it was probable, were I to depart, the fleet could not sail the Shadow seas without me, and would be left as sitting ducks upon the real waters here. So the crews were either dead or prisoners, whatever I did.

Random had been right.

I drew forth Bleys' Trump and concentrated till it moved.

"Yes?" he said, and his voice was agitated. I could almost hear the sounds of battle about him.

"We're in trouble," I said. "Seventy-three ships made it through, and Caine has called on us to surrender by noon."

"Damn his eyes!" said Bleys. "I haven't made it as far as you. We're in the middle of a fight now. An enormous cavalry force is cutting us to pieces. So I can't counsel you fairly. I've got my own problems. Do as you see fit. They're coming again!" And the contact was broken.

I drew forth Gérard's, and sought contact.

When we spoke it seemed I could see a shore line behind him. I seemed to recognize it. If my guess was correct, he was in southern waters. I don't like to remember our conversation. I asked him if he could help me against Caine, and if he would.

"I only agreed to let you by," he said. "That is why I withdrew to the south. I couldn't reach you in time if I wanted to. I did not agree to help you kill our brother."

And before I could reply, he was gone. He was right, of course. He'd agreed to give me an opportunity, not to fight my battle for me.

What then did that leave me?

I lit a cigarette. I paced the deck. It was no longer morning. The mists had long vanished and the sun warmed my shoulders. Soon it would be noon. Perhaps two hours. . . .

I fingered my cards, weighed the deck in my hand. I could try a contest of wills through them, with either Eric or Caine. There was that power present, and perhaps even others of which I knew nothing. They had been so designed, at the command of Oberon, by the hand of the mad artist Dworkin Barimen, that wild-eyed hunchback who had been a sorcerer, priest, or psychiatrist—the stories conflicted on this point—from some distant Shadow where Dad had saved him from a disastrous fate he had brought upon himself. The details were unknown, but he had always been a bit off his rocker since that time. Still, he was a great artist, and it was undeniable that he possessed some strange power. He had vanished ages ago, after creating the cards and tracing the Pattern in Amber. We had often speculated about him, but no one seemed to know his whereabouts. Perhaps Dad had done him in, to keep his secrets secret.

Caine would be ready for such an attack, and I probably couldn't break him, though I might be able to hold him. Even then, though, his captains had doubtless been given the order to attack.

Eric would surely be ready for anything, but if there was nothing else left to do, I might as well try it. I had nothing to lose but my soul.

Then there was the card for Amber itself. I could take my self there with it and try an assassination, but I figured the odds were about a million to one against my living to effect it.

I was willing to die fighting, but it was senseless for all these men to go down with me. Perhaps my blood was tainted, despite my power over the Pattern. A true prince of Amber should have had no such qualms. I decided then that my centuries on the Shadow Earth had changed me, softened me perhaps, had done something to me which made me unlike my brothers.

I decided to surrender the fleet and then transport myself to Amber and challenge Eric to a final duel. He'd be foolish to accept. But what the hell—I had nothing else left to do.

I turned to make my wishes known to my officers, and the power fell upon me, and I was stricken speechless.

I felt the contact and I finally managed to mutter "Who?" through clenched teeth. There was no reply, but a twisting thing bored slowly within my mind and I wrestled with it there.

After a time when he saw that I could not be broken without a long struggle, I heard Eric's voice upon the wind:

"How goes the world with thee, brother?" he inquired.

"Poorly," I said or thought, and he chuckled, though his voice seemed strained by the efforts of our striving.

"Too bad," he told me. "Had you come back and supported me, I would have done well by you. Now, of course, it is too late. Now, I will only rejoice when I have broken both you and Bleys."

I did not reply at once, but fought him with all the power I possessed. He withdrew slightly before it, but he succeeded in holding me where I stood.

If either of us dared divert his attention for an instant, we could come into physical contact or one of us get the upper hand on the mental plane. I could see him now, clearly, in his chambers in the palace. Whichever of us made such a move, though, he would fall beneath the other's control.

So we glared at each other and struggled internally. Well, he had solved one of my problems, by attacking me first. He held my Trump in his left hand and his brows were furrowed. I sought for an edge, but couldn't find one. People were talking to me but I couldn't hear their words as I stood there backed against the rail.

What time was it?

All sense of time had departed since the beginning of the struggle. Could two hours have passed? Was that it? I couldn't be sure.

"I feel your troubled thought," said Eric. "Yes, I am coordinated with Caine. He contacted me after your parley. I can hold you thus while your fleet is demolished around you and sent down to Rebma to rot. The fishes will eat your men."

"Wait," I said. "They are guiltless. Bleys and I have misled them, and they think we are in the right. Their deaths would serve no purpose. I was preparing to surrender the fleet."

"Then you should not have taken so long," he replied, "for now it is too late. I cannot call Caine to countermand my orders, without releasing you, and the moment I release you I will fall beneath your mental domination or suffer physical assault. Our minds are too proximate."

"Supposing I give you my word that I won't do this thing?"

"Any man would be forsworn to gain a kingdom," said Eric.

"Can't you read the thought? Can't you feel it within my mind? I'll keep my word!"

"I feel there is a strange compassion for these men you have duped, and I know not what may have caused such a bond, but no. You know it yourself. Even if you are sincere at this moment—as you well may be—the temptation will be too great the instant the opportunity occurs. You know it yourself. I can't risk it."

And I knew it. Amber burned too strongly in the blood of us.

"Your swordsmanship has increased remarkably," he commented. "I see that your exile has done you some good in that respect. You are closer to being my equal now than anyone save Benedict, who may well be dead."

"Don't flatter yourself," I said. "I know I can take you now. In fact—"

"Don't bother. I won't duel with you at this late date," and he smiled, reading my thought, which burned all too clearly.

"I more than half wish you had stood by me," he said. "I could have used you more than any of the others. Julian I spit upon. Caine is a coward. Gérard is strong, but stupid."

I decided to put in the only good word I might.

"Listen," I said. "I conned Random into coming here with me. He wasn't hot on the idea. I think he would have supported you, had you asked him."

"That bastard!" he said. "I wouldn't trust him to empty chamber pots. One day I'd find a piranha in mine. No thanks. I might have pardoned him, save for your present recommendation. You'd like me to clasp him to my bosom and call him brother now, wouldn't you? Oh no! You leap too quickly to his defense. It reveals his true attitude, of which he has doubtless made you aware. Let us forget Random in the courts of clemency."

I smelled smoke then and heard the sounds of metal on metal. That would mean that Caine had come upon us and was doing his job.

"Good," said Eric, catching it from my mind.

"Stop them! Please! My men don't have a chance against that many!"

"Not even were you to yield—" and he bit it off and cursed. I caught the thought, then. He could have asked me to yield in return for their lives, and then let Caine continue with the slaughter. He would have liked to have done that, but he'd let those first words slip out in the heat of his passion.

I chuckled at his irritation.

"I'll have you soon, anyhow," he said. "As soon as they take the flagship."

"Until then," I said, "try this!" And I hit him with everything I had, boring into his mind, hurting him with my hatred. I felt his pain and it drove me harder. For all the years of exile I'd spent, I lashed at him, seeking at least this payment. For his putting me through the plague, I beat at the barriers of his sanity, seeking this vengeance. For the auto accident, for which I knew he had been responsible, I struck at him, seeking some measure of anguish in return for my hurt.

His control began to slip and my frenzy increased. I bore down upon him and his hold upon me began to slacken.

Finally, "You devil!" he cried, and moved his hand to cover the card that he held.

The contact was broken, and I stood there shaking.

I had done it. I had bested him in a contest of wills. No longer would I fear my tyrant brother in any form of single combat. I was stronger than he.

I sucked in several deep breaths and stood erect, ready for the moment the coldness of a new mental attack occurred. I knew that it wouldn't, though, not from Eric. I sensed that he feared my fury.

I looked about me and there was fighting. There was already blood on the decks. A ship had come alongside us and we were being boarded. Another vessel was attempting the same maneuver on the opposite side. A bolt whistled by my head.

I drew my blade and leaped into the fray.

I don't know how many I slew that day. I lost count somewhere after number twelve or thirteen. It was more than twice that, on that engagement alone, though. The strength with which a prince of Amber is naturally endowed, which had allowed me to lift a Mercedes, served me that day, so that I could raise a man with one hand and hurl him over the rail.

We slew everyone aboard both boarding ships and opened their hatches and sent them down to Rebma where Random would be amused by the carnage. My crew had been cut in half in the battle, and I had suffered innumerable nicks and scratches, but nothing serious. We went to the aid of a sister vessel and knocked off another of Caine's raiders.

The survivors of the rescued vessel came aboard the flagship and I had a full crew once more.

"Blood!" I called out. "Give me blood and vengeance this day, my warriors, and you will be remembered in Amber forever!"

And as a man, they raised their weapons and cried out, "Blood!" And gallons—no, rivers—of it were let that day. We destroyed two more of Caine's raiders, replenishing our numbers from those of the survivors of our own fleet. As we headed toward a sixth, I climbed the mainmast and tried to take a quick count.

We looked to be outnumbered three to one. There seemed to be between forty-five and fifty-five remaining of my fleet.

We took the sixth, and we didn't have to look for the seventh and the eighth. They came to us. We took them too, but I received several wounds in the fighting that again left me with half a crew. My left shoulder and my right thigh had been cut deeply, and a slash along my right hip was hurting.

As we sent those ships to the bottom, two more moved toward us.

We fled and gained an ally in one of my own ships which had been victorious in its own recent battle. We combined crews once more, this time transferring the standard to the other vessel, which had been less damaged than my own, which had begun shipping water badly and was beginning to list to starboard.

We were allowed no breathing space, as another vessel neared and the men attempted to board.

My men were tired, and I was getting that way. Fortunately the other crew wasn't in such great shape either. Before the second of Caine's vessels came to its aid, we had overwhelmed it, boarded, and transferred the standard again. That ship had been in even better shape.

We took the next and I was left with a good ship, forty men, and gasping.

There was no one in sight to come to our aid now. All of my surviving ships were engaged by at least one of Caine's. A raider was heading toward us and we fled.

We gained perhaps twenty minutes this way. I tried to sail into Shadow, but it's a hard, slow thing that near to Amber. It's much easier to get this close than it is to depart, because Amber is the center, the nexus. If I'd had another ten minutes, I could have made it.

I did, though.

As the vessel hove nearer, I saw another one off in the distance turning in our direction. It bore the black and green standard beneath Eric's colors and the white unicorn. It was Caine's ship. He wanted to be there for the kill.

We took the first one and didn't even have time to open its hatches before Caine was upon us. I was left standing on the bloody deck, with a dozen men about me, and Caine moved to the bow of his ship and called upon me to surrender.

"Will you grant my men their lives if I do this thing?" I asked him.

"Yes," he said. "I'd lose a few crewmen myself if I didn't, and there's no need for that."

"On your word as a prince?" I asked.

He thought about it a moment, then nodded.

"Very well," he said. "Have your men lay down their arms and board my vessel when I come alongside."

I sheathed my blade and nodded about me.

"You have fought the good fight, and I love you for it," I said. "But we have lost in this place." I dried my hands on my cloak as I spoke and wiped them carefully, as I'd hate to smudge a work of art. "Lay down your arms and know that your exploits of this day will never be forgotten. One day I will praise you before the court of Amber."

The men, the nine big red ones and the three remaining hairy ones, wept as they put down their arms.

"Do not fear that all is lost in the struggle for the city," I said. "We have lost only one engagement and the battle still continues elsewhere. My brother Bleys hacks his way toward Amber at this moment. Caine will keep his word to spare your lives when he sees that I have gone to join with Bleys upon the land, for he would not have knowledge that he was forsworn come into Amber. I am sorry that I cannot take you with me."

And with this, I drew Bleys' Trump from the pack and held it low and before me, out of sight of the other vessel.

Just as Caine came alongside, there was movement beneath that cold, cold surface.

"Who?" Bleys asked.

"Corwin," I said. "How fare you?"

"We won the battle, but lost many troops. We're resting now before we renew the march. How go things with you?"

"I think we've destroyed nearly half of Caine's fleet, but he's won the day. He's about to board me now. Give me escape."

He held forth his hand and I touched it and collapsed into his arms.

"This is getting to be a habit," I muttered, and then I saw that he was wounded too, about the head, and there was a bandage around his left hand. "Had to grab the wrong end of a saber," he remarked, as he saw my eyes fall upon it. "It smarts."

I caught my breath and then we walked to his tent, where he opened a bottle of wine and gave me bread, cheese, and some dried meat. He still had plenty of cigarettes and I smoked one as a medical officer dressed my wounds.

He still had around a hundred and eighty thousand men behind him. As I stood on a hilltop and the evening began around me, it seemed as if I looked out over every camp I had ever stood within, stretching on and on over the miles and the centuries without end. I suddenly felt tears come into my eyes, for the men who are not like the lords of Amber, living but a brief span and passing into dust, that so many of them must meet their ends upon the battlefields of the world.

I returned to Bleys' tent and we finished the bottle of wine.

VII

That night there was a bad storm. It hadn't let up when dawn struggled to cross the world's palm with silver, and it continued on through the day's march.

It is a very demoralizing thing to tramp along and be rained on, a cold rain at that. How I've always hated the mud, through which it seems I've spent centuries marching!

We sought after a Shadow way that was free of rain, but nothing we did seemed to matter.

We could march to Amber, but we would do it with our clothing sticking to us, to the drumbeat of the thunder, with the flashing of the lightning at our backs.

The next night the temperature plummeted, and in the morning I stared past the stiff flags and regarded a world gone white beneath a gray sky, filled with flurries. My breath went back in plumes behind me.

The troops were ill-equipped for this, save for the hairy ones, and we got them all moving quickly, to prevent frostbite. The big red guys suffered. Theirs had been a very warm world.

We were attacked by tiger, polar bear, and wolf that day. The tiger Bleys killed measured over fourteen feet from tail tip to nose.

We marched on well into the night, and the thaw began. Bleys pushed the troops to get them out of the cold Shadows. The Trump for Amber indicated that a warm, dry autumn prevailed there, and we were nearing the real Earth.

By midnight on that second night we'd marched through slush and sleet, cold rains, warm rains, and on into a dry world.

The orders were given to make camp then, with triple security cordons. Considering the tired condition of the men, we were ripe for an attack. But the troops were staggering and couldn't be pushed much further.

The attack came several hours later, and Julian led it, I learned later from the description given by survivors.

He headed commando raids against our most vulnerable campsites on the periphery of the main body. Had I known it to be Julian, I would have used his Trump to try to hold him, but I only knew it after the fact.

We'd lost perhaps two thousand men in the abrupt winter, and I didn't yet know how many Julian had accounted for.

It seemed the troops were beginning to get demoralized, but they followed when we ordered them ahead.

The next day was one continuous ambush. A body of men the size of ours could not be allowed to deviate sufficiently to try to deal with the harassing raids Julian led against our flanks. We got some of his men, but not enough—one for every ten of ours, perhaps.

By high noon we were crossing the valley that paralleled the seacoast. The Forest of Arden was to the north and our left. Amber lay directly ahead. The breezes were cool and filled with the odors of earth and its sweet growing things. A few leaves fell. Amber lay eighty miles distant and was but a shimmer above the horizon.

That afternoon, with a gathering of clouds and but the lightest of rains, the bolts began to fall from the heavens. Then the storm ceased and the sun came forth to dry things off.

After a time, we smelled the smoke.

After another time, we saw it, flapping skyward all about us.

Then the sheets of flame began to rise and fall. They moved toward us, with their crunching, constant footsteps; and as they came nearer, we began to feel the heat, and somewhere, way back along the lines, a panic arose. There were cries, and the columns swelled and welled foward.

We began to run.

Flakes of ash were falling about us now and the smoke grew thicker. We sprinted ahead and the flames rushed even closer. The sheets of light and heat flapped a steady, welling thunder as we ran, and the waves of warmth beat upon us, washed over us. Soon they were right there alongside us, and the trees blackened and the leaves flaked down, and some of the smaller trees began to sway. For as far ahead as we could see, our way was an alley of fires.

We ran faster, for soon things would be worse.

And we were not mistaken.

Big trees began to topple across our path. We leaped over them, we circled around them. At least, we were on a trail. . . .

The heat became stifling and the breath came heavy in our lungs. Deer and wolves and foxes and rabbits darted past us, fleeing with us, ignoring our presence and that of their natural enemies. The air above the smoke seemed filled with crying birds. Their droppings fell among us, went unnoticed.

To burn this ancient wood, as venerable as the Forest of Arden, seemed almost an act of sacrilege to me. But Eric was prince in Amber, and soon to be king. I suppose I might have, too. . . .

My eyebrows and hair were singed. My throat felt like a chimney. How many would this assault cost us? I wondered.

Seventy miles of wooded valley lay between us and Amber, and over thirty behind us, going back to the forest's end.

"Bleys!" I gasped. "Two or three miles ahead of us the trail forks! The right branch comes more quickly to the river Oisen, which goes down to the sea! I think it's our one chance! The whole Valley of Garnath is going to be burned! Our only hope lies in reaching the water!"

He nodded.

We raced on, but the fires outpaced us.

We made it to the fork, though, beating out flames on our smoldering clothing, wiping ashes from our eyes, spitting such from our mouths, running hands through our hair when the flamelets nested there.

"Only about a quarter mile more," I said.

I had been struck several times by falling boughs. All the exposed areas of my skin pulsed with a more than feverish pain, and many of the covered areas as well. We ran through burning grasses, heading down a long slope, and when we reached the bottom we saw the water, and our speed increased, though we didn't think it possible. We plunged in and let the cold wetness embrace us.

Bleys and I contrived to float as near together as possible as the currents took us and we were swept along the twisting course of the Oisen. The interlocked branches of the trees overhead had become as the beams in a cathedral of fire. As they broke apart and collapsed in places, we had to turn onto our bellies and swim or dive for the deepest places, depending on how near we were. The waters about us were filled with hissing and blackened debris, and at our backs our surviving troops' heads in the river seemed as a strip of floating coconuts.

The waters were dark and cold and our wounds began to ache, and we shivered and our teeth chattered.

It was several miles before we left the burning wood and reached the low, flat, treeless place that led on to the sea. It would be a perfect place for Julian to be waiting, with archers, I decided. I mentioned this to Bleys and he agreed, but he didn't reckon there was much we could do about it. I was forced to agree.

The woods burned all around us, and we swam and we drifted.

It seemed like hours, but must have been less, before my fears began to materialize and the first volley of arrows descended.

I dove, and I swam underwater for a long distance. Since I was going with the current, I made it quite a way along the river before I had to surface once more.

As I did, more arrows fell about me.

The gods knew how long this gauntlet of death might be drawn, but I didn't want to stick around and find out.

I gulped air and dove once more.

I touched bottom, I felt my way among rocks.

I moved along for as far as I could, then headed toward the right bank, exhaling as I rose.

I burst through the surface, gasped, took a deep breath and went down again, without sticking around to get the lay of the land.

I swam on till my lungs were bursting, and surfaced then.

This time I wasn't quite so lucky. I took an arrow through my left biceps. I managed to dive and break off the shaft when I struck bottom. Then I pulled out the head and continued on by means of the frog kick and under-body sculling with my right hand. The next time up I'd be a sitting duck, I knew.

So I forced myself on, till the red flashes crossed my eyeballs and the blackness crept into my head. I must have stayed down for three minutes.

When I surfaced this time, though, nothing happened, and I trod water and gasped.

I made my way to the left bank and grabbed hold of the trailing undergrowth.

I looked all around me. We were running short on trees at this point, and the fires hadn't gotten this far. Both banks seemed empty, but so did the river. Could I have been the only survivor? It didn't seem possible. After all, there had been so many of us when the last march began.

I was half dead with fatigue and my entire body was laced with aches and pains. Every inch of my skin seemed to have been burned, but the waters were so cold that I was shaking and probably blue. I'd have to leave the river soon, if I wanted to live. I felt I could manage a few more underwater expeditions, and I decided to chance them before departing from the sheltering depths.

Somehow I managed four more laps, and I felt then that I might not come up again if I tried a fifth. So I hung onto a rock and caught my breath, then crawled ashore.

I rolled onto my back and looked all around. I didn't recognize the locale. The fires hadn't reached it yet, though. There was a thick clump of bushes off to my right and I crawled toward it, crawled into it, fell flat on my face and went to sleep.

When I awoke, I wished I hadn't. Every inch of me ached, and I was sick. I lay there for hours, half delirious, and finally managed to stagger back to the river for a long drink of water. Then I headed back for the thicket, made it, and slept again.

I was still sore when consciousness came once more, but a little bit stronger. I walked to the river and back, and by means of my icy Trump found that Bleys was still alive.

"Where are you?" he asked, when I had made the contact.

"Damned if I know," I replied. "Lucky to be anywhere at all. Near the sea, though. I can hear the waves and I know the smell."

"You're near the river?"

"Yes."

"Which bank?

"Left, as you'd face the sea. North."

"Then stay put," he told me, "and I'll send someone after you. I'm assembling our forces now. I've already got over two thousand together, and Julian won't come near us. More keep straggling in every minute."

"Okay," I said, and that was it.

I stayed put. I slept as I did so.

I heard them bashing about in the bushes and was alert. I pushed some fronds aside and peered forth.

It was three of the big red guys.

So I straightened my gear and brushed all my garments, ran a hand through my hair, stood erect and swayed, took several deep breaths, and stepped forth.

"I am here," I announced.

Two of them did double-takes, blades in their hands, as I said it.

But they recovered, smiled, paid me deference, and conducted me back to the camp. It was perhaps two miles distant. I made it without leaning.

Bleys appeared and said, "We've got over three thousand now." Then he called for a medical officer to take care of me again.

We were undisturbed all through the night, and the rest of our troops straggled in that night and the following day.

We had perhaps five thousand by then. We could see Amber in the distance.

We slept another night and on the following morning we set forth.

By afternoon we had made maybe fifteen miles. We marched along the beach, and there was no sign of Julian anywhere.

The feeling of pain from my burns began to subside. My thigh was healthy, but my shoulder and arm still hurt from here to hell and back again.

We marched along the beach, and thre was no sign of Julian anywhere.

The feeling of pain from my burns began to subside. My thigh was healthy, but my shoulder and arm still hurt from here to hell and back again.

We marched on, and soon we were within forty miles of Amber. The weather stayed clement, and all of the wood to our left was a desolate, blackened ruin. The fire had destroyed most of the timber in the valley, so for once there was a thing in our favor. Julian nor anybody else could ambush us. We'd see them coming a mile off. We made another ten miles ere the sun fell and we bivouacked on the beach.

The next day. I remembered that Eric's coronation was near at hand and I reminded Bleys. We had almost lost count of the days, but realized we still had a few remaining.

We led a speed-march till noon, then rested. By then, we were twenty-five miles away from the foot of Kolvir. By twilight, the distance was ten.

And we kept on. We marched till midnight and we bivouacked once again. By that time, I was beginning to feel fairly alive once more. I practiced a few cuts with my blade and could almost manage them. The next day, I felt even better.

We marched until we came to the foot of Kolvir, where we were met by all of Julian's forces, combined with many from Caine's fleet who now stood as foot soldiers.

Bleys stood there and called things, like Robert E. Lee at Chancellorsville, and we took them.

We had maybe three thousand men when we had finished off everything Julian had to throw against us. Julian, of course, escaped.

But we had won. There was celebration that night. We had won.

I was very afraid by then, and I made my fears known to Bleys. Three thousand men against Kolvir.

I had lost the fleet, and Bleys had lost over ninety-eight percent of his foot soldiers. I did not look upon these as rejoiceable items.

I didn't like it.

But the next day we began the ascent. There was a stairway, allowing for the men to go two abreast along it. This would narrow soon, however, forcing us to go single file.

We made it a hundred yards up Kolvir, then two, then three.

Then the storm blew in from the sea, and we held tight and were lashed by it.

Afterward, a couple of hundred men were missing.

We struggled on and the rains came down. The way grew steeper, more slippery. A quarter of the way up Kolvir we met with a column of armed men descending. The first of these traded blows with the leader of our vanguard, and two men fell. Two steps were gained, and another man fell.

This went on for over an hour, and by then we were about a third of the way up and our line was wearing back toward Bleys and myself. It was good that our big red warriors were stronger than Eric's troops. There would come a clash of arms, a cry, and a man would be brought by. Sometimes he would be red, occasionally furry, but more often he wore Eric's colors.

We made it to the halfway point, fighting for every step. Once we reached the top, there would be the broad stair of which the one to Rebma had been but an image. It would lead up to the Great Arch, which was the eastern entranceway to Amber.

Perhaps fifty of our vanguard remained. Then forty, thirty, twenty, a dozen. . . .

We were about two-thirds of the way up by then, and the stair zigged and zagged its way back and forth across the face of Kolvir. The eastern stair is seldom used. It is almost a decoration. Our original plans had been to cut through the now blackened valley and then circle, climbing, and to take the western way over the mountains and enter Amber from behind. The fire and Julian had changed all this. We'd never have made it up and around. It was now a frontal assault or nothing. And it wasn't going to be nothing.

Three more of Eric's warriors fell and we gained four steps. Then our front man made the long descent and we lost one.

The breeze was sharp and cool from off the sea, and birds were collecting at the foot of the mountain. The sun broke through the clouds, as Eric apparently put aside his weathermaking now that we were engaged with his force.

We gained six steps and lost another man.

It was strange and sad and wild. . . .

Bleys stood before me, and soon his turn would come. Then mine, should he perish.

Six of the vanguard remained.

Ten steps . . .

Then five remained.

We pushed on, slowly, and there was blood on every step for as far back as I could see. There's a moral there, somewhere.

The fifth man slew four before he fell himself, so bringing us to another zig, or zag, as the case may be.

Onward and upward, our third man fighting with a blade in either hand. It was good that he fought in a holy war, for there was real zeal behind each blow. He took three before he died.

The next wasn't as zealous, or as good with his blades. He fell immediately, and then there were two.

Bleys drew his long, filigreed blade, and its edge sparkled in the sun.

"Soon, brother," he said, "we will see what they can do against a prince."

"Only one, I hope," I replied, and he chuckled.

I'd say we were three-quarters of the way there when Bleys' turn finally came.

He leaped forward, immediately dislodging the first man to face him. The point of his blade found the throat of the second, and the flat of it fell alongside the head of the third, dislodging him also. He dueled a moment with the fourth and dispatched him.

My own blade was in my hand, ready, as I watched and advanced.

He was good, even better than I remembered him to be. He advanced like a whirlwind, and his blade was alive with light. They fell before it—how they fell, my friend! Whatever else you might say of Bleys, on that day he acquitted himself as became his rank. I wondered how long he could keep going.

He'd a dagger in his left hand, which he used with brutal efficiency whenever he could manage a corps à corps. He left it in the throat of his eleventh victim.

I could see no end to the column which opposed us. I decided that it must stretch all the way to the landing at the top. I hoped my turn wouldn't come. I almost believed it.

Three more men plummeted past me and we came to a small landing and a turn. He cleared the landing and began the ascent. For half an hour I watched him, and they died and they died. I could hear the murmurs of awe from the men behind me. I almost thought he could make it to the top.

He used every trick available. He baffled blades and eyes with his cloak. He tripped the warriors. He seized wrists and twisted, with his full strength.

We made it to another landing. There was some blood on his sleeve by then, but he smiled constantly, and the warriors behind the warriors he killed were ashen. This helped him, too. And perhaps the fact that I stood ready to fill the gap also contributed to their fears and so slowed them, worked on their nerves. They'd heard of the naval engagement, I later learned.

Bleys worked his way to the next landing, cleared it, turned again, began to ascend. I hadn't thought he could make it that far, then. I didn't think I could make it as far as he had. It was the most phenomenal display of swordsmanship and endurance I'd seen since Benedict had held the pass above Arden against the Moonriders out of Ghenesh.

He was tiring, though, I could see that, too. If only there were some way for me to relieve him, to spell him for a time. . . .

But there wasn't. So I followed, fearing every stroke might be his last.

I knew that he was weakening. We were within a hundred feet of the top at that point.

I suddenly felt for him. He was my brother and he'd done well by me. I don't think he thought he'd make it then, yet he was fighting on . . . in effect, giving me my chance for the throne.

He killed three more men, and his blade moved more slowly each time. He fought with the fourth for perhaps five minutes before he took him. I was certain that the next would be his last.

He wasn't, though.

As he slew that man, I transferred my blade from my right hand to my left, drew my dagger with my right and threw it.

It went in up to the hilt, in the throat of the next man.

Bleys sprang over two steps and hamstrung the man before him, casting him downward.

Then he cut upward, ripping open the belly of the one behind that one.

I rushed to fill the gap, to be right behind him and ready. He didn't need me yet, though.

He took the next two, with a new burst of energy. I called for another dagger and one was passed to me from somewhere along the line.

I kept it really till he slowed once more, and I used it on the man he fought.

The man was lunging as it spun in, so the hilt rather than the blade caught him. It struck against his head, though, and Bleys pushed against his shoulder and he fell. But the next man leaped forward, and though he impaled himself, he struck Bleys upon the shoulder and they went over the edge together.

By reflex, almost without knowing what I was doing, yet knowing fully in one of those microsecond decisions you justify after the fact, my left hand leaped to my belt, whipped out my pack of the Trumps and cast them toward Bleys as he seemed to hang there for an instant —so rapidly did my muscles and perceptions respond—and I cried out, "Catch them, you fool!"

And he did.

I didn't have time to see what happened next, as I parried and thrust.

Then began the final lap of our journey up Kolvir.

Let's just say I made it and was gasping, as my troops came over the edge to support me there on the landing.

We consolidated our forces and pressed ahead.

It took us an hour to reach the Great Arch.

We passed through. We entered Amber.

Wherever Eric was, I'm sure he'd never guessed we'd make it this far.

And I wondered where Bleys was? Had he gotten a chance to grab a Trump and use it, before he reached the bottom? I guessed that I'd never know.

We had underestimated, all the way around. We were outnumbered now, and the only thing left to do was to fight on for as long as we could hold out. Why had I done such a foolish thing as throw Bleys my Trumps? I knew he had none of his own and that's what had dictated my response, conditioned perhaps by my years on the Shadow Earth. But I might have used them to escape, if things went badly.

Things went badly.

We fought on until twilight, and by then there was only a small band of us remaining.

We were surrounded at a point a thousand yards within Amber, and still far from the palace. We were fighting a defensive fight, and one by one we died. We were overwhelmed.

Llewella or Deirdre would have given me sanctuary. Why had I done it?

I killed another man and put the question out of my mind.

The sun went down and darkness filled the sky. We were down to a few hundred by then, and not much closer to the palace.

Then I saw Eric and heard him shouting orders. If only I could reach him!

But I couldn't.

I'd probably have surrendered, to save my remaining troops, who had served me far too well.

But there was no one to surrender to, no one asking for a surrender. Eric couldn't even hear me if I cried out. He was out of the way, directing.

So we fought on, and I was down to a hundred men.

Let's be brief.

They killed everyone but me.

At me they threw nets and unleashed blunted arrows.

Finally, I fell and was clubbed and hog-tied, and then everything went away but a nightmare which attached itself and wouldn't let go, no matter what.

We had lost.

I awoke in a dungeon far below Amber, sorry that I had made it that far.

The fact that I still lived meant that Eric had plans for me. I visualized racks and braces, flames and tongs. I foresaw my coming degradation as I lay there on the damp straw.

How long had I been unconscious? I did not know.

I searched my cell for a means of committing suicide. I found nothing that would serve this purpose.

All my wounds blazed like suns, and I was so very tired.

I lay me down and slept once more.

I awakened, and still no one came to me. There was none to buy, none to torture.

Also, there was nothing for me to eat.

I lay there, wrapped in my cloak, and I reviewed everything that had happened since I'd awakened in Greenwood and refused my hypo. Better, perhaps, if I hadn't.

I knew despair.

Soon Eric would be crowned king in Amber. This thing might already have occurred.

But sleep was so lovely a thing, and I so tired.

It was the first real chance I'd had to rest and forget my wounds.

The cell was so dark and smelly and damp.

VIII

How many times I awakened and returned to sleep, I do not know. Twice I found bread and meat and water on a tray by the door. Both times, I emptied the tray. My cell was almost pitch dark and very chilly. I waited there, and I waited.

Then they came for me.

The door swung open and a feeble light entered. I blinked at it as I was called forth.

The corridor without was filled to overflowing with armed men, so I wasn't about to try anything.

I rubbed at the stubble on my chin and went where they took me.

After a long walk, we came to the hall of the spiral stair and began to ascend. I asked no questions as we moved, and no one offered me any information.

When we reached the top, I was conducted further into the palace proper. They took me to a warm, clean room and ordered me to strip, which I did. Then I entered a steaming tub of water, and a servant came forth and scrubbed me and shaved me and trimmed my hair.

When I was dry again, I was given fresh garments, of black and of silver.

I donned them, and a black cloak was hung about my shoulders, its clasp a silver rose.

"You are ready," said the sergeant of the guard. "Come this way."

I followed him, and the guard followed me.

I was taken far to the back of the palace where a smith placed manacles about my wrists, fetters on my ankles, with chains upon them too heavy for me to break. Had I resisted, I knew I would have been beaten unconscious and the result would have been the same. I had no desire to be beaten unconscious again, so I complied.

Then the chains were taken up by several of the guards, and I was led back toward the front of the palace. I had no eyes for the magnificence that lay all about me. I was a prisoner. I would probably soon be dead or on the rack. There was nothing I could do right now. A glance out of the window showed me that it was early evening, and there was no place for nostalgia as I passed through rooms where we had played as children.

I was led up a long corridor and into the great dining room.

There were tables all over the place, and people seated all about them, many of whom I knew.

All the fine gowns and suits of Amber burned about me on the bodies of the nobles, and there was music beneath the torchlight and food already upon the tables, though no one was eating yet.

I saw faces that I recognized, like Flora's, and some strange faces. There was the minstrel, Lord Rein—yes, he had been knighted, by me—whom I had not seen in centuries. He turned his eyes away when my gaze fell upon him.

I was taken to the foot of the huge center table and seated there.

The guards stayed and stood behind me. They fastened the ends of the chains to rings fresh-set in the floor. The seat at the head of my table was as yet unoccupied.

I did not recognize the woman to my right, but the man to my left was Julian. I ignored him and stared at the lady, a little wisp of a blonde.

"Good evening," I said. "I don't believe we've been introduced. My name is Corwin."

She looked at the man at her right for support, a heavy, redheaded guy with lots of freckles. He looked away and suddenly became engaged in an animated conversation with the woman to his right.

"It's all right to talk with me, honest," I said. "It's not contagious."

She managed a weak smile and said, "I'm Carmel. How are you, Prince Corwin?"

"That's a sweet name," I replied, "and I'm just fine. What's a nice girl like you doing in a place like this?"

She took a quick drink of water.

"Corwin," said Julian, louder than necessary. "I think the lady finds you offensive and obnoxious."

"What's she said to you so far this evening?" and he didn't blush. He whitened.

"That will be enough from you."

I stretched then, and rattled my chains on purpose. Outside of the effect it produced, it also showed me how much slack I had. Not enough, of course. Eric had been careful.

"Come closer and whisper me your objections, brother," I said.

But he didn't.

I had been the last to be seated, so I knew the time was near at hand. And it was.

There came five trumpet notes from six trumpets and Eric entered the hall.

Everybody stood.

Except for me.

The guards had to drag me to my feet by means of the chains and hold me there.

Eric smiled and descended the stair to my right. I could barely see his own colors beneath the ermine robe that he wore.

He moved to the head of the table and stood before his chair. A servant came and stood behind him, and the wine stewards made their rounds, pouring.

When all the glasses were filled, he raised his.

"May you dwell forever in Amber," he said, "which endureth forever," and everyone raised his glass.

Except for me.

"Pick it up!" said Julian.

"Shove it up," said I.

He didn't, only glared. But I leaned forward quickly then and raised my glass.

There were a couple hundred poeple between us, but my voice carried. And Eric's eyes were upon me all the while, as I said, "To Eric, who sits at the foot of the table!"

No one moved to touch me as Julian emptied his glass upon the floor. All the others did the same, but I managed to quaff most of mine, before it was struck from my hand.

Eric seated himself then and the nobles followed suit, and I was released to fall into my chair.

The serving began, and since I was hungry I ate as well as the rest of them, and better than most.

There was constant music and the meal lasted for over two hours. No one said a word to me during the whole time, and I said nothing more myself. But my presence was felt, and our table was quieter than the others.

Caine sat farther up along the table. At Eric's right hand. I gathered that Julian was out of favor. Neither Random nor Deirdre was present. There were many other nobles whom I recognized, some of whom I had once counted as friends, but none of these would return my glances.

I gathered then that it only required a small formality for Eric to be king in Amber.

And this followed shortly.

After dinner, there were no speeches. Eric simply stood.

There came another flash of trumpets and a raucous sound upon the air.

Then there was a procession, leading all the way to the throne room of Amber.

I knew what was coming next.

Eric stood before the throne and everybody bowed.

Except for me, that is, and I was forced to my knees anyway.

Today was the day of his coronation.

There was silence. Then Caine bore in the cushion which held the crown, the crown of Amber. He knelt and froze in that position, offering it.

Then I was jerked to my feet and dragged forward. I knew what was about to happen. It came upon me in a flash, and I fought. But I was beaten down and brought to my knees at the foot of the stair before the throne.

The music rose up softly—it was "Greensleeves"—and somewhere at my back Julian said, "Behold the crowning of a new king in Amber!" Then to me, in a whisper, "Take up the crown and hand it to Eric. He will crown himself."

I stared at the crown of Amber upon the crimson cushion Caine held.

It was wrought of silver and had seven high points, each topped by a gem stone. It was studded with emeralds, and there were two huge rubies at either temple.

I didn't move, thinking of the times I had seen the face of our father beneath it.

"No," I said simply, and I felt a blow upon my left cheek.

"Take it and give it to Eric," he repeated.

I tried to strike at him, but my chains were drawn tight. I was struck again.

I stared at the high sharp peaks.

"Very well," I finally said, and reached for it.

I held it in both hands for a moment then quickly placed it on my own head and declared, "I crown me, Corwin, king of Amber!"

It was removed immediately and replaced upon the cushion. Several blows fell upon my back. There came a murmuring throughout the hall.

"Now pick it up and try it again," said Julian. "Take it and hand it to Eric."

Another blow fell.

"Okay," I told him, feeling my shirt grow wet.

This time I hurled it, hoping to put out one of Eric's eyes.

He caught it in his right hand and smiled down at me as I was beaten.

"Thank you," he said. "Now hear me, all you present, and those of you who listen in Shadow. I assume the crown and throne this day. I take into my hand the scepter of the kingdom of Amber. I have won the throne fairly, and I take it and hold it by the right of my blood."

"Liar!" I cried, and a hand was clapped over my mouth.

"I crown myself Eric the First, King of Amber."

"Long live the king!" cried the nobles, three times.

Then he leaned forward and whispered to me, "Your eyes have looked upon the fairest sight they will ever behold. . . . Guards! Take Corwin away to the stithy, and let his eyes be burnt from out his head! Let him remember the sights of this day as the last he might ever see! Then cast him into the darkness of the deepest dungeon beneath Amber, and let his name be forgotten!"

I spat and was beaten.

I fought every step of the way, but was taken forth from the hall. No one would look upon me as I went, and the last thing I remember was the sight of Eric seated upon his throne, pronouncing his blessing upon the nobles of Amber, and smiling.

That which he said was done to me, and mercifully I fainted before it was finished.

I have no idea how much later it was that I awakened within absolute blackness and felt the terrible pains within my head. Perhaps it was then that I pronounced the curse, or perhaps it had been at the time that the white-hot irons had descended. I don't remember. But I knew that Eric would never rest easy upon the throne, for the curse of a prince of Amber, pronounced in a fullness of fury, is always potent.

I clawed at the straw, in the absolute blackness of my cell, and no tears came. That was the horror of it. After a time—only you and I, gods, know how long—sleep came again.

When I awakened, there was still the pain. I rose to my feet. I measured off the dimensions of my cell. Four paces in width, five in length. There was a lavatory hole in the floor and a straw-tick mattress in a corner. The door contained a small slot at the bottom, and behind it there was a tray which held a stale piece of bread and a bottle of water. I ate and I drank, but I was not refreshed.

My head ached so, and there was nothing of peace within me.

I slept as much as I could, and no one came to see me. I awakened and crossed my cell and felt for food and ate it when I found it. I slept as much as I could.

After seven sleeps, the pain was gone from out my eye sockets. I hated my brother who was king in Amber. Better he had killed me.

I wondered at the popular reaction, but could not guess.

When the darkness reached as far as Amber, however, I knew that Eric would have his regrets. This much I knew, and this comforted me.

Thus began my days of darkness, and I had no way of measuring their passage. Even if I had had eyes, I could not have distinguished day from night in that place.

Time went on its way, ignoring me. There were occasions when I broke into a sweat over this and shivered. Had I been there months? Only hours? Or weeks? Or had it been years?

I forgot all about time. I slept, I paced (I knew exactly where to place my feet and when to turn), and I reflected upon things I had done and hadn't done. Sometimes I would sit cross-legged and breathe slowly and deeply, and empty my mind and keep it that way for as long as I could. This helped—thinking of nothing.

Eric had been clever. Although the power lived within me, now it was useless. A blind man cannot walk among Shadows.

My beard had grown down to my chest and my hair was long. I was always hungry at first, but after a time my appetite waned. Sometimes I grew dizzy when I stood up too rapidly.

I could still see, in my nightmares, but this hurt me even more when I awakened.

Later, though, I felt somewhat distant from the events which had led up to this. It was almost as though they had happened to a different person. And this, too, was true.

I had lost a lot of weight. I could visualize myself, pallid and thin. I couldn't even cry, though I felt like it a couple of times. There was something wrong with my tear ducts. It was a dreadful thing that any man should be brought to this.

Then one day there came a light scratching upon the door. I ignored it.

It came again, and still I did not respond.

Then I heard my name whispered, in the interrogative.

I crossed the cell.

"Yes?" I replied.

"It's me, Rein," he said. "How are you?"

I laughed at that.

"Fine! Oh just fine!" I said. "Steak and champagne every night, and dancing girls. God! You should make the scene sometime!"

"I'm sorry," he said, "that there is nothing I can do for you," and I could feel the pain in his voice.

"I know," I said.

"I would if I could," he told me.

"I know that, too."

"I brought you something. Here."

The little gate at the bottom of the cell door creaked slightly as it swung inward several times.

"What is it?" I asked.

"Some clean clothes," he said, "and three loaves of fresh bread, a head of cheese, some beef, two bottles of wine, a carton of cigarettes, and a lot of matches."

My voice caught in my throat.

"Thanks, Rein. You're all right. How did you arrange this?"

"I know the guard who's standing duty this shift. He won't talk. He owes me too much."

"He might try to cancel his debts by squealing," I said. "So don't do it again—much as I appreciate it. Needless to say, I'll dispose of the evidence."

"I wish it had turned out different, Corwin."

"You and me both. Thanks for thinking of me when you were ordered not to."

"That part was easy," he said.

"How long have I been in this place?"

"Four months and ten days," he said.

"So what's new in Amber?"

"Eric reigns. That's all."

"Where's Julian?"

"Back in the Forest of Arden with his guard."

"Why?"

"Some strange things made it through Shadow recently."

"I see. How about Caine?"

"He's still in Amber, enjoying himself. Wenching and drinking, mostly."

"And Gérard?"

"He's admiral of the entire fleet."

I sighed with a bit of relief. I was afraid his withdrawal during the naval engagement might have cost him something with Eric.

"And what of Random?"

"He's up the hall aways."

"What? He was taken?"

"Yes. He walked the Pattern in Rebma and showed up here, with a cross bow. He wounded Eric before he was taken."

"Really? Why wasn't he slain?"

"Well, rumor has it he's married a noblewoman of Rebma. Eric didn't want to court an incident with Rebma at this point. Moire has quite a kingdom, and there is talk that Eric is even considering asking her to be his queen. All gossip, of course. But interesting."

"Yes," I said.

"She liked you, didn't she?"

"Somewhat. How did you hear?"

"I was present when Random was sentenced. I got to speak with him for a moment. The Lady Vialle, who claims to be his wife, has asked to join him in prison. Eric is not yet certain how to reply."

I thought upon the blind girl, whom I had never met, and I wondered at this.

"How long ago did all this happen?" I asked.

"Mm. Thirty-four days," he replied. "That was when Random showed up. A week later, Vialle made her request."

"She must be a strange woman, if she really loves Random."

"Those were my sentiments," he replied. "I can't think of a more unusual combination."

"If you should get to see him again, give him my regards and my regrets."

"Yes."

"How fare my sisters?"

"Deirdre and Llewella remain in Rebma. The Lady Florimel has been enjoying Eric's favors and stands high in the present court. I do not know where Fiona is presently.

"Has anything more been heard of Bleys? I am sure that he died."

"He must have died," said Rein. "His body was never recovered, though."

"What of Benedict?"

"As absent as ever."

"How about Brand?"

"No word."

"Then I guess that covers the whole family tree, as it stands at present. Have you written any new ballads?"

"No," he said. "I'm still working on 'The Siege of Amber,' but it will be an underground hit, if at all."

I reached my hand out through the tiny gate at the bottom of the door.

"I would clasp hands with thee," I said, and I felt his hand touch mine.

"It was good of thee to do this thing for me. Don't do it again, though. It would be foolish to risk Eric's wrath."

He squeezed my hand, muttered something, and was gone.

I found his CARE package and stuffed myself with the meat, which was the most perishable item. I ate a lot of the bread, to accompany it, and I realized that I had almost forgotten how good good food can taste. Then I grew drowsy and slept. I don't think I slept very long, and when I awoke I opened one of the bottles of wine.

It didn't take as much as usual, in my weakened condition, to get me kind of high. I had a cigarette, sat down on my mattress, leaned back against the wall, and mused.

I remembered Rein as a child. I was already full grown by then and he was a candidate for court jester. A thin, wise kid. People had kidded him too much. Me included. But I wrote music, composed ballads, and he'd picked up a lute somewhere and had taught himself how to use it. Soon we were singing with voices together raised and all like that, and before long I took a liking to him and we worked together, practicing the martial arts. He was lousy at them, but I felt kind of sorry for the way I had treated him earlier, what with the way he had dug my stuff, so I forced the fake graces upon him and also made him a passable saber man. I'd never regretted it, and I guess he didn't either. Before long, he became minstrel to the court of Amber. I had called him my page all that while, and when the wars beckoned, against the dark things out of Shadow called Weirmonken, I made him my squire and we had ridden off to the wars together. I knighted him upon the battlefield, at Jones Falls, and he had deserved it. After that, he had gone on to become my better when it came to the ways of words and music. His colors were crimson and his words golden. I loved him, as one of my two or three friends in Amber. I didn't think he'd take the risk he had to bring me a decent meal, though. I didn't think anyone would. I had another drink and smoked another cigarette, in his name, to celebrate him. He was a good man. I wondered how long he would survive.

I threw all the butts into the head and also—eventually—the empty bottle. I didn't want anything around to show that I had been "enjoying" myself, should a sudden inspection be held. I ate all the good food he had brought me, and I felt surfeited for the first time since I had been in durance. I saved the last bottle for one massive spell of drunkenness and forgetfulness.

And after that time had passed, I returned to my cycle of recriminations.

I hoped, mainly, that Eric had no measure of our complete powers. He was king in Amber, granted, but he didn't know everything. Not yet. Not the way Dad had known. There was a million-in-one shot that might still work in my favor. So much so, and so different that at least it served to grant me my small purchase upon sanity, there in the grip of despair.

But maybe I did go mad for a time, I don't know. There are days that are great blanks to me now, as I stand here on the brink of Chaos. God knows what they held, and I'll never see a shrink to find out.

There are none of you, good doctors, could cope with my family, anyway.

I lay there and I paced there, within the numbing darkness. I grew quite sensitive to sounds. I listened to the scurry of rats' feet through straw, the distant moaning of other prisoners, the echoes of a guard's footsteps as he approached with a tray of food. I began estimating distances and direction from things like this.

I suppose I became more sensitive to odors also, but I tried not to think about them too much. Aside from the imaginable nauseating ones there was, for a long while, what I would swear to be the odor of decaying flesh. I wondered. If I were to die, how long would it be before someone took notice? How many chunks of bread and bowls of slop would go uneaten before the guard thought to check within after my continued existence?

The answer to that one could be very important.

The death odor was around for a long while. I tried to think in terms of time again, and it seemed that it persisted for over a week.

Though I rationed myself carefully, resisting the compulsion, the handy temptation, for as long as I could, I finally found myself down to my final pack of cigarettes.

I tore it open and lit one. I had had a carton of Salems and I had smoked eleven packs. That was two hundred and twenty cigarettes. I had once timed myself with one, and it had taken me seven minutes to smoke it. That made for a total of one thousand five hundred and forty minutes spent smoking, or twenty-five hours and forty minutes. I was sure I had spent at least an hour between cigarettes, more like an hour and a half. Say an hour and a half. Now figure that I was sleeping six to eight hours per day. That left sixteen to eighteen waking hours. I guessed I was smoking ten or twelve per day. So that meant maybe three weeks had passed since Rein's visit. He had told me it was four months and ten days since the coronation, which meant that it was now around five months.

I nursed my last pack, enjoying each one like a love affair. When they were all gone, I felt depressed.

Then a lot more time must have passed.

I got to wondering about Eric. How was he making out as liege? What problems was he encountering? What was he up to right now? Why hadn't he been around to torment me? Could I ever truly be forgotten in Amber, even by imperial decree? Never, I decided.

And what of my brothers? Why had none of them contacted me? It would be so easy to draw forth my Trump and break Eric's decree.

No one did, though.

I thought for a long while upon Moire, the last woman I had loved. What was she doing? Did she think of me ever? Probably not.

Maybe she was Eric's mistress by now, or his queen. Did she ever speak to him of me? Again, probably not.

And what of my sisters? Forget it. Bitches all, they.

I had been blinded once before, by a cannon flashback in the eighteenth century on the Shadow Earth. But it had only lasted for around a month and my sight had returned. Eric had had a permanent thing in mind, however, when he had given his order. I still perspired and shuddered, and sometimes woke up screaming, whenever memory of the white-hot irons returned to me—hung there before my eyes—and then the contact!

I moaned softly and continued to pace.

There was absolutely nothing I could do. That was the most horrible part of the whole thing. I was as helpless as an embryo. To be born again into sight and fury was a thing for which I would give my soul. Even for an hour, with a blade in my hand, to duel once again with my brother.

I lay back on my mat and slept. When I awakened, there was food, and I ate once again and paced. My fingernails and my toenails had grown long. My beard was very long and my hair fell across my eyes, constantly. I felt filthy, and I itched all the time. I wondered whether I had fleas.

That a prince of Amber could be brought to this state drew a terrible emotion from the center of my being, wherever that may be. I had been reared to think of us as invincible entities, clean and cool and diamond-hard, like our pictures on the Trumps. Obviously, we were not.

At least, we were enough like other men to have our resources.

I played mental games, I told myself stories, I reviewed pleasant memories—there were many of these. I recalled the elements: wind, rain, snow, the summer's warmth, and the spring's cool breezes. I had had a small airplane on the Shadow Earth, and when I flew it I had enjoyed the sensation. I recalled the glistening panoramas of color and distance, the miniaturization of cities, the broad blue sweep of sky, the herds of clouds (where were they now?) and the clean expanse of the ocean beneath my wings. I remembered women I had loved, parties, military engagements. And when all was done, and I could help it no longer, I thought of Amber.

One time, when I did so, my tear glands began to function again. I wept.

After an interminable time, a time filled with blackness and many sleeps, I heard footsteps which paused before the door to my cell, and I heard the sound of a key within the lock.

It was a time so long after Rein's visit that I had forgotten the taste of the wine and the cigarettes. I could not really estimate its span, but it had been long.

There were two men in the corridor. I could tell this from their footsteps even before I heard the sounds of their voices.

One of the voices I recognized.

The door swung open and Julian said my name.

I didn't answer right away, and he repeated it.

"Corwin? Come here."

Since I didn't have much choice in the matter, I drew myself erect and advanced. I stopped when I knew I was near him.

"What do you want?" I asked.

"Come with me." And he took my arm.

We walked along the corridor, and he said nothing and I'd be damned if I'd ask him any questions.

From the echoes, I could tell when we entered the big hall. Soon after, he guided me up the stair.

Up, and into the palace proper we went.

I was taken to a room and seated in a chair. A barber set to work cutting my hair and my beard. I didn't recognize his voice when he asked me if I wanted the beard trimmed or removed.

"Cut it off," I said, and a manicurist set to work on my nails, all twenty of them.

Then I was bathed, and someone helped me to dress in clean garments. They hung loose on me. I was deloused also, but forget that.

Then I was led into another black place filled with music and the odors of good food and the sounds of many voices and some laughter. I recognized it to be the dining room.

The voices subsided a bit as Julian led me in and seated me.

I sat there until the trumpet notes, to which I was forced to rise.

I heard the toast called out:

"To Eric the First, King of Amber! Long live the king!"

I didn't drink to that, but no one seemed to notice. It was Caine's voice that had called out the toast, from far up along the table.

I ate as much as I could, because it was the best meal I had been offered since the coronation. I gathered from conversation overheard that today was the anniversary of Eric's coronation, which meant I had spent an entire year in the dungeons.

No one spoke to me, and I didn't make any overtures. I was present as a ghost only. To humiliate me, and to serve as a reminder to my brothers, no doubt, as to the price of defying our liege. And everyone had been ordered to forget me.

It went on well into the night. Someone kept me well provided with wine, which was something, and I sat there and listened to the music of all the dances.

The tables had been removed by this time, and I was seated off somewhere in a corner.

I got stinking drunk and was half dragged, half carried back to my cell in the morning, when the whole thing was over save for the cleaning up. My only regret was that I hadn't gotten sick enough to dirty the floor or someone's pretty garments.

Thus ended the first year of darkness.

IX

I shall not bore you with repetition. My second year was pretty much like my first, with the same finale. Ditto for the third. Rein came twice that second year, with a basket of goodies and a mouthful of gossip. Both times I forbade him ever to come again. The third year he came down six times, every other month, and each time I forbade him anew and ate his food and heard what he had to say.

Something was wrong in Amber. Strange *things* walked through Shadow and presented themselves, with violence, to all and sundry. They were destroyed, of course. Eric was still trying to figure out how they had occurred. I did not mention my curse, though I later rejoiced in the fact that it had come to pass.

Random, like myself, was still a prisoner. His wife *had* joined him. The positions of my brothers and sisters remained unchanged. This bolstered me through the third anniversary of the coronation, and it made me feel almost alive again.

It . . .

It! One day it was there, and it made me feel so good that I immediately broke out the final bottle of wine Rein had brought me and opened the last pack of cigarettes, which I had been saving.

I smoked them and sipped and enjoyed the feeling that I had somehow beaten Eric. If he found this out, I felt it might be fatal. But I knew he didn't know.

So I rejoiced, smoking, drinking and reveling in the light of that which had occurred.

Yes, the *light*.

I'd discovered a tiny patch of brightness, off somewhere to my right.

Do you know what that meant to me?

Well, let's take it like this: I had awakened in a hospital bed and learned that I had recovered all too soon. Dig?

I heal faster than others who have been broken. All the lords and ladies of Amber have something of this capacity.

I'd lived through the Plague, I'd lived through the march on Moscow. . . .

I regenerate faster and better than anybody I've ever known.

Napoleon had once made a remark about it. So had General MacArthur.

With nerve tissue it takes me a bit longer, that's all.

My sight was returning to me, that's what it meant—that lovely patch of brightness, off somewhere to my right.

After a time, I knew that it was the little barred area in the door to my cell.

I had grown new eyes, my fingers told me. It had taken me over three years, but I had done it. It was the billion-in-one thing I spoke of earlier, the thing which even Eric could not properly assess, because of the variances of powers among the individual members of the family. I had beaten him to this extent: I had learned that I could grow new eyeballs. I had always known that I could regenerate nerve tissues, given sufficient time. I had been left paraplegic from a spine injury received during the Franco-Prussian wars. After two years, it had gone away. I had had my hope—a wild one, I'll admit —that I could do what I had done then, with my burned-out orbs. And I had been right. They felt intact, and the sight was returning, slowly.

How long till the next anniversary of Eric's coronation? I stopped pacing and my heart beat faster. As soon as someone saw that I'd recovered my eyes, I'd lose them again.

Therefore, I'd have to escape before the four years had passed.

How?

I hadn't thought about it much up to this time, because even if I could figure a way to get out of my cell, I'd never make it out of Amber—or out of the palace, for that matter—without eyes or aid, and neither were available to me.

Now, though . . .

The door of my cell was a big, heavy, brass-bound thing, with only a tiny grille at a height of about five feet for purposes of looking in to see whether I was still alive, if anyone cared. Even if I succeeded in removing it, I could tell that I couldn't reach out far enough to touch the lock. There was a little swinging gate at the bottom of the door, large enough to push my food through and that's about all. The hinges were either on the outside or in between the door and the jamb, I couldn't tell for sure. Either way, I couldn't get at them. There were no windows and no other doors.

It was still almost like being blind, save for that feeble reassuring light through the grille. I knew my sight hadn't returned fully. That was still a long way off. But even if it had, it was nearly pitch dark in there. I knew this because I knew the dungeons under Amber.

I lit a cigarette, paced some more, and assessed my possessions, seeking anything that might be of aid. There was my clothing, my sleeping mat, and all the damp straw I wanted. I also had matches, but I quickly rejected the notion of setting fire to the straw. I doubted anyone would come and open the door if I did. Most likely the guard would come and laugh, if he came at all. I had a spoon I'd picked up at the last banquet. I'd wanted a knife, really, but Julian had caught me trying to lift one and snatched it away. What he didn't know, though, was that that was my second attempt. I already had the spoon tucked inside my boot.

So what good was it?

I'd heard these stories of guys digging their way out of cells with the damnedest things—belt buckles (which I didn't have)—etc. But I didn't have time to try the Count of Monte Cristo bit. I needed out in a matter of months, or my new eyes wouldn't mean anything.

The door was mainly wood. Oak. It was bound with four metal strips. One went around it near the top, one near the bottom, right above the gate, and there were two which ran from top to bottom, passing along either side of the foot-wide grille. The door opened outward, I knew, and the lock was to my left. My memories told me the door was about two inches thick, and I recalled the approximate position of the lock, which I verified by leaning against the door and feeling the tension at that point. I knew that the door was also barred, but I could worry about that later. I might be able to raise it by sliding the handle of the spoon upward between the door's edge and the jamb.

I knelt on my sleeping mat and with the spoon I traced a box about that area which contained the lock. I worked until my hand was quite sore—maybe a couple of hours. Then I ran my fingernail over the surface of the wood. I hadn't scarred it much, but it was a beginning. I switched the spoon to my left hand and continued until it, too, began to ache.

I kept hoping that Rein would show up. I was sure I could talk him into giving me his dagger if I really pressed the matter. He didn't put in an appearance, though, so I just kept grinding away.

Day after day I worked, until I was perhaps half an inch into the wood. Each time I'd hear a guard's footsteps I'd move the pallet back to the far wall and lie on it with my back to the door. When he had passed, I'd resume work. Then I had to stop for a while, as much as I hated to. Even though I had wrapped them in cloth torn from my garments, my hands had blistered and the blisters had broken, and after a time the raw flesh underneath began to bleed. So I took a break to let them heal. I decided to devote the time to planning what I'd do after I got out.

When I'd worked my way far enough through the door, I'd raise the bar. The sound of it falling would probably bring a guard. By then, though, I'd be out. A couple of good kicks would break out the piece I was working on and the lock could stay right where it was if it wanted to. The door would swing open then and I would face the guard. He would be armed and I wouldn't. I'd have to take him.

He might be overconfident, thinking I couldn't see. On the other hand, he might be a bit afraid, if he recalled how I had entered into Amber. Either way he would die and I would then be armed. I gripped my right biceps with my left hand and my fingertips touched. Gods! I was emaciated! Whatever, I was of the blood of Amber, and I felt that even in that condition I could take any ordinary man. Maybe I was kidding myself, but I'd have to try it.

Then if I succeeded, with a blade in my hand, nothing could keep me from reaching the Pattern. I'd walk it, and when I made it to the center, I could transport myself to any Shadow world I chose. There I would recuperate, and this time I would not rush things. If it took me a century, I'd have everything letter-perfect before I moved against Amber again. After all, I was technically its liege. Hadn't I crowned myself in the presence of all, before Eric had done the same? I'd make good my claim to the throne!

If only it weren't impossible to walk into Shadow from Amber itself! Then I wouldn't have to fool around with the Pattern. But my Amber is the center of all, and you just don't depart it that easily.

After, say, a month my hands had healed and I was developing large callouses from my scraping activites. I heard a guard's footsteps and removed myself to the far side of the cell. There was a brief creak and my meal was slipped beneath the door. Then there were footsteps again, this time diminishing in the distance.

I returned to the door. Without looking, I knew what was on the tray: a chunk of stale bread, a crock of water, and a piece of cheese if I was lucky. I positioned the mat, knelt on it and felt at the groove. I was about halfway through.

Then I heard the chuckle.

It came from behind me.

I turned, not needing eyes to tell me that someone else was present. There was a man standing near the left wall, giggling.

"Who is it?" I asked, and my voice sounded strange. I realized then that these were the first words I had spoken in a long while.

"Escape," he said. "Trying to escape." And he chuckled again.

"How did you get in here?"

"Walked," he replied.

"From where? How?"

I struck a match and it hurt my eyes, but I held it.

He was a small man. Tiny, might be an even better word. He was around five feet tall and a hunchback. His hair and beard were as heavy as my own. The only distinguishing features in that great mass of fur were his long, hook nose and his almost black eyes, now squinted against the light.

"Dworkin!" I said.

He chuckled again.

"That's my name. What's yours?"

"Don't you know me, Dworkin?" I struck another match and held it near my face. "Look hard. Forget the beard and the hair. Add a hundred pounds to my frame. You drew me, in exquisite detail, on several packs of playing cards."

"Corwin," he said at last. "I remember you. Yes."

"I had thought you were dead."

"I'm not, though. See?" and he pirouetted before me. "How is your father? Have you seen him recently? Did he put you here?"

"Oberon is no more," I replied. "My brother Eric reigns in Amber, and I am his prisoner."

"Then I have seniority," he told me, "for I am Oberon's prisoner."

"Oh? None of us knew that Dad had locked you up."

I heard him weeping.

"Yes," he said after a time. "He didn't trust me."

"Why not?"

"I told him I'd thought of a way to destroy Amber. I described it to him, and he locked me in."

"That wasn't very nice," I said.

"I know," he agreed, "but he did give me a pretty apartment and lots of things to do research with. Only he stopped coming to visit me after a time. He used to bring men who showed me splotches of ink and made me tell stories about them. That was fun, until I told a story I didn't like and turned the man into a frog. The king was angry when I wouldn't turn him back, and it's been so long since I've seen anybody that I'd even turn him back now, if he still wanted me to. Once—"

"How did you get here, into my cell?" I asked again.

"I told you. I walked."

"Through the wall?"

"Of course not. Through the Shadow wall."

"No man can walk through Shadows in Amber. There are no Shadows in Amber."

"Well, I cheated," he admitted.

"How?"

"I designed a new Trump and stepped through it, to see what was on this side of the wall. Oh my!—I just remembered. . . . I can't get back without it. I'll have to make another. Have you got anything to eat? And something to draw with? And something to draw on?"

"Have a piece of bread," I said, and handed it to him, "and here's a piece of cheese to go along with it."

"Thank you, Corwin," and he wolfed them down and drank all my water afterward. "Now, if you'll give me a pen and a piece of parchment, I'll be returning to my own rooms. I want to finish a book I was reading. It's been nice talking to you. Too bad about Eric. I'll stop back again some time and we'll talk some more. If you see your father, please tell him not to be angry with me because I'll—"

"I don't have a pen, or parchment," I observed.

"Goodness," he said, "that's hardly civilized."

"I know. But then, Eric isn't very."

"Well, what have you got? I prefer my own apartment to this place. At least, it's better lighted."

"You have dined with me," I said, "and now I am going to ask you a favor. If you will grant me this respect, I promise that I will do everything I can to make things right between you and Dad."

"What is it that you want?" he asked.

"Long have I admired your work," I said, "and there is something

I have always desired as a work of your hand. Do you recall the Lighthouse of Cabra?"

"Of course. I've been there many times. I know the keeper, Jopin. I used to play chess with him."

"More than anything else I can think of," I told him, "for most of my adult life, I have longed to see one of your magical sketches of that great gray tower."

"A very simple subject," he said, "and rather an appealing one, at that. I did some preliminary sketches in the past, but I never got beyond that point. Other work kept getting in the way. I'll fetch you one, if you'd like."

"No," I said. "I'd like something more enduring, to keep me company here in my cell—to comfort me, and any others who may later occupy this place."

"Commendable," he said. "What have you in mind as the medium."

"I have a stylus here," I told him (the spoon was fairly sharp by then), "and I'd like to see it traced upon the far wall, so that I might look at it as I take my rest."

He was silent a moment, then, "The illumination is quite poor," he remarked.

"I have several books of matches," I replied. "I'll light them and hold them for you. We might even burn some of this straw if we run low."

"Those are hardly ideal working conditions. . . ."

"I know," I said, "and I apologize for them, great Dworkin, but they are the best I have to offer. A work of art by your hand would brighten my humble existence beyond measure."

He chuckled again.

"Very well. But you must promise me that you will provide light afterwards, so that I may sketch myself a way back to my own chambers."

"Agreed," I said, and I felt in my pocket.

I had three full packages of matches and part of a fourth.

I pressed the spoon into his hand and led him to the wall.

"Do you have the feel of the instrument?" I asked him.

"Yes, it's a sharpened spoon, isn't it?"

"Yes. I'll make a light as soon as you say you are ready. You'll have to sketch rapidly, because my supply of matches is limited. I'll allot half for the lighthouse and the other half for your own business."

"All right," he said, and I struck a match and he began to trace lines upon the moist gray wall.

First he did an upright rectangle to frame and contain the thing. Then with several deft strokes, the lighthouse began to appear. It was amazing, daft as he was, his skill was intact. I held each match at its barest base, spat on my left thumb and forefinger, and when I could hold it no longer in my right I took hold of the blackened end and inverted it, letting the match burn away completely before I struck another.

When the first book of matches was gone, he had finished the tower and was working on the sea and sky. I encouraged him, I murmured appreciation at every stroke.

"Great, really great," I said, when it appeared to be almost finished. Then he made me waste another match while he signed it. I was almost through the second book by then.

"Now let's admire it," he said.

"If you want to get back to your own apartments, you'll have to leave the admiring to me," I told him. "We're too low on matches to be art critics at this point."

He pouted a bit, but moved to the other wall and began sketching as soon as I struck a light.

He sketched a tiny study, a skull on the desk, a globe beside it, walls full of books all around.

"Now that's good," he said, when I had finished the third pack and was starting on the remaining partial pack.

It took him six more to finish up and one to sign it.

He gazed at it while the eighth match burned—there were only two remaining—then he took a step forward and was gone.

The match was burning my fingertips by then and I dropped it and it sizzled when it hit the straw and went out.

I stood there shaking, full of mixed feelings, and then I heard his voice and felt his presence at my side. He was back again.

"I just thought of something," he said. "How can you see the picture when it's so dark in here?"

"Oh. I can see in the dark," I told him. "I've lived with it so long that it has become my friend."

"I see. I just wondered. Give me a light so I can go back now."

"Very well," I agreed, considering my second to last match. "But you'd better bring your own illumination next time you stop around. I'll be out of matches after this."

"All right." And I struck a light and he considered his drawing, walked toward it, and vanished once more.

I turned quickly and considered the Lighthouse of Cabra before the match failed. Yes, the power was there. I could feel it.

Would my final match serve me, though?

No, I didn't think it would. A longer period of concentration than that was required for me to use a Trump as a gateway.

What could I burn? The straw was too damp and might not take fire. It would be horrible to have the gateway—my road to freedom —right there with me and not be able to use it.

I needed a flame that would last awhile.

My sleeping roll! It was a cloth liner stuffed with straw. That straw would be drier, and the cloth would burn, too.

I cleared half the floor, down to the bare stone. Then I sought the sharpened spoon, to use to cut the liner. I cursed then. Dworkin had carried it off with him.

I twisted and tore at the thing.

Finally, it came open and I pulled out the dry straw from the middle. I made a little heap of it and I set the liner nearby, to use as extra fuel if I needed it. The less smoke the better though. It would attract attention if a guard passed this way. This wasn't too likely, though, since I had just recently been fed, and I got one meal a day.

I struck my last match, then used it to set fire to the cardboard book that had contained it. When this got going. I used it on the straw.

It almost didn't take. The straw was damper than I'd thought, even though it came from the center of my mat. But finally there was a glow, and then a flame. It took two of the other empty matchbooks to achieve this, so I was glad I hadn't thrown them down the john.

I tossed on the third, held the liner in my left hand, and stood and faced the drawing.

The glow spread up the wall as the flames danced higher, and I concentrated on the tower and recalled it. I thought I heard the cry of a gull. I sniffed something like a salt breeze, and the place became more real as I stared.

I tossed the liner onto the fire, and the flames subsided for a moment, then sprang higher. I didn't remove my eyes from the drawing as I did this.

The magic was still there, in Dworkin's hand, for soon the lighthouse seemed as real to me as my cell. Then it seemed the only reality, and the cell but a Shadow at my back. I heard the splashing of the waves and felt something like the afternoon sun upon me.

I stepped forward, but my foot did not descend into the fire.

I stood upon the sandy, rock-strewn edge of the small island Cabra, which held the great gray lighthouse that lit a path for the ships of Amber by night. A flock of frightened gulls wheeled and screamed about me, and my laughter was one with the booming of the surf and the free song of the wind. Amber lay forty-three miles behind my left shoulder.

I had escaped.

X

I made my way to the lighthouse and climbed the stone stair that led to the door on its western face. It was high, wide, heavy, and water-tight. Also, it was locked. There was a small quay about three hundred yards behind me. Two boats were moored at it. One was a row-boat and the other was a sailboat with a cabin. They swayed gently, and beneath the sun the water was mica behind them. I paused for a moment to regard them. It had been so long since I had seen anything that for an instant they seemed more than real, and I caught a sob within my throat and swallowed it.

I turned and knocked on the door.

After what seemed too long a wait, I knocked again.

Finally, I heard a noise within and the door swung open, creaking on its three dark hinges.

Jopin, the keeper, regarded me through bloodshot eyes and I smelled whisky upon his breath. He was about five and a half feet tall and so stooped that he reminded me somewhat of Dworkin. His beard was as long as mine, so of course it seemed longer, and it was the color of smoke, save for a few yellow stains near his dry-looking lips. His skin was as porous as an orange rind and the elements had darkened it to resemble a fine old piece of furniture. His dark eyes squinted, focused. As with many people who are hard of hearing, he spoke rather loudly.

"Who are you? What do you want?" he asked.

If I was that unrecognizable in my emaciated, hairy condition, I decided that I might as well maintain my anonymity.

"I am a traveler from the south and I was shipwrecked recently," I said. "I clung to a piece of wood for many days and was finally washed ashore here. I slept on the beach all morning. It was only recently that I recovered sufficient strength to walk to your light-house."

He moved forward and took my arm. He threw his other arm around my shoulders.

"Come in, come in then," he said. "Lean on me. Take it easy. Come this way."

He led me to his quarters, which were extraordinarily messy, being strewn with many old books, charts, maps, and pieces of nautical equipment. He wasn't any too steady himself, so I didn't lean too hard, just enough to maintain the impression of weakness I had tried to convey as I'd leaned against his doorframe.

He led me to a daybed, suggested I lie down, and left to secure the door and fetch me something to eat.

I removed my boots, by my feet were so filthy that I put them back on again. If I'd been drifting about very long, I wouldn't be dirty. I didn't want to give away my story, so I drew a blanket that was there over me and leaned back, really resting.

Jopin returned shortly with a pitcher of water, a pitcher of beer, a great slice of beef, and half a loaf of bread upon a square wooden tray. He swept clear the top of a small table, which he then kicked into a position beside the couch. The he set the tray down on it and bade me eat and drink.

I did. I stuffed myself. I glutted myself. I ate everything in sight. I emptied both pitchers.

Then I felt tremendously tired. Jopin nodded when he saw it come over me, and he told me to go to sleep. Before I knew it, I had.

When I awakened, it was night time and I felt considerably better than I had in many weeks. I got to my feet and retraced my earlier route and departed the building. It was chilly out there, but the sky was crystal clear and there seemed to be a million stars. The lens at the top of the tower blazed at my back, then went dark, blazed, then went dark. The water was cold, but I just had to cleanse myself. I bathed and washed my clothing and wrung it out. I must have spent an hour doing that. Then I went back to the lighthouse, hung my clothing over the back of an old chair to dry out, crawled beneath the blanket, slept again.

In the morning, when I awoke, Jopin was already up. He prepared me a hearty breakfast, and I treated it the same way as I had the dinner of the previous evening. Then I borrowed a razor, a mirror, and a pair of scissors and gave myself a shave and a sort of haircut. I bathed again afterward, and when I donned my salty, stiff, clean garments I felt almost human again.

Jopin stared at me when I returned from the sea and said, "You look kinda familiar, fella," and I shrugged.

"Now tell me about your wreck."

So I did. Out of whole cloth. What a disaster I detailed! Down to the snapping of the mainmast, yet.

He patted me on the shoulder and poured me a drink. He lit the cigar he had given me.

"You just rest easy here," he told me. "I'll take you ashore any time you like, or I'll signal you a passing ship if you see one you recognize."

I took him up on his offered hospitality. It was too much of a lifesaver not to. I ate his food and drank his drinks and let him give me a clean shirt which was too big for him. It had belonged to a friend of his who'd drowned at sea.

I stayed with him for three months, as I recovered my strength. I helped him around the place—tending the light on nights when he felt like getting smashed, and cleaning up all the rooms in the house—even to the extent of painting two of them and replacing five cracked windowpanes—and watching the sea with him on stormy nights.

He was apolitical, I learned. He didn't care who reigned in Amber. So far as he was concerned, the whole bloody crew of us was rotten. So long as he could tend his lighthouse and eat and drink of good food and brew, and consider his nautical charts in peace, he didn't give half a damn what happened ashore. I came to be rather fond of him, and since I knew something of old charts and maps also, we spent many a good evening correcting a few. I had sailed far into the north many years ago, and I gave him a new chart based on my recollections of the voyage. This seemed to please him immensely, as did my descriptions of those waters.

"Corey," (that was how I'd named myself), "I'd like to sail with you one day," he said. "I hadn't realized you were skipper of your own vessel one time."

"Who knows?" I told him. "You were once a captain yourself, weren't you?"

"How'd you know?" he asked.

Actually, I'd remembered, but I gestured about me in reply.

"All these things you've collected," I said, "and your fondness for the charts. Also, you bear yourself like a man who once held a command."

He smiled.

"Yes," he told me, "that's true. I had a command for over a hundred years. That seems long ago. . . . Let's have another drink."

I sipped mine and sort of put it aside. I must have gained over forty pounds in the months I had spent with him. Any day now, I was expecting him to recognize me as a member of the family. Maybe he would turn me in to Eric if he did—and maybe not. Now that we'd established this much of camaraderie, I had a feeling that he might not do it. I didn't want to take the chance and find out.

Sometimes as I sat tending the light I wondered, "How long should I stay here?"

Not too much longer, I decided, adding a drop of grease to a swivel bearing. Not much longer at all. The time was drawing near when I should take to the road and walk among Shadows once again.

Then one day I felt the pressure, gentle and questing at first. I couldn't tell for sure who it was.

I immediately stood stock still, closed my eyes and made my mind go blank. It was about five minutes before the questing presence withdrew.

I paced then and wondered, and I smiled when I realized the shortness of my course. Unconsciously, I had been pacing out the dimensions of my cell back in Amber.

Someone had just tried to reach me, via my Trump. Was it Eric? Had he finally become aware of my absence and decided to try locating me in this manner? I wasn't sure. I felt that he might fear mental contact with me again. Julian, then? Or Gérard? Caine? Whoever it had been, I had closed him out completely, I knew that. And I would refuse such contact with any of my family. I might be missing some important news or a helpful call, but I couldn't afford to take the chance. The attempted contact and my blocking efforts left me with a chill. I shuddered. I thought about the thing all the rest of the day and decided that the time had come for me to move on. It wouldn't do for me to remain this close to Amber while I was so vulnerable. I had recovered sufficiently to make my way among Shadows, to seek for the place where I had to go if Amber were ever to be mine. I had been lulled into something close to peace by old Jopin's ministrations. It would be a pain to leave him, for in the months of our association I had come to like the old guy. So that evening, after we'd finished a game of chess, I told him of my plans to depart.

He poured us two drinks then raised his and said, "Good luck to you, Corwin. I hope to see you again one day."

I didn't question the fact that he had called me by my proper name, and he smiled as he realized that I hadn't let it slip by.

"You've been all right, Jopin," I told him. "If I should succeed in what I'm about to try, I won't forget what you did for me."

He shook his head.

"I don't want anything," he said. "I'm happy right where I am, doing exactly what I'm doing. I enjoy running this damned tower. It's my whole life. If you should succeed in whatever you're about—no, don't tell me about it, please! I don't want to know!—I'll be hoping you'll stop around for a game of chess sometime."

"I will," I promised.

"You can take the *Butterfly* in the morning, if you'd like."

"Thanks."

The *Butterfly* was his sailboat.

"Before you go," he said, "I suggest you take my spyglass, climb the tower, and look back on the Vale of Garnath."

"What's there to see?"

He shrugged.

"You'll have to make up your own mind about that."

I nodded.

"Okay, I will."

We then proceeded to get pleasantly high and turned in for the night. I'd miss old Jopin. With the exception of Rein, he was the only friend I'd found since my return. I wondered vaguely about the valley which had been a sheet of flame the last time I had crossed it. What could it be that was so unusual about it now, these four years later?

Troubled by dreams of werewolves and Sabbats, I slept, and the full moon rose above the world.

At the crack of dawn I did the same. Jopin was still sleeping, which was good, because I don't really like to say good-by, and I had a funny feeling that I would never see him again.

I climbed the tower to the room that housed the big light, spyglass at my side. I moved to the window facing the shore and focused on the valley.

There was a mist hanging above the wood. It was a cold, gray, wet-looking thing that clung to the tops of the small, gnarly trees. The trees were dark, and their branches twisted together like the fingers of wrestling hands. Dark things darted among them, and from the patterns of their flight I knew they were not birds. Bats, probably. There was something evil present in that great wood, I knew, and then I recognized it. It was myself.

I had done this thing with my curse. I had transformed the peaceful Valley of Garnath into what it now represented: it was a symbol of my hate for Eric and for all those others who had stood by and let him get away with his power grab, let him blind me. I didn't like the looks of that forest, and as I stared at it I realized how my hate had objectified itself. I knew it because it was a part of me.

I had created a new entranceway into the real world. Garnath was now a pathway through Shadows. Shadows dark and grim. Only the dangerous, the malicious might walk that pathway. This was the source of the *things* Rein had mentioned, the things that troubled Eric. Good in a way—if they kept him occupied. But as I swung the glass, I couldn't escape the feeling that I had done a very bad thing indeed. At the time, I'd had no idea that I'd ever see the light of day's bright skies again. Now that I did, I realized that I'd unleashed a thing that would take an awful lot of undoing. Even now, strange shapes seemed to move within that place. I had done a thing which had never been done before, not during the whole of Oberon's reign: I had opened a new way to Amber. And I had opened it only to the worst. A day would come when the liege of Amber—whoever he might be—would be faced with the problem of closing that dreadful way. I knew this as I stared, realizing the thing to be a product of my own pain, anger, and hate. If I won out in Amber one day, I might have to cope with my own handiwork, which is always a devilish thing to attempt. I lowered the glass and sighed.

So be it, I decided. In the meantime, it would give Eric something to have insomnia over.

I grabbed a quick bit to eat, outfitted the *Butterfly* as rapidly as I could, hoisted some canvas, cast off, and set sail. Jopin was usually up by that hour, but maybe he didn't like good-bys either.

I headed her out to sea, knowing where I was going but not real certain how to get there. I'd be sailing through Shadow and strange waters, but it would be better than the overland route, what with my handiwork abroad in the realm.

I had set sail for a land near as sparkling as Amber itself, an almost immortal place, a place that did not really exist, not any longer. It was a place which had vanished into Chaos ages ago, but of which a Shadow must somewhere survive. All I had to do was find it, recognize it, and make it mine once again, as it had been in days long gone by. Then, with my own forces to back me up, I would do another thing Amber had never known. I didn't know how yet, but I promised myself that guns would blaze within the immortal city on the day of my return.

As I sailed into Shadow, a white bird of my desire came and sat upon my right shoulder, and I wrote a note and tied it to its leg and sent it on its way. The note said, "I am coming," and it was signed by me.

I would never rest until I held vengeance and the throne within my hand, and good night sweet prince to anybody who stood between me and these things.

The sun hung on my left and the winds bellied the sails and propelled me onward. I cursed once and then laughed.

I was free and I was running, but I had made it this far. I now had the chance I'd wanted all along.

A black bird of my desire came and sat on my left shoulder, and I wrote a note and tied it to its leg and sent it off into the west.

It said, "Eric—I'll be back," and it was signed: "Corwin, Lord of Amber."

A demon wind propelled me east of the sun.

THE GUNS OF AVALON

To Bob and Phyllis Rozman

I

I stood there on the beach and said, "Good-by, *Butterfly*," and the ship slowly turned, then headed out toward deep water. It would make it back into port at the lighthouse of Cabra, I knew, for that place lay near to Shadow.

Turning away, I regarded the black line of trees near at hand, knowing that a long walk lay ahead of me. I moved in that direction, making the necessary adjustments as I advanced. A pre-dawn chill lay upon the silent forest, and this was good.

I was perhaps fifty pounds underweight and still occasionally experienced double vision, but I was improving. I had escaped the dungeons of Amber and recuperated somewhat, with the assistance of mad Dworkin and drunken Jopin, in that order. Now I had to find me a place, a place resembling another place—one which no longer existed. I located the path. I took it.

After a time, I stopped at a hollow tree that had to be there. I reached inside and drew forth my silvered blade and strapped it to my waist. It mattered not that it had been somewhere in Amber. It was here now, for the wood that I walked was in Shadow.

I continued for several hours, the unseen sun somewhere behind my left shoulder. Then I rested awhile, then moved on. It was good to see the leaves and the rocks and the dead tree trunks, the live ones, the grass, the dark earth. It was good to smell all the little smells of life, and to hear its buzzing/humming/chirping sounds. Gods! How I treasured my eyes! Having them back again after nearly four years of blackness was a thing for which I lacked words And to be walking free . . .

I went on, my tattered cloak flapping in the morning breeze. I must have looked over fifty years old, my face creased, my form sparse, lean. Who would have known me for what I was?

As I walked, walked in Shadow, moved toward a place, I did not reach that place. It must be that I had grown somewhat soft. Here is what happened—

I came upon seven men by the side of the road, and six of them were dead, lying in various stages of red dismemberment. The seventh was in a semi-reclined position, his back against the mossy bole of an ancient oak. He held his blade across his lap and there was a large wet wound in his right side, from which the blood still flowed. He wore no armor, though some of the others did. His gray eyes were open, though glassy. His knuckles were skinned and his breathing was slow. From beneath shaggy brows, he watched the crows eat out the eyes of the dead. He did not seem to see me.

I raised my cowl and lowered my head to hide my face. I moved nearer.

I knew him, or someone very like him, once.

His blade twitched and the point rose as I advanced.

"I'm a friend," I said. "Would you like a drink of water?"

He hesitated a moment, then nodded.

"Yes."

I opened my canteen and passed it to him.

He drank and coughed, drank some more.

"Sir, I thank you," he said as he passed it back. "I only regret it were not stronger. Damn this cut!"

"I've some of that, too. If you're sure you can handle it."

He held out his hand and I unstoppered a small flask and gave it to him. He must have coughed for twenty seconds after a slug of that stuff Jopin drinks.

Then the left side of his mouth smiled and he winked lightly.

"Much better," he said. "Mind if I pour a drop of this onto my side? I hate to waste good whisky, but—"

"Use it all, if you have to. On second thought, though, your hand looks shaky. Maybe I'd better do the pouring."

He nodded, and I opened his leather jacket and with my dagger cut away at his shirt until I had exposed the wound. It was nasty-looking, deep, running from front to back a couple inches above the top of his hip. He had other, less serious gashes on his arms, chest, and shoulders.

The blood kept oozing from the big one, and I blotted it a bit and wiped it clean with my kerchief.

His entire body jerked, one great spasm, and then he settled down to shivering. But he did not cry out. I had not thought he would. I folded the kerchief and pressed it in place on the wound. I tied it there, with a long strip I had torn from the bottom of my cloak.

"Want another drink?" I asked him.

"Of water," he said. "Then I fear I must sleep."

He drank, then his head leaned forward until his chin was resting upon his breast. He slept, and I made him a pillow and covered him over with dead men's cloaks.

Then I sat there at his side and watched the pretty black birds.

He had not recognized me. But then, who would? Had I revealed myself to him, he might possibly have known me. We had never really met, I guess, this wounded man and I. But in a peculiar sense, we were acquainted.

I was walking in Shadow, seeking a place, a very special place. It had been destroyed once, but I had the power to re-create it, for Amber casts an infinity of shadows. A child of Amber may walk among them, and such was my heritage. You may call them parallel worlds if you wish, alternate universes if you would, the products of a deranged mind if you care to. I call them shadows, as do all who possess the power to walk among them. We select a possibility and we walk until we reach it. So, in a sense, we create it. Let's leave it at that for now.

I had sailed, had begun this walk toward Avalon.

Centuries before, I had lived there. It is a long, complicated, proud and painful story, and I may go into it later on, if I live to finish much more of this telling.

I was drawing nearer to my Avalon when I came upon the wounded knight and the six dead men. Had I chosen to walk on by, I could have reached a place where the six men lay dead and the knight stood unwounded—or a place where he lay dead and they stood laughing. Some would say it did not really matter, since all these things are possibilities, and therefore all of them exist somewhere in Shadow.

Any of my brothers and sisters—with the possible exceptions of Gérard and Benedict—would not even have given a second glance. I have become somewhat chickenhearted, however. I was not always that way, but perhaps the shadow Earth, where I spent so many years, mellowed me a bit, and maybe my hitch in the dungeons of Amber reminded me somewhat of the quality of human suffering. I do not know. I only know that I could not pass by the hurt I saw on the form of someone much like someone who had once been a friend. If I were to speak my name in this man's ear, I might hear myself reviled, I would certainly hear a tale of woe.

So, all right. I would pay this much of the price: I would get him back on his feet, then I would cut out. No harm done, and perhaps some small good within this Other.

I sat there, watching him, and after several hours, he awakened.

"Hello," I said, unstoppering my canteen. "Have another drink?"

"Thank you." He extended a hand.

I watched him drink, and when he handed it back he said, "Excuse me for not introducing myself. I was not in good manner. . ."

"I know you," I said. "Call me Corey."

He looked as if he were about to say, "Corey of What?" but thought better of it and nodded.

"Very well, Sir Corey," he demoted me."I wish to thank you."

"I am thanked by the fact that you are looking better," I told him. "Want something to eat?"

"Yes, please."

"I have some dried meat here and some bread that could be fresher," I said. "Also a big hunk of cheese. Eat all you want."

I passed it to him and he did.

"What of yourself, Sir Corey?" he inquired.

"I've already eaten, while you were asleep."

I looked about me, significantly. He smiled.

". . . And you knocked off all six of them by yourself?" I said. He nodded.

"Good show. What am I going to do with you now?"

He tried to see my face, failed.

"I do not understand," he said.

"Where are you headed?"

"I have friends," he said, "some five leagues to the north. I was going in that direction when this thing happened. And I doubt very much that any man, or the Devil himself, could bear me on his back for one league. And I could stand, Sir Corey, you'd a better idea as to my size."

I rose, drew my blade, and felled a sapling—about two inches in diameter—with one cut. Then I stripped it and hacked it to the proper length.

I did it again, and with the belts and cloaks of dead men I rigged a stretcher.

He watched until I was finished, then commented:

"You swing a deadly blade, Sir Corey—and a silver one, it would seem. . ."

"Are you up to some traveling?" I asked him.

Five leagues is roughly fifteen miles.

"What of the dead?" he inquired.

"You want to maybe give them a decent Christian burial?" I said. "Screw them! Nature takes care of its own. Let's get out of here. They stink already."

"I'd like at least to see them covered over. They fought well."

I sighed.

"All right, if it will help you to sleep nights. I haven't a spade, so I'll build them a cairn. It's going to be a common burial, though."

"Good enough," he said.

I laid the six bodies out, side by side. I heard him mumbling something, which I guessed to be a prayer for the dead.

I ringed them around with stones. There were plenty of stones in the vicinity, so I worked quickly, choosing the largest so that things would go faster. That is were I made a mistake. One of them must have weighed around four hundred pounds, and I did not roll it. I hefted it and set it in place.

I heard a sharp intake of breath from his direction, and I realized that he had noted this.

I cursed then:

"Damn near ruptured myself on that one!" I said, and I selected smaller stones after that.

When I had finished, I said, "All right. Are you ready to move?"

"Yes."

I raised him in my arms and set him on the stretcher. He clenched his teeth as I did so.

"Where do we go?" I asked.

He gestured.

"Head back to the trail. Follow it to the left until it forks. Then go right at that place. How do you propose to . . . ?"

I scooped the stretcher up in my arms, holding him as you would a baby, cradle and all. Then I turned and walked back to the trail, carrying him.

"Corey?" he said.

"Yes?"

"You are one of the strongest men I have ever met—and it seems I should know you."

I did not answer him immediately. Then I said, "I try to keep in good condition. Clean living and all."

". . . And your voice sounds rather familiar."

He was staring upward, still trying to see my face.

I decided to get off the subject fast.

"Who are these friends of yours I am taking you to?"

"We are headed for the Keep of Ganelon."

"That ratfink!" I said, almost dropping him.

"While I do not understand the word you have used, I take it to be a term of opprobrium," he said, "from the tone of your voice. If such is the case, I must be his defender in—"

"Hold on," I said. "I've a feeling we're talking about two different guys with the same name. Sorry."

Through the stretcher, I felt a certain tension go out of him.

"That is doubtless the case," he said.

So I carried him until we reached the trail, and there I turned to the left.

He dropped off to sleep again, and I made better time after that, taking the fork he had told me about and sprinting while he snored. I began wondering about the six fellows who had tried to do him in and almost succeeded. I hoped that they did not have any friends beating about the bushes.

I slowed my pace back to a walk when his breathing changed.

"I was asleep," he said.

". . . And snoring," I added.

"How far have you borne me?"

"Around two leagues, I'd say."

"And you are not tired?"

"Some," I said, "but not enough to need rest just yet."

"Mon Dieu!" he said. "I am pleased never to have had you for an enemy. Are you certain you are not the Devil?"

"Yeah, sure," I said. "Don't you smell the brimstone? And my right hoof is killing me."

He actually sniffed a couple times before he chuckled, which hurt my feelings a bit.

Actually, we had traveled over four leagues, as I reckoned it. I was hoping he would sleep again and not be too concerned about distances. My arms were beginning to ache.

"Who were those six men you slew?" I asked him.

"Wardens of the Circle," he replied, "and they were no longer men, but men possessed. Now pray to God, Sir Corey, that their souls be at peace."

"Wardens of the Circle?" I asked. "What Circle?"

"The dark Circle—the place of iniquity and loathsome beasts . . ." He took a deep breath. "The source of the illness that lies upon the land."

"This land doesn't look especially ill to me," I said.

"We are far from that place, and the realm of Ganelon is still too strong for the invaders. But the Circle widens. I feel that the last battle will be fought here."

"You have aroused my curiosity as to this thing."

"Sir Corey, if you know not of it 'twere better you forgot it, skirted the Circle, and went your way. Though I should dearly love to fight by your side, this is not your fight—and who can tell the outcome?"

The trail began winding upward. Then, through a break in the trees, I saw a distant thing that made me pause and caused me to recall another, similar place.

"What . . . ?" asked my charge, turning. Then, "Why, you moved much more quickly than I had guessed. That is our destination, the Keep of Ganelon."

I thought then about a Ganelon. I did not want to, but I did. He had been a traitorous assassin and I had exiled him from Avalon centuries before. I had actually cast him through Shadow into another time and place, as my brother Eric had later done to me. I hoped it was not to this place that I had sent him. While not very likely, it was possible. Though he was a mortal man with his allotted span, and I had exiled him from that place perhaps six hundred years ago, it was possible that it was only a few years past in terms of this world. Time, too, is a function of Shadow, and even Dworkin did not know all of its ins and outs. Or perhaps he did. Maybe that is what drove him mad. The most difficult thing about Time, I have learned, is doing it. In any case, I felt that this could not be my old enemy and former trusted aide, for *he* would certainly not be resisting any wave of iniquity that was sweeping across the land. He would be right in there pitching for the loathsome beasts, I felt sure.

A thing that caused me difficulty was the man that I carried. His counterpart had been alive in Avalon at the time of the exiling, meaning that the time lag could be just about right.

I did not care to encounter the Ganelon I had known and be recognized by him. He knew nothing of Shadow. He would only know that I had worked some dark magic on him, as an alternative to killing him, and while he had survived that alternative it might have been the rougher of the two.

But the man in my arms needed a place of rest and shelter, so I trudged forward.

I wondered, though . . .

There did seem to be something about me that lent itself to recognition by this man. If there were some memories of a shadow of myself in this place that was like yet not like Avalon, what form did they take? How would they condition a reception of the actual me should I be discovered?

The sun was beginning to sink. A cool breeze began, hinting of a chilly night to come. My ward was snoring once more, so I decided to sprint most of the remaining distance. I did not like the feeling that this forest after dark might become a place crawling with unclean denizens of some damned Circle that I knew nothing about, but who seemed to be on the make when it came to this particular piece of real estate.

So I ran through lengthening shadows, dismissing rising notions of pursuit, ambush, surveillance, until I could do so no longer. They had achieved the strength of a premonition, and then I heard the noises at my back: a soft pat-pat-pat, as of footfalls.

I set the stretcher down, and I drew my blade as I turned.

There were two of them, cats.

Their markings were precisely those of Siamese cats, only these were the size of tigers. Their eyes were of a solid, sun-bright yellow, pupilless. They seated themselves on their haunches as I turned, and they stared at me and did not blink.

They were about thirty paces away. I stood sideways between them and the stretcher, my blade raised.

Then the one to the left opened its mouth. I did not know whether to expect a purr or a roar.

Instead, it spoke. It said, "Man, most mortal."

The voice was not human-sounding. It was too high-pitched.

"Yet still it lives," said the second, sounding much like the first.

"Slay it here," said the first.

"What of the one who guards it with the blade I like not at all?"

"Mortal man?"

"Come find out," I said, softly.

"It is thin, and perhaps it is old."

"Yet it bore the other from the cairn to this place, rapidly and without rest. Let us flank it."

I sprang forward as they moved, and the one to my right leaped toward me.

My blade split its skull and continued on into the shoulder. As I turned, yanking it free, the other swept past me, heading toward the stretcher. I swung wildly.

My blade fell upon its back and passed completely through its body. It emitted a shriek that grated like chalk on a blackboard as it fell in two pieces and began to burn. The other was burning also.

But the one I had halved was not yet dead. Its head turned toward me and those blazing eyes met my own and held them.

"I die the final death," it said, "and so I know you, Opener. Why do you slay us?"

And then the flames consumed its head.

I turned, cleaned my blade and sheathed it, picked up the stretcher, ignored all questions, and continued on.

A small knowledge had begun within me, as to what the thing was, what it had meant.

And I still sometimes see that burning cat head in dreams, and then I awaken, wet and shivering, and the night seems darker, and filled with shapes I cannot define.

The Keep of Ganelon had a moat about it, and a drawbridge, which was raised. There was a tower at each of the four corners where its high walls met. From within those walls many other towers reaching even higher, tickling the bellies of low, dark clouds, occluding the early stars, casting shadows of jet down the high hill the place occupied. Several of the towers were already lighted, and the wind bore me the faint sound of voices.

I stood before the drawbridge, lowered my charge to the ground, cupped my hands about my mouth, and called out:

"Hola! Ganelon! Two travelers are stranded in the night!"

I heard the clink of metal on stone. I felt that I was being studied from somewhere above. I squinted upward, but my eyes were still far from normal.

"Who is there?" the voice came down, big and booming.

"Lance, who is wounded, and I, Corey of Cabra, who bore him here."

I waited as he called this information to another sentry, and I heard more voices raised as the message was passed along the line.

After a pause of several minutes, a reply came back in the same manner.

Then the guard called down:

"Stay clear! We're going to lower the drawbridge! You may enter!"

The creaking began as he spoke, and in a brief time the thing banged to earth on our side of the moat. I raised my charge once more and walked across it.

Thus did I bear Sir Lancelot du Lac to the Keep of Ganelon, whom I trusted like a brother. That is to say, not at all.

There was a rush of people about me, and I found myself ringed by armed men. There was no hostility present, however, only concern. I had entered a large, cobbled courtyard, lit by torches and filled with bedrolls. I could smell sweat, smoke, horses, and the odors of cooking. A small army was bivouacked there.

Many had approached me and stood staring and murmuring, but then there came up two who were fully arrayed, as for battle, and one of them touched my shoulder.

"Come this way," he said.

I followed and they flanked me. The ring of people parted as we passed. The drawbridge was already creaking back into place. We moved toward the main complex of dark stone.

Inside, we walked along a hallway and passed what appeared to be a reception chamber. Then we came upon a stairway. The man to my right indicated that I should mount it. On the second floor, we stopped before a heavy wooden door and the guard knocked upon it.

"Come in," called out a voice which unfortunately seemed very familiar.

We entered.

He sat at a heavy wooden table near a wide window overlooking the courtyard. He wore a brown leather jacket over a black shirt, and his trousers were also black. They were bloused over the tops of his dark boots. He had about his waist a wide belt which held a hoof-hilted dagger. A short sword lay on the table before him. His hair and beard were red, with a sprinkling of white. His eyes were dark as ebony.

He looked at me, then turned his attention to a pair of guards who entered with the stretcher.

"Put him on my bed," he said. Then "Roderick, tend to him."

His physician, Roderick, was an old guy who didn't look as if he would do much harm, which relieved me somewhat. I had not fetched Lance all that distance to have him bled.

Then Ganelon turned to me once more.

"Where did you find him?" he asked.

"Five leagues to the south of here."

"Who are you?"

"They call me Corey," I said.

He studied me too closely, and his worm-like lips twitched toward a smile beneath his mustache.

"What is your part in this thing?" he asked.

"I don't know what you mean," I said.

I had let my shoulders sag a bit. I spoke slowly, softly, and with a slight falter. My beard was longer than his, and lightened by dust. I imagined I looked like an older man. His attitude on appraisal tended to indicate that he thought I was.

"I am asking you why you helped him," he said.

"Brotherhood of man, and all that," I replied.

"You are a foreigner?"

I nodded.

"Well, you are welcome here for so long as you wish to stay."

"Thanks. I will probably move on tomorrow."

"Now join me in a glass of wine and tell me of the circumstances under which you found him."

So I did.

Ganelon let me speak without interrupting, and those piercing eyes of his were on me all the while. While I had always felt laceration by means of the eyeballs to be a trite expression, it did not feel so that night. He stabbed at me with them. I wondered what he knew and what he was guessing concerning me.

Then fatigue sprang and seized me by the scuff of the neck. The exertion, the wine, the warm room—all of these worked together, and suddenly it was as if I were standing off in the corner somewhere and listening to myself, watching myself, feeling dissociated. While I was capable of great exertion in short bursts, I realized that I was

still very low when it came to stamina. I also noticed that my hand
was trembling.

"I'm sorry," I heard myself saying. "The day's labors are beginning to get to me . . ."

"Of course," said Ganelon. "I will talk with you more on the morrow. Sleep now. Sleep well."

Then he called in one of the guards and ordered him to conduct
me to a chamber. I must have staggered on the way, because I
remember the guard's hand on my elbow, steering me.

That night I slept the sleep of the dead. It was a big, black thing,
about fourteen hours long.

In the morning, I ached all over.

I bathed myself. There was a basin on the high dresser, and soap
and a washcloth someone had thoughtfully set beside it. My throat
felt packed with sawdust and my eyes were full of fuzz.

I sat down and assessed myself.

There had been a day when I could have carried Lance the entire
distance without going to pieces afterward. There had been a day
when I had fought my way up the face of Kolvir and into the heart
of Amber itself.

Those days were gone. I suddenly felt like the wreck I must have
looked.

Something would have to be done.

I had been putting on weight and picking up strength slowly. The
process would have to be accelerated.

A week or two of clean living and violent exercise could help a lot,
I decided. Ganelon had not given any real indication of having recognized me. All right. I would take advantage of the hospitality he
had offered.

With that resolve, I sought out the kitchen and conned a hearty
breakfast. Well, it was really around lunchtime, but let's call things
by their proper names. I had a strong desire for a smoke and felt a
certain perverse joy in the fact that I was out of tobacco. The Fates
were conspiring to keep me true to myself.

I strolled out into the courtyard and a brisk, bright day. For a long
while, I watched the men who were quartered there as they went
through their training regime.

There were bowmen off at the far end, thwanging away at targets
fastened to bales of hay. I noted that they employed thumb rings and

an oriental grip on the bowstring, rather than the three-fingered technique with which I was more comfortable. It made me wonder a bit about this Shadow. The swordsmen used both the edges and points of their weapons, and there was a variety of blades and fencing techniques in evidence. I tried to estimate, and guessed there were perhaps eight hundred of them about—and I had no idea as to how many of them there might be out of sight. Their complexions, their hair, their eyes, varied from pale to quite dark. I heard many strange accents above the thwanging and the clanging, though most spoke the language of Avalon, which is of the tongue of Amber.

As I stood watching, one swordsman raised his hand, lowered his blade, mopped his brow, and stepped back. His opponent did not seem especially winded. This was my chance for some of the exercise I was seeking.

I moved forward, smiled, and said, "I'm Corey of Cabra. I was watching you."

I turned my attention to the big, dark man who was grinning at his resting buddy.

"Mind if I practice with you while your friend rests?" I asked him.

He kept grinning and pointed at his mouth and his ear. I tried several other languages, but none of them worked. So I pointed at the blade and at him and back to myself until he got the idea. His opponent seemed to think it was a good one, as the smaller fellow offered me his blade.

I took it into my hands. It was shorter and a lot heavier than Grayswandir. (That is the name of my blade, which I know I have not mentioned up until now. It is a story in itself, and I may or may not go into it before you learn what brought me to this final pass. But, should you hear me refer to it by name again, you will know what I am talking about.)

I swung my blade a few times to test it, removed my cloak, tossed it off to the side, and struck an *en garde*.

The big fellow attacked. I parried and attacked. He parried and riposted. I parried the riposte, feinted, and attacked. Et cetera. After five minutes, I knew that he was good. And I knew that I was better. He stopped me twice so that I could teach him a maneuver I had used. He learned both very quickly. After fifteen minutes, though, his grin widened. I guess that was around the point where he broke down most opponents by virtue of sheer staying power, if they were good enough to resist his attacks up until then. He had stamina, I'll say that. After twenty minutes, a puzzled look came onto his face. I just didn't look as if I could stand up that long. But then, what can any man really know of that which lies within a scion of Amber?

After twenty-five minutes, he was sheathed in sweat, but he continued on. My brother Random looks and acts, on occasion, like an asthmatic, teen-age hood—but once we had fenced together for over twenty-six hours, to see who would call it quits. (If you're curious, it was me. I had had a date lined up for the next day and had wanted to arrive in reasonably good condition.) We could have gone on. While I was not up to a performance like that just then, I knew that I could outlast the man I faced. After all, he was only human.

After about half an hour, when he was breathing heavily and slowing down on his counterstrokes and I knew that in a few minutes he might guess that I was pulling mine, I raised my hand and lowered my blade as I had seen his previous opponent do. He ground to a halt also, then rushed forward and embraced me. I did not understand what he said, but I gathered that he was pleased with the workout. So was I.

The horrible thing was, I felt it. I found myself slightly heady.

But I needed more. I promised me I would kill myself with exercise that day, glut myself with food that night, sleep deeply, wake, and do it again.

So I went over to where the archers stood. After a time, I borrowed a bow, and in my three-fingered style unleashed perhaps a hundred arrows. I did not do too badly. Then, for a time, I watched the men on horseback, with their lances, shields, maces. I moved on. I watched some practice in hand-to-hand combat.

Finally, I wrestled three men in succession. Then I did feel beat. Absolutely. Entirely.

I sat down on a bench in the shade, sweating, breathing heavily. I wondered about Lance, about Ganelon, about supper. After perhaps ten minutes, I made my way back to the room I had been given and I bathed again.

By then I was ravenously hungry, so I set forth to find me dinner and information.

Before I had gone very far from the door, one of the guards whom I recognized from the previous evening—the one who had guided me to my chamber—approached and said, "Lord Ganelon bids you dine with him in his quarters, at the ringing of the dinner bell."

I thanked him, said I would be there, returned to my chamber, and rested on my bed until it was time. Then I made my way forth once again.

I was beginning to ache deeply and I had a few additional bruises. I decided this was a good thing, would help me to seem older. I banged on Ganelon's door and a boy admitted me, then dashed off to join another youth who was spreading a table near to the fireplace.

Ganelon wore a green shirt and trousers, green boots and belt, sat in a high-backed chair. He rose as I entered, walked forward to greet me.

"Sir Corey, I've heard report of your doings this day," he said, clasping my hand. "It makes your carrying Lance seem more believable. I must say you're more a man than you look—meaning no offense by that."

I chuckled.

"No offense."

He led me to a chair, handed me a glass of pale wine that was a bit too sweet for my taste, then said, "Looking at you, I'd say I could push you over with one hand—but you carried Lance five leagues and killed two of those bastard cats on the way. And he told me about the cairn you built, of big stones—"

"How is Lance feeling today?" I interrupted.

"I had to place a guard in his chamber to be sure he rested. The muscle-bound clod wanted to get up and walk around. He'll stay there all week, though, by God!"

"Then he must be feeling better."

He nodded.

"Here's to his health."

"I'll drink to that."

We drank. Then: "Had I an army of men like you and Lance," he said, "the story might have been different."

"What story?"

"The Circle and its Wardens," he said. "You've not heard of it?"

"Lance mentioned it. That's all."

One boy tended an enormous chunk of beef on a spit above a low fire. Occasionally, he sloshed some wine over it as he turned the shaft. Whenever the odor drifted my way, my stomach would rumble and Ganelon would chuckle. The other boy left the room to fetch bread from the kitchen.

Ganelon was silent a long while. He finished his wine and poured himself another glass. I sipped slowly at my first.

"Have you ever heard of Avalon?" he finally asked.

"Yes," I replied. "There is a verse I heard long ago from a passing bard: 'Beyond the River of the Blessed, there we sat down, yea, we wept, when we remembered Avalon. Our swords were shattered in our hands and we hung our shields on the oak tree. The silver towers were fallen, into a sea of blood. How many miles to Avalon? None, I say, and all. The silver towers are fallen.'"

"Avalon fallen . . . ?" he said.

"I think the man was mad. I know of no Avalon. His verse stayed in my mind, though."

Ganelon averted his face and did not speak again for several minutes. When he did, his voice was altered.

"There was," he said. "There was such a place. I lived there, years ago. I did not know it was fallen."

"How came you here from that place?" I asked him.

"I was exiled by its sorcerer Lord, Corwin of Amber. He sent me through darkness and madness to this place, that I might suffer and die here—and I *have* suffered and come near to the final lay many a time. I've tried to find the way back, but nobody knows it. I've spoken with sorcerers, and even a captured creature of the Circle before we slew the thing. But none knew the road to Avalon. It is as the bard said, 'No miles, and all,'" he misquoted my lyric. "Do you recall the bard's name?"

"I am sorry, but I do not."

"Where is this Cabra place you hie from?"

"Far to the east, across the waters," I said. "Very far. It is an island kingdom."

"Any chance they could furnish us with some troops? I can afford to pay quite a bit."

I shook my head.

"It is a small place with a small militia, and it would be several months' travel both ways—sea and land. They have never fought as mercenaries, and for that matter they are not very warlike."

"Then you seem to differ a great deal from your countrymen," he said, looking at me once more.

I sipped my wine.

"I was an arms instructor," I said, "to the Royal Guard."

"Then you might be inclined to hire out, to help train my troops?"

"I'll stay a few weeks and do that," I said.

He nodded a tight-lipped microsecond of a smile, then, "It saddens me to hear this indication that fair Avalon is gone," he said. "But if it is so, it means that my exiler is also likely dead." He drained his wineglass. "So even the demon came to a time when he could not defend his own," he mused. "That's a heartening thought. It means we might have a chance here, against these demons."

"Begging your pardon," I said, sticking my neck out for what I thought good reason, "if you were referring to that Corwin of Amber, he did not die when whatever happened happened."

The glass snapped in his hand.

"You know Corwin?" he said.

"No, but I know of him," I replied. "Several years ago, I met one of his brothers—a fellow named Brand. He told me of the place called Amber, and of the battle in which Corwin and a brother of his named Bleys led a horde against their brother Eric, who held the city. Bleys fell from the mountain Kolvir and Corwin was taken prisoner. Corwin's eyes were put out after Eric's coronation, and he was cast into the dungeons beneath Amber, where he may yet remain if he has not since died."

Ganelon's face was drained of color as I spoke.

"All those names you mentioned—Brand, Bleys, Eric," he said. "I heard him mention them in days long gone by. How long ago did you hear of this thing?"

"It was about four years back."

"He deserved better."

"After what he did to you?"

"Well," said the man, "I've had a lot of time to think about it, and it is not as if I gave him no cause for what he did. He was strong—stronger than you or Lance, even—and clever. Also, he could be merry on occasion. Eric should have killed him quickly, not the way that he did. I've no love for him, but my hate's died down a bit. The demon deserved better than he got, that's all."

The second boy returned with a basket of bread. The one who had prepared the meat removed it from the spit and set it on a platter in the center of the table.

Ganelon nodded toward it.

"Let's eat," he said.

He rose and moved to the table.

I followed. We did not talk much during the meal.

After stuffing myself until my stomach would hold no more and soaking down its contents with another glass of too-sweet wine, I began to yawn. Ganelon cursed after the third one.

"Damn it, Corey! Stop that! It's contagious!"

He stifled a yawn of his own.

"Let's take some air," he said, rising.

So we walked out along the walls, passing the sentries in their rounds. They would come to attention and salute Ganelon as soon as they saw who it was approaching, and he would give them a word of greeting and we would move on. We came to a battlement, where we paused to rest, seating ourselves on the stone, sucking in the evening air, cool and damp and full of the forest, and noting the appearance of the stars, one by one, in the darkening sky. The stone was cold beneath me. Far off in the distance, I thought I could detect the shimmer of the sea. I heard a night bird, from somewhere below us. Ganelon produced a pipe and tobacco from a pouch he wore at his belt. He filled it, tamped it, and struck a flame. His face would have been satanic in the spark light, save for whatever turned his mouth downward and drew the muscles in his cheeks up into that angle formed by the inner corners of his eyes and the sharp bridge of his nose. A devil is supposed to have an evil grin, and this one looked too morose.

I smelled the smoke. After a time, he began to speak, softly and very slowly at first:

"I remember Avalon," he began. "My birth there was not ignoble, but virtue was never one of my strong points. I went through my inheritance quickly and I took to the roads where I waylaid travelers. Later, I joined with a band of other men such as myself. When I discovered I was the strongest and most fit to lead, I became the leader. There were prices on all our heads. Mine was the highest."

He spoke more rapidly now, and his voice grew more refined and his choice of words came as an echo from out of his past.

"Yes, I remember Avalon," he said, "a place of silver and shade and cool waters, where the stars shone like bonfires at night and the green of day was always the green of spring. Youth, love, beauty—I knew them in Avalon. Proud steeds, bright metal, soft lips, dark ale. Honor . . ."

He shook his head.

"One later day," he said, "when war commenced within the realm, the ruler offered full pardon to any outlaws who would follow him in battle against the insurgents. This was Corwin. I threw in with him and rode off to the wars. I became an officer, and then—later—a member of his staff. We won the battles, put down the uprising. Then Corwin ruled peacefully once more, and I remained at his court. Those were the good years. There later came some border skirmishes, but these we always won. He trusted me to handle such things for him. Then he granted a Dukedom to dignify the House of a minor noble whose daughter he desired in marriage. I had wanted that Dukedom, and he had long hinted it might one day be mine. I was furious, and I betrayed my command the next time I was dispatched to settle a dispute along the southern border, where something was always stirring. Many of my men died, and the invaders entered into the realm. Before they could be routed, Lord Corwin himself had to take up arms once more. The invaders had come through in great strength, and I thought they would conquer the realm. I hoped they would. But Corwin, again, with his foxy tactics, prevailed. I fled, but was captured and taken to him for sentencing. I cursed him and spat at him. I would not bow. I hated the ground he trod, and a condemned man has no reason not to put up the best front he can, to go out like a man. Corwin said he would show me a measure of mercy for favors past. I told him to shove his mercy, and then I realized that he was mocking me. He ordered me released and he approached me. I knew he could kill me with his hands. I tried to fight with him, but to no avail. He stuck me once and I fell. When I awakened, I was strapped across his horse's rump. He rode along, jibing at me the while. I would not reply to anything he said, but we rode through wondrous lands and lands out of nightmare, which is one way I learned of his sorcerous power—for no traveler I have ever met has passed through the places I saw that day. Then he pronounced my exile, released me in this place, turned, and rode away."

He paused to relight his pipe, which had gone out, puffed upon it for a time, went on: "Many a bruising, cudgeling, biting, and beating did I take in this place at the hands of man and beast, only barely preserving my life. He had left me in the wickedest portion of the realm. But then one day my fortunes took a turn. An armored knight bade me depart the roadway that he might pass. At that point, I cared not whether I lived or died, so I called him a pock-marked whoreson and bade him go to the Devil. He charged me and I seized his lance and pushed its point into the ground, so unhorsing him. I drew him a smile beneath his chin with his own dagger, and thus obtained me mounting and weapons. Then did I set about paying back those who had used me poorly. I took up my old trade on the highways once again and I gained me another band of followers. We grew. When there were hundreds of us our needs were considerable. We would ride into a small town and make it ours. The local militia would fear us. This, too, was a good life, though not so splendid as the Avalon I never shall know again. All the roadside inns came to fear the thunder of our mounts, and travelers would soil their britches when they heard us coming. Ha! This lasted for several years. Large parties of armed men were sent to track us and destroy us, but always we evaded them or ambushed them. Then one day there was the dark Circle, and no one really knows why."

He puffed more vigorously on his pipe, stared off into the distance.

"I am told it began as a tiny ring of toadstools, far to the west. A child was found dead in its center, and the man who found her—her father—died of convulsions several days later. The spot was immediately said to be accursed. It grew quickly in the months that followed, until it was half a league across. The grasses darkened and shone like metal within it, but did not die. The trees twisted and their leaves blackened. They swayed when there was no wind, and bats danced and darted among them. In the twilight, strange shapes could be seen moving—always *within* the Circle, mind you—and there were lights, as of small fires, throughout the night. The Circle continued to grow, and those who lived near it fled—mostly. A few remained. It was said that those who remained had struck some bargain with the dark things. And the Circle continued to widen, spreading like the ripple from a rock cast into a pond. More and more people remained, living, within it. I have spoken with these people, fought with them, slain them. It is as if there is something dead inside them all. Their voices lack the thrust and dip of men chewing over their words and tasting them. They seldom do much with their faces, but wear them like death masks. They began to leave the Circle in bands, marauding. They slew wantonly. They committed many atrocities and defiled places of worship. They put things to the torch when they left them. They never stole objects of silver. Then, after many months, other creatures than men began to come forth—strangely formed, like the hellcats you slew. Then the

Circle slowed in its growth, almost halting, as though it were nearing some sort of limit. But now all manner of raiders emerged from it—some even faring forth during the day—laying waste to the countryside about its borders. When they had devastated the land about its entire circumference, the Circle moved to encompass those areas also. And so its growth began again, in this fashion. The old king, Uther, who had long hunted me forgot all about me and set his forces to patrolling that damned Circle. It was beginning to worry me, also, as I did not relish the notion of being seized by some hell-spawned bloodsucker as I slept. So I got together fifty-five of my men—that was all who would volunteer, and I wanted no cowards—and we rode into that place one afternoon. We came upon a pack of those dead-faced men burning a live goat on a stone altar and we lit into the lot of them. We took one prisoner and tied him to his own altar and questioned him there. He told us that the Circle would grow until it covered the entire land, from ocean to ocean. One day it would close with itself on the other side of the world. We had best join with them, if we wished to save our hides. Then one of my men stabbed him and he died. He really died, for I know a dead man when I see one. I've made it happen often enough. But as his blood fell upon the stone, his mouth opened and out came the loudest laugh I ever heard in my life. It was like thunder all about us. Then he sat up, unbreathing, and began to burn. As he burned, his form changed, until it was like that of the burning goat—only larger—there upon the altar. Then a voice came from the thing. It said, 'Flee, mortal man! But you shall never leave this Circle!' And believe me, we fled! The sky grew black with bats and other—things. We heard the sound of hoofbeats. We rode with our blades in our hands, killing everything that came near us. There were cats such as you slew, and snakes and hopping things, and God knows what all else. As we neared the edge of the Circle, one of King Uther's patrols saw us and came to our aid. Sixteen of the fifty-five who had ridden in with me rode back out. And the patrol lost perhaps thirty men itself. When they saw who I was, they hustled me off to court. Here. This used to be Uther's palace. Told him what I had done, what I had seen and heard. He did with me as Corwin had. He offered full pardon to me and to my men if we would join with him against the Wardens of the Circle. Having gone through what I had gone through, I realized that the thing had to be stopped. So I agreed. Then I fell ill, I am told that I was delirious for three days. I was as weak as a child after my recovery, and I learned that everyone who had entered the Circle had been likewise taken. Three had died. I visited the rest of my men, told them the story, and they were enlisted. The patrols about the Circle were strengthened. But it would not be contained. In the years that followed, the Circle grew. We fought many skirmishes. I was promoted until I stood at Uther's right hand, as once I had at Corwin's. Then the skirmishes became more than skirmishes. Larger and larger parties emerged from that hellhole. We lost a few battles. They took some of our outposts. Then one night an army emerged, an army—a horde—of both men and the other things that dwelled there. That night we met the largest force we had ever engaged. King Uther himself rode to battle, against my advice—for he was advanced in years—and he fell that night and the land was without a ruler. I wanted my captain, Lancelot, to sit in stewardship, for I knew him to be a far more honorable man than myself. . . . And it is strange here. I had known a Lancelot, just like him, in Avalon—but this man knew me not when first we met. It is strange. . . . At any rate, he declined, and the position was thrust upon me. I hate it, but here I am. I have held them back for over three years now. All my instincts tell me to flee. What do I owe these damned people? What do I care if the bloody Circle widens? I could cross over the sea to some land it would never reach during my lifetime, and then forget the whole thing. Damn it! I didn't want this responsibility! Now it is mine, though!"

"Why?" I asked him, and the sound of my own voice was strange to me.

There was silence.

He emptied his pipe. He refilled it. He relit it. He puffed it.

There was more silence.

Then, "I don't know," he said. "I'd stab a man in the back for a pair of shoes, if he had them and I needed them to keep my feet from freezing. I once did, that's how I know. But . . . this is different. This is a thing hurting everybody, and I'm the only one who can do the job. God damn it! I know they're going the bury me here one day, along with all the rest of them. But I can't pull out. I've got to hold that thing back as long as I can."

My head was cleared by the cold night air, which gave my consciousness a second wind, so to speak, though my body felt mildly anesthetized about me.

"Couldn't Lance lead them?" I asked.

"I'd say so. He's good man. But there is another reason. I think that goat-thing, whatever it was, on the altar, is a bit afraid of me. I had gone in there and it had told me I'd never make it back out again, but I did. I lived through the sickness that followed after. It knows it's me that has been fighting it all along. We won that great bloody engagement on the night Uther died, and I met the thing again in a different form and it knew me. Maybe this is a part of what is holding it back now."

"What form?"

"A thing with a manlike shape, but with goat horns and red eyes. It was mounted on a piebald stallion. We fought for a time, but the tide of the battle swept us apart. Which was a good thing, too, for it was winning. It spoke again, as we swaggered swords, and I knew that head-filling voice. It called me a fool and told me I could never hope to win. But when morning came, the field was ours and we drove them back to the Circle, slaying them as they fled. The rider of the piebald escaped. There have been other sallyings forth since then, but none such as that night's. If I were to leave this land, another such army—one that is readying even now—would come forth. That thing would somehow know of my departure—just as it knew that Lance was bringing me another report on the disposition of troops within the Circle, sending those Wardens to destroy him as he returned. It knows of you by now, and surely it must wonder over this development. It must wonder who you are, for all your strength. I will stay here and fight it till I fall. I must. Do not ask me why. I only hope that before that day comes, I at least learn how this thing came to pass—*why* that Circle is out there."

Then there came a fluttering near to my head. I ducked quickly to avoid whatever it was. It was not necessary, though. It was only a bird. A white bird. It landed on my left shoulder and stood there, making small noises. I held up my wrist and it hopped over onto it. There was a note tied to its leg. I unfastened it, read it, crumpled it in my hand. Then I studied invisible things distant.

"What is the matter, Sir Corey?" cried Ganelon.

The note, which I had sent on ahead to my destination, written in my own hand, transmitted by a bird of my desire, could only reach the place that had to be my next stop. This was not precisely the place that I had in mind. However, I could read my own omens.

"What is it?" he asked. "What is it that you hold? A message?"

I nodded. I handed it to him. I could not very well throw it away, since he had seen me take it.

It read, "I am coming," and it bore my signature.

Ganelon puffed his pipe and read it in the glow.

"*He* lives? And he would come *here?*" he said.

"So it would seem."

"This is very strange," he said. "I do not understand it at all . . ."

"It sounds like a promise of assistance," I said, dismissing the bird, which cooed twice, then circled my head and departed.

Ganelon shook his head.

"I do not understand."

"Why number the teeth of a horse you may receive for nothing?" I said. "You have only succeeded in containing that thing."

"True," he said. "Perhaps he could destroy it."

"And perhaps it's just a joke," I told him. "A cruel one."

He shook his head again.

"No. That is not his style. I wonder what he is after?"

"Sleep on it," I suggested.

"There is little else that I can do, just now," he said, stifling a yawn.

We rose then and walked the wall. We said our good nights, and I staggered off toward the pit of sleep and fell headlong into it.

II

Day. More aches. More pains.

Someone had left me a new cloak, a brown one, which I decided was a good thing. Especially if I put on more weight and Ganelon recalled my colors. I did not shave my beard, because he had known me in a slightly less hairy condition. I took pains to disguise my voice whenever he was about. I hid Grayswandir beneath my bed.

For all of the following week I drove myself ruthlessly. I worked and sweated and strove until the aches subsided and my muscles grew firm once more. I think I put on fifteen pounds that week. Slowly, very slowly, I began feeling like my old self.

The country was called Lorraine, and so was she. If I happened to be in the mood to hand you a line, I would tell you we met in a meadow behind the castle, she gathering flowers and me walking there for exercise and fresh air. Crap.

I guess a polite term would be camp follower. I met her at the end of a hard day's work, spent mainly with the saber and the mace. She was standing off on the side lines waiting for her date when I first caught sight of her. She smiled and I smiled back, nodded, winked, and passed her by. The next day I saw her again, and I said "Hello" as I passed her. That's all.

Well, I kept running into her. By the end of my second week, when my aches were gone and I was over a hundred-eighty pounds and feeling that way again, I arranged to be with her one evening. By then, I was aware of her status and it was fine, so far as I was concerned. But we did not do the usual thing that night. No.

Instead, we talked, and then something else happened.

Her hair was rust-colored with a few strands of gray in it. I guessed she was under thirty, though. Eyes, very blue. Slightly pointed chin. Clean, even teeth inside a mouth that smiled at me a lot. Her voice was somewhat nasal, her hair was too long, her make-up laid on too heavily over too much tiredness, her complexion too freckled, her choice in clothing too bright and tight. But I liked her. I did not think I'd actually feel that way when I asked her out that night because, as I said, liking her was not what I had in mind.

There was no place to go but my chamber, so we had gone there. I had become a captain, and I took advantage of my rank by having dinner brought to us, and an extra bottle of wine.

"The men are afraid of you," she said. "They say you never grow tired."

"I do," I said, "believe me."

"Of course," she said, shaking her too-long locks and smiling. "Don't we all?"

"I daresay," I replied.

"How old are you?"

"How old are *you?*"

"A gentlemen would not ask that question."

"Neither would a lady."

"When you first came here, they thought you were over fifty."

"And . . . ?"

"And now they have no idea. Forty-five? Forty?"

"No," I said.

"I didn't think so. But your beard fooled everyone."

"Beards often do that."

"You look better every day. Bigger . . ."

"Thanks. I feel better than I did when I arrived."

"Sir Corey of Cabra," she said. "Where's Cabra? What's Cabra? Will you take me there with you, if I ask you nicely?"

"I'd tell you so," I said, "but I'd be lying."

"I know. But it would be nice to hear."

"Okay. I'll take you there with me. It's a lousy place."

"Are you really as good as the men say?"

"I'm afraid not. Are you?"

"Not really. Do you want to go to bed now?"

"No. I'd rather talk. Have a glass of wine."

"Thank you. . . . Your health."

"Yours."

"Why is it you are such a good swordsman?"

"Aptitude and good teachers."

". . . And you carried Lance all that distance and slew those beasts . . ."

"Stories grow with the telling."

"But I have watched you. You *are* better than the others. That is why Ganelon made you whatever deal he did. He knows a good thing when he sees it. I've had many friends who were swordsmen, and I've watched them at practice. You could cut them to pieces. The men say you are a good teacher. They like you, even if you do scare them."

"Why do I frighten them? Because I am strong? There are many strong men in the world. Because I can stand up and swing a blade for a long while?"

"They think there is something supernatural involved."

I laughed.

"No, I'm just the second-best swordsman around. Pardon me— maybe the third. But I try harder."

"Who's better?"

"Eric of Amber, possibly."

"Who is he?"

"A supernatural creature."

"He's the best?"

"No."

"Who is?"

"Benedict of Amber."

"Is he one, too?"

"If he is still alive, he is."

"Strange, that's what you are," she said. "And why? Tell me. *Are* you a supernatural creature?"

"Let's have another glass of wine."

"It'll go to my head."

"Good."

I poured them.

"We are all going to die," she said.

"Eventually."

"I mean here, soon, fighting this thing."

"Why do you say that?"

"It's too strong."

"Then why stick around?"

"I've no place else to go. That's why I asked you about Cabra."

"And why you came here tonight?"

"No. I came to see what you were like."

"I am an athlete who is breaking training. Were you born around here?"

"Yes. In the wood."

"Why'd you pick up with these guys?"

"Why not? It's better than getting pig shit on my heels every day."

"Never have a man of your own? Steady, I mean?"

"Yes. He's dead. He's the one who found . . . the Fairy Ring."

"I'm sorry."

"I'm not. He used to get drunk whenever he could borrow or steal enough to afford it and then come home and beat me. I was glad when I met Ganelon."

"So you think that the thing is too strong, that we are going to lose to it?"

"Yes."

"You may be right. But I think you're wrong."

She shrugged.

"You'll be fighting with us?"

"I'm afraid so."

"Nobody knew for sure, or would say if they did. That might prove interesting. I'd like to see you fight with the goat-man."

"Why?"

"Because he seems to be their leader. If you killed him, we'd have more of a chance. You might be able to do it."

"I have to," I said.

"Special reason?"

"Yes."

"Private one?"

"Yes."

"Good luck."

"Thanks."

She finished her wine, so I poured her another.

"I know *he* is a supernatural creature," she said.

"Let's get off the subject."

"All right. But will you do me a thing?"

"Name it."

"Put on armor tomorrow, pick up a lance, get hold of a horse, and trounce that big cavalry officer Harald."

"Why?"

"He beat me last week, just like Jarl used to. Can you do it?"

"Yes."

"Will you?"

"Why not? Consider him trounced."

She came over and leaned against me.

"I love you," she said.

"Crap."

"All right. How about, 'I like you'?"

"Good enough. I—"

Then a chill and numbing wind blew along my spine. I stiffened and resisted what was to come by blanking my mind completely.

Someone was looking for me. It was someone of the House of Amber, doubtless, and he was using my Trump or something very like it. There was no mistaking the sensation. If it was Eric, then he had more guts than I gave him credit for, since I had almost napalmed his brain the last time we had been in contact. It could not be Random, unless he was out of prison, which I doubted. If it was Julian or Caine, they could go to hell. Bleys was probably dead. Possibly Benedict, too. That left Gérard, Brand, and our sisters. Of these, only Gérard might mean me well. So I resisted discovery, successfully. It took me perhaps five minutes, and when it was finished I was shaking and sweating and Lorraine was staring at me strangely.

"What happened?" she asked. "You aren't drunk yet, and neither am I."

"Just a spell I sometimes get," I said. "It's a disease I picked up in the islands."

"I saw a face," she said. "Perhaps it was on the floor, maybe it was in my head. It was an old man. The collar of his garment was green and he looked a lot like you, except that his beard was gray."

I slapped her then.

"You're lying! You couldn't have . . ."

"I'm just telling you what I saw! Don't hit me! I don't know what it meant! Who was he?"

"I think it was my father. God, it's strange . . ."

"What happened?" she repeated.

"A spell," I said. I said. "I sometimes get them, and people think they see my father on the castle wall or floor. Don't worry about it. It's not contagious."

"Crap," she said. "You're lying to me."

"I know. But please forget the whole thing."

"Why should I?"

"Because you like me," I told her. "Remember? And because I'm going to trounce Harald for you tomorrow."

"That's true," she said, and I started shaking again and she fetched a blanket from the bed and put it about my shoulders.

She handed me my wine and I drank it. She sat beside me and rested her head on my shoulder, so I put my arm about her. A devil wind began to scream and I heard the rapid rattle of the rainfall that came with it. For a second, it seemed that something beat against the shutters. Lorraine whimpered slightly.

"I do not like what is happening tonight," she said.

"Neither do I. Go bar the door. It's only bolted right now."

As she did this, I moved our seat so that it faced my single window. I fetched Grayswandir out from beneath the bed and unsheathed it. Then I extinguished every light in the room, save for a single candle on the table to my right.

I reseated myself, my blade across my knees.

"What are we doing?" Lorraine asked, as she came and sat down at my left.

"Waiting," I said.

"For what?"

"I am not positive, but this is certainly the night for it."

She shuddered and drew near.

"You know, perhaps you had better leave," I said.

"I know," she said, "but I'm afraid to go out. You'll be able to protect me if I stay here, won't you?"

I shook my head.

"I don't even know if I'll be able to protect myself."

She touched Grayswandir.

"What a beautiful blade! I've never seen one like it."

"There isn't another," I said, and each time that I shifted a little, the light fell differently upon it, so that one moment it seemed filmed over with unhuman blood of an orange tint and the next it lay there cold and white as snow or a woman's breast, quivering in my hand each time a little chill took me.

I wondered how it was that Lorraine had seen something I had not during the attempted contact. She could not simply have imagined anything that close to home.

"There is something strange about *you*," I said.

She was silent for four or five flickerings of the candle, then said, "I've a touch of the second sight. My mother had more of it. People say my grandmother was a sorceress. I don't know any of that business, though. Well, not much of it. I haven't done it for years. I always wind up losing more than I gain."

Then she was silent again, and I asked her, "What do you mean?"

"I used a spell to get my first man," she said, "and look what he turned out to be. If I hadn't, I'd have been a lot better off. I wanted a pretty daughter, and I made that happen—"

She stopped abruptly and I realized she was crying.

"What's the matter? I don't understand . . ."

"I thought you knew," she said.

"No, I'm afraid not."

"She was the little girl in the Fairy Circle. I thought you knew . . ."

"I'm sorry."

"I wish I didn't have the touch. I never use it any more. But it won't let me alone. It still brings me dreams and signs, and they are never over things I can do anything about. I wish it would go away and devil somebody else!"

"That's the one thing it will not do, Lorraine. I'm afraid you are stuck with it."

"How do you know?"

"I've known people like you in the past, that's all."

"You've a touch of it yourself, haven't you?"

"Yes."

"Then you feel that there is something out there now, don't you?"

"Yes."

"So do I. Do you know what it is doing?"

"It's looking for me."

"Yes, I feel that, too. Why?"

"Perhaps to test my strength. It knows that I am here. If I am a new ally come to Ganelon, it must wonder what I represent, who I am . . ."

"Is it the horned one himself?"

"I don't know. I think not, though."

"Why not?"

"If I am really he who would destroy it, it would be foolish to seek me out here in the keep of its enemy where I am surrounded by strength. I would say one of its minions is looking for me. Perhaps, somehow, that is what my father's ghost . . . I do not know. If its servant finds me and names me, it will know what preparations to make. If it finds me and destroys me, it will have solved the problem. If I destroy the servant, it will know that much more about my strength. Whichever way it works out, the horned one will be something ahead. So why should it risk its own pronged dome at this stage in the game?"

We waited, there in the shadow-clad chamber, as the taper burned away the minutes.

She asked me, "What did you mean when you said, if it finds you and names you . . . ? Names you what?"

"The one who almost did not come here," I said.

"You think that it might know you from somewhere, somehow?" she asked.

"I think it might," I said.

She drew away from me then.

"Don't be afraid," I said. "I won't hurt you."

"I am afraid, and you will hurt me!" she said. "I know it! But I want you! Why do I want you?"

"I don't know," I said.

"There is something out there now!" she said, sounding slightly hysterical. "It's near! It's very near! Listen! Listen!"

"Shut up!" I said, as a cold, prickly feeling came to rest on the back of my neck and coiled about my throat. "Get over on the far side of the room, behind the bed!"

"I'm afraid of the dark," she said.

"Do it, or I'll have to knock you out and carry you. You'll be in my way here."

I could hear a heavy flapping above the storm, and there came a scratching on the stone of the wall as she moved to obey me.

Then I was looking into two hot, red eyes which were looking back into my own. I dropped mine quickly. The thing stood there on the ledge outside the window and regarded me.

It was well over six feet in height, with great branches of antlers growing out of its forehead. Nude, its flesh was a uniform ash-gray in color. It appeared to be sexless, and it had gray, leathery wings extending far out behind it and joining with the night. It held a short, heavy sword of dark metal in its right hand, and there were runes carved all along the blade. With its left hand, it clutched at the lattice.

"Enter at your peril," I said loudly, and I raised the point of Grayswandir to indicate its breast.

It chuckled. It just stood there and chuckled and giggled at me. It tried to meet my eyes once more, but I would not let it. If it looked into my eyes for long, it would know me, as the hellcat had known me.

When it spoke, it sounded like a bassoon blowing words.

"You are not the one," it said, "for you are smaller and older. Yet . . . That blade . . . It could be his. Who are you?"

"Who are you?" I asked.

"Strygalldwir is my name. Conjure with it and I will eat your heart and liver."

"Conjure with it? I can't even pronounce it," I said, "and my cirrhosis would give you indigestion. Go away."

"Who are you?" it repeated.

"Misli, gammi gra'dil, Strygalldwir," I said, and it jumped as if given a hotfoot.

"You seek to drive me forth with such a simple spell?" it asked when it settled again. "I am not one of the lesser ones."

"It seemed to make you a bit uncomfortable."

"Who are you?" it said again.

"None of your business, Charlie. Ladybird, Ladybird, fly away home—"

"Four times must I ask you and four times be refused before I may enter and slay you. Who are you?"

"No," I said, standing. "Come on in and burn!"

Then it tore away the latticework, and the wind that accompanied it into the chamber extinguished the candle.

I lunged forward, and there were sparks between us when Grayswandir met the dark rune-sword. We clashed, then I sprang back. My eyes had adjusted to the half dark, so the loss of the light did not blind me. The creature saw well enough, also. It was stronger than a man, but then so am I. We circled the room. An icy wind moved about us, and when we passed the window again, cold droplets lashed my face. The first time that I cut the creature—a long slash across the breast—it remained silent, though tiny flames danced about the edges of the wound. The second time that I cut it—high upon the arm —it cried out, cursing me.

"Tonight I will suck the marrow from your bones!" it said. "I will dry them and work them most cunningly into instruments of music! Whenever I play upon them, your spirit will writhe in bodiless agony!"

"You burn prettily," I said.

It slowed for a fraction of a second and my opportunity was there.

I beat that dark blade aside and my lunge was perfect. The center of its breast was my target. I ran it through.

It howled then, but did not fall. Grayswandir was torn from my grasp and flames bloomed about the wound. It stood there wearing them. It advanced a step toward me and I picked up a small chair and held it between us.

"I do not keep my heart where men do," it said.

Then it lunged, but I blocked the blow with chair and caught it in the right eye with one of the legs. I threw the chair to the side then, and stepping forward, seized its right wrist and turned it over. I struck the elbow with the edge of my hand, as hard as I could. There came a sharp crack and the rune-sword clattered to the floor. Then its left hand struck my head and I fell.

It leaped for the blade, and I seized its ankle and jerked.

It sprawled, and I threw myself atop it and found its throat. I turned my head into the hollow of my shoulder, chin against my breast, as it clawed for my face with its left hand.

As my death grip tightened, its eyes sought mine, and this time I did not avoid them. There came a tiny shock at the base of my brain, as we both knew that we knew.

"You!" it managed to gasp, before I twisted my hands hard and the life went out of those red red eyes.

I stood, put my foot upon its carcass, and withdrew Grayswandir.

The thing burst into flames when my blade came free, and kept burning until there was nothing remaining but a charred spot upon the floor.

Then Lorraine came over and I put my arm about her and she asked me to take her back to her quarters and to bed. So I did, but we didn't do anything but lie there together until she had cried herself to sleep. That is how I met Lorraine.

Lance and Ganelon and I sat atop our mounts on a high hill, the late morning sun hitting us in the back, and we looked down into the place. Its appearance confirmed things for me.

It was akin to that twisted wood that filled the valley to the south of Amber.

Oh my father! What have I wrought? I said within my heart, but there was no answer other than the dark Circle that lay beneath me and spread for as far as the eye could see.

Through the bars of my visor, I looked down upon it—charred-seeming, desolate, and smelling of decay. I lived inside my visor these days. The men looked upon it as an affectation, but my rank gave me the right to be eccentric. I had worn it for over two weeks, since my battle with Strygalldwir. I had put it on the following morning before I trounced Harald to keep my promise to Lorraine, and I had decided that as my girth increased I had better keep my face concealed.

I weighed perhaps fourteen stone now, and felt like my old self again. If I could help clean up this mess in the land called Lorraine, I knew that I would have a chance at least to try what I most wanted, and perhaps succeed.

"So that's it," I said. "I don't see any troops mustering."

"I believe we will have to ride north," said Lance, "and we will doubtless only see them after dark."

"How far north?"

"Three or four leagues. They move about a bit."

We had ridden for two days to reach the Circle. We had met a patrol earlier that morning and learned that the troops inside the thing continued to muster every night. They went through various drills and then were gone—to someplace deeper inside—with the coming of morning. A perpetual thunderhead, I learned, rode above the Circle, though the storm never broke.

"Shall we breakfast here and then ride north?" I asked.

"Why not?" said Ganelon. "I'm starved and we've time."

So we dismounted and ate dried meat and drank from our canteen.

"I still do not understand that note," said Ganelon, after belching, patting his stomach, and lighting his pipe. "Will he stand beside us in the final battle, or will he not? Where is he, if he intends to help? The day of conflict draws nearer and nearer."

"Forget him," I said. "It was probably a joke."

"I can't, damn it!" he said. "There is something passing strange about the whole business!"

"What is it?" asked Lance, and for the first time I realized that Ganelon had not told him.

"My old liege, Lord Corwin, sends an odd message by carrier bird, saying he is coming. I had thought him dead, but he sent this message," Ganelon told him. "I still do not know what to make of it."

"Corwin?" said Lance, and I held my breath. "Corwin of Amber?"

"Yes, Amber and Avalon."

"Forget his message."

"Why?"

"He is a man without honor, and his promise means nothing."

"You know him?"

"I know of him. Long ago, he ruled in this land. Do you not recall the stories of the demon lordling? They are the same. That was Corwin, in days before my days. The best thing he did was abdicate and flee when the resistance grew too strong against him."

That was not true!

Or was it?

Amber casts an infinity of shadows, and my Avalon had cast many of its own, because of my presence there. I might be known on many earths that I had never trod, for shadows of myself had walked them, mimicking imperfectly my deeds and my thoughts.

"No," said Ganelon, "I never paid heed to the old stories. I wonder if it *could* have been the same man, ruling here. That is interesting."

"Very," I agreed, to keep my hand in things. "But if he ruled so long ago, surely he must be dead or decrepit by now."

"He was a sorcerer," said Lance.

"The one I knew certainly was," said Ganelon, "for he banished me from a land neither art nor artifice can discover now."

"You never spoke of this before," said Lance. "How did it occur?"

"None of your business," said Ganelon, and Lance was silent once again.

I hauled out my own pipe—I had obtained one two days earlier—and Lance did the same. It was a clay job and drew hot and hard. We lit up, and the three of us sat there smoking.

"Well, he did the smart thing," said Ganelon. "Let's forget it now."

We did not, of course. But we stayed away from the subject after that.

If it had not been for the dark thing behind us, it would have been quite pleasant, just sitting there, relaxing. Suddenly, I felt close to the two of them. I wanted to say something, but I could not think what. Ganelon solved that by bringing up current business once more.

"So you want to hit them before they hit us?" he said.

"That's right," I replied. "Take the fight to their home territory."

"The trouble is that it *is* their home territory," he said. "They know it better than we do now, and who knows what powers they might be able to call on there?"

"Kill the horned one and they will crumble," I said.

"Perhaps. Perhaps not. Maybe you could do it," said Ganelon. "Unless I got lucky, though, I don't know whether I could. He's too mean to die easily. While I think I'm still as good a man as I was some years ago, I may be fooling myself. Perhaps I've grown soft. I never wanted this damn stay-at-home job!"

"I know," I said.

"I know," said Lance.

"Lance," said Ganelon, "should we do as our friend here says? Should we attack?"

He could have shrugged and equivocated. He did not.

"Yes," he said. "They almost had us last time. It was very close the night King Uther died. If we do not attack them now, I feel they may defeat us next time. Oh, it would not be easy, and we would hurt them badly. But I think they could do it. Let us see what we can see now, then make our plans for an attack."

"All right," said Ganelon. "I am sick of waiting, too. Tell me that again after we return and I'll go along with it."

So we did that thing.

We rode north that afternoon, and we hid ourselves in the hills and looked down upon the Circle. Within it, they worshipped, after their fashion, and they drilled. I estimated around four thousand troops. We had about twenty-five hundred. They also had weird flying, hopping, crawling things that made noises in the night. We had stout hearts. Yeah.

All that I needed was a few minutes alone with their leader, and it would be decided, one way or another. The whole thing down there. I had done it, and it was up to me to undo it, if I could.

I was afraid that I could not.

In a fit of passion, compounded of rage, horror, and pain, I had unleashed this thing, and it was reflected somewhere in every earth in existence. Such is the blood curse of a Prince of Amber.

We watched them all that night, the Wardens of the Circle, and in the morning we departed.

The verdict was, attack!

So we rode all the way back and nothing followed us. When we reached the Keep of Ganelon, we fell to planning. Our troops were ready—over-ready, perhaps—and we decided to strike within a fortnight.

As I lay with Lorraine, I told her of these things. For I felt that she should know. I possessed the power to spirit her away into Shadow—that very night, if she would agree. She did not.

"I'll stay with you," she said.

"Okay."

I did not tell her that I felt everything lay within my hands, but I have a feeling she knew and that for some reason she trusted me. I would not have, but that was her affair.

"You know how things might be," I said.

"I know," she said, and I knew that she knew and that was it. We turned our attention to other subjects, and later we slept.

She'd had a dream.

In the morning, she said to me, "I had a dream."

"What about?" I asked.

"The coming battle," she told me. "I see you and the horned one locked in combat."

"Who wins?"

"I don't know. But as you slept, I did a thing that might help you."

"I wish you had not," I said. "I can take care of myself."

"Then I dreamed of my own death, in this time."

"Let me take you away to a place I know."

"No, my place is here," she told me.

"I don't pretend to own you," I said, "but I can save you from whatever you've dreamed. That much lies within my power, believe me."

"I do believe you, but I will not go."

"You're a damned fool."

"Let me stay."

"As you wish . . . Listen, I'll even send you to Cabra . . ."

"No."

"You're a damned fool."

"I know. I love you."

". . . And a stupid one. The word is 'like.' Remember?"

"You'll do it," she said.

"Go to hell," I said.

Then she wept, softly, until I comforted her once again.

That was Lorraine.

III

I thought back, one morning, upon all that had gone before. I thought of my brothers and sisters as though they were playing cards, which I knew was wrong. I thought back to the rest home where I had awakened, back to the battle for Amber, back to my walking the Pattern in Rebma, and back to that time with Moire, who just might be Eric's by now. I thought of Bleys and of Random, Deirdre, Caine, Gérard, and Eric, that morning. It was the morning of the battle, of course, and we were camped in the hills near the Circle. We had been attacked several times along the way, but they had been brief, guerrilla affairs. We had dispatched our assailants and continued. When we reached the area we had decided upon, we made our camp, posted guards, and retired. We slept undisturbed. I awoke wondering whether my brothers and sisters thought of me as I thought of them. It was a very sad thought.

In the privacy of a small grove, my helmet filled with soapy water, I shaved my beard. Then I dressed, slowly, in my private and tattered colors. I was as hard as stone, dark as soil, and mean as hell once more. Today would be the day. I donned my visor, put on chain mail, buckled my belt, and hung Grayswandir at my side. Then I fastened my cloak at my neck with a silver rose and was discovered by a messenger who had been looking for me to tell me that things were about ready.

I kissed Lorraine, who had insisted on coming along. Then I mounted my horse, a roan named Star, and rode off toward the front.

There I met with Ganelon and with Lance. They said, "We are ready."

I called for my officers and briefed them. They saluted, turned and rode away.

"Soon," said Lance, lighting his pipe.

"How is your arm?"

"Fine, now," he replied, "after that workout you gave it yesterday. Perfect."

I opened my visor and lit my own pipe.

"You've shaved your beard," said Lance. "I cannot picture you without it."

"The helm fits better this way," I said.

"Good fortune to us all," said Ganelon. "I know no gods, but if any care to be with us, I welcome them."

"There is but one God," said Lance. "I pray that He be with us."

"Amen," said Ganelon, lighting his pipe. "For today."

"It will be ours," said Lance.

"Yes," said I, as the sun stirred the east and the birds of morning the air, "it has that feel to it."

We emptied our pipes when we had finished and tucked them away at our belts. Then we secured ourselves with final tightenings and claspings of our armor and Ganelon said, "Let us be about it."

My officers reported back to me. My sections were ready.

We filed down the hillside, and we assembled outside the Circle. Nothing stirred within it, and no troops were visible.

"I wonder about Corwin," Ganelon said to me.

"He is with us," I told him, and he looked at me strangely, seemed to notice the rose for the first time, then nodded brusquely.

"Lance," he said, when we had assembled. "Give the order."

And Lance drew his blade. His cried "Charge!" echoed about us.

We were half a mile inside the Circle before anything happened. There were five hundred of us in the lead, all mounted. A dark cavalry appeared, and we met them. After five minutes, they broke and we rode on.

Then we heard the thunder.

There was lightning, and the rain began to fall.

The thunderhead had finally broken.

A thin line of foot soldiers, pikemen mainly, barred our way, waiting stoically. Maybe we all smelled the trap, but we bore down upon them.

Then the cavalry hit our flanks.

We wheeled, and the fighting began in earnest.

It was perhaps twenty minutes later . . .

We held out, waiting for the main body to arrive.

Then the two hundred or so of us rode on . . .

Men. It was men that we slew, that slew us—gray-faced, dour-countenanced men. I wanted more. One more . . .

Theirs must have been a semi-metaphysical problem in logistics. How much could be diverted through this Gateway? I was not sure. Soon . . .

We topped a rise, and far ahead and below us lay a dark citadel.

I raised my blade.

As we descended, they attacked.

They hissed and they croaked and they flapped. They meant, to me, that he was running low on people. Grayswandir became a flame in my hand, a thunderbolt, a portable electric chair. I slew them as fast as they approached, and they burned as they died. To my right, I saw Lance draw a similar line of chaos, and he was muttering beneath his breath. Prayers for the dead, no doubt. To my left, Ganelon laid about him, and a wake of fires followed behind his horse's tail. Through the flashing lightning, the citadel loomed larger.

The hundred or so of us stormed ahead, and the abominations fell by the wayside.

When we reached the gate, we were faced an infantry of men and beasts. We charged.

They outnumbered us, but we had little choice. Perhaps we had preceded our own infantry by too much. But I thought not. Time, as I saw it, was all important now.

"I've got to get through!" I cried. "He's inside!"

"He's mine!" said Lance.

"You're both welcome to him!" said Ganelon, laying about him. "Cross when you can! I'm with you!"

We slew and we slew and we slew, and then the tide turned in their favor. They pressed us, all the ugly things that were more or less than human, mixed in with human troops. We were drawn up into a tight knot, defending ourselves on all sides, when our bedraggled infantry arrived and began hacking. We pressed for the gate once more and made it this time, all forty or fifty of us.

We won through, and then there were troops in the courtyard to be slain.

The dozen or so of us who made it to the foot of the dark tower were faced by a final guard contingent.

"Go it!" cried Ganelon, as we leaped from our horses and waded into them.

"Go it!" cried Lance, and I guess they both meant me, or each other.

I took it to mean me, and I broke away from the fray and raced up the stairs.

He would be there, in the highest tower, I knew; and I would have to face him, and face him down. I did not know whether I could, but I had to try, because I was the only one who knew where he really came from—and I was the one who put him there.

I came to a heavy wooden door at the top of the stairs. I tried it but it was secured from the other side. So I kicked it as hard as I could.

It fell inward with a crash.

I saw him there by the window, a man-formed body dressed in light armor, goat head upon those massive shoulders.

I crossed the threshold and stopped.

He had turned to stare as the door had fallen, and now he sought my eyes through steel.

"Mortal man, you have come too far," he said. "Or *are* you mortal man?" and there was a blade in his hand.

"Ask Strygalldwir," I said.

"You are the one who slew him," he stated. "Did he name you?"

"Maybe."

There were footsteps on the stairs behind me. I stepped to the left of the doorway.

Ganelon burst into the chamber and I called "Halt!" and he did.

"This is the thing," he said. "What is it?"

"My sin against a thing I loved," I said. "Stay away from it. It's mine."

"You're welcome to it."

He stood stock still.

"Did you really mean that?" asked the creature.

"Find out," I said, and leaped forward.

But it did not fence with me. Instead, it did what any mortal fencer would consider foolish.

It hurled its blade at me, point forward, like a thunderbolt. And the sound of its passage came like a clap of thunder. The elements outside the tower echoed it, a deafening response.

With Grayswandir, I parried that blade as though it were an ordinary thrust. It embedded itself in the floor and burst into flame. Without, the lightning responded.

For an instant, the light was as blinding as a magnesium flare, and in that moment the creature was upon me.

It pinned my arms to my sides, and its horns struck against my visor, once, twice . . .

Then I threw my strength against those arms, and their grip began to weaken.

I dropped Grayswandir, and with a final heave broke the hold it had upon me.

In that moment, however, our eyes met.

Then we both struck, and we both reeled back.

"Lord of Amber," it said then, "why do you strive with me? It was you who gave us this passage, this way . . ."

"I regret a rash act and seek to undo it."

"Too late—and this a strange place to begin."

It struck again, so quickly that it got through my guard. I was slammed back against the wall. Its speed was deadly.

And then it raised its hand and made a sign, and I had a vision of the courts of Chaos come upon me—a vision that made my hackles rise, made a chill wind blow across my soul, to know what I had done.

". . . You see?" it was saying. "You gave us this Gateway. Help us now, and we will restore to you that which is yours."

For a moment I was swayed. It was possible that it could do just what it had offered, if I would help.

But it would be a threat forever after. Allies briefly, we would be at each other's throats after we got what we wanted—and those dark forces would be much stronger by then. Still, if I held the city . . .

"Do we have a bargain?" came the sharp, near-bleat of the question.

I thought upon the shadows, and of the places beyond Shadow . . .

Slowly, I reached up and unbuckled my helm . . .

Then I hurled it, just as the creature seemed to relax. I think Ganelon was moving forward by then.

I leaped across the chamber and drove it back against the wall.

"No!" I cried.

Its manlike hands found my throat at about the same instant mine wrapped about its own.

I squeezed, with all my strength, and twisted. I guess it did the same.

I heard something snap like a dry stick. I wondered whose neck had broken. Mine sure hurt.

I opened my eyes and there was the sky. I was lying on my back on a blanket on the ground.

"I'm afraid he's going to live," said Ganelon, and I turned my head, slowly, in the direction of his voice.

He was seated on the edge of the blanket, sword across his knees. Lorrained was with him.

"How goes it?" I said.

"We've won," he told me. "You've kept your promise. When you killed that thing, it was all over. The men fell senseless, the creatures burned."

"Good."

"I have been sitting here wondering why I no longer hate you."

"Have you reached any conclusions?"

"No, not really. Maybe it's because we're a lot alike. I don't know."

I smiled at Lorraine.

"I'm glad you're very poor when it comes to prophecy. The battle is over and you're still alive."

"The death has already begun," she said, not returning my smile.

"What do you mean?"

"They still tell stories of how the Lord Corwin had my grandfather executed—drawn and quartered publicly—for leading one of the early uprisings against him."

"That wasn't me," I said. "It was one of my shadows."

But she shook her head and said, "Corwin of Amber, I am what I am," and she rose and left me then.

"What was it?" asked Ganelon, ignoring her departure. "What was the thing in the tower?"

"Mine," I said; "one of those things which was released when I laid my curse upon Amber. I opened the way then for that which lies beyond Shadow to enter the real world. The paths of least resistance are followed in these things, through the shadows to Amber. Here, the path was the Circle. Elsewhere, it might be some different thing. I have closed their way through this place now. You may rest easy here."

"That is why you came here?"

"No," I said. "Not really. I was but passing on the road to Avalon when I came upon Lance. I could not let him lie there, and after I took him to you I became involved in this piece of my handiwork."

"Avalon? Then you lied when you said it was destroyed?"

I shook my head.

"Not so. Our Avalon feel, but in Shadow I may find its like once more."

"Take me with you."

"Are you mad?"

"No, I would look once again on the land of my birth, no matter what the peril."

"I do not go to dwell there," I said, "but to arm for battle. In Avalon there is a pink powder the jewelers use. I ignited a sample of it one time in Amber. I go there only to obtain it and to build guns that I may lay siege to Amber and gain the throne that is mine."

"What of those things from beyond Shadow you spoke of."

"I will deal with them afterwards. Should I lose this time, they they are Eric's problem."

"You said that he had blinded you and cast you into the dungeons."

"That is true. I grew new eyes. I escaped."

"You *are* a demon."

"This has often been said. I no longer deny it."

"You will take me with you?"

"If you really wish to come. It will differ from the Avalon you knew, however."

"To Amber!"

"You *are* mad!"

"No. Long have I wished to look upon that fabled city. After I have seen Avalon once again I will want to turn my hand to something new. Was I not a good general?"

"Yes."

"Then you will teach me of these things you call guns, and I will help you in the greatest battle. I've not too many good years remaining before me, I know. Take me with you."

"Your bones may bleach at the foot of Kolvir, beside my own."

"What battle is certain? I will chance it."

"As you would. You may come."

"Thank you, Lord."

We camped there that night, rode back to the keep in the morning. Then I sought after Lorraine. I learned that she had run off with one of her former lovers, an officer named Melkin. Although she had been upset, I resented the fact that she had not given me the opportunity to explain something of which she only knew rumors. I decided to follow them.

I mounted Star, turned my stiff neck in the direction they had supposedly taken, and rode on after. In a way, I could not blame her. I had not been received back at the keep as the slayer of the horned one might have been were he anyone else. The stories of their Corwin lingered on, and the demon tag was on all of them. The men I had worked with, fought beside, now looked at me with glances holding something more than fear—glances only, for they quickly dropped their eyes or turned them to another thing. Perhaps they feared that I wished to stay and reign over them. They might have been relieved, all save Ganelon, when I took to the trail. Ganelon, I think, feared that I would not return for him as I had promised. This, I feel, is the reason that he offered to ride with me. But it was a thing that I had to do by myself.

Lorraine had come to mean something to me, I was surprised to discover, and I found myself quite hurt by her action. I felt that she owed me a hearing before she went her way. Then if she still chose her mortal captain, they could have my blessing. If not, I realized that I wanted to keep her with me. Fair Avalon would be postponed for so long as it took me to resolve this to ending or continuance.

I rode along the trail and the birds sang in the trees about me. The day was bright with a sky-blue, tree-green peace, for the scourge had been lifted from the land. In my heart, there was something like a bit of joy that I had undone at least a small portion of the rottenness I had wrought. Evil? Hell, I've done more of it than most men, but I had picked up a conscience too, somewhere along the way, and I let it enjoy one of its rare moments of satisfaction. Once I held Amber, I could allow it a little more leeway, I felt. Ha!

I was heading north, and the terrain was foreign to me. I followed a clearly marked trail, which bore the signs of two riders' recent passage. I followed all that day, through dusk and into evening, dismounting periodically to inspect the way. Finally, my eyes played too many tricks on me, so I located a small glen—several hundred yards to the left of the trail—and there I camped for the night. It was the pains in my neck, doubtless, that made me dream of the horned one and relive that battle. "Help us now, and we will restore to you that which is yours," it said. I awoke suddenly at that point, with a curse on my lips.

When morning paled the sky, I mounted and continued on. It had been a cold night, and the day still held me in hands out of the north. The grasses sparkled with a light frost and my cloak was damp from having been used as a bedroll.

By noon, something of warmth had returned to the world and the trail was fresher. I was gaining on them.

When I found her, I leaped down from my mount and ran to where she lay, beneath a wild rosebush without flowers, the thorns of which had scratched her cheek and shoulder. Dead, she had not been so for long, for the blood was still damp upon her breast where the blade had entered, and her flesh yet warm.

There were no rocks with which to build her a cairn, so I cut away the sod with Grayswandir and laid her there to rest. He had removed her bracelets, her rings, and her jeweled combs, which had held all she possessed of fortune. I had to close her eyes before I covered her over with my cloak, and here my hand faltered and my own eyes grew dim. It took me a long while.

I rode on, and it was not long before I overtook him, riding as though he were pursued by the Devil, which he was. I spoke not a word when I unhorsed him, nor afterward, and I did not use my blade, though he drew his own. I hurled his broken body into a high oak tree, and when I looked back it was dark with birds.

I replaced her rings, her bracelets, her combs, before I closed the grave, and that was Lorraine. All that she had ever been or wanted to be had come to this, and that is the whole story of how we met and how we parted, Lorraine and I, in the land called Lorraine, and it is like onto my life, I guess, for a Prince of Amber is part and party to all the rottenness that is in the world, which is why whenever I do speak of my conscience, something else within me must answer, "Ha!" In the mirrors of the many judgments, my hands are the color of blood. I am a part of the evil which exists to oppose other evils. I destroy Melkins when I find them, and on that Great Day of which prophets speak but in which they do not truely believe, on that day when the world is completely cleansed of evil, then I, too, will go down into darkness, swallowing curses. Perhaps even sooner than that, I now judge. But whatever . . . Until that time, I shall not wash my hands nor let them hang useless.

Turning, I rode back to the Keep of Ganelon, who knew but would never understand.

IV

Riding, riding, through the wild, weird ways that led to Avalon, we went, Ganelon and I, down alleys of dream and of nightmare beneath the brass bark of the sun and the hot, white isles of night, till these were gold and diamond chips and the moon swam like a swan. Day belled forth the green of spring, we crossed a mighty river and the mountains before us were frosted by night. I unleashed an arrow of my desire into the midnight and it took fire overhead, burned its way like a meteor into the north. The only dragon we encountered was lame and limped away quickly to hide, singeing daisies as it panted and wheezed. Migrations of bright birds arrowed our destination, and crystalline voices from lakes echoed our words as we passed. I sang as we rode, and after a time, Ganelon joined me. We had been traveling for over a week, and the land and the sky and the breezes told me we were near to Avalon now.

We camped in a wood near a lake as the sun slid behind stone and the day died down and ceased. I went off to the lake to bathe while Ganelon unpacked our gear. The water was cold and bracing. I splashed about in it for a long while.

I thought I heard several cries as I bathed, but I could not be certain. It was a weird wood and I was not overly concerned. However, I dressed quickly and hurried back to the camp.

As I walked, I heard it again: a whine, a plea. Drawing nearer, I realized that a conversation was in progress.

Then I entered the small clearing we had chosen. Our gear was spread about and the beginnings of a campfire had been laid.

Ganelon squatted on his haunches beneath an oak tree. The man hung from it.

He was young and fair of hair and complexion. Beyond that, it was hard to say at a glance. It is difficult, I discovered, to obtain a clear initial impression as to a man's features and size when he is hanging upside down several feet above the ground.

His hands had been tied behind his back and he hung from a low bough by a rope that had been knotted about his right ankle.

He was talking—brief, rapid phrases in response to Ganelon's questions—and his face was moist with spittle and sweat. He did not hang limply, but swung back and forth. There was an abrasion on his cheek and several spots of blood on his shirt front.

Halting, I restrained myself from interrupting for a moment and watched. Ganelon would not have put him where he was without a reason, so I was not immediately overwhelmed with sympathy for the fellow. Whatever it was that had prompted Ganelon to question him thus, I knew that I, too, would be interested in the information. I was also interested in whatever the session would show me concerning Ganelon, who was now something of an ally. And a few more minutes upside down could not do that much additional damage . . .

As his body slowed, Ganelon prodded him in the sternum with the tip of his blade and set him to swinging violently once again. This broke the skin lightly and another red spot appeared. At this, the boy cried out. From his complexion, I could see now that he was a youth. Ganelon extended his blade and held its point several inches beyond the place the boy's throat would come to on the backswing. At the last moment, he snatched it back and chuckled as the boy writhed and cried out, "Please!"

"The rest," said Ganelon. "Tell me everything."

"That's all!" said the other. "I know no more!"

"Why not?"

"They swept on by me then! I could not see!"

"Why did you not follow?"

"They were mounted. I was on foot."

"Why did you not follow on foot then?"

"I was dazed."

"Dazed? You were afraid! You deserted!"

"No!"

Ganelon held his blade forth, snapped it away again at the final moment.

"No!" cried the youth.

Ganelon moved the blade again.

"Yes!" the boy screamed. "I was afraid!"

"And you fled then?"

"Yes! I kept running! I've been fleeing ever since . . ."

"And you know nothing of how things went after that?"

"No."

"You lie!"

He moved the blade again.

"No!" said the boy. "Please . . ."

I stepped forward then.

"Ganelon," I said.

He glanced at me and grinned, lowering the blade. The boy sought my eyes.

"What have we here?" I asked.

"Ha!" he said, slapping the inside of the youth's thigh so that he cried out. "A thief, a deserter—with an interesting tale to tell."

"Then cut him down and let me hear it," I said.

Ganelon turned and cut through the cord with one swipe of his blade. The boy fell to the ground and began sobbing.

"I caught him trying to steal our supplies and thought to question him about the area," Ganelon said. "He's come from Avalon— quickly."

"What do you mean?"

"He was a foot soldier in a battle that took place there two nights ago. He turned coward during the fighting and deserted."

The youth began to mouth a denial and Ganelon kicked him.

"Silence!" he said. "I'm telling it now—as you told me!"

The boy moved sideways like a crab and looked at me with wide, pleading eyes.

"Battle? Who was fighting?" I asked.

Ganelon smiled grimly.

"It sounds somewhat familiar," he said. "The forces of Avalon were engaged in what seems to have been the largest—and perhaps final—of a long series of confrontations with beings not quite natural."

"Oh?"

I studied the boy and his eyes dropped, but I saw that fear was there before they fell.

". . . Women," Ganelon said. "Pale furies out of some hell, lovely and cold. Armed and armored. Long, light hair. Eyes like ice. Mounted on white, fire-breathing steeds that fed on human flesh, they came forth by night from a warren of caves in the mountains an earthquake opened several years ago. They raided, taking young men back with them as captives, killing all others. Many appeared later as a soulless infantry, following their van. This sounds very like the men of the Circle we knew."

"But many of those lived when they were freed," I said. "They did not seem soulless then, only somewhat as I once did—amnesiac. It seems strange," I went on, "that they did not block off these caves during the day, since the riders only came forth by night . . ."

"The deserter tells me this was tried," said Ganelon, "and they always burst forth after a time, stronger than before."

The boy was ashen, but he nodded when I looked toward him inquiringly.

"Their General, whom he calls the Protector, routed them many times," Ganelon continued. "He even spent part of a night with their leader, a pale bitch named Lintra—whether in dalliance or parlay, I'm not certain. But nothing came of this. The raids continued and her forces grew stronger. The Protector finally decided to mass an all-out attack, in hopes of destroying them utterly. It was during that battle that this one fled," he said, indicating the youth with a gesture of his blade, "which is why we do not know the ending to the story."

"Is that the way it was?" I asked him.

The boy looked away from the weapon's point, met my eyes for a moment, then nodded slowly.

"Interesting," I said to Ganelon. "Very. I've a feeling their problem is linked to the one we just solved. I wish I knew how their fight turned out."

Ganelon nodded, shifted his grip on his weapon.

"Well, if we're finished with him now . . ." he said.

"Hold. I presume he was trying to steal something to eat?"

"Yes."

"Free his hands. We'll feed him."

"But he tried to steal from us."

"Did you not say that you had once killed a man for a pair of shoes?"

"Yes, but that was different."

"How so?"

"I got away with it."

I laughed. It broke me up completely, and I could not stop laughing. He looked irritated, then puzzled. Then he began laughing himself.

The youth regarded us as if we were a pair of maniacs.

"All right," said Ganelon finally, "all right," and he stooped, turned the boy with a single push, and severed the cord that bound his wrists.

"Come, lad," he said. "I'll fetch you something to eat," and he moved to our gear and opened several food parcels.

The boy rose and limped slowly after him. He seized the food that was offered and began eating quickly and noisily, not taking his eyes off Ganelon. His information, if true, presented me with several complications, the foremost being that it would probably be more difficult to obtain what I wanted in a war-ravaged land. It also lent weight to my fears as to the nature and extent of the disruption pattern.

I helped Ganelon build a small fire.

"How does this affect our plans?" he asked.

I saw no real choice. All of the shadows near to what I desired would be similarly involved. I could lay my course for one which did not possess such involvement, but in reaching it I would have achieved the wrong place. That which I desired would not be available there. If the forays of chaos kept occurring on my desire-walk through Shadow, then they were bound up with the nature of the desire and would have to be dealt with, one way or another, sooner or later. They could not be avoided. Such was the nature of the game, and I could not complain because I had laid down the rules.

"We go on," I said. "It is the place of my desire."

The youth let out a brief cry, and then—perhaps from some feeling of indebtedness for my having prevented Ganelon from poking holes in him—warned, "Do not go to Avalon, sir! There is nothing there that you could desire! You will be slain!"

I smiled to him and thanked him. Ganelon chuckled then and said, "Let us take him back with us to stand a deserter's trial."

At this, the youth scrambled to his feet and began running.

Still laughing, Ganelon drew his dagger and cocked his arm to throw it. I struck his arm and his cast went wide of its mark. The youth vanished within the wood and Ganelon continued to laugh.

He retrieved the dagger from where it had fallen and said, "You should have let me kill him, you know."

"I decided against it."

He shrugged.

"If he returns and cuts our throats tonight you may find yourself feeling somewhat different."

"I should imagine. But he will not, you know that."

He shrugged again, skewering a piece of meat and warming it over the flames.

"Well, war has taught him to show a good pair of heels," he acknowledged. "Perhaps we *will* awaken in the morning."

He took a bite and began to chew. It seemed like a good idea and I fetched some for myself.

Much later, I was awakened from a troubled sleep to stare at stars through a screen of leaves. Some omen-making portion of my mind had seized upon the youth and used us both badly. It was a long while before I could get back to sleep.

In the morning we kicked dirt over the ashes and rode on. We made it into the mountains that afternoon and passed through them the following day. There were occasional signs of recent passage on the trail we followed, but we encountered no one.

The following day we passed several farmhouses and cottages, not pausing at any of them. I had opted against the wild, demonic route I had followed when I exiled Ganelon. While quite brief, I knew that he would have found it massively disconcerting. I had wanted this time to think, so such a journeying was not called for. Now, however, the long route was nearing its end. We achieved Amber's sky that afternoon, and I admired it in silence. It might almost be the Forest of Arden through which we rode. There were no horn notes, however, no Julian, no Morgenstern, no stormhounds to harry us, as there had been in Arden when last I passed that way. There were only the bird notes in the great-boled trees, the complaint of a squirrel, the bark of a fox, the plash of a waterfall, the whites and blues and pinks of flowers in the shade.

The breezes of the afternoon were gentle and cool; they lulled me so that I was unprepared for the row of fresh graves beside the trail that came into sight when we rounded a bend. Near by, there was a torn and trampled glen. We tarried them briefly but learned nothing more than had been immediately apparent.

We passed another such place farther along, and several fire-charred groves. The trail was well worn by then and the side brush trampled and broken, as by the passage of many men and beasts. The smell of ashes was occasionally upon the air, and we hurried past the partly eaten carcass of a horse now well ripened where it lay.

The sky of Amber no longer heartened me, though the way was clear for a long while after that.

The day was running to evening and the forest had thinned considerably when Ganelon noted the smoke trails to the southeast. We took the first side path that seemed to lead in that direction, although it was tangent to Avalon proper. It was difficult to estimate the distance, but we could tell that we would not reach the place until after nightfall.

"Their army—still encamped?" Ganelon wondered.

"Or that of their conqueror."

He shook his head and loosened his blade in its scabbard.

Toward twilight, I left the trail to follow a sound of running water to its source. It was a clear, clean stream that had made its way down from the mountains and still bore something of their chill within it. I bathed there, trimming my new beard and cleaning the dust of travel from my garments as well. As we were nearing this end of our journeying, it was my wish to arrive with what small splendor I could muster. Appreciating this, Ganelon even splashed water over his face and blew his nose loudly.

Standing on the bank, blinking my rinsed eyes at the heavens, I saw the moon resolve itself sharp and clear, the fuzziness fading from its edges. This was the first time it had happened. My breathing jerked to a halt and I kept staring. Then I scanned the sky for early stars, traced the edges of clouds, the distant mountains, the farthest trees. I looked back at the moon, and it still held clear and steady. My eyesight was normal once again.

Ganelon drew back at the sound of my laughter, and he never inquired as to its cause.

Suppressing an impulse to sing, I remounted and headed back toward the trail once again. The shadows deepened as we rode, and clusters of stars bloomed among the branches overhead. I inhaled a big piece of the night, held it a moment, released it. I was myself once again and the feeling was good.

Ganelon drew up beside me and said in a low voice, "There will doubtless be sentries."

"Yes," I said.

"Then hadn't we better leave the trail?"

"No. I would rather not seem furtive. It matters not to me whether we arrive with an escort. We are simply two travelers."

"They may require the reason for our travels."

"Then let us be mercenaries who have heard of strife in the realm and come seeking employment."

"Yes. We look the part. Let us hope they pause long enough to notice."

"If they cannot see us that well, then we are poor targets."

"True, but I am not fully comforted by the thought."

I listened to the sounds of the horses' hoofs on the trail. The way was not straight. It twisted, curved, and wandered for a time, then took an upward turn. As we mounted the rise it followed, the trees thinned even more.

We came to the top of a hill then, and into a fairly open area. Advancing, we achieved a sudden view that covered several miles. We drew rein at an abrupt drop that curved its way into a gradual slope after ten or fifteen precipitous meters, sweeping downward to a large plain perhaps a mile distant, then continuing on through a hilly, sporadically wooded area. The plain was dotted with campfires and there were a few tents toward the center of things. A large number of horses grazed near by, and I guessed there were several hundred men sitting beside the fires or moving about the compound.

Ganelon sighed.

"At least they seem to be normal men," he said.

"Yes."

". . . And if they are normal military men, we are probably being watched right now. This is too good a vantage to leave unposted."

"Yes."

There came a noise from behind us. We began to turn, just as a near by voice said, "Don't move!"

I continued to turn my head, and I saw four men. Two of them held crossbows trained on us and the other two had blades in their hands. One of these advanced two paces.

"Dismount!" he ordered. "On this side! Slowly!"

We climbed down from our mounts and faced him, keeping our hands away from our weapons.

"Who are you? Where are you from?" he asked.

"We are mercenaries," I replied, "from Lorraine. We heard there was fighting here, and we are seeking employment. We were headed for that camp below. It is yours, I hope?"

". . . And if I said no, that we are a patrol for a force about to invade that camp?"

I shrugged. "In that case, is your side interested in hiring a couple of men?"

He spat. "The Protector has no need for your sort," he said. Then, "From what direction do you ride?"

"East," I said.

"Did you meet with any—difficulty—recently?"

"No," I said. "Should we have?"

"Hard to say," he decided. "Remove your weapons. I'm going to send you down to the camp. They will want to question you about anything you may have seen in the east—anything unusual."

"We've seen nothing unusual," I said.

"Whatever, they will probably feed you. Though I doubt you will be hired. You have come a bit late for the fighting. Remove your weapons now."

He called two more men from within the trees while we unbuckled our sword belts. He instructed them to escort us below, on foot. We were to lead our horses. The men took our weapons, and as we turned to go our interrogator cried out, "Wait!"

I turned back toward him.

"You. What is your name?" he asked me.

"Corey," I said.

"Stand still."

He approached, drawing very near. He stared at me for perhaps ten seconds.

"What is the matter?" I asked.

Instead of replying, he fumbled with a pouch at his belt. He withdrew a handful of coins and held them close to his eyes.

"Damn! It's too dark," he said, "and we can't make a light."

"For what?" I said.

"Oh, it is not of any great importance," he told me. "You struck me as familiar, though, and I was trying to think why. You look like the head stamped on some of our old coins. A few of them are still about.

"Doesn't he?" he addressed the nearest bowman.

The man lowered his crossbow and advanced. He squinted at me from a few paces' distance.

"Yes," he said then, "he does."

"Who was it—the one we're thinking of?"

"One of those old men. Before my time. I don't remember."

"Me neither. Well . . ." He shrugged. "No importance. Go ahead, Corey. Answer their questions honestly and you'll not be harmed."

I turned away and left him there in the moonlight, gazing after me and scratching the top of his head.

The men who guarded us were not the talkative sort. Which was just as well.

All the way down the hill I wondered about the boy's story and the resolution of the conflict he had described, for I had achieved the physical analogue of the world of my desire and would now have to operate within the prevailing situations.

The camp had the pleasant smell of man and beast, wood smoke, roasting meat, leather and oil, all intermingled in the firelight where men talked, honed weapons, repaired gear, ate, gamed, slept, drank, and watched us as we led our mounts through their midst escorted in the direction of a nearly central trio of tattered tents. A sphere of silence expanded about us as we went.

We were halted before the second-largest tent and one of our guards spoke with a man who was pacing the area. The man shook his head several times and gestured in the direction of the largest tent. The exchange lasted for several minutes, then our guard returned and spoke with the other guard who waited at our left. Finally, our man nodded and approached me while the other summoned a man from the nearest campfire.

"The officers are all at a meeting in the Protector's tent," he said. "We are going to hobble your horses and put them to graze. Unstrap your things and set them here. You will have to wait to see the captain."

I nodded, and we set about unstowing our belongings and rubbing the horses down. I patted Star on the neck and watched a small man with a limp lead him and Ganelon's mount Firedrake off toward the other horses. We sat on our packs then and waited. One of the guards brought us some hot tea and accepted a pipeful of my tobacco. They moved then to a spot somewhat to our rear.

I watched the big tent, sipped my tea, and thought of Amber and a small night club in the Rue de Char et Pain in Brussels, on the shadow Earth I had so long inhabited. Once I obtained the jewelers rouge I needed from here, I would be heading for Brussels to deal with the arms merchants of the Gun Bourse once again. My order would be complicated and expensive, I realized, because some ammunition manufacturer would have to be persuaded to set up a special production line. I knew dealers on that Earth other than Interarmco, thanks to my itinerant military background in that place, and I estimated that it would only take me a few months to get outfitted there. I began considering the details and time passed quickly and pleasantly.

After what was probably an hour and a half, the shadows stirred within the large tent. It was several minutes after that before the entrance flap was thrown aside and men began to emerge, slowly, talking among themselves, glancing back within. The last two tarried at the threshold, still talking with someone who remained inside. The rest of them passed into the other tents.

The two at the entrance edged their way outside, still facing the interior. I could hear the sounds of their voices, although I could not make out what was being said. As they drifted farther outside, the man with whom they were speaking moved also and I caught a glimpse of him. The light was at his back and the two officers blocked most of my view, but I could see that he was thin and very tall.

Our guards had not yet stirred, indicating to me that one of the two officers was the captain mentioned earlier. I continued to stare, willing them to move farther and grant me a better look at their superior.

After a time they did, and a few moments later he took a step forward.

At first, I could not tell whether it was just a play of light and shadow . . . But no! He moved again and I had a clear view for a moment. He was missing his right arm, from a point just below the elbow. It was so heavily bandaged that I guessed the loss to have been quite recent.

Then his large left hand made a downward, sweeping gesture and hovered a good distance out from his body. The stump twitched at the same moment, and so did something at the back of my mind. His hair was long and straight and brown, and I saw the the way that his jaw jutted . . .

He stepped outside then, and a breeze caught the cloak he wore and caused it to flare to his right. I saw that his shirt was yellow, his trousers brown. The cloak itself was a flame-like orange, and he caught its edge with an unnaturally rapid movement of his left hand and drew it back to cover his stump.

I stood quickly, and his head snapped in my direction.

Our gazes met, and neither of us moved for several heartbeats after that.

The two officers turned and stared, and then he pushed them aside and was striding toward me. I heard Ganelon grunt and climb quickly to his feet. Our guards were taken by surprise, also.

He halted several paces before me and his hazel eyes swept over me. He seldom smiled, but he managed a faint one this time.

"Come with me," he said, and he turned back toward his tent.

We followed him, leaving our gear where it lay.

He dismissed the two officers with a glance, halted beside the tent's entrance and motioned us in. He followed and let the flap fall behind him. My eyes took in his bedroll, a small table, benches, weapons, a campaign chest. There was an oil lamp on the table, as well as books, maps, a bottle, and some cups. Another lamp flickered atop the chest.

He clasped my hand and smiled again.

"Corwin," he said, "and still alive."

"Benedict," I said, smiling myself, "and breathing yet. It has been devilish long."

"Indeed. Who is your friend?"

"His name is Ganelon."

"Ganelon," he said, nodding toward him but not offering to clasp hands.

He moved to the table then and poured three cups of wine. He passed one to me, another to Ganelon, raised the third himself.

"To your health, brother," he said.

"To yours."

We drank.

Then, "Be seated," he said, gesturing toward the nearest bench and seating himself at the table, "and welcome to Avalon."

"Thank you—Protector."

He grimaced.

"The sobriquet is not unearned," he said flatly, continuing to study my face. "I wonder whether their earlier protector could say the same?"

"It was not really this place," I said, "and I believe that he could."

He shrugged.

"Of course," he said. "Enough of that! Where have you been?

What have you been doing? Why have you come here? Tell me of yourself. It has been too long."

I nodded. It was unfortunate, but family etiquette as well as the balance of power required that I answer his questions before asking any of my own. He was my elder, and I had—albeit unknowing—intruded in his sphere of influence. It was not that I begrudged him the courtesy. He was one of the few among my many relatives whom I respected and even liked. It was that I was itching to question him. It had been, as he had said, too long.

And how much should I tell him now? I had no notion where his sympathies might lie. I did not desire to discover the reasons for his self-imposed exile from Amber by mentioning the wrong things. I would have to begin with something fairly neutral and sound him out as I went along.

"There must be a beginning," he said then. "I care not what face you put upon it."

"There are many beginnings," I said. "It is difficult . . . I suppose I should go all the way back and take it from there."

I took another sip of the wine.

"Yes," I decided. "That seems simplest—though it was only comparatively recently that I recalled much of what had occurred.

"It was several years after the defeat of the Moonriders out of Ghenesh and your departure that Eric and I had a major falling out," I began. "Yes, it was a quarrel over the succession. Dad had been making abdication noises again, and he still refused to name a successor. Naturally, the old arguments were resumed as to who was more legitimate. Of course, you and Eric are both my elders, but while Faiella, mother to Eric and myself, was his wife after the death of Clymnea, they—"

"Enough!" cried Benedict, slapping the table so hard that it cracked.

The lamp danced and sputtered, but by some small miracle was not upset. The tent's entrance flap was immediately pushed aside and a concerned guard peered in. Benedict glanced at him and he withdrew.

"I do not wish to sit in on our respective bastardy proceedings," Benedict said softly. "That obscene pastime was one of the reasons I initially absented myself from felicity. Please continue your story without the benefit of footnotes."

"Well—yes," I said, coughing lightly. "As I was saying, we had some rather bitter arguments concerning the whole matter. Then one evening it went beyond mere words. We fought."

"A duel?"

"Nothing that formal. A simultaneous decision to murder one another is more like it. At any rate, we fought for a long while and Eric finally got the upper hand and proceeded to pulverize me. At the risk of getting ahead of my story, I have to add that all of this was only recalled to me about five years ago."

Benedict nodded, as though he understood.

"I can only conjecture as to what occurred immediately after I lost consciousness," I went on. "But Eric stopped short of killing me himself. When I awakened, I was on a shadow Earth in a place called London. The plague was rampant at the time, and I had contracted it. I recovered with no memory of anything prior to London. I dwelled on that shadow world for centuries, seeking some clue as to my identity. I traveled all over it, often as part of some military campaign. I attended their universities, I spoke with some of their wisest men, I consulted famous physicians. But nowhere could I find the key to my past. It was obvious to me that I was not like other men and I took great pains to conceal this fact. I was furious because I could have anything that I wanted except what I wanted most—my own identity, my memories.

"The years passed, but this anger and this longing did not. It took an accident that fractured my skull to set off the changes that led to the return of my first recollections. This was approximately five years ago, and the irony of it is that I have good reason to believe Eric was responsible for the accident. Flora had apparently been resident on that shadow Earth all along, keeping watch over me.

"To return to conjecture, Eric must have stayed his hand at the last moment, desiring my death, but not wanting it traceable to him. So he transported me through Shadow to a place of sudden, almost certain death—doubtless to return and say that we had argued and I had ridden off in a huff, muttering something about going away again. We had been hunting in the Forest of Arden that day—just the two of us, together."

"I find it strange," Benedict interrupted, "that two rivals such as yourselves should elect to hunt together under such circumstances."

I took a sip of wine and smiled.

"Perhaps it was a trifle more contrived than I made it sound," I said. "Perhaps we both welcomed the opportunity to hunt together—just the two of us."

"I see," he said. "So it is possible that your situations could have been reversed?"

"Well," I said, "that is difficult to say. I do not believe I would have gone that far. I am talking as of now, of course. People do change, you know. Back then . . . ? Yes, I might have done the same thing to him. I cannot say for certain, but it is possible."

He nodded again, and I felt a flash of anger which passed quickly into amusement.

"Fortunately, I am not out to justify my own motives for anything," I continued. "To go on with my guesswork, I believe that Eric kept tabs on me after that, doubtless disappointed at first that I had survived, but satisfied as to my harmlessness. So he arranged to have Flora keep an eye on me, and the world turned peacefully for a long while. Then, presumably, Dad abdicated and disappeared without the question of the succession having been settled—"

"The hell he did!" said Benedict. "There was no abdication. He just vanished. One morning he simply was not in his chambers. His bed had not even been slept in. There were no messages. He had been seen entering the suite the evening before, but no one saw him depart. And even this was not considered strange for a long while. At first it was simply thought that he was sojourning in Shadow once again, perhaps to seek another bride. It was a long while before anyone dared suspect foul play or chose to construe this as a novel form of abdication."

"I was not aware of this," I said. "Your sources of information seem to have been closer to the heart of things than mine were."

He only nodded, giving rise to uneasy speculations on my part as to his contact in Amber. For all I knew, he could be pro-Eric these days.

"When was the last time you were back there yourself?" I ventured.

"A little over twenty years ago," he replied, "but I keep in touch."

Not with anyone who had cared to mention it to me! He must have known that as he said it, so did he mean me to take it as a caution—or a threat? My mind raced. Of course he possessed a set of the Major Trumps. I fanned them mentally and went through them like mad. Random had professed ignorance as to his whereabouts. Brand had been missing a long while. I had had indication that he was still alive, imprisoned in some unpleasant place or other and in no position to report on the happenings in Amber. Flora could not have been his contact, as she had been in virtual exile in Shadow herself until recently. Llewella was in Rebma. Deirdre was in Rebma also, and had been out of favor in Amber when last I saw her. Fiona? Julian had told me she was "somewhere to the south." He was uncertain as to precisely where. Who did that leave?

Eric himself, Julian, Gérard, or Caine, as I saw it. Scratch Eric. He would not have passed along the details of Dad's non-abdication in a manner that would allow things to be taken as Benedict had taken them. Julian supported Eric, but was not without personal ambitions of the highest order. He would pass along information if it might benefit him to do so. Ditto for Caine. Gérard, on the other hand, had always struck me as more interested in the welfare of Amber itself than in the question of who sat on its throne. He was not over-fond of Eric, though, and had once been willing to support either Bleys or myself over him. I believed he would have considered Benedict's awareness of events to be something in the nature of an insurance policy for the realm. Yes, it was almost certainly one of these three. Julian hated me, Caine neither liked nor disliked me especially, and Gérard and I shared fond memories that went all the way back to my childhood. I would have to find out who it was, quickly—and he was not yet ready to tell me, of course, knowing nothing of my present motives. A liaison with Amber could be used to hurt me or benefit me in short order, depending upon his desire and the person on the other end. It was therefore both sword and shield to him, and I was somewhat hurt that he had chosen to display these accoutrements so quickly. I chose to take it that his recent injury had served to make him abnormally wary, for I had certainly never given him cause for distress. Still, this caused me to feel abnormally wary also, a sad thing to know when meeting one's brother again for the first time in many years.

"It is interesting," I said, swirling the wine within my cup. "In this light, then, it appears that everyone may have acted prematurely."

"Not everyone," he said.

I felt my face redden.

"Your pardon," I said.

He nodded curtly.

"Please continue your telling."

"Well, to continue my chain of assumptions," I said, "when Eric decided that the throne had been vacant long enough and the time had come to make his move, he must also have decided that my amnesia was not sufficient and that it would be better to see my claim quitted entirely. At this time, he arranged for me to have an accident off on that shadow Earth, an accident which should have proven fatal but did not."

"How do you know this? How much of it is guesswork?"

"Flora as much as admitted it to me—including her own complicity in the thing—when I questioned her later."

"Very interesting. Go on."

"The bash on my head provided what even Sigmund Freud had been unable to obtain for me earlier," I said. "There returned to me small recollections that grew stronger and stronger—especially after I encountered Flora and was exposed to all manner of things that stimulated my memory. I was able to convince her that it had fully returned, so her speech was open as to people and things. Then Random showed up, fleeing from something—"

"Fleeing? From what? Why?"

"From some strange creatures out of Shadow. I never found out why."

"Interesting," he said, and I had to agree. I had thought of it often, back in the cell, wondering just why Random had entered, stage left, pursued by Furies, in the first place. From the moment we met until the moment we parted, we had been in some sort of peril; I had been preoccupied with my own troubles and he had volunteered nothing concerning his abrupt appearance. It had crossed my mind, of course, at the time of his arrival, but I was uncertain as to whether it was something of which I might be expected to have knowledge, and I let it go at that. Events then submerged it until later in my cell and again the present moment. Interesting? Indeed. Also, troubling.

"I managed to take in Random as to my condition," I continued. "He believed I was seeking the throne, when all that I was consciously seeking was my memory. He agreed to help me return to Amber, and he succeeded in getting me back. Well, almost," I corrected. "We wound up in Rebma. By then, I had told Random my true condition, and he proposed my walking the Pattern again as a means of restoring it fully. The opporturnity was there, and I took it. It proved effective, and I used the power of the Pattern to transport myself into Amber."

He smiled.

"At this point, Random must have been a very unhappy man," he said.

"He was not exactly singing with glee," I said. "He had accepted Moire's judgment, that he wed a woman of her choosing—a blind girl named Vialle—and remain there with her for at least a year. I left him behind, and I later learned that he had done this thing. Deirdre was also there. We had encountered her along the way, in flight from Amber, and the three of us had entered Rebma together. She remained behind, also."

I finished my wine and Benedict nodded toward the bottle. It was almost empty, though, so he fetched a fresh bottle from his chest and we refilled our cups. I took a long swallow. It was better wine than the previous. Must have been his private stock.

"In the palace," I went on, "I made my way to the library, where I obtained a pack of the Tarots. This was my main reason for venturing there. I was surprised by Eric before I could do much else and we fought, there in the library. I succeeded in wounding him and believe I could have finished him, save that reinforcements arrived and I was forced to flee. I contacted Bleys then, who gave me passage to him in Shadow. You may have heard the rest from your own sources. How Bleys and I threw in together, assaulted Amber, lost. He fell from the face of Kolvir. I tossed him my Tarots and he caught them. I understand that his body was never found. But it was a long way down—though I believe the tide was high by then. I do not know whether he died that day or not."

"Neither do I," said Benedict.

"So I was imprisoned and Eric was crowned. I was prevailed upon to assist in the coronation, despite a small demurrer on my part. I did succeed in crowning myself before that bastard—genealogically speaking—had it back and placed it on his own head. Then he had me blinded and sent to the dungeons."

He leaned forward and studied my face.

"Yes," he said, "I had heard that. How was it done?"

"Hot irons," I said, wincing involuntarily and repressing an impulse to clutch at my eyes. "I passed out partway through the ordeal."

"Was there actual contact with the eyeballs?"

"Yes," I said. "I think so."

"And how long did the regeneration take?"

"It was close to four years before I could see again," I said, "and my vision is just getting back to normal now. So—about five years altogether, I would say."

He leaned back, sighed, and smiled faintly.

"Good," he said. "You give me some small hope. Others of us have lost portions of their anatomy and experienced regeneration also, of course, but I never lost anything significant—until now."

"Oh yes," I said. "It is a most impressive record. I reviewed it regularly for years. A collection of bits and pieces, many of them forgotten I daresay, but by the principals and myself: fingertips, toes, ear lobes. I would say that there is hope for your arm. Not for a long while, of course.

"It is a good thing that you are ambidextrous," I added.

His smile went on and off and he took a drink of wine. No, he was not ready to tell me what had happened to him.

I took another sip of my own. I did not want to tell him about Dworkin as something of an ace in the hole. None of us understood the man's full power, and he was obviously mad. But he could be manipulated. Even Dad had apparently come to fear him after a time, and had had him locked away. What was it that he had told me back in my cell? That Dad had had him confined after he had announced his discovery of a means for destroying all of Amber. If this was not just the rambling of a psychotic and was the real reason for his being where he was, then Dad had been far more generous than I would have been. The man was too dangerous to let live. On the other hand, though, Dad had been trying to cure him of his condition. Dworkin had spoken of doctors, men he had frightened away or destroyed when he had turned his powers against them. Most of my memories of him were of a wise, kindly old man, quite devoted to Dad and the rest of the family. It would be difficult readily to destroy someone like that if there was some hope. He had been confined to what should have been inescapable quarters. Yet when he had grown bored one day, he had simply walked out. No man can walk through Shadow in Amber, the very absence of Shadow, so he had done something I did not understand, something involving the principle behind the Trumps, and had left his quarters. Before he returned to them, I managed to persuade him to provide me with a similar exit from my own cell, one that transported me to the lighthouse of

Cabra, where I recovered somewhat, then set out upon the voyage that took me to Lorraine. Most likely he was still undetected. As I understood it, our family had always possessed special powers, but it was he who analyzed them and formalized their functions by means of the Pattern and the Tarots. He had often tried to discuss the matter, but it had seemed awfully abstract and boring to most of us. We are a very pragmatic family, damn it! Brand was the only one who seemed to have had any interest in the subject. And Fiona. I had almost forgotten. Sometimes Fiona would listen. And Dad. Dad knew an awful lot of things that he never discussed. He never had much time for us, and there were so many things about him that we did not know. But he was probably as well versed as Dworkin in whatever principles were involved. Their main difference was one of application. Dworkin was an artist. I do not really know what Dad was. He never encouraged intimacy, though he was not an unkind father. Whenever he took note of us, he was quite lavish with gifts and diversions. But he left our upbringing to various members of his court. He tolerated us, I feel, as occasionally inevitable consequences of passion. Actually, I am quite surprised that the family is not much larger. The thirteen of us, plus two brothers and a sister I knew who were now dead, represent close to fifteen hundred years of parental production. There had been a few others also, of whom I had heard, long before us, who had not survived. Not a tremendous batting average for so lusty a liege, but then none of us had proved excessively fertile either. As soon as we were able to fend for ourselves and walk in Shadow, Dad had encouraged us to do so, find places where we would be happy and settle there. This was my connection with the Avalon which is no more. So far as I knew, Dad's own origins were known only to himself. I had never encountered anyone whose memory stretched back to a time when there had been no Oberon. Strange? Not to know where one's own father comes from, when one has had centuries in which to exercise one's curiosity? Yes. But he was secretive, powerful, shrewd—traits we all possess to some degree. He wanted us well situated and satisfied, I feel—but never so endowed as to present a threat to his own reign. There was in him, I guessed, an element of uneasiness, a not unjustifiable sense of caution with respect to our learning too much concerning himself and times long gone by. I do not believe that he had ever truly envisioned a time when he would not rule in Amber. He occasionally spoke.

jokingly or grumblingly, of abdication. But I always felt this to be a calculated thing, to see what responses it would provoke. He must have realized the state of affairs his passing would produce, but refused to believe that the situation would ever occur. And no one of us really knew all of his duties and responsibilities, his secret commitments. As distasteful as I found the admission, I was coming to feel that none of us was really fit to take the throne. I would have liked to blame Dad for this inadequacy, but unfortunately I had known Freud too long not to feel self-conscious about it. Also, I was now beginning to wonder about the validity of any of our claims. If there had been no abdication and he did indeed still live, then the best any of us could really hope to do was sit in regency. I would not look forward—especially from the throne—to his returning and finding things otherwise. Let's face it, I was afraid of him, and not without cause. Only a fool does not fear a genuine power that he does not understand. But whether the title be king or regent, my claim on it was stronger than Eric's and I was still determined to have it. If a power out of Dad's dark past, which none of us really understood, could serve to secure it, and if Dworkin did represent such a power, then he must remain hidden until he could be employed on my behalf.

Even, I asked myself, if the power he represented was the power to destroy Amber itself, and with it to shatter the shadow worlds and capsize all of existence as I understood it?

Especially then, I answered myself. For who else could be trusted with such power?

We are indeed a very pragmatic family.

More wine, and then I fumbled with my pipe, cleaning it, repacking it.

"That, basically, is my story to date," I said, regarding my handiwork, rising and taking a light from the lamp. "After I recovered my sight, I managed to escape, fled Amber, tarried for a time in a place called Lorraine, whare I encountered Ganelon, then came here."

"Why?"

I reseated myself and looked at him again.

"Because it is near to the Avalon I once knew," I said.

I had purposely refrained from mentioning any earlier acquaintanceship with Ganelon, and hoped that he would take a cue from it. This shadow was near enough to our Avalon so that

Ganelon should be familiar with its topography and most of its customs. For whatever it was worth, it seemed politic to keep this information from Benedict.

He passed over it as I thought he might, buried there where it was beside more interesting digging.

"And of your escape?" he asked. "How did you manage that?"

"I had help, of course," I admitted, "in getting out of the cell. Once out— Well, there are still a few passages of which Eric is unaware."

"I see," he said, nodding—hoping, naturally, that I would go on to mention my partisans' names, but knowing better than to ask.

I puffed my pipe and leaned back, smiling.

"It is good to have friends," he said, as if in agreement with some unvoiced thought I might be entertaining.

"I guess that we all have a few of them in Amber."

"I like to think so," he said. Then, "I understand you left the partly whittled cell door locked behind you, had set fire to your bedding, and had drawn pictures on the wall."

"Yes," I said. "Prolonged confinement does something to a man's mind. At least, it did to mine. There are long periods during which I know I was irrational."

"I do not envy you the experience, brother," he said. "Not at all. What are your plans now?"

"They are still uncertain."

"Do you feel that you might wish to remain here?"

"I do not know," I said. "What is the state of affairs here?"

"I am in charge," he said—a simple statement of fact, not a boast. "I believe I have just succeeded in destroying the only major threat to the realm. If I am correct, then a reasonably tranquil period should be at hand. The price was high"—he glanced at what remained of his arm—"but will have been worth it—as shall be seen before very long, when things have returned to normal."

He then proceeded to relate what was basically the same situation the youth had described, going on to tell how they had won the battle. The leader of the hellmaids slain, her riders had bolted and fled. Most of them were also slain then, and the caverns had been sealed once more. Benedict had decided to maintain a small force in the field for mopping-up purposes, his scouts the while combing the area for survivors.

He made no mention of the meeting between himself and their leader, Lintra.

"Who slew their leader?" I asked him.

"I managed it," he said, making a sudden movement with his stump, "though I hesitated a moment too long on my first blow."

I glanced away and so did Ganelon. When I looked back, his face had returned to normal and he had lowered his arm.

"We looked for you. Did you know that, Corwin?" he asked. "Brand searched for you in many shadows, as did Gérard. You guessed correctly as to what Eric said after your disappearance that day. We were inclined to look farther than his word, however. We tried your Trump repeatedly, but there was no response. It must be that brain damage can block it. That is interesting. Your failure to respond to the Trump led us to believe you had died. Then Julian, Caine, and Random joined the search."

"All that? Really? I am astonished."

He smiled.

"Oh," I said then, and smiled myself.

Their joining the hunt at that point meant that it was not my welfare that concerned them, but the possibility of obtaining evidence of fratricide against Eric, so as to displace him or blackmail him.

"I sought for you in the vicinity of Avalon," he continued, "and I found this place and was taken by it. It was in a pitiful condition in those days, and for generations I worked to restore it to its former glory. While I began this in memory of you, I developed a fondness for this land and its people. They came to consider me their protector, and so did I."

I was troubled as well as touched by this. Was he implying that I had fouled things up terribly and that he had tarried here to put them in order—so as to clean up after his kid brother this one last time? Or did he mean that he realized I had loved this place—or a place very much like it—and that he had worked to set it in good order as something I might have wished done? Perhaps I was becoming oversensitive.

"It is good to know that I was sought," I said, "and it is very good to know that you are the defender of this land. I would like to see this place, for it does remind me of the Avalon that I knew. Would you have any objections to my visiting here?"

"That is all that you wish to do? Visit?"

"That is all that I had in mind."

"Know then that what is remembered of the shadow of yourself that once reigned here is not good. Children are not named Corwin in this place, nor am I brother to any Corwin here."

"I understand," I said. "My name is Corey. Can we be old friends?"

He nodded.

"Old friends of mine are always welcome to visit here," he said.

I smiled and nodded. I felt insulted that he would entertain the notion that I had designs upon this shadow of a shadow: I, who had—albeit but for an instant—felt the cold fire of Amber's crown upon my brow.

I wondered what his attitude would have been had he known of my responsibility, when it came down to basics, for the raids. For that matter, I suppose, I was also responsible for the loss of his arm. I preferred to push things one step farther back, however, and hold Eric responsible. After all, it was his action that had prompted my curse.

Still, I hoped that Benedict would never find out.

I wanted very badly to know where he stood with respect to Eric. Would he support him, throw his weight behind me, or just stay out of the way when I made my move? Conversely, I was certain that he wondered whether my ambitions were dead or still smoldering—and if the latter, what my plans were for stoking them. So . . .

Who was going to raise the matter?

I took several good puffs on my pipe, finished my wine, poured some more, puffed again. I listened to the sounds of the camp, the wind, my stomach . . .

Benedict took a sip of wine.

Then, "What are your long-range plans?" he asked me, almost casually.

I could say that I had not made up my mind yet, that I was simply happy to be free, alive, seeing. . . . I could tell him that that was enough for me, for now, that I had no special plans. . . .

. . . And he would know that I lied in my teeth. For he knew me better than that.

So, "You know what my plans are," I said.

"If you were to ask for my support," he said, "I would deny it. Amber is in bad enough shape without another power grab."

"Eric is a usurper."

"I choose to look upon him as regent only. At this time, any of us who claims the throne is guilty of usurpation."

"Then you believe Dad still lives?"

"Yes. Alive and distressed. He has made several attempts to communicate."

I succeeded in keeping my face from showing anything. So I was not the only one, then. To reveal my experiences at this point would sound hypocritical, opportunistic, or a flat lie—since in our seeming contact of five years ago he had given me the go-ahead to take the throne. Of course, he could have been referring to a regency then. . . .

"You did not lend support to Eric when he took the throne," I said. "Would you give it to him now that he holds it, if an attempt were made to unseat him?"

"It is as I said," he told me. "I look upon him as regent. I do not say that I approve of this, but I desire no further strife in Amber."

"Then you *would* support him?"

"I have said all that I have to say on the matter. You are welcome to visit my Avalon, but not to use it as a staging area for an invasion of Amber. Does that clarify matters with respect to anything you may have in mind?"

"It clarifies matters," I said.

"This being the case, do you still wish to visit here?"

"I do not know," I said. "Does your desire to avoid strife in Amber work both ways?"

"What do you mean?"

"I mean that if I were returned to Amber against my will, I would damn well create as much strife as I could to prevent a recurrence of my previous situation."

The lines went out of his face and he slowly lowered his eyes.

"I did not mean to imply that I would betray you. Do you think that I am without feelings, Corwin? I would not see you imprisoned again, blinded—or worse. You are always welcome to visit here, and you may leave your fears along with your ambitions at the border."

"Then I would still like to visit," I said. "I have no army, nor did I come here to recruit one."

"Then you know that you are most welcome."

"Thank you, Benedict. While I did not to expect to find you here, I am glad that I did."

He reddened faintly and nodded.

"It pleases me, also," he said. "Am I the first of us you have seen —since your escape?"

I nodded.

"Yes, and I am curious as to how everyone is faring. Any major reports?"

"No new deaths," he said.

We both chuckled, and I knew that I would have to turn up the family gossip on my own. It had been worth the attempt, though.

"I am planning on remaining in the field for a time," he said, "and continuing my patrols until I am satisfied that none of the invaders remain. It could be another week before we withdraw."

"Oh? Then it was not a total victory?"

"I believe that it was, but I never take unnecessary chances. It is worth a little more time to be certain."

"Prudent," I said, nodding.

". . . So unless you have a strong desire to remain here in camp, I see no reason why you should not proceed on toward town and get near the center of things. I maintain several residences about Avalon. I have in mind for your use a small manor house that I have found pleasant. It is not far from town."

"I look forward to seeing it."

"I will provide you with a map and a letter to my steward in the morning."

"Thank you, Benedict."

"I will join you there as soon as I have finished here," he said, "and in the meantime, I have messengers passing that way daily. I will keep in touch with you through them."

"Very good."

"Then find yourselves a comfortable piece of ground," he said. "You'll not miss the breakfast call, I'm sure."

"I seldom do," I said. "Is it all right if we sleep at that spot where we left our gear?"

"Certainly," he said, and we finished the wine.

As we left his tent, I seized the flap up high when I opened it and was able to squeeze it several inches to the side when I cast it before me. Benedict bade us good night and turned away as he let it fall, not noticing the gap of several inches that I had created along its one side.

I made my bed up a good distance to the right of our equipment, facing in the direction of Benedict's tent, and I moved the gear itself as I rummaged through it. Ganelon shot me a quizzical look, but I simply nodded and made a movement with my eyes toward the tent. He glanced that way, returned the nod, and proceeded to spread his own blankets farther to the right.

I measured it with my eyes, walked over, and said, "You know, I'd much rather sleep here. Would you mind switching with me?" I added a wink for emphasis.

"Makes no difference to me," he said, shrugging.

The campfires had died or were dying, and most of the company had turned in. The guard only paid us heed a couple of times around. The camp was very quiet and there were no clouds to obscure the brilliance of the stars. I was tired, and the smells of the smoke and the damp earth came pleasantly to my nostrils, reminding me of other times and places such as this and the rest at the day's end.

Instead of closing my eyes, however, I fetched my pack and propped my back against it, filled my pipe again, and struck it to life.

I adjusted my position twice as he paced within the tent. Once, he vanished from my field of vision and remained hidden for several moments. But the far light moved then, and I knew that he had opened the chest. Then he came into sight once more and cleared the table, dropped back for an instant, returned and reseated himself in his earlier position. I moved so that I could keep sight of his left arm.

He was paging through a book, or sorting something of about that size.

Cards, maybe?

Naturally.

I would have given a lot for one glimpse of the Trump that he finally settled upon and held before him. I would have given a lot to have Grayswandir beneath my hand, in case another person suddenly came into the tent by means other than the entrance through which I spied. My palms and the soles of my feet tingled, in anticipation of flight or combat.

But he remained alone.

He sat there unmoving for perhaps a quarter of an hour, and when he finally stirred it was only to replace the cards somewhere in his chest and to extinguish the lamps.

The guard continued on his monotonous rounds and Ganelon began to snore.

I emptied my pipe and rolled over onto my side.

Tomorrow, I told myself. If I wake up here tomorrow, everything will be all right . . .

V

I sucked on a blade of grass and watched the mill wheel turn. I was lying on my stomach on the stream's opposite bank, my head propped in my hands. There was a tiny rainbow in the mist above the froth and boil at the foot of the waterfall, an occasional droplet found its way to me. The steady splashing and the sound of the wheel drowned out all other noises in the wood. The mill was deserted today, and I contemplated it because I had not seen its like in ages. Watching the wheel and listening to the water were more than just relaxing. It was somewhat hypnotic.

It was our third day at Benedict's place, and Ganelon was off in town seeking amusement. I had accompanied him on the previous day and learned what I wanted to know at that time. Now I had no time for sight-seeing. I had to think and act quickly. There had been no difficulty at the camp. Benedict had seen us fed and had furnished us with the map and the letter he had promised. We had departed at sunrise and arrived at the manor around midday. We were well received, and after settling into the quarters we were shown, we had made our way into town, where we had spent the balance of the day.

Benedict was planning to remain in the field for several more days. I would have to be done with the task I had set myself before he came home. So a hellride was in order. There was no time for leisurely journeying. I had to remember the proper shadows and be under way soon.

It would have been refreshing, being in this place that was so like my Avalon, except that my thwarted purposes were reaching the point of obsession. Realizing this was not tantamount to controlling it, however. Familiar sights and sounds had diverted me only briefly, then I had turned once more to my planning.

It should work out neatly, as I saw it. This one journey should solve two of my problems, if I could manage it without arousing sus-

picion. It meant that I would definitely be gone overnight, but I had
anticipated this and had already instructed Ganelon to cover for me.

My head nodding with each creak of the wheel, I forced everything else from my mind and set about remembering the necessary
texture of the sand, its coloration, the temperature, the winds, the
touch of salt in the air, the clouds . . .

I slept then and I dreamed, but not of the place that I sought.

I regarded a big roulette wheel, and we were all of us on it—my
brothers, my sisters, myself, and others whom I knew or had known
—rising and falling, each with his allotted section. We were all
shouting for it to stop for us and wailing as we passed the top and
headed down once more. The wheel had begun to slow and I was on
the rise. A fair-haired youth hung upside down before me, shouting
pleas and warnings that were drowned in the cacophony of voices.
His face darkened, writhed, became a horrible thing to behold, and I
slashed at the cord that bound his ankle and he fell from sight. The
wheel slowed even more as I neared the top, and I saw Lorraine
then. She was gesturing, beckoning frantically, and calling my name.
I leaned toward her, seeing her clearly, wanting her, wanting to help
her. But as the wheel continued its turning she passed from my sight.

"Corwin!"

I tried to ignore her cry, for I was almost to the top. It came again,
but I tensed myself and prepared to spring upward. If it did not stop
for me, I was going to try gimmicking the damned thing, even though
falling off would mean my total ruin. I readied myself for the leap.
Another click . . .

"Corwin!"

It receded, returned, faded, and I was looking toward the water
wheel again with my name echoing in my ears and mingling, merging, fading into the sound of the stream.

I blinked my eyes and ran my fingers through my hair. A number
of dandelions fell about my shoulders as I did so, and I heard a giggle from somewhere behind me.

I turned quickly and stared.

She stood about a dozen paces from me, a tall, slender girl with
dark eyes and close-cropped brown hair. She wore a fencing jacket
and held a rapier in her right hand, a mask in her left. She was looking at me and laughing. Her teeth were white, even, and a trifle long;
a band of freckles crossed her small nose and the upper portions of

her well-tanned cheeks. There was that air of vitality about her which is attractive in ways different from mere comeliness. Especially, perhaps, when viewed from the vantage of many years.

She saluted me with her blade.

"En garde, Corwin!" she said.

"Who the Devil are you?" I asked, just then noticing a jacket, mask, and rapier beside me in the grass.

"No questions, no answers," she said. "Not till we've fenced."

She fitted her mask over her head then and waited.

I rose and picked up the jacket. I could see that it would be easier to fence than argue with her. The fact that she knew my name disturbed me, and the more that I thought of it the more she seemed somehow familiar. It was best to humor her, I decided, shrugging into the jacket and buckling it.

I picked up the blade, pulled on the mask.

"All right," I said, sketching a brief salute and advancing. "All right."

She moved forward then and we met. I let her carry the attack.

She came on very fast with a beat-feint-feint-thrust. My riposte was twice as fast, but she was able to parry it and come back with equal speed. I began a slow retreat then, drawing her out. She laughed and came on, pressing me hard. She was good and she knew it. She wanted to show off. She almost got through twice, too, in the same way—low-line—which I did not like at all. I caught her with a stop-thrust as soon as I could after that. She cursed softly, good-naturedly, as she acknowledged it and came right back at me. I do not ordinarily like to fence with women, no matter how good they are, but this time I discovered that I was enjoying myself. The skill and grace with which she carried the attacks and bore them gave me pleasure to behold and respond to, and I found myself contemplating the mind that lay behind that style. At first, I had wanted to tire her quickly, to conclude the match and question her. Now I found myself desiring to prolong the encounter.

She did not tire readily. There was small cause for concern on that count. I lost track of time as we stamped back and forth along the bank of the stream, our blades clicking steadily.

A long while must have passed, though, before she stamped her heel and threw up her blade in a final salute. She tore off her mask then and gave me another smile.

"Thank you!" she said, breathing heavily.

I returned the salute and drew off the bird cage. I turned and fumbled with the jacket buckles, and before I realized it she had approached and kissed me on the cheek. She had not had to stand tiptoe to do it either. I felt momentarily confused, but I smiled. Before I could say anything, she had taken my arm and turned me back in the direction from which we had come.

"I've brought us a picnic basket," she said.

"Very good. I am hungry. I am also curious . . ."

"I will tell you anything that you want to hear," she said merrily.

"How about telling me your name?" I said.

"Dara," she replied. "My name is Dara, after my grandmother."

She glanced at me as she said it, as though hoping for a reaction. I almost hated to disappoint her, but I nodded and repeated it, then, "Why did you call me Corwin?" I asked.

"Because that is your name," she said. "I recognized you."

"From where?"

She released my arm.

"Here it is," she said, reaching behind a tree and raising a basket that had been resting upon the ridges of exposed roots.

"I hope the ants didn't get to it," she said, moving to a shaded area beside the stream and spreading a cloth upon the ground.

I hung the fencing gear on a nearby shrub.

"You seem to carry quite a few things around with you," I observed.

"My horse is back that way," she said, gesturing downstream with her head.

She returned her attention to weighting down the cloth and unpacking the basket.

"Why way back there?" I asked.

"So that I could sneak up on you, of course. If you'd heard a horse clomping around you'd have been awake sure as hell."

"You're probably right," I said.

She paused as though pondering deeply, then spoiled it with a giggle.

"But you didn't the first time, though. Still . . ."

"The first time?" I said, seeing she wanted me to ask it.

"Yes, I almost rode over you awhile back," she said. "You were sound asleep. When I saw who it was, I went back for a picnic basket and the fencing gear."

"Oh. I see."

"Come and sit down now," she said. "And open the bottle, will you?"

She put a bottle beside my place and carefully unwrapped two crystal goblets, which she then set in the center of the cloth.

I moved to my place and sat down.

"That is Benedict's best crystal," I noted, as I opened the bottle.

"Yes," she said. "Do be careful not to upset them when you pour —and I don't think we should clink them together."

"No, I don't think we should," I said, and I poured.

She raised her glass.

"To the reunion," she said.

"What reunion?"

"Ours."

"I have never met you before."

"Don't be so prosaic," she said, and took a drink.

I shrugged.

"To the reunion."

She began to eat then, so I did too. She was so enjoying the air of mystery she had created that I wanted to cooperate, just to keep her happy.

"Now where could I have met you?" I ventured. "Was it some great court? A harem, perhaps . . . ?"

"Perhaps it was in Amber," she said. "There you were . . ."

"Amber?" I said, remembering that I was holding Benedict's crystal and confining my emotions to my voice. "Just who are you, anyway?"

". . . There you were—handsome, conceited, admired by all the ladies," she continued, "and there I was—a mousy little thing, admiring you from afar. Gray, or pastel—not vivid—little Dara—a late bloomer, I hasten to add—eating her heart out for you—"

I muttered a mild obscenity and she laughed again.

"That wasn't it?" she asked.

"No," I said, taking another bite of beef and bread. "More likely it was that brothel where I sprained by back. I was drunk that night—"

"You remember!" she cried. "It was a part-time job. I used to break horses during the day."

"I give up," I said, and I poured more wine.

The really irritating thing was that there *was* something damnably familiar about her. But from her appearance and her behavior, I guessed her age at about seventeen. This pretty much precluded our paths ever having crossed.

"Did Benedict teach you your fencing?" I asked.

"Yes."

"What is he to you?"

"My lover, of course," she replied. "He keeps me in jewels and furs—and he fences with me."

She laughed again.

I continued to study her face.

Yes, it was possible. . . .

"I am hurt," I said, finally.

"Why?" she asked.

"Benedict didn't give me a cigar."

"Cigar?"

"You are his daughter, aren't you?"

She redened, but she shook her head.

"No," she said. "But you are getting close."

"Granddaughter?" I said.

"Well . . . sort of."

"I am afraid that I do not understand."

"Grandfather is what he likes me to call him. Actually, though, he was my grandmother's father."

"I see. Are there any others at home like you?"

"No, I am the only one."

"What of your mother—and your grandmother?"

"Dead, both of them."

"How did they die?"

"Violently. Both times it happened while he was back in Amber. I believe that is why he has not returned there for a long while now. He does not like to leave me unprotected—even though he knows that I can take care of myself. You know that I can, too, don't you?"

I nodded. It explained several things, one of them being why he was Protector here. He had to keep her somewhere, and he certainly would not want to take her back to Amber. He would not even want her existence known to the rest of us. She could be made into an easy armlock. And it would be out of keeping to make me aware of her so readily.

So, "I do not believe that you are supposed to be here," I said, "and I feel that Benedict would be quite angry if he knew that you were."

"You are just the same as he is! I am an adult, damn it!"

"Have you heard me deny it? You *are* supposed to be someplace else, though, aren't you?"

She filled her mouth instead of answering. So I did, too. After several uncomfortable minutes of chewing, I decided to start on a fresh subject.

"How did you recognize me?" I asked.

She swallowed, took a drink of wine, grinned.

"From your picture, of course," she said.

"What picture?"

"On the card," she said. "We used to play with them when I was very small. I learned all my relatives that way. You and Eric are the other good swordsmen, I knew that. That is why I—"

"You have a set of the Trumps?" I interrupted.

"No," she said, pouting. "He wouldn't give me a set—and I know he has several, too."

"Really? Where does he keep them?"

She narrowed her eyes, focusing them on my own. Damn! I hadn't meant to sound that eager.

But, "He has a set with him most of the time," she said, "and I have no idea where he keeps the others. Why? Won't he let you see them?"

"I haven't asked him," I told her. "Do you understand their significance?"

"There were certain things I was not allowed to do when I was near them. I gather that they have a special use, but he never told me what it is. They are quite important, aren't they?"

"Yes."

"I thought so. He is always so careful with them. Do you have a set?"

"Yes, but it's out on loan just now."

"I see. And you would like to use them for something complicated and sinister."

I shrugged.

"I would like to use them, but for very dull, uncomplicated purposes."

"Such as?"

I shook my head.

"If Benedict does not want you to know their function yet, I am not about to tell you."

She made a small growling noise.

"You're afraid of him," she said.

"I have considerable respect for Benedict, not to mention some affection."

She laughed.

"Is he a better fighter than you, a better swordsman?"

I looked away. She must have just gotten back from someplace fairly removed from things. The townspeople I'd met had all known about Benedict's arm. It was not the sort of news that traveled slowly. I certainly was not going to be the first to tell her.

"Have it as you would," I said. "Where have you been?"

"The village," she said, "in the mountains. Grandpa took me there to stay with some friends of his called Tecys. Do you know the Tecys?"

"No, I don't."

"I've been here before," she said. "He always takes me to stay with them in the village when there is any sort of trouble here. The place has no name. I just call it the village. It is quite strange—the people, as well as the village. They seem to—sort of—worship us. They treat me as if I were something holy, and they never tell me anything I want to know. It is not a long ride, but the mountains are different, the sky is different—everything!—and it is as if there were no way back, once I am there. I had tried coming back on my own before, but I just got lost. Grandpa always had to come for me, and then the way was easy. The Tecys follow all of his instructions concerning me. They treat him as if he were some sort of god."

"He is," I said, "to them."

"You said that you do not know them."

"I don't have to. I know Benedict."

"How does he do it? Tell me."

I shook my head.

"How did you do it?" I asked her. "How did you get back here this time?"

She finished her wine and held out the glass. When I looked up from refilling it, her head was cocked toward her right shoulder, her brows were furrowed, and her eyes were focused on something far away.

"I do not really know," she said, raising the glass and sipping from it automatically. "I am not quite certain how I went about it. . . ."

With her left hand, she began to toy with her knife, finally picking it up.

"I was mad, mad as hell for having been packed off again," she said. "I told him that I wanted to stay here and fight, but he took me riding with him and after a time we arrived at the village. I do not know how. It was not a long ride, and suddenly we were there. I know this area. I was born here, I grew up here. I've ridden all over, hundreds of leagues in all directions. I was never able to find it when I went looking. But it seemed only a brief while that we rode, and suddenly we were at the Tecys' again. But it had been several years, and I can be more determined about things now that I am grown. I resolved to return by myself."

With the knife, she began scraping and digging at the ground beside her, not seeming to notice what she was doing.

"I waited till nightfall," she went on, "and studied the stars to take my direction. It was an unreal feeling. The stars were all different. I didn't recognize any of the constellations. I went back inside and thought about it. I was a little bit afraid and did not know what to do. I spent the next day trying to get more information out of the Tecys and the other people in the village. But it was like a bad dream. Either they were stupid or they were purposely trying to confuse me. Not only was there no way to get from here to there, they had no idea where 'here' was and were none too certain about 'there.' That night I checked the stars again, to be sure about what I had seen, and I was about ready to begin believing them."

She moved the knife back and forth as if honing it now, smoothing the soil and packing it flat. Then she began to trace designs.

"For the next several days, I tried to find my way back," she continued. "I thought I could locate our trail and backtrack along it, but it just sort of vanished. Then I did the only other thing I could think of. Each morning I struck out in a different direction, rode until noon, then headed back. I came across nothing that was familiar. It was totally bewildering. Each night I went to sleep more angry and upset over the way things were turning out—and more determined to find my own way back to Avalon. I had to show Grandpa that he could no longer dump me like a child and expect me to stay put.

"Then, after about a week, I began having dreams. Nightmares, sort of. Did you ever dream that you were running and running and not going anyplace? That is sort of what it was like—with the burning spider web. Only it wasn't really a spider web, there was no spider and it wasn't burning. But I was caught in this thing, going around it and through it. But I wasn't really moving. That is not completely right, but I do not know how else to put it. And I had to keep trying—actually, I wanted to—to move about it. When I woke up I was tired, as if I had actually been exerting myself all night long. This went on for many nights, and each night it seemed stronger and longer and more real.

"Then this morning I got up, the dream still dancing in my head, and I knew that I could ride home. I set out, still half dreaming, it seemed. I rode the entire distance without stopping once, and this time I paid no special heed to my surroundings, but kept thinking of Avalon—and as I rode, things kept getting more and more familiar until I was here again. Only then did it seem as if I were fully awake. Now the village and the Tecys, that sky, those stars, the woods, the mountains, they all seem like a dream to me. I am not at all certain that I could find my way back there. Is that not strange? Can you tell me what happened?"

I rose and circled the remains of our lunch. I sat down beside her.

"Do you remember the looks of the burning spider web that really wasn't a spider web, or burning?" I asked her.

"Yes—sort of," she said.

"Give me that knife," I said.

She passed it to me.

With its point, I began adding to her doodling in the dirt, extending lines, rubbing some out, adding others. She did not say a word the entire time, but she watched every move that I made. When I had finished, I put the knife aside and waited for a long, silent while.

Then, finally, she spoke very softly.

"Yes, that is it," she said turning away from the design to stare at me. "How did you know? How did you know what I had dreamed?"

"Because" I said, "you dreamed a thing that is inscribed in your very genes. Why, how, I do not know. It demonstrates, however, that you are indeed a daughter of Amber. What you did was walk in Shadow. What you dreamed was the Great Pattern of Amber. By its power do those of the blood royal hold dominion over shadows. Do you understand what I am talking about?"

"I am not certain," she said. "I do not think so. I have heard Grandpa cursing shadows, but I never understood what he meant."

"Then you do not know where Amber truly lies."

"No. He was always evasive. He told me of Amber and of the family. But I do not even know the direction in which Amber lies. I only know that it is far."

"It lies in all directions," I said, "or any direction one chooses. One need but—"

"Yes!" she interrupted. "I had forgotten, or thought he was just being mysterious or humoring me, Brand said exactly the same thing a long while ago. What does it mean, though?"

"Brand! When was Brand here?"

"Years ago," she said, "when I was just a little girl. He used to visit here often. I was very much in love with him and I pestered him mercilessly. He used to tell me stories, teach me games . . ."

"When was the last time you saw him?"

"Oh, eight or nine years ago, I'd say."

"Have you met any of the others?"

"Yes," she said. "Julian and Gérard were here not too long ago. Just a few months back."

I suddenly felt very insecure. Benedict had certainly been quiet about a lot of things. I would rather have been ill advised than kept totally ignorant of affairs. It makes it easier for you to be angry when you find out. The trouble with Benedict was that he was too honest, though. He would rather tell me nothing than lie to me. I felt something unpleasant coming my way, however, and knew that there could be no dawdling now, that I would have to move as quickly as possible. Yes, it had to be a hard hellride for the stones. Still, there was more to be learned here before I essayed it. Time . . . Damn!

"Was that the first time that you met them?" I asked.

"Yes," she said, "and my feelings were very hurt." She paused, sighed. "Grandpa would not let me speak of our being related. He introduced me as his ward. And he refused to tell me why. Damn it!"

"I'm sure he had some very good reasons."

"Oh, I am too. But it does not make you feel any better, when you have been waiting all your life to meet your relatives. Do *you* know why he treated me like that?"

"These are trying times in Amber," I said, "and things will get worse before they get better. The fewer people who know of your existence, the less chance there is of your getting involved and coming to harm. He did it only to protect you."

She made a spitting noise.

"I do not need protecting," she said. "I can take care of myself."

"You are a fine fencer," I said. "Unfortunately, life is more complicated than a fair dueling situation."

"I know that. I'm not a child. But—"

" 'But' nothing! He did the same thing I'd do if you were mine. He's protecting himself as well as you. I'm surprised he let Brand know about you. He's going to be damned mad that I found out."

Her head jerked and she stared at me, eyes wide.

"But you wouldn't do anything to hurt us," she said. "We—we're related . . ."

"How the hell do you know why I'm here or what I'm thinking?" I said. "You might have just stuck both your necks in nooses!"

"You *are* joking, aren't you?" she said, slowly raising her left hand between us.

"I don't know," I said. "I need not be—and I wouldn't be talking about it if I did have something rotten in mind, would I?"

"No . . . I guess not," she said.

"I am going to tell you something Benedict should have told you long ago," I said. "Never trust a relative. It is far worse than trusting strangers. With a stranger there is a possibility that you might be safe."

"You really mean that, don't you?"

"Yes."

"Yourself included?"

I smiled.

"Of course it does not apply to me. I am the soul of honor, kindness, mercy, and goodness. Trust me in all things."

"I will," she said, and I laughed.

"I will," she insisted. "You would not hurt us. I know that."

"Tell me about Gérard and Julian," I said, feeling uncomfortable, as always, in the presence of unsolicited trust. "What was the reason for their visit?"

She was silent for a moment, still studying me, then, "I have been telling you quite a few things," she said, "haven't I? You are right. One can never be too careful. I believe that it is your turn to talk again."

"Good. You are learning how to deal with us. What do you want to know?"

"Where is the village, really? And Amber? They are somehow alike, aren't they? What did you mean when you said that Amber lies in all directions, or any? What are shadows?"

I got to my feet and looked down at her. I held out my hand. She looked very young and more than a little frightened then, but she took it.

"Where . . . ?" she asked, rising.

"This way," I said, and I took her to stand at the place where I had slept and regarded the falls and the water wheel.

She began to say something, but I stopped her.

"Look. Just look," I said.

So we stood there looking at the rushing, the splashing, the turning while I ordered my mind. Then, "Come," I said, turning her by the elbow and walking her toward the wood.

As we moved among the trees, a cloud obscured the sun and the shadows deepened. The voices of the birds grew more shrill and a dampness came up out of the ground. As we passed from tree to tree, their leaves became longer and broader. When the sun appeared again, its light came more yellow, and beyond a turning of the way we encountered hanging vines. The bird cries grew hoarser, more numerous. Our trail took an upward turn, and I led her past an outcropping of flint and onto higher ground. A distant, barely perceptible rumble seemed to come from behind us. The sky was a different blue as we moved through an open place, and we frightened a large, brown lizard that had been sunning itself on a rock. As we took a turn about another mass of stone, she said, "I did not know this was here. I have never been this way before." But I did not answer her, for I was busy shifting the stuff of Shadow.

Then we faced the wood once more, but now the way led uphill through it. Now the trees were tropical giants, interspersed with ferns, and new noises—barks, hisses, and buzzes—were to be heard. Moving up this trail, the rumble grew louder about us, the very ground beginning to vibrate with it. Dara held tightly to my arm, saying nothing now, but searching everything with her eyes. There were big, flat, pale flowers and puddles where the moisture dripped from overhead. The temperature had risen considerably and we were perspiring quite a bit. Now the rumble grew to a mighty roar, and when at length we emerged from the wood again, it was a sound like steady thunder that fell against us. I guided her to the edge of the precipice and gestured outward and down.

It plunged for over a thousand feet: a mighty cataract that smote the gray river like an anvil. The currents were rapid and strong, bearing bubbles and flecks of foam a great distance before they finally dissolved. Across from us, perhaps half a mile distant, partly screened by rainbow and mist, like an island slapped by a Titan, a gigantic wheel slowly rotated, ponderous and gleaming. High overhead, enormous birds rode like drifting crucifixes the currents of the air.

We stood there for a fairly long while. Conversation was impossible, which was just as well. After a time, when she turned from it to look at me, narrow-eyed, speculative, I nodded and gestured with my eyes toward the wood. Turning then, we made our way back in the direction from which we had come.

Our return was the same process in reverse, and I managed it with greater ease. When conversation became possible once more, Dara still kept her silence, apparently realizing by then that I was a part of the process of change going on around us.

It was not until we stood beside our own stream once more, watching the small mill wheel in its turning, that she spoke.

"Was that place like the village?"

"Yes. A shadow."

"And like Amber?"

"No. Amber casts Shadow. It can be sliced to any shape, if you know how. That place was a shadow, your village was a shadow—and *this* place is a shadow. Any place that you can imagine exists somewhere in Shadow."

". . . And you and Grandpa and the others can go about in these shadows, picking and choosing what you desire?"

"Yes."

"That is what I did, then coming back from the village."

"Yes."

Her face became a study in realization. Her almost-black eyebrows dropped half an inch and her nostrils flared with a quick inhalation.

"I can do it, too . . ." she said. "Go anywhere, do anything I want!"

"The ability lies within you," I said.

She kissed me then, a sudden, impulsive thing, then rotated away, her hair bobbing on her slim neck as she tried to look at everything at once.

"Then I can do anything," she said, coming to a standstill.

"There are limitations, dangers . . ."

"That is life," she said. "How do I learn to control it?"

"The Great Pattern of Amber is the key. You must walk it in order to gain the ability. It is inscribed on the floor in a chamber beneath the palace in Amber. It is quite large. You must begin on the outside and walk it to its center without stopping. There is considerable resistance and the feat is quite an ordeal. If you stop, if you attempt to depart the Pattern before completing it, it will destroy you. Complete it, though, and your power over Shadow will be subject to your conscious control."

She raced to our picnic site and studied the pattern we had drawn on the ground there.

I followed more slowly. As I drew near, she said, "I must go to Amber and walk it!"

"I am certain that Benedict plans for you to do so, eventually," I said.

"Eventually?" she said. "Now! I must walk it now! Why did he never tell me of these things?"

"Because you cannot do it yet. Conditions in Amber are such that it would be dangerous to both of you to allow your existence to become known there. Amber is barred to you, temporarily."

"It is not fair!" she said, turning to glare at me.

"Of course not," I said. "But that is the way things stand just now. Don't blame me."

The words came somewhat stickily to my lips. Part of the blame, of course, was mine.

"It would almost be better if you had not told me of these things," she said, "if I cannot have them."

"It is not as bad as all that," I said. "The situation in Amber will become stable again—before too very long."

"How will I learn of it?"

"Benedict will know. He will tell you then."

"He has not seen fit to tell me much of anything!"

"To what end? Just to make you feel bad? You know that he has been good to you, that he cares for you. When the time is ready, he will move on your behalf."

"And if he does not? Will you help me then?"

"I will do what I can."

"How will I able to find you? To let you know?"

I smiled. It had gotten to this point without my half trying. No need to tell her the really important part. Just enough to be possibly useful to me later. . . .

"The cards," I said, "the family Trumps. They are more than a mere sentimental affectation. They are means of communication. Get hold of mine, stare at it, concentrate on it, try to keep all other thoughts out of your mind, pretend that it is really me and begin talking to me then. You will find that it really is, and that I am answering you."

"Those are all the things Grandpa told me not to do when I handle the cards!"

"Of course."

"How does it work?"

"Another time," I said. "A thing for a thing. Remember? I have told you now of Amber and of Shadow. Tell me of the visit here by Gérard and Julian."

"Yes," she said. "There is not really much to tell, though. One morning, five or six months ago, Grandpa simply stopped what he was doing. He was pruning some trees back in the orchard—he likes to do that himself—and I was helping him. He was up on a ladder, snipping away, and suddenly he just stopped, lowered the clippers, and did not move for several minutes. I thought that he was just resting, and I kept on with my raking. Then I heard him talking—not just muttering—but talking as though he were carrying on a conversation. At first, I thought he was talking to me, and I asked him what he had said. He ignored me, though. Now that I know about the Trumps, I realize that he must have been talking to one of them just then. Probably Julian. Anyway, he climbed down from the ladder quite quickly after that, told me he had to go away for a day or so, and started back toward the manor. He stopped before he had gone very far, though, and returned. That was when he told me that if Julian and Gérard were to visit here that I was to be introduced as his ward, the orphaned daughter of a faithful servant. He rode away a short while later, leading two spare horses. He was wearing his blade.

"He returned in the middle of the night, bringing both of them with him. Gérard was barely conscious. His left leg was broken, and the entire left side of his body was badly bruised. Julian was quite battered also, but he had no broken bones. They remained with us for the better part of a month, and they healed quickly. Then they borrowed two horses and departed. I have not seen them since."

"What did they say as to how they had been injured?"

"Only that they had been in an accident. They would not discuss it with me."

"Where? Where did it happen?"

"On the black road. I overheard them talking about it several times."

"Where is this black road?"

"I do not know."

"What did they say about it?"

"They cursed it a lot. That was all."

Looking down, I saw that there was some wine left in the bottle. I stooped and poured two final drinks, passed her one.

"To the reunion," I said, and smiled.

". . . The reunion," she agreed, and we drank.

She began cleaning the area and I assisted her, my earlier sense of urgency upon me once again.

"How long should I wait before I try to reach you?" she asked.

"Three months. Give me three months."

"Where will you be then?"

"In Amber, I hope."

"How long will you be staying here?"

"Not very. In fact, I have to take a little trip right now. I should be back tomorrow, though. I will probably only be staying for a few days after that."

"I wish you would stay longer."

"I wish that I could. I would like to, now that I have met you."

She reddened and turned what seemed all of her attention to repacking the basket. I gathered up the fencing gear.

"Are you going back to the manor now?" she said.

"To the stables. I'll be leaving immediately."

She picked up the basket.

"We will go together then. My horse is this way."

I nodded and followed her toward a footpath to our right.

"I suppose," she said, "that it would be best for me not to mention any of this to anybody, Grandpa in particular?"

"That would be prudent."

The splash and gurgle of the stream, as it flowed to the river, on its way to the sea, faded, faded, was gone, and only the creak of the land-locked wheel that cut it as it went, remained for a time in the air.

VI

Steady movement is more important than speed, much of the time. So long as there is a regular progression of stimuli to get your mental hooks into, there is room for later movement. Once this begins, its rate is a matter of discretion.

So I moved slowly, but steadily, using my discretion. No sense in tiring Star unnecessarily. Rapid shifts are hard enough on people. Animals, who are not so good at lying to themselves, have a rougher time of it, sometimes going completely berserk.

I crossed the stream at a small wooden bridge and moved parallel to it for a time. My intention was to skirt the town itself, but to follow the general direction of the watercourse until I reached the vicinity of the coast. It was midafternoon. My way was shaded, cool. Grayswandir hung at my side.

I bore west, coming at length to the hills that rose there. I refrained from beginning the shift until after I had reached a point that looked down upon the city that represented the largest concentration of population in this realm that was like my Avalon. The city bore the same name, and several thousand people lived there, worked there. Several of the silver towers were missing, and the stream cut the city at a somewhat different angle farther south, having widened or been widened eightfold by then. There was some smoke from the stithies and the public houses, stirred lightly by breezes from the south; people, mounted, afoot, driving wagons, driving coaches, moved through the narrow streets, entered and departed shops, hostels, residences; flocks of birds wheeled, descended, rose about the place where horses were tethered; a few bright pennons and banners stirred listlessly; the waters sparkled and there was a haze in the air. I was too far away to hear the sounds of voices, and of clanking, hammering, sawing, rattling, and creaking as anything other than a generalized hum. While I could distinguish no individual odors, had I still been blind I would have known by sniffing the air that a city was near.

Seeing it from up there, a certain nostalgia came over me, a wistful rag-tail of a dream accompanied by a faint longing for the place that was this place's namesake to me in a vanished shadow and of long ago, where life had been just as simple and I happier than I was at that moment.

But one does not live as long as I have lived without achieving that quality of consciousness which strips naïve feelings as they occur and is generally loathe to participate in the creation of sentimentality.

Those days were passed, that thing done with, and it was Amber now that held me completely. I turned and continued southward, confirmed in my desire to succeed. Amber, I do not forget . . .

The sun became a dazzling, bright blister above my head and the winds began to scream about me. The sky grew more and more yellow and glaring as I rode, until it was as if a desert stretched from horizon to horizon overhead. The hills grew rockier as I descended toward the lowlands, exhibiting wind-sculpted forms of grotesque shape and somber coloration. A dust storm struck me as I emerged from the foothills, so that I had to muffle my face with my cloak and narrow my eyes to slits. Star whinnied, snuffled repeatedly, plodded on. Sand, stone, winds, and the sky more orange then, a slate-like crop of clouds toward which the sun was heading . . .

Then long shadows, the dying of the wind, stillness . . . Only the click of hoof on rock and the sounds of breathing . . . Dimness, as they rush together and the sun is foiled by clouds . . . The walls of the day shaken by thunder . . . An unnatural clarity of distant objects . . . A cool, blue, and electric feeling in the air . . . Thunder again . . .

Now, a rippling, glassy curtain to my right as the rain advances . . . Blue fracture lines within the clouds . . . The temperature plummeting, our pace steady, the world a monochromatic backdrop now . . .

Gonging thunder, flashing white, the curtain flaring toward us now . . . Two hundred meters . . . One-fifty . . . Enough!

Its bottommost edge plowing, furrowing, frothing . . . The moist smell of the earth . . . Star's whinny . . . A burst of speed . . .

Small rivulets of water creeping outward, sinking, staining the ground . . . Now bubbling muddily, now trickling . . . Now a steady flow . . . Streamlets all about us, splashing . . .

High ground ahead, and Star's muscles bunching and relaxing, bunching and relaxing beneath me, as he leaps the rills and freshets, plunges through a racing, roiling sheet, and strikes the slope, hoofs sparking against stones as we mount higher, the voice of the gurgling, eddying flow beneath us deepening to a steady roar . .

Higher, then, and dry, pausing to wring out the corners of my cloak. . . . Below, behind, and to the right a gray, storm-tossed sea laps at the foot of the cliff we hold . . .

Inland now toward clover fields and evenings, the boom of the surf at my back . . .

Pursuing falling stars into the darkening east and eventual silence and night . . .

Clear the sky and bright the stars, but a few small wisps of cloud . . .

A howling pack of red-eyed things, twisting along our trail . . . Shadow . . . Green-eyed . . . Shadow . . . Yellow . . . Shadow . . . Gone . . .

But dark peaks with skirts of snow, jostling one another about me . . . Frozen snow, as dry as dust, lifted in waves by the icy blasts of the heights . . . Powdery snow, flour-like . . . Memory here, of the Italian Alps, of skiing . . . Waves of snow drifting across stone faces . . . A white fire within the night air . . My feet rapidly numbing within my wet boots . . . Star bewildered and snorting, testing each step and shaking his head as if in disbelief . . .

So shadows beyond the rock, a gentler slope, a dying wind, less snow . . .

A twisting trail, a corkscrew trail, an adit into warmth . . . Down, down, down the night, beneath the changing stars . . .

Far the snows of an hour ago, now scrubby plants and level plain . . . Far, and the night birds stagger into the air, wheeling above the carrion feast, shedding hoarse notes of protest as we pass . . .

Slow again, to the place where the grasses wave, stirred by the less cold breeze . . . The cough of a hunting cat . . . The shadowy flight of a bounding, deer-like beast . . . Stars sliding into place and feelings in my feet once more . . .

Star rearing, neighing, racing ahead from some unseen thing . . . A long time in the soothing then, and longer still till the shivers go . . .

Now icicles of a partial moon falling on distant treetops . . . Moist earth exhaling a luminescent mist . . . Moths dancing in the night light . . .

The ground momentarily buckling and swaying, as if mountains were shifting their feet . . . To every star its double . . . A halo round the dumbbell moon . . . The plain, the air above it, filled with fleeing shapes . . .

The earth, a wound-down clock, ticks and grows still . . . Stability . . . Inertia . . . The stars and the moon reunited with their spirits . . .

Skirting the growing fringe of trees, west . . . Impressions of a sleeping jungle: delirium of serpents under oilcloth . . .

West, west . . . Somewhere a river with broad, clean banks to ease my passage to the sea . . .

Thud of hoofs, shuttling of shadows . . . The night air upon my face . . . A glimpse of bright beings on high, dark walls, shining towers . . . The air is sweetened . . . Vision swims . . . Shadows . . .

We are merged, centaur-like, Star and I, under a single skin of sweat . . . We take the air and give it back in mutual explosions of exertion . . . Neck clothed in thunder, terrible the glory of the nostrils . . . Swallowing the ground . . .

Laughing, the smell of the waters upon us, the trees very near to our left . . .

Then among them . . . Sleek bark, hanging vines, broad leaves, droplets of moisture . . . Spider web in the moonlight, struggling shapes within . . . Spongy turf . . . Phosphorent fungus on fallen trees . . .

A clear space . . . Long grasses rustling . . .

More trees . . .

Again, the riversmell . . .

Sounds, later . . . Sounds . . . The glassy chuckling of water . . .

Closer, louder, beside it at last . . . The heavens buckling and bending in its belly, and the trees . . . Clean, with a cold, damp tang . . . Leftward beside it pacing it now . . . Easy and flowing, we follow . . .

To drink . . . Splashing in its shallows, then hock-high with head depressed, Star, in it, drinking like a pump, blasting spray from his nostrils . . . Upriver, it laps at my boots . . . Dripping from my hair running down my arms . . . Star's head turning, at the laughter . . .

Then downriver again, clean, slow, winding .. Then straight, widening, slowing . . .

Trees thickening then thinning . . .

Long, steady, slow . . .

A faint light in the east . . .

Sloping downward now and fewer trees . . . Rockier, and the darkness made whole once again . . .

The first, dim hint of the sea, lost an odor later . . . Clicking, on, in the nightsend chill . . . Again, an instant's salt . . .

Rock, and an absence of trees . . . Hard, steep, bleak, down . . . Ever-increasing precipitousness . . .

Flashing between walls of stone . . . Dislodged pebbles vanishing in the now racing current their splashes drowned in the roar's echoes . . . Deeper the defile, widening . . .

Down, down . . .

Farther still . . .

Now pale once more the east, gentler the slope . . . Again, the touch of salt, stronger . . .

Shale and grit . . . Around a corner, down, and brighter still . . .

Steady, soft and loose the footing . . .

The breeze and the light, the breeze and the light . . . Beyond a crop of rock . . .

Draw rein.

Below me lay the stark seaboard, where rank upon rank of rolling dunes, harassed by the winds out of the southwest, tossed spumes of sand that partly obliterated the distant outlines of the bleak morning sea.

I watched the pink film spread across the water from the east. Here and there, the shifting sands revealed dark patches of gravel. Rugged masses of rock reared above the swell of the waves. Between the massive dunes—hundreds of feet in height—and myself, there high above that evil coast, lay a smashed and pitted plain of angular rocks and gravel, just now emerging from hell or night into dawn's first glow, and alive with shadows.

Yes, it was right.

I dismounted and watched the sun force a bleak and glaring day upon the prospect. It was the hard, white light I had sought. Here, *sans* humans, was the necessary place, just as I had seen it decades earlier on the shadow Earth of my exile. No bulldozers, sifters, broom-wielding blacks; no maximum-security city of Oranjemund.

No X-ray machines, barbed wire, or armed guards. None of these things here. No. For this shadow had never known a Sir Ernest Oppenheimer, and there had never been a Consolidated Diamond Mines of South West Africa, nor a government to approve their amalgamation of coastal mining interests. Here was the desert called Namib in that place some four hundred miles to the northwest of Cape Town, a strip of dunes and rock ranging from a couple to a dozen miles in width and running along that forsaken coast line for perhaps three hundred miles on the seaward side of the Richtersveld Mountains, within whose shadow I now stood. Here, unlike any conventional mine, the diamonds were scattered as casually as bird droppings across the sand. I, of course, had brought along a rake and a sieve.

I broke out the rations and prepared breakfast. It was going to be a hot, dusty day.

As I worked the dunes, I thought of Doyle, the little wispy-haired jeweler with the brick-red complexion and wens on his cheeks, back in Avalon. Jewelers rouge? Why did I want all that jewelers rouge—enough to supply an army of jewelers for a dozen lifetimes? I had shrugged. What was it to him what I wanted it for, so long as I was able to pay for it? Well, if there was some new use of the stuff and good money to be made, a man would be a fool . . . In other words, he would be unable to furnish me with such a quantity within a week? Small, square chuckles had escaped through the gaps in his smile. A week? Oh, no! Of course not! That was ridiculous, out of the question. . . . I saw. Well, a quick thanks and perhaps his competitor up the way might be able to produce the stuff, and might also be interested in a few uncut diamonds I was expecting in a matter of days. . . . Diamonds, did I say? Wait. He was always interested in diamonds himself. . . . Yes, but he was sadly deficient in the jewelers rouge department. A raised hand. It might be that he had spoken hastily with respect to his ability to produce the polishing material. It was the quantity that had disturbed him. But the ingredients were plentiful and the formula fairly simple. Yes, there was no real reason why something could not be worked out. Within a week, at that. Now, about the diamonds . . .

Before I left his shop, something had been worked out.

I have met many persons who thought that gunpowder explodes, which of course is incorrect. It burns rapidly, building up gas pressure which ejects a bullet from the mouth of a shell and drives it through the barrel of a weapon, after having been ignited by the primer, which does the actual exploding when the firing pin is driven into it. Now, with typical family foresight, I had experimented with a variety of combustibles over the years. My disappointment at the discovery that gunpowder would not ignite in Amber, and that all of the primers I tested were equally inert there, was a thing mitigated only by the knowledge that none of my relatives could bring firearms into Amber either. It was much later, during a visit to Amber, after polishing a bracelet I had brought for Deirdre, that I discovered this wonderful property of jewelers rouge from Avalon when I disposed of the polishing cloth in a fireplace. Fortunately, the quantity involved was small, and I was alone at the time.

It made an excellent primer, straight from the container. When cut with a sufficient quantity of inert material, it could also be made to burn properly.

I kept this bit of information to myself, feeling that one day it would be used to decide certain basic issues in Amber. Unfortunately, Eric and I had our run-in before that day arrived and it went into storage along with all my other memories. When things finally did clear for me, my fortunes were quickly cast with those of Bleys, who was preparing an assault on Amber. He had not really needed me then, but had taken me in on the enterprise, I feel, so that he could keep an eye on me. Had I furnished him with guns, he would have been invincible and I would have been unnecessary. More important, had we succeeded in seizing Amber in accordance with his plans, the situation would have become strained indeed, with the bulk of the occupying forces, as well as the officers' loyalty, his. Then I would have required something to adjust the balance of power more equitably. A few bombs and automatic weapons, say.

Had I been my whole self even a month earlier, things would have been quite different. I could have been sitting in Amber, rather than being scorched, abraded, and desiccated, with another hellride before me and a knot of troubles to be worked out after that.

I spat sand so that I would not choke when I laughed. Hell, we make our own ifs. I had better things to think about than what could have happened. Like Eric . . .

I remember that day, Eric. I was in chains and I had been forced to my knees before the throne. I had already crowned myself, to mock you, and been beaten for it. The second time I had the crown in my hands, I threw it at you. But you caught it and smiled. I was glad that it was not damaged when it failed to damage you. Such a beautiful thing. . . . All of silver, with its seven high points, and studded with emeralds to beat all diamonds. Two large rubies at either temple. . . . You crowned yourself that day, all arrogance and hasty pomp. The first words that you spoke then were whispered to me, before the echoes of "Long live the king!" had died within the hall. I remember every one of them. "Your eyes have looked upon the fairest sight they ever will behold," you said. Then, "Guards!" you ordered. "Take Corwin away to the stithy, and let his eyes be burnt from out his head! Let him remember the sights of this day as the last he might ever see! Then cast him into the darkness of the deepest dungeon beneath Amber, and let his name be forgotten!"

"Now you reign in Amber," I said aloud. "But I have my eyes, and I have neither forgotten nor been forgotten."

No, I thought. Wrap yourself in the kingship, Eric. The walls of Amber are high and thick. Stay behind them. Ring yourself with the futile steel of blades. Ant-like, you armor your house in dust. You know now that you will never be secure so long as I live, and I have told you that I will be back. I am coming, Eric. I will bring me up guns out of Avalon, and I will break down your doors and smite your defenders. Then it will be as it was, briefly, another time, before your men came to you and saved you. That day I had only a few drops of your blood. This time, I will have it all.

I uncovered another rough diamond, the sixteenth or so, and flipped it into the sack at my waist.

As I faced the setting sun, I wondered about Benedict, Julian, and Gérard. What was the connection? Whatever, I did not like any combination of interests which involved Julian. Gérard was all right. I had been able to sleep back at the camp when I had thought that it was he whom Benedict was contacting. If he was now allied with Julian, though, it was cause for increased uneasiness. If anyone hated me even more than Eric, it was Julian. If he knew where I was, then my danger was great. I was not yet ready for a confrontation.

I supposed Benedict could find a moral justification for selling me out at this point. After all, he knew that whatever I did—and he knew that I was going to do something—would result in strife in Amber. I could understand, even sympathize with his feelings. He was dedicated to the preservation of the realm. Unlike Julian, he was a man of principle, and I regretted having to be at odds with him. My hope was that my coup would be as quick and painless as a tooth extraction under gas, and that we would be back on the same side again soon afterward. Having met Dara now, I also wanted it this way for her sake.

He had told me too little for comfort. I had no way of knowing whether he really intended to remain in the field the entire week, or whether he was even now cooperating with the forces of Amber in the laying of my trap, the walling of my prison, the digging of my grave. I had to hurry though I longed to linger in Avalon.

I envied Ganelon, in whatever tavern or brothel he drank, whored, or fought, on whatever hillside he hunted. He had come home. Should I leave him to his pleasures, despite his offer to accompany me to Amber? But no, he would be questioned on my departure— used badly, if Julian had anything to do with it—and then become an outcast in what must seem his own land to him, if they let him go at all. Then he would doubtless become an outlaw again, and the third time would probably prove his undoing. No, I would keep my promise. He would come with me, if that was what he still wanted. If he had changed his mind, well— I even envied him the prospect of outlawry in Avalon. I would have liked to remain longer, to ride with Dara in the hills, tramp about the countryside, sail upon the rivers. . . .

I thought about the girl. The knowledge of her existence changed things somewhat. I was not certain how. Despite our major hatreds and petty animosities, we Amberites are a very family-conscious bunch, always eager for news of one another, desirous to know everyone's position in the changing picture. A pause for gossip has doubtless stayed a few death blows among us. I sometimes think of us as a gang of mean little old ladies in a combination rest home and obstacle course.

I could not fit Dara into things yet because she did not know where she fit herself. Oh, she would learn eventually. She would receive superb tutelage once her existence became known. Now that I had brought her awareness of her uniqueness it would only be a matter of time before this occurred and she joined in the games. I had felt somewhat serpent-like at points during our conversation in the grove—but hell, she had a right to know. She was bound to find out sooner or later, and the sooner she did the sooner she could start shoring up her defenses. It was for her own benefit.

Of course, it was possible—even likely—that her mother and grandmother had lived their lives in ignorance of their heritage . . .

And where had it gotten them? They died violently, she had said.

Was it possible, I wondered, that the long arm of Amber had reached for them out of Shadow? And that it might strike again?

Benedict could be a tough and mean and nasty as any of us when he wanted to be. Tougher, even. He would fight to protect his own, doubtless even kill one of us if he thought it necessary. He must have assumed that keeping her existence a secret and keeping her ignorant would protect her. He would be angry with me when he found out what I had done, which was another reason for clearing out in a hurry. But I had not told her what I had out of sheer perverseness. I wanted her to survive, and I did not feel he was handling things properly. When I returned, she would have had time to think things over. She would have many questions and I would seize the opportunity to caution her at length and to give specifics.

I gnashed my teeth.

None of this should be necessary. When I ruled in Amber, things would be different. They had to be . . .

Why had no one ever come up with a way to change the basic nature of man? Even the erasure of all my memories and a new life in a new world had resulted in the same old Corwin. It I were not happy with what I was it could be a proposition worthy of despair.

In a quiet part of the river, I washed away the dust, the sweat, wondering the while about the black road which had so injured my brothers. There were many things that I needed to know.

As I bathed, Grayswandir was never far from my hand. One of us is capable of tracking another through Shadow, when the trail is still warm. As it was, my bath was undisturbed, though I used Grayswandir three times on the way back, on less mundane things than brothers.

But this was to be expected, as I had accelerated the pace considerably. . . .

It was still dark, though dawn was not too far away, when I entered the stables at my brother's manor. I tended Star, who had grown somewhat wild, talking to him and soothing him as I rubbed him down, then putting out a good supply of food and water. Ganelon's Firedrake greeted me from the opposite stall. I cleaned up at the pump to the rear of the stable, trying to decide where I was going to catch a little sleep.

I needed some rest. A few hours' worth would hold me for a time, but I refused to take them beneath Benedict's roof. I would not be taken that easily, and while I had often said that I wanted to die in bed, what I really meant was that in my old age I wanted to be stepped on by an elephant while making love.

I was not averse to drinking his booze, though, and I wanted a belt of something strong. The manor was dark; I entered quietly and I found the sideboard.

I poured a stiff one, tossed it off, poured another, and carried it to the window. I could see for a great distance. The manor stood on a hillside and Benedict had landscaped the place well.

"'White in the moon the long road lies,'" I recited, surprised at the sound of my own voice. "'The moon stands blank above. . .'"

"So it does. So it does, Corwin my lad," I heard Ganelon say.

"I didn't see you sitting there," I said softly, not turning from the window.

"That's because I'm sitting so still," he said.

"Oh," I said. "How drunk are you?"

"Hardly at all," he said, "now. But if you would care to be a good fellow and fetch me a drink . . ."

I turned.

"Why can't you get your own?"

"It hurts to move."

"All right."

I went and poured him one, carried it to him. He raised it slowly, nodded his thanks, took a sip.

"Ah, that's good!" he sighed. "May it numb things a bit."

"You were in a fight," I decided.

"Aye," he said. "Several."

"Then bear your wounds like a good trooper and let me save my sympathy."

"But I won!"

"God! Where did you leave the bodies?"

"Oh, they are not that bad off. 'Twas a girl did this to me."

"Then I'd say you got your money's worth."

"'Twas not that sort of thing at all. I believe I've embarrassed us."

"Us? How?"

"I did not know she was the lady of the house. I came in feeling jolly, and I thought her some serving wench . . ."

"Dara?" I said, tensing.

"Aye, the same. I slapped her on the rump and went for a kiss or two—" He groaned. "Then she picked me up. She raised me off the ground and held me up over her head. Then she told me she was the lady of the house. Then she let me fall. . . . I'm eighteen stone if I'm a pebble, man, and it was a long way down."

He took another drink, and I chuckled.

"She laughed, too," he said ruefully. "She helped me up then and was not unkind, and of course I apologized— That brother of yours must be quite a man. I never met a girl that strong. The things she could do to a man. . . ." There was awe in his voice. He shook his head slowly and tossed back the rest of his drink. "It was frightening —not to mention embarrassing," he concluded.

"She accepted your apology?"

"Oh, yes. She was quite gracious about the whole thing. She told me to forget all about it, and said that she would, too."

"Then why are you not in bed sleeping it off?"

"I was waiting up, in case you came in at an odd hour. I wanted to catch you right away."

"Well, you have."

He rose slowly and picked up his glass.

"Let's go outside," he said.

"Good idea."

He picked up the brandy decanter on the way out, which I also thought was a good idea, and we followed a path through the garden behind the house. Finally he heaved himself onto an old stone bench at the foot of a large oak tree, where he refilled both our glasses and took a drink from his own.

"Ah! He has good taste in liquor, too, your brother," he said.

I seated myself beside him and filled my pipe.

"After I told her I was sorry and introduced myself, we got to talking for a time," he said. "As soon as she learned I was with you, she wanted to know all sorts of things about Amber and shadows and you and the rest of your family."

"Did you tell her anything?" I said, striking a light.

"Couldn't have if I wanted to," he said. "I had none of the answers."

"Good."

"It got me to thinking, though. I do not believe Benedict tells her too much, and I can see why. I would be careful what I say around her, Corwin. She seems over-curious."

I nodded, puffing.

"There is a reason for it," I said. "A very good reason. I am glad to know, though, that you keep your wits about you even when you have been drinking. Thanks for telling me."

He shrugged and took a drink.

"A good bashing is a sobering thing. Also, your welfare is my welfare."

"True. Does this version of Avalon meet with your approval?"

"Version? It *is* my Avalon," he said. "A new generation of people is in the land, but it is the same place. I visited the Field of Thorns today, where I put down Jack Hailey's bunch in your service. It was the same place."

"The Field of Thorns . . ." I said, remembering.

"Yes, this is my Avalon," he continued, "and I'll be coming back here for my old age, if we live through Amber."

"You still want to come along?"

"All my life I've wanted to see Amber—well, since I first heard of it. That was from you, in happier times."

"I do not really remember what I said. It must have been a good telling."

"We were both wonderfully drunk that night, and it seemed but a brief while that you talked—weeping some of the time—telling me of the mighty mountain Kolvir and the green and golden spires of the city, of the promenades, the decks, the terrace, the flowers, the fountains. . . . It seemed but a brief while, but it was most of the night for before we staggered off to bed the morning had begun. God! I could almost draw you a map of the place! I must see it before I die."

"I do not remember that night," I said slowly. "I must have been very, very drunk."

He chuckled.

"We had some good times here in the old days," he said. "And they do remember us here. But as people who lived very long ago— and they have many of the stories wrong. But hell! How many people get their stories right from day to day?"

I said nothing, smoking, thinking back.

". . . All of which leads me to a question or two," he said.

"Shoot."

"Will your attack on Amber put you at great odds with your brother Benedict?"

"I really wish that I knew the answer to that one," I said. "I think that it will, initially. But my move should be completed before he can reach Amber from here, in response to any distress call that goes out. That is, reach Amber with reinforcements. He could get there in no time at all, personally, if someone on the other end were helping. But that would serve little purpose. No. Rather than tear Amber apart, he will support whoever can hold it together, I am certain. Once I have ousted Eric, he will want the strife to stop right there and he will go along with my holding the throne, just to put an end to it. He will not really approve of the seizure in the first place, of course."

"That is what I am getting at. Will there be bad blood between you afterward as a result of that?"

"I do not believe so. This is purely a matter of politics, and we have known one another most of our lives, he and I, and have always been on better terms with each other than either of us with Eric."

"I see. Since you and I are in this together and Avalon seems to be Benedict's now, I was wondering what his feelings would be about my returning here one day. Would he hate me for having helped you?"

"I doubt that very much. He has never been that sort of person."

"Then let me carry things a step further. God knows I am an experienced military man, and if we succeed in taking Amber he will have ample evidence of the fact. With his right arm injured the way that it is and all, do you think he might consider taking me on as a field commander for his militia? I know this area so well. I could take him to the Field of Thorns and describe that battle. Hell! I would serve him well—as well as I served you."

He laughed then.

"Pardon me. Better than I served you."

I chuckled, sipped my drink.

"It would be tricky," I said. "Of course I like the idea. But I am not too certain that you could ever enjoy his trust. It would seem too obvious a ploy on my part."

"Damn politics! That is not what I meant! Soldiering is all that I know, and I love Avalon!"

"I believe you. But would he?"

"With only one arm he will be needing a good man about. He could—"

I began to laugh and restrained myself quickly, for the sound of laughter seems to carry for a good distance. Also, Ganelon's feelings were involved.

"I am sorry," I said. "Excuse me, please. You do not understand. You do not really understand who it was we talked with in the tent that night. He may have seemed an ordinary man to you—a handicapped one, at that. But this is not so. I fear Benedict. He is unlike any other being in Shadow or reality. He is the Master of Arms for Amber. Can you conceive of a millennium? A thousand years? Several of them? Can you understand a man who, for almost every day of a lifetime like that, has spent some time dwelling with weapons, tactics, strategies? Because you see him in a tiny kingdom, commanding a small militia, with a well-pruned orchard in his back yard, do not be deceived. All that there is of military science thunders in his head. He has often journeyed from shadow to shadow, witnessing variation after variation on the same battle, with but slightly altered circumstances, in order to test his theories of warfare. He has commanded armies so vast that you could watch them march by day after day and see no end to the columns. Although he is inconvenienced by the loss of his arm, I would not wish to fight with him either with weapons or barehanded. It is fortunate that he has no designs upon the throne, or he would be occupying it right now. If he were, I believe that I would give up at this moment and pay him homage. I fear Benedict."

Ganelon was silent for a long while, and I took another drink, for my throat had become dry.

"I did not realize this, of course," he said then. "I will be happy if he just lets me come back to Avalon."

"That much he will do. I know."

"Dara told me she had a message from him today. He has decided to cut short his stay in the field. He will probably be returning tomorrow."

"Damn!" I said, standing. "We will have to move soon, then. I hope Doyle has that stuff ready. We must go to him in the morning and expedite matters. I want to be away from here before Benedict gets back!"

"You have the pretties then?"

"Yes."

"May I see them?"

I undid the sack at my belt and passed it to him. He opened it and withdrew several stones, holding them in the palm of his left hand and turning them slowly with his fingertips.

"They do not look like much," he said, "from what I can see of them in this light. Wait! There's a glimmer! No . . ."

"They are in the rough, of course. You are holding a fortune in your hands."

"Amazing," he said, dropping them back in the sack and refastening it. "It was so easy for you."

"It was not all that easy."

"Still, to gather a fortune so quickly seems somehow unfair."

He passed it back.

"I will see that you are provided with a fortune when our labors are done," I said. "That should prove some compensation, should Benedict not offer you a position."

"Now that I know who he is, I am more determined than ever to work for him one day."

"We will see what can be done."

"Yes. Thank you, Corwin. How shall we work our departure?"

"I want you to go and get some rest, for I will roust you out of bed early. Star and Firedrake will take unkindly to the notion of draft duty, I fear, but we will then borrow one of Benedict's wagons and head into town. Before this, I will try to arrange a good smoke screen here for our orderly withdrawal. We will then hurry Doyle the jeweler about his task, obtain our cargo, and depart into Shadow as quickly as possible. The greater our head start, the more difficult it will be for Benedict to track us. If I can get half a day's lead into Shadow, it will be practically impossible for him."

"Why should he be so eager to come after us in the first place?"

"He does no trust me worth a damn—and justly so. He is waiting for me to make my move. He knows there is something I need here, but he does not know what. He wants to find out, so that he can seal off another threat to Amber. As soon as he realizes we have gone for good, he will know what we have it and he will come looking."

Ganelon yawned, stretched, finished his drink.

"Yes," he said then. "We'd best rest now, to be in condition for the hurrying. Now that you have told me more about Benedict, I am less surprised by the other thing I meant to tell you—though no less discomfited."

"That being . . . ?"

He rose to his feet, picked up the decanter carefully, then pointed down the path.

"If you continue on in that direction," he said, "passing the hedge that marks the end of this bower and entering the woods that lie below—and then go on for another two hundred paces or so—you come to a place where there is a little grove of saplings off to the left, standing in a sudden declivity perhaps four feet lower than the level of the trail itself. Down in it, stamped down and strewn over with leaves and twigs, there is a fresh grave. I found it while taking the air earlier, when I paused to relieve myself down there."

"How do you know it is a grave?"

He chuckled.

"When holes have bodies in them that is how they are generally called. It was quite shallow, and I poked around a bit with a stick. There are four bodies in there—three men and a woman."

"How recently dead?"

"Very. A few days, I'd judge."

"You left it as you found it?"

"I'm not a fool, Corwin."

"Sorry. But this troubles me considerably, because I don't understand it at all."

"Obviously they gave Benedict some trouble and he returned the favor."

"Perhaps. What were they like? How did they die?"

"Nothing special about them. They were in their middle years, and their throats had been cut—save for one fellow who got it in the guts."

"Strange. Yes, it is good that we are leaving soon. We have enough problems of our own without getting involved in the local ones."

"Agreed. So let us be off to bed."

"You go ahead. I am not quite ready yet."

"Take your own advice and get some rest," he said, turning back toward the manor. "Don't sit up and worry."

"I won't."

"Good night, then."

"See you in the morning."

I watched him return along the path. He was right, of course, but I was not yet ready to surrender my consciousness. I went over my plans again, to be certain there was nothing I was overlooking, finished my drink and set the glass on the bench. I rose then and strolled, trailing wisps of tobacco smoke about me. There was a bit of moonlight from over my shoulder and dawn was still a few hours' distant, as I reckoned it. I was firm in my resolve to spend the rest of the night out of doors, and I thought to find me a good place to sack out.

Of course, I eventually wandered down the path and into the grove of saplings. A little poking around showed me that there had been some recent digging, but I was in no mood to exhume bodies by moonlight and was perfectly willing to take Ganelon's word as to what he had found there. I am not even certain why I went there. Morbid streak, I guess. I did decide against sleeping in the vicinity, though.

I made my way into the northwest corner of the garden, finding an area that was out of line of sight from the manor. There were high hedgerows and the grass was long, soft, and sweet-smelling. I spread my cloak, sat down upon it, and pulled off my boots. I put my feet down into the cool grass and sighed.

Not too much longer, I decided. Shadows to diamonds to guns to Amber. I was on my way. A year ago I had been rotting in a cell, crossing and recrossing the line between sanity and madness so many times that I had all but rubbed it out. Now I was free, strong, sighted, and had a plan. Now I was a threat seeking fulfillment once again, a deadlier threat than I had been previously. This time I did not have my fortunes tied up with the plans of another. Now I was responsible for my own success or failure.

The feeling was good, as was the grass, as was the alcohol which had now seeped through my system and warmed me with a pleasant flame. I cleaned my pipe, put it away, stretched, yawned, and was about to recline.

I detected a distant movement, propped myself on my elbows and watched for it again. I did not have long to wait. A figure was passing slowly along the path, pausing frequently, moving quietly. It vanished beneath the tree where Ganelon and I had been sitting, and did not emerge again for a long while. Then it continued on for several dozen paces, stopped and seemed to be staring in my direction. Then it advanced toward me.

Passing about a clump of shrubbery and emerging from the shadows, her face was suddenly touched by the moonlight. Apparently aware of this, she smiled in my direction, slowing as she came near, stopping when she stood before me.

She said, "I take it your quarters are not to your liking, Lord Corwin."

"Not at all," I said. "It is such a beautiful night that it appealed to the outdoorsman in me."

"Something must have appealed to you last night, also," she said, "despite the rain," and she seated herself beside me on my cloak. "Did you sleep indoors or out?"

"I spent it out," I said. "But I did not sleep. In fact, I have not slept since I saw you last."

"Where have you been?"

"Down by the seaside, sifting sand."

"Sounds depressing."

"It was."

"I have been doing a lot of thinking, since we walked in Shadow."

"I would imagine."

"I have not done too much sleeping either. That was why I heard you come in, heard you talking with Ganelon, knew you were out here somewhere when he came back alone."

"You were right."

"I must get to Amber, you know. And walk the Pattern."

"I know. You will."

"Soon, Corwin. Soon!"

"You are young, Dara. There is plenty of time."

"Damn it! I have been waiting all my life—without even knowing about it! Is there no way I can go now?"

"No."

"Why not? You could take me on a quick journey through shadows, take me to Amber, let me walk the Pattern . . ."

"If we are not slain immediately, we might be fortunate enough to be given adjoining cells for a time—or racks—before we are executed."

"Whatever for? You are a Prince of the City. You have a right to do as you please."

I laughed.

"I am an outlaw, dear. If I return to Amber I will be executed, if I am lucky. Or something much worse if I am not. But seeing as how things turned out last time, I should think they would kill me quickly. This courtesy would doubtless also be extended to my companions."

"Oberon would not do such a thing."

"Given sufficient provocation, I believe that he would. But the question does not really arise. Oberon is no more, and my brother Eric sits on the throne and calls himself liege."

"When did this occur?"

"Several years ago, as time is measured in Amber."

"Why would he want to kill you?"

"To keep me from killing him, of course."

"Would you?"

"Yes, and I will. Soon, too, I think."

She turned to face me then.

"Why?"

"So that I can occupy the throne myself. It is rightly mine, you see. Eric has usurped it. I am just recently escaped from torture and several years' imprisonment at his hands. He made the mistake, however, of allowing himself the luxury of keeping me alive so that he could contemplate my wretchedness. He never thought that I would get free and return to challenge him again. Neither did I, for that matter. But since I have been fortunate enough to obtain a second chance, I shall be careful not to make the same mistake he did."

"But he is your brother."

"Few are more aware of that fact than he and I, I assure you."

"How soon do you expect to accomplish—your objectives?"

"As I said the other day, if you can get hold of the Trumps, contact me in about three months. If you cannot, and things come about according to my plans, I will get in touch with you fairly early in my reign. You should have your chance to take the Pattern before another year passes."

"And if you fail?"

"Then you will have a longer wait ahead of you. Until Eric has assured the permanency of his own reign, and until Benedict has acknowledged him king. You see, Benedict is not willing to do this. He has remained away from Amber for a long while, and for all Eric knows, he is no longer among the living. Should he put in an appearance now, he is going to have to take a position either for or against Eric. Should he come out for him, then the continuance of Eric's reign will be assured—and Benedict does not want to be responsible for that. Should he come out against him, there will be strife—and he does not want to be responsible for that either. He has no desire for the crown himself. Only by remaining out of the picture entirely can he assure the measure of tranquility that does prevail. Were he to appear and refuse to take either position, *he* could possibly get away with it, but it would be tantamount to denying Eric's kingship and would still lead to trouble. Were he to appear with you, he would be surrendering his will, for Eric would put pressure on him through you."

"Then if you lose I might never get to Amber!"

"I am only describing the situation as I see it. There are doubtless many factors of which I am unaware. I have been out of circulation for a long while."

"You *must* win!" she said. Then, suddenly, "Would Grandpa support you?"

"I doubt it. But the situation would be quite different. I am aware of his existence, and of yours. I will not ask his support. So long as he does not oppose me, I will be satisfied. And if I am quick, efficient, and successful, he will not oppose me. He will not like my having found out about you, but when he sees that I mean you no harm all will be well on that count."

"Why would you not use me? It seems the logical thing to do."

"It is. But I've discovered I like you," I said, "so that's out of the question."

She laughed.

"I've charmed you!" she said.

I chuckled.

"In your own delicate way, at sword's point, yes."

Abruptly, she sobered.

"Grandpa is coming back tomorrow," she said. "Did your man Ganelon tell you?"

"Yes."

"How does that affect whatever you are about?"

"I intend to be hell and gone out of here before he returns."

"What will he do?"

"The first thing that he will do will be to get very angry with you for being here. Then he will want to know how you managed your return and how much you have told me about yourself."

"What should I tell him?"

"Tell him the truth about how you got back. That will give him something to think about. As to your status, your woman's intuition cautioned you concerning my trustworthiness, and you took the same line with me as you did with Julian and Gérard. As to my whereabouts, Ganelon and I borrowed a wagon and headed into town, saying that we would not be back until quite late."

"Where will you really be going?"

"Into town, briefly. But we will not be coming back. I want as much of a head start as possible because he can track me through Shadow, up to a point."

"I will delay him as best I can for you. Were you not going to see me before you left?"

"I was going to have this talk with you in the morning. You got it ahead of time by being restless."

"Then I am glad that I was—restless. How are you going to conquer Amber?"

I shook my head. "No, dear Dara. All scheming princes must keep a few small secrets. That's one of mine."

"I am surprised to learn there is so much distrust and plotting in Amber."

"Why? The same conflicts exist everywhere, in various forms. They are all about you, always, for all places take their form from Amber."

"It is difficult to understand . . ."

"One day you will. Leave it at that for now."

"Then tell me another thing. Since I am able to negotiate shadows somewhat, even without having taken the Pattern, tell me more precisely how you go about it. I want to get better at it."

"No!" I said. "I will not have you fooling with Shadow until you are ready. It is dangerous even after you have taken the Pattern. To do it before is foolhardy. You were lucky, but do not try it again. I'll even help, by not telling you anything more about it."

"All right!" she said. "Sorry. I guess I can wait."

"I guess you can. No hard feelings?"

"No. Well—" She laughed. "They wouldn't do me any good, I guess. You must know what you are talking about. I am glad that you care what happens to me."

I grunted, and she reached out and touched my cheek. At this, I turned my head again and her face was moving slowly toward my own, smile gone and lips parting, eyes almost closed. As we kissed, I felt her arms slide about my neck and shoulders and mine found their way into a similar position around her. My surprise was lost in the sweetness, gave way to warmth and a certain excitement.

If Benedict ever found out, he was going to be more than just irritated with me. . . .

VII

The wagon creaked, monotonously, and the sun was already well into the west, though it still poured hot streams of daylight upon us. Back among the cases, Ganelon snored, and I envied him his noisy occupation. He had been sleeping for several hours, and this was my third day without rest.

We were perhaps fifteen miles out of the city, and heading into the northeast. Doyle had not had my order completely ready, but Ganelon and I had persuaded him to close up his shop and accelerate his production. This involved several additional hours' curseworthy delay. I had been too keyed-up to sleep then and was unable to do so now, so I was edging my way through shadows.

I forced back the fatigue and the evening and found some clouds to shade me. We moved along a dry, deeply rutted, clay road. It was an ugly shade of yellow, and it cracked and crumbled as we went. Brown grasses hung limply on either side of the way, and the trees were short, twisted things, their barks thick and shaggy. We passed numerous outcrops of shale.

I had paid Doyle well for his compounds, and had also purchased a handsome bracelet to be delivered to Dara the following day. My diamonds were at my belt, Grayswandir near to my hand. Star and Firedrake walked steadily, strongly. I was on my way to having it made.

I wondered whether Benedict had returned yet. I wondered how long he would remain deceived as to my whereabouts. I was by no means out of danger from him. He could follow a trail for a great distance through Shadow, and I was leaving him a good one. I had little choice in the matter, though. I needed the wagon, I was stuck with our present speed, and I was in no condition to manage another hellride. I handled the shifts slowly and carefully, very conscious of my dulled senses and growing weariness counting on the gradual accumulation of change and distance to build up a barrier between

Benedict and myself, hoping that it would soon become an impenetrable one.

I found my way from late afternoon back to noontide within the next two miles, but kept it a cloudy noon, for it was only its light that I desired, not its heat. Then I managed to locate a small breeze. It increased the probability of rain, but it was worth it. You can't have everything.

I was fighting back drowsiness by then, and the temptation was great to awaken Ganelon and simply add more miles to our distance by letting him drive while I slept. But I was afraid to try it this early in the journey. There were still too many things to do.

I wanted more daylight, but I also wanted a better road, and I was sick of that goddamned yellow clay, and I had to do something about those clouds, and I had to keep in mind where we were headed. . . .

I rubbed my eyes, I took several deep breaths. Things were starting to jump around inside my head, and the steady clop-clop of the horses' hoofs and the creaking of the wagon were starting to have a soporific effect. I was already numb to the jolting and the swaying. The reins hung loosely in my hands, and I had already nodded and let them slip once. Fortunately, the horses seemed to have a good idea as to what was expected of them.

After a time, we mounted a long, easy slope that led down into mid-morning. By then, the sky was quite dark, and it took several miles and half a dozen twistings of the road to dissipate the cloud cover somewhat. A storm could turn our way into a river of mud quite quickly. I winced at the thought, let the sky alone and concentrated on the road once more.

We came to a dilapidated bridge leading across a dry stream bed. On its other side, the road was smoother, less yellow. As we proceeded, it grew darker, flatter, harder, and the grass came green beside it.

By then though, it had begun raining.

I fought with this for a time determined not to surrender my grass and the dark, easy road. My head ached, but the shower ended within a quarter of a mile and the sun came out once more.

The sun . . . oh yes, the sun.

We rattled on, finally coming to a dip in the road that kept twisting its way down among brighter trees. We descended into a cool valley, where we eventually crossed another small bridge, this one with a narrow band of water drifting along the middle of the bed beneath it. I had wrapped the reins about my wrist by then, because I kept nodding. As from a great distance, I focused my concentration, straightening, sorting . . .

Birds queried the day, tentatively, from within the woods to my right. Glistening droplets of dew clung to the grass, the leaves. A chill came into the air, and the rays of the morning sun slanted down through the trees . . .

But my body was not fooled by the awakening within this shadow, and I was relieved finally to hear Ganelon stir and curse. If he had not come around before much longer I would have had to awaken him.

Good enough. I tugged gently on the reins and the horses got the idea and halted. I put on the brake, as we were still on an incline, and located a water bottle.

"Here!" said Ganelon, as I drank. "Leave a drop for me!"

I passed the bottle back to him.

"You are taking over now," I told him. "I have to get some sleep."

He drank for half a minute, then let out an explosive exhalation.

"Right," he said, swinging himself over the edge of the wagon and down. "But bide a moment. Nature summons."

He stepped off the road, and I crawled back onto the bed of the wagon and stretched out where he had lain, folding my cloak into a pillow.

Moments later, I heard him climb onto the driver's seat, and there was a jolt as he released the brake. I heard him cluck his tongue and snap the reins lightly.

"Is it morning?" he called back to me.

"Yes."

"God! I've slept all day and all night!"

I chuckled.

"No. I did a little shadow-shifting," I said. "You only slept six or seven hours."

"I don't understand. But never mind, I believe you. Where are we now?"

"Still heading northeast," I said, "around twenty miles out of the city and maybe a dozen or so from Benedict's place. We have moved through Shadow, also."

"What am I to do now?"

"Just keep following the road. We need the distance."

"Could Benedict still reach us?"

"I think so. That's why we can't give the horses their rest yet."

"All right. Is there anything special I should be alert for?"

"No."

"When should I rouse you?"

"Never."

He was silent then, and as I waited for my consciousness to be consumed, I thought of Dara, of course. I had been thinking of her on and off all day.

The thing had been quite unpremeditated on my part. I had not even thought of her as a woman until she came into my arms and revised my thinking on the subject. A moment later, and my spinal nerves took over, reducing much of what passes for cerebration down to its basics, as Freud had once said to me. I could not blame it on the alcohol, as I had not had that much and it had not affected me especially. Why did I want to blame it on anything? Because I felt somewhat guilty, that was why. She was too distant a relation for me to really think of her as one. That was not it. I did not feel I had taken unfair advantage of her, for she had known what she was doing when she came looking for me. It was the circumstances that made me question my own motives, even in the midst of things. I had wanted to do more than simply win her confidence and a measure of friendship when I had first spoken with her and taken her on that walk into Shadow. I was trying to alienate some of her loyalty, trust, and affection from Benedict and transfer it to myself. I had wanted her on my side, as a possible ally in what might become an enemy camp. I had hoped to be able to use her, should the need arise when the going got rough. All this was true. But I did not want to believe that I had had her as I did just to further this end. I suspected there was some truth to it, though, and it made me uncomfortable and more than a little ignoble. Why? I had done plenty of things in my time that many would consider much worse, and I was not especialy troubled by these. I wrestled with it, not liking to admit it but already knowing the answer. I cared for the girl. It was as simple as that. It was different from the friendship I had felt for Lorraine, with its element of world-weary understanding between two veterans about it, or the air of casual sensuality that had existed briefly between Moire and myself, back before I had taken the Pattern for the second time. It was quite different. I had known her so briefly that it was most illogical. I was a man with centuries behind me. Yet . . . I had not felt this way in centuries. I had forgotten the feeling, until now. I did not want to be in love with her. Not now. Later, perhaps. Better yet, not at all. She was all wrong for me. She was a child. Everything that she would want to do, everything that she would find new and fascinating, I had already done. No, it was all wrong. I had no business falling in love with her. I should not let myself . . .

Ganelon hummed some bawdy tune, badly. The wagon jounced and creaked, took a turn uphill. The sun fell upon my face, and I covered my eyes with my forearm. Somewhere thereabout, oblivion fixed its grip and squeezed.

When I awoke, it was past noon and I was feeling grimy. I took a long drink of water, poured some in the palm of my hand, and rubbed it in my eyes. I combed my hair with my fingers. I took a look at our surroundings.

There was greenery about us, small stands of trees and open spaces where tall grasses grew. It was till a dirt road that we traveled, hardpacked and fairly smooth. The sky was clear, but for a few small clouds, and shade alternated with sunlight fairly regularly. There was a light breeze.

"Back among the living. Good!" said Ganelon, as I climbed over the front wall and took a seat beside him.

"The horses are getting tired, Corwin, and I'd like to stretch my legs a bit," he said. "I'm also getting very hungry. Aren't you?"

"Yes. Pull off into that shady place to the left and we'll stop awhile."

"I would like to go on a bit farther than that," he said.

"For any special reason?"

"Yes. I want to show you something."

"Go ahead."

We clopped along for perhaps half a mile, then came to a bend in the road that took us in a more northerly direction. Before very long we came to a hill, and when we had mounted it there was another hill, leading even higher.

"How much farther do you want to go?" I said.

"Let's take this next hill," he replied. "We might be able to see it from up there."

"All right."

The horses strained against the steepness of that second hill, and I got out and pushed from behind. When we finally reached the top, I felt even grimier from the mixture of sweat and dust, but I was fully awake once more. Ganelon reined in the horses and put on the brake. He climbed back in the wagon and up onto a crate then. He stood, facing to the left, and shaded his eyes.

"Come up here, Corwin," he called.

I climbed over the tailgate and he squatted and extended a hand. I took it, and he helped me up onto the crate, where I stood beside him. He pointed, and I followed the gesture.

Perhaps three-quarters of a mile distant, running from left to right for as far as I could see, was a wide, black band. We were several hundred yards higher than the thing and had a decent view of, I would say, half a mile of its length. It was several hundred feet across, and though it curved and turned twice that I could see, its width appeared to remain constant. There were trees within it, and they were totally black. There seemed to be some movement. I could not say what it was. Perhaps it was only the wind rippling the black grasses near its edge. But there was also a definite sensation of flowing within it, like current in a flat, dark river.

"What is it?" I said.

"I thought perhaps you could tell me," Ganelon replied. "I had thought it a part of your shadow-sorceries."

I shook my head slowly.

"I was quite drowsy, but I would remember if I had arranged for anything that strange to occur. How did you know it was there?"

"We skirted it several times as you slept, then edged away again. I did not like the feeling at all. It was a very familiar one. Does it not remind you of something?"

"Yes. Yes, it does. Unfortunately."

He nodded.

"It's like that damned Circle back in Lorraine. That's what it's like."

"The black road . . ." I said.

"What?"

"The black road," I repeated. "I did not know what she was referring to when she mentioned it, but now I begin to understand. This is not good at all."

"Another ill omen?"

"I am afraid so."

He cursed, then, "Will it cause us any immediate trouble?" he asked.

"I don't believe so, but I am not certain."

He climbed down from the crate and I followed.

"Let's find some forage for the horses then," he said, "and tend to our own bellies as well."

"Yes."

We moved forward and he took the reins. We found a good spot at the foot of the hill.

We tarried there for the better part of an hour, talking mainly of Avalon. We did not speak again of the black road, though I thought of it quite a bit. I had to get a closer look at the thing, of course.

When we were ready to move on, I took the reins again. The horses, somewhat refreshed, moved out at a good pace.

Ganelon sat beside me on the left, still in a talkative mood. I was only just then beginning to realize how much this strange homecoming had meant to him. He had revisited many of his old haunts from the days of his outlawry, as well as four battlefields where he had distinguished himself greatly after he had achieved respectability. I was in many ways moved by his reminiscences. An unusual mixture of gold and clay, this man. He should have been an Amberite.

The miles slid by quickly and we were drawing near to the black road again when I felt a familiar mental jab. I passed the reins to Ganelon.

"Take them!" I said. "Drive!"

"What is it?"

"Later! Just drive!"

"Should I hurry?"

"No. Keep it normal. Don't say anything for a while."

I closed my eyes and rested my head in my hands, emptying my mind and building a wall around the emptiness. No one home. Out to lunch. No solicitors. This property is vacant. Do not disturb. Trespassers will be prosecuted. Beware of dog. Falling rock. Slippery when wet. To be razed for urban renewal . . .

It eased, then came on again, hard, and I blocked it again. There followed a third wave. I stopped that one, too.

Then it was gone.

I sighed, massaged my eyeballs.

"It's all right now," I said.

"What happened?"

"Someone tried to reach me by a very special means. It was almost certainly Benedict. He must just now have found out any of a number of things that could make him want to stop us. I'll take the reins again now. I fear he will be on our trail soon."

Ganelon handed them over.

"What are our chances of escaping him?"

"Pretty fair now, I'd say, that we've got more distance behind us. I am going to shuffle some more shadows as soon as my head stops spinning."

I guided us on, and our way twisted and wound, paralleling that black road for a time, then heading in closer to it. Finally, we were only a few hundred yards away from it.

Ganelon studied it in silence for a long while, then said, "It reminds me too much of that other place. The little tongues of mist that lick about things, the feeling that something is always moving just at the corner of your eye . . .

I bit my lip. I began to perspire heavily. I was trying to shift away from the thing now and there was some sort of resistance. It was not the same feeling of monolithic immovability as occurs when you try to move through Shadow in Amber. It was altogether different. It was a feeling of—inescapability.

We moved through Shadow all right. The sun drifted higher in the heavens, heading back toward noonday—for I did not relish the thought of nightfall beside that black strip—and the sky lost something of its blue and the trees shot higher about us and mountains appeared in the distance.

Was it that the road cut through Shadow itself?

It must. Why else would Julian and Gérard have located it and been sufficiently intrigued to explore the thing?

It was unfortunate, but I feared we had much in common, that road and I.

Damn it!

We moved beside it for a long while, gradually moving closer together, also. Soon, only about a hundred feet separated us. Fifty . . .

. . . And, as I had felt they eventually must, our paths finally intersected.

I drew rein. I packed my pipe and lit it, smoked as I studied the thing. Star and Firedrake obviously did not approve of the black area that cut across our way. They had whinnied and tried to pull off to the side.

It was a long, diagonal cut across the black place if we wanted to keep to the road. Also, part of the terrain was hidden from our sight by a series of low, stone hills. There were heavy grasses at the edge of the black and patches of it, here and there, about the foot of the hills. Bits of mist scudded among them and faint, vaporous clouds hovered in all the hollows. The sky, seen through the atmosphere that hung about the place, was several shades darker, with a smeared, sooty tone to it. A silence that was not the same as stillness lay upon it, almost as though some unseen entity were poised, holding its breath.

Then we heard a scream. It was a girl's voice. The old lady in distress trick?

It came from somewhere to the right, beyond those hills. It smelled fishy. But hell! It could be real.

I tossed the reins to Ganelon and jumped to the ground, taking Grayswandir into my hand.

"I'm going to investigate," I said, moving off to the right and leaping the gulley that ran beside the road.

"Hurry back."

I plowed through some brush and scrambled up a rocky slope. I pushed my way through more shrubbery on its down side and mounted another, higher slope. The scream came again as I was climbing it, and this time I heard other sounds as well.

Then I reached the top and was able to see for a good distance.

The black area began about forty feet below me, and the scene I sought was laid about a hundred-fifty feet within it.

It was a monochromatic sight, save for the flames. A woman, all in white, black hair hanging loose, down to her waist, was bound to one of those dark trees, smoldering branches heaped around her feet. Half a dozen hairy, albino men, almost completely naked and continuing the process of undressing as they moved, shuffled about, muttering and chuckling, poking at the woman and the fire with sticks that they carried and clutching at their loins repeatedly. The flames were high enough now to singe the woman's garments, causing them to smolder. Her long dress was sufficiently torn and disarrayed so that I could see she possessed a lovely, voluptuous form, though the smoke wrapped her in such a manner that I was unable to see her face.

I rushed forward, entering the area of the black road, leaping over the long, twining grasses, and charged into the group, beheading the nearest man and running another through before they knew I was upon them. The others turned and flailed at me with their sticks, shouting as they swung them.

Grayswandir ate off big chunks of them, until they fell apart and were silent. Their juices were black.

I turned, holding my breath, and kicked away the front of the fire. Then I moved in close to the lady and cut her bonds. She fell into my arms, sobbing.

It was only then that I noticed her face—or, rather, her lack of once. She wore a full, ivory mask, oval and curving, featureless, save for two tiny rectangular grilles for her eyes.

I drew her away from the smoke and the gore. She clung to me, breathing heavily, thrusting her entire body against me. After what seemed an appropriate period of time, I attempted to disentangle myself. But she would not release me, and she was surprisingly strong.

"It is all right now," I said, or something equally trite and apt, but she did not reply.

She kept shifting her grip upon my body, with rough caressing movements and a rather disconcerting effect. Her desirability was enhanced, from instant to instant. I found myself stroking her hair, and the rest of her as well.

"It is all right now," I repeated. "Who are you? Why were they burning you? Who were they?"

But she did not reply. She had stopped sobbing, but her breathing was still heavy, although in a different way.

"Why do you wear this mask?"

I reached for it and she jerked her head back.

This did not seem especially important, though. While some cold, logical part of me knew that the passion was irrational, I was as powerless as the gods of the Epicureans. I wanted her and I was ready to have her.

Then I heard Ganelon cry out my name and I tried to turn in that direction.

But she restrained me. I was amazed at her strength.

"Child of Amber," came her half-familiar voice. "We owe you this for what you have given us, and we will have all of you now."

Ganelon's voice came to me again, a steady stream of profanities.

I exerted all my strength against that grip and it weakened. My hand shot forward and I tore away the mask.

There came a brief cry of anger as I freed myself, and four final, fading words as the mask came away:

"Amber must be destroyed!"

There was no face behind the mask. There was nothing there at all.

Her garment collapsed and hung limply over my arm. She—or it —had vanished.

Turning quickly, I saw that Ganelon was sprawled at the edge of the black, his legs twisted unnaturally. His blade rose and fell slowly, but I could not see at what he was striking. I ran toward him.

The black grasses, over which I had leaped, were twined about his ankles and legs. Even as he hacked at them, others lashed about as though seeking to capture his sword arm. He had succeeded in partly freeing his right leg, and I leaned far forward and managed to finish the job.

I moved to a position behind him, out of reach of the grasses, and tossed away the mask, which I just then realized I was still clutching. It fell to earth beyond the edge of the black and immediately began to smolder.

Catching him under the arms, I strove to drag Ganelon back. The stuff resisted fiercely, but at last I tore him free. I carried him then, leaping over the remaining dark grasses that separated us from the more docile, green variety beyond the road.

He regained his footing and continued to lean heavily against me, bending forward and slapping at his leggings.

"They're numb," he said. "My legs are asleep."

I helped him back to the wagon. He transferred his grip to its side and began stamping his feet.

"They're tingling," he announced. "It's starting to come back. . . . Oow!"

Finally, he limped to the front of the wagon. I helped him climb onto the seat and followed him up.

He sighed.

"That's better," he said. "They're coming along now. That stuff just sucked the strength out of them. Out of the rest of me, too. What happened?"

"Our bad omen made good on its promise."

"What now?"

I picked up the reins and released the brake.

"We go across," I said. "I have to find out more about this thing. Keep your blade handy."

He grunted and laid the weapon across his knees. The horses did not like the idea of going on, but I flicked their flanks lightly with the whip and they began to move.

We entered the black area, and it was like riding into a World War II newsreel. Remote though near at hand, stark, depressing, grim. Even the creaking and the hoof falls were somehow muffled, made to seem more distant. A faint, persistent ringing began in my ears. The grasses beside the road stirred as we passed, though I kept well away from them. We passed through several patches of mist. They were odorless, but our breathing grew labored on each occasion. As we neared the first hill, I began the shift that would take us through Shadow.

We rounded the hill.

Nothing.

The dark, miasmal prospect was unaltered.

I grew angry then. I drew the Pattern from memory and held it blazing before my mind's eye. I essayed the shift once more.

Immediately, my head began to ache. A pain shot from my forehead to the back of my skull and hung there like a hot wire. But this only fanned my anger and caused me to try even harder to shift the black road into nothingness.

Things wavered. The mists thickened, rolled across the road in billows. Outlines grew indistinct. I shook the reins. The horse moved after. My head began to throb, felt as if were about to come apart.

Instead, momentarily, everything else did . . . .

The ground shook, cracking in places, but it was more than just that. Everything seemed to undergo a spasmodic shudder, and the cracking was more than mere fracture lines in the ground.

It was a though someone had suddenly kicked the leg of a table on which a loosely assembled jigsaw puzzle lay. Gaps appeared in the entire prospect: here, a green bough; there, a sparkle of water, a glimpse of blue sky, absolute blackness, white nothingness, the front of a brick building, faces behind a window, fire, a piece of star-filled sky . . .

The horses were galloping by then, and I had all I could do to keep from screaming for the pain.

A babble of mixed noises—animal, human, mechanical—washed over us. It seemed that I could hear Ganelon cursing, but I could not be certain.

I thought that I would pass out from the pain, but I determined, out of sheer stubbornness and anger, to persist until I did. I concentrated on the Pattern as a dying man might cry out to his God, and I threw my entire will against the existence of the black road.

Then the pressure was off and the horses were plunging wildly, dragging us into a green field. Ganelon snatched at the reins, but I drew on them myself and shouted to the horses until they halted.

We had crossed the black road.

I turned immediately and looked back. The scene had the wavering quality of something seen through troubled waters. Our path through it stood clean and steady, however, like a bridge or a dam, and the grasses at its edge were green.

"That was worse," Ganelon said, "than the ride you took me on when you exiled me."

"I think so, too," I said, and I spoke to the horses gently, finally persuading them to return to the dirt road and continue on along it.

The world was brighter here, and the trees that we soon moved among were great pines. The air was fresh with their fragrance. Squirrels and birds moved within them. The soil was darker, richer. We seemed to be at a higher altitude than we had been before the crossing. It pleased me that we had indeed shifted—and in the direction I had desired.

Our way curved, ran back a bit, straightened. Every now and then we caught a glimpse of the black road. It was not too far off to our right. We were still running roughly parallel to it. The thing definitely cut through Shadow. From what we saw of it, it appeared to have settled back down to being its normal, sinister self once more.

My headache faded and my heart grew somewhat lighter. We achieved higher ground and a pleasant view over a large area of hills and forest, reminding me of parts of Pennsylvania I had enjoyed driving through years earlier.

I stretched; then, "How are your legs now?" I asked.

"All right," Ganelon said, looking back along our trail. "I can see for a great distance, Corwin . . ."

"Yes?"

"I see a horseman, coming very fast."

I stood and turned. I think I might have groaned as I dropped back into the seat and shook the reins.

He was still too far to tell for certain—on the other side of the black road. But who else could it be, pushing along at that speed on our trail?

I cursed then.

We were nearing the crest of the rise. I turned to Ganelon and said, "Get ready for another hellride."

"It's Benedict?"

"I think so. We lost too much time back there. He can move awfully fast—especially through Shadow—all alone like that."

"Do you think you can still lose him?"

"We'll find out," I said. "Real soon now."

I clucked to the horses and shook the reins again. We reached the top and a blast of icy air struck us. We leveled off and the shadow of a boulder to our left darkened the sky. When we had passed it, the darkness remained and crystals of fine-textured snow stung our faces and hands.

Within a few moments, we were heading downward once more and the snowfall became a blinding blizzard. The wind screamed in our ears and the wagon rattled and skidded. I leveled us quickly. There were drifts all about by then and the road was white. Our breath fumed and ice glistened on trees and rocks.

Motion and temporary bafflement of the senses. That was what it took . . .

We raced on, and the wind slammed and bit and cried out. Drifts began to cover the road.

We rounded a bend and emerged from the storm. The world was still a glacéed-over thing and an occasional flake flitted by, but the sun pulled free of the clouds, pouring light upon the land, and we headed downward once more. . . .

. . . Passing through a fog and emerging in a barren, though snowless waste of rock and pitted land. . . .

. . . We bore to the the right, regained the sun, followed a twisted course on a level plain, winding among tall, featureless stands of blue-gray stone. . . .

. . . Where far off to our right the black road paced us.

Waves of heat washed over us and the land steamed. Bubbles popped in boiling stews that filled the craters, adding their fumes to the dank air. Shallow puddles lay like a handful of old, bronze coins.

The horses raced, half-maddened now, as geysers began to erupt along the trail. Scalding waters spewed across the roadway, narrowly missing us, running in steaming, slick sheets. The sky was brass and the sun was a mushy apple. The wind was a panting dog with bad breath.

The ground trembled, and far off to our left a mountain blew its top toward the heavens and hurled fires after it. An ear-splitting crash temporarily deafened us and concussion waves kept beating against our bodies. The wagon swayed and shimmied.

The ground continued to shake and the winds slammed us with near-hurricane force as we rushed toward a row of black-topped hills. We left what there was of a roadway when it turned in the wrong direction and headed, bumping and shuddering, across the plain itself. The hills continued to grow, dancing in the troubled air.

I turned when I felt Ganelon's hand on my arm. He was shouting something, but I could not hear him. Then he pointed back and I followed his gesture. I saw nothing that I had not expected to see. The air was turbulent, filled with dust, debris, ashes. I shrugged and returned my attention to the hills.

A greater darkness occurred at the base of the nearest hill. I made for it.

It grew before me as the ground slanted downward once more, an enormous cavern mouth, curtained by a steady fall of dust and gravel.

I cracked the whip in the air and we raced across the final five or six hundred yards and plunged into it.

I began slowing the horses immediately, letting them relax into a walk.

We continued to move downward, turned a corner, and came into a wide, high grotto. Light leaked down from holes high above, dappling stalactites and falling upon quivering green pools. The ground continued to shake, and my hearing took a turn for the better as I saw a massive stalagmite crumble and heard the faint tinkle of its fall.

We crossed a black-bottomed chasm on a bridge that might have been limestone, which shattered behind us and vanished.

Bits of rock rained down from overhead and sometimes large stones fell. Patches of green and red fungus glowed in corners and cracks, streaks of minerals sparkled and bent, large crystals and flat flowers of pale stone added to the moist, eerie beauty of the place.

We wheeled through caverns like chains of bubbles and coursed a whitecrested torrent until it vanished into a black hole.

A long, corkscrew gallery took us upward once more, and I heard Ganelon's voice, faint and echoing, "I thought that I glimpsed movement—that might be a rider—at the crest of the mountain—just for an instant—back there."

We moved into a slightly brighter chamber.

"If it was Benedict, he's got a hard act to follow," I shouted, and there came the tremors and muffled crashings as more things collapsed behind us.

We proceeded onward and upward, until finally openings began to occur overhead, giving upon patches of clear blue sky. The hoof clicks and the sounds of the wagon gradually assumed a normal volume and their echoes came to us also. The tremors ceased, small birds darted above us, and the light increased in intensity.

Then another twisting of the way, and our exit lay before us, a wide, low opening onto day. We had to duck our heads as we passed beneath the jagged lintel.

We bounced up and over a jutting lip of moss-covered stone, then looked upon a bed of gravel that lay like a scythed track upon the hillside, passing among gigantic trees, vanishing within them, below. I made a clicking noise with my tongue, encouraging the horses on their way.

"They are very tired now," Ganelon remarked.

"I know. Soon they will get to rest, one way or another."

The gravel crunched beneath our wheels. The smell of the trees was good.

"Have you noticed it? Down there, off to the right?"

"What . . . ?" I began, turning my head. Then, "Oh," I finished.

The infernal black road was with us still, perhaps a mile distant.

"How many shadows does it cut across?" I mused.

"All of them, it would seem," Ganelon suggested.

I shook my head slowly.

"I hope not," I said.

We proceeded downward, beneath a blue sky and a golden sun westering in a normal way.

"I was almost afraid to come out of that cave," Ganelon said after a time. "No telling what would be on this side."

"The horses couldn't take much more. I had to let up. If that was Benedict we saw, his horse had better be in very good condition. He was pushing it hard. Then to have it face all that. . . . I think he would fall back."

"Maybe it's used to it," Ganelon said, as we crunched around a bend to the right, losing sight of the cave mouth.

"There is always that possibility," I said, and I thought of Dara again, wondering what she was doing at that moment.

We wove our way steadily downward, shifting slowly and imperceptibly. Our trail kept drifting to the right, and I cursed when I realized we were nearing the black road.

"Damn! It's as persistent as an insurance salesman!" I said, feeling my anger turn to something like hatred. "When the time is right, I am going to destroy that thing!"

Ganelon did not reply. He was taking a long drink of water. He passed me the bottle and I did, too.

At length, we achieved level terrain, and the trail continued to twist and curve at the least excuse. It allowed the horses to take it easy and it would slow a mounted pursuer.

About an hour later, I began to feel comfortable and we stopped to eat. We had just about finished our meal when Ganelon—who had not removed his gaze from the hillside—stood and shaded his eyes.

"No," I said, leaping to my feet. "I don't believe it."

A lone rider had emerged from the mouth of the cave. I watched as he halted for a moment, then continued on down the trail.

"What do we do now?" Ganelon asked.

"Let's pick up our stuff and get moving again. We can at least delay the inevitable a little longer. I want more time to think."

We rolled once more, still moving at a moderate pace, though my mind was racing at full speed. There had to be a way to stop him. Preferably, without killing him.

But I couldn't think of any.

Except for the black road, which was edging nearer once more, we had come into a lovely afternoon in a beautiful place. It was a shame to dampen it with blood, particularly if it might be my blood. Even with his blade in his left hand, I was afraid to face him. Ganelon would be of no use to me. Benedict would barely notice him.

I shifted as we took another turning. Moments later, a faint smell of smoke came to my nostrils. I shifted slightly again.

"He's coming fast!" Ganelon announced. "I just saw— There's smoke! Flames! The woods are on fire!"

I laughed and looked back. Half the hillside swam under smoke and an orange thing raced through the green, its crackling just then reaching my ears. Of their own accord, the horses increased their pace.

"Corwin! Did you——?"

"Yes! If it were steeper and there were no trees, I'd have tried an avalanche."

The air was momentarily filled with birds. We drew nearer the black way. Firedrake tossed his head and whinnied. There were flecks of foam on his muzzle. He tried to bolt, then reared and pawed the air. Star made a frightened noise and pulled to the right. I fought a moment, regained control, decided to let them run a bit.

"He's still coming!" cried Ganelon.

I cursed and we ran. Eventually, our path brought us alongside the black road. We were on a long straightaway, and a glance back showed me that the whole hillside was ablaze, the trail running like a nasty scar down its middle. It was then that I saw the rider. He was almost halfway down and moving like something in the Kentucky Derby. God! What a horse that had to be! I wondered what shadow had borne him.

I drew on the reins, gently at first, then harder, until finally we began to slow. We were only a few hundred feet from the black road by then, and I had seen to it that there was a place not too far ahead where the gap narrowed to thirty or forty. I managed to rein in the horses when we reached it, and they stood there quivering. I handed the reins to Ganelon, drew Grayswandir, and stepped down to the road.

Why not? It was a good, clear, level area, and perhaps that black, blasted slice of land, contrasting with the colors of life and growth immediately beside it, appealed to some morbid instinct in me.

"What now?" Ganelon asked.

"We cannot shake him," I said, "and if he makes it through the fire he will be here in a few minutes. There is no sense to running any farther. I'll meet him here."

Ganelon twisted the reins around a side bar and reached for his blade.

"No," I said. "You cannot affect the outcome one way or the other. Here is what I want you to do: Take the wagon on up the road and wait there with it. If things are resolved to my satisfaction, we will be continuing on. If they are not, surrender immediately to

Benedict. It is me that he wants, and he will be the only one left who can take you back to Avalon. He will do it, too. You will at least retire to your homeland that way."

He hesitated.

"Go on," I told him. "Do as I said."

He looked down at the ground. He unwound the reins. He looked at me.

"Good luck," he said, and he shook the horses forward.

I backed off the trail, moved to a position before a small stand of saplings, and waited. I kept Grayswandir in my hand, glanced once at the black road, then fixed my eyes on the trail.

Before long, he appeared up near the flame line, smoke and fire all about him, burning branches falling. It was Benedict all right, his face partly muffled, the stump of his right arm upraised to shield his eyes, coming like some ghastly escapee from hell. Bursting through a shower of sparks and cinders, he came into the clear and plunged on down the trail.

Soon, I could hear the hoofbeats. A gentlemanly thing to do would be to sheathe my blade while I waited. If I did that, though, I might not have a chance to draw it again.

I found myself wondering how Benedict would be wearing his blade and what sort it would be. Straight? Curved? Long? Short? He could use them all with equal facility. He had taught me how to fence. . . .

It might be smart as well as gentlemanly to sheathe Grayswandir. He might be willing to talk first—and this way I was asking for trouble. As the hoofbeats grew louder, though, I realized I was afraid to put it away.

I wiped my palm only before he came into view. He had slowed for the turn, and he must have seen me at the same instant I saw him. He rode straight toward me, slowing. But halting did not appear to be his immediate aim.

It was almost a mystical experience. I do not know how else to put it. My mind outran time as he neared, and it was as though I had an eternity to ponder the approach of this man who was my brother. His garments were filthy, his face blackened, the stump of his right arm raised, gesturing anywhere. The great beast that he rode was striped, black and red, with a wild red mane and tail. But it really was a horse, and its eyes rolled and there was foam at its mouth and its breathing was painful to hear. I saw then that he wore his blade slung across his back, for its shaft protruded high above his right shoulder. Still slowing, eyes fixed upon me, he departed the road, bearing slightly toward my left, jerked the reins once and released them, keeping control of the horse with his knees. His left hand went up in a salute-like movement that passed above his head and seized the hilt of his weapon. It came free without a sound, describing a beautiful arc above him and coming to rest in a lethal position out from his minuscule line of edge that gleamed like a filament of mirror. The picture he presented was burned into my mind with a kind of magnificence, a certain splendor that was strangely moving. The blade was a long, scythe-like affair that I had seen him use before. Only then we had stood as allies against a mutual foe I had begun to believe unbeatable. Benedict has proved otherwise that night. Now that I saw it raised against me I was overwhelmed with a sense of my own mortality, which I had never experienced before in this fashion. It was as though a layer had been stripped from the world and I had a sudden, full understanding of death itself.

The moment was gone. I backed into the grove. I had stood there so that I could take advantage of the trees. I dropped back about twelve feet among them and took two steps to my left. The horse reared at the last possible moment and snorted and whinnied, moist nostrils flaring. It turned aside, tearing up turf. Benedict's arm moved with near-invisible speed, like the tongue of a toad, and his blade passed through a sapling I'd guess at three inches in diameter. The tree continued to stand upright for a moment, then slowly toppled.

His boots struck the earth and he strode toward me. I had wanted the grove for this reason, also, to make him come to me in a place where a long blade would be hampered by branches and boles.

But as he advanced, he swung the weapon, almost casually, back and forth, and the trees fell about him as he passed. If only he were not so infernally competent. If only he were not Benedict. . . .

"Benedict," I said, in a normal voice, "she is an adult now, and she is capable of making up her own mind about things."

But he gave no sign of having heard me. He just kept coming, swinging that great blade from side to side. It made an almost ringing sound as it passed through the air, followed by a soft *thukk!* as it bit through another tree, slowing only slightly.

I raised Grayswandir to point at his breast.

"Come no farther, Benedict," I said. "I do not wish to fight with you."

He moved his blade into an attack position and said one word: "Murderer!"

His hand twitched then and my blade was almost simultaneously beaten aside. I parried the ensuing thrust and he brushed my riposte aside and was at me again.

This time I did not even bother to riposte. I simply parried, re-treated, and stepped behind a tree.

"I don't understand," I said, beating down his blade as it slid by the trunk and nearly skewered me. "I have not murdered anyone recently. Certainly not in Avalon."

Another *thukk!* and the tree was falling toward me. I got out of its way and retreated, parrying.

"Murderer," he said again.

"I don't know what you are talking about, Benedict."

"Liar!"

I stood my ground then and held it. Damn it! It was senseless to die for the wrong reason! I riposted as fast as I could, seeking open-ings everywhere. There were none.

"At least tell me!" I shouted. "Please!"

But he seemed to be finished with talking. He pressed forward and I had to fall back once more. It was like trying to fence with a gla-cier. I became convinced then that he was out of his mind, not that that helped me any. With anybody else, an insane madness would cause the loss of some control in a fight. But Benedict had hammered out his reflexes over the centuries, and I seriously believed that the removal of his cerebral cortex would not have altered his movements from their state of perfection.

He drove me steadily back, and I dodged among trees and he cut them down and kept coming. I made the mistake of attacking and barely stopped his counterthrusts inches from my breast. I fought down the first wave of panic that came to me when I saw that he was driving me back toward the edge of the grove. Soon he would have me in the open, with no trees to slow him.

My attention was focused on him so completely that I did not real-ize what was then to occur until it did.

With a mighty cry, Ganelon sprang from somewhere, wrapping his arms about Benedict and pinning his sword arm to his side.

Even had I really wanted to, though, I did not have the opportunity to kill him then. He was too fast, and Ganelon was not aware of the man's strength.

Benedict twisted to his right, interposing Ganelon between us, and at the same time brought the stump of his arm around like a club, striking Ganelon in the left temple. Then he pulled his left arm free, seized Ganelon by his belt, swept him off his feet, and threw him at me. As I stepped aside, he retrieved his blade from where it had fallen near his feet and came at me again. I barely had time to glance and see that Ganelon had landed in a heap some ten paces to my rear.

I parried and resumed my retreat. I only had one trick remaining, and it saddened me that if it failed Amber would be deprived of its rightful liege.

It is somewhat more difficult to fence with a good left-hander than a good right-hander, and this worked against me also. But I had to experiment a bit. There was something I had to learn, even if it meant taking a chance.

I took a long step back, moving momentarily out of range, then leaned forward and attacked. It was a very calculated thing, and very fast.

One unexpected result, which I am certain was at least partly luck, was that I got through, even though I missed my target. For an instant, Grayswandir rode high off one of his parries and nicked his left ear. This slowed him slightly for a few moments, but not enough to matter. If anything, it served to strengthen his defense. I continued to press my attack, but there was simply no getting through then. It was only a small cut, but the blood ran down to his ear lobe and spattered off, a few drops at a time. It could even be distracting, if I permitted myself to do more than take note of it.

Then I did what I feared, but had to try. I left him a small opening, just for a moment, knowing that he would come right through it toward my heart.

He did, and I parried it at the last instant. I do not like to think about how close he came that time.

Then I began to yield once more, giving ground, backing out of the grove. Parrying and retreating, I moved past the spot where Ganelon lay. I fell back another fifteen feet or so, fighting defensively, conservatively.

Then I gave Benedict another opening.

He drove in, as he had before, and I managed to stop him again.

He pressed the attack even harder after that, pushing me back to the edge of the black road.

There, I stopped and held my ground, shifting my position to the spot I had chosen. I would have to hold him just a few moments longer, to set him up. . . .

They were very rough moments, but I fought furiously and readied myself.

Then I gave him the same opening again.

I knew he would come in the same as before, and my right leg was across and back behind my left, then straightening, as he did. I gave his blade but the barest beat to the side as I sprang backward onto the black road, immediately extending my arm full length to discourage a balaestra.

Then he did what I had hoped. He beat at my blade and advanced normally when I dropped it into quarte . . .

. . . causing him to step into the patch of black grasses over which I had leaped.

I dared not look down at first. I simply stood my ground and gave the flora a chance.

It only took a few moments. Benedict became aware of it the next time that he tried to move. I saw the puzzled expression flash across his face, then the strain. It had him, I knew.

I doubted, though, that it could hold him very long, so I moved immediately.

I danced to the right, out of range of his blade, rushed forward and sprang across the grasses, off the black road once again. He tried to turn, but they had twined themselves about his legs all the way up to his knees. He swayed for a moment, but retained his balance.

I passed behind him and to his right. One easy thrust and he was a dead man, but of course there was no reason to do it now.

He swung his arm back behind his neck and turned his head, pointing the blade at me. He began pulling his left leg free.

But I feinted toward his right, and when he moved to parry it I slapped him across the back of the neck with the flat of Grayswandir.

It stunned him, and I was able to move in and punch him in the kidney with my left hand. He bent slightly and I blocked his sword arm and struck him in the back of the neck again, this time with my fist, hard. He fell, unconscious, and I removed his blade from his hand and cast it aside. The blood from his left ear lobe trailed down his neck like some exotic earring.

I put Grayswandir aside, seized Benedict under the armpits, and dragged him back from the black road. The grasses resisted mightily, but I strained against them and finally had him free.

Ganelon had gotten to his feet by then. He limped up and stood beside me, looking down at Benedict.

"What a fellow he is," he said. "What a fellow he is. . . . What are we going to do with him?"

I picked him up in a fireman's carry and stood.

"Take him back toward the wagon right now," I said. "Will you bring the blades?"

"All right."

I headed up the road and Benedict remained unconscious—which was good, because I did not want to have to hit him again if I could help it. I deposited him at the base of a sturdy tree beside the road near the wagon.

I resheathed our blades when Ganelon came up, and set him to stripping ropes from several of the cases. While he did this, I searched Benedict and found what I was looking for.

I bound him to the tree then, while Ganelon fetched his horse. We tethered it to a nearby bush, upon which I also hung his blade.

Then I mounted to the driver's seat of the wagon and Ganelon came up alongside.

"Are you just going to leave him there?" he asked.

"For now," I said.

We moved on up the road. I did not look back, but Ganelon did.

"He hasn't moved yet," he reported. Then, "Nobody ever just took me and threw me like that. With one hand yet."

"That's why I told you to wait with the wagon, and not to fight with him if I lost."

"What is to become of him now?"

"I will see that he is taken care of, soon."

"He will be all right, though?"

I nodded.

"Good."

We continued on for perhaps two miles and I halted the horses. I climbed down.

"Don't be upset by anything that happens," I said. "I am going to make arrangements for Benedict now."

I moved off the road and stood in the shade, taking out the deck of Trumps Benedict had been carrying. I riffled through them, located Gérard, and removed him from the pack. The rest I returned to the silk-lined, wooden case, inlaid with bone, in which Benedict had carried them.

I held Gérard's Trump before me and regarded it.

After a time, it grew warm, real, seemed to stir. I felt Gérard's actual presence. He was in Amber. He was walking down a street that I recognized. He looks a lot like me, only larger, heavier. I saw that he still wore his beard.

He halted and stared.

"Corwin!"

"Yes, Gérard. You are looking well."

"Your eyes! You can see?"

"Yes, I can see again."

"Where are you?"

"Come to me now and I will show you."

His gaze tightened.

"I am not certain that I can do that, Corwin. I am very involved just now."

"It is Benedict," I said. "You are the only one I can trust to help him."

"Benedict? He is in trouble?"

"Yes."

"Then why does he not summon me himself?"

"He is unable to. He is restrained."

"Why? How?"

"It is too long and involved to go into now. Believe me, he needs your help, right away."

He raked his beard with his upper teeth.

"And you cannot handle it yourself?"

"Absolutely not."

"And you think I can?"

"I know you can."

He loosened his blade in its scabbard.

"I would not like to think this is some sort of trick, Corwin."

"I assure you it is not. With all the time I have had to think, I would have come up with something a little more subtle."

He sighed. Then he nodded.

"All right. I'm coming to you."

"Come ahead."

He stood for a moment, then took a step forward.

He stood beside me. He reached out and clasped my shoulder. He smiled.

"Corwin," he said. "I'm glad you've your eyes back."

I looked away.

"So am I. So am I."

"Who is that in the wagon?"

"A friend. His name is Ganelon."

"Where is Benedict? What is the problem?"

I gestured.

"Back there," I said. "About two miles down the road. He is bound to a tree. His horse is tethered near by."

"Then why are you here?"

"I am fleeing."

"From what?"

"Benedict. I'm the one who bound him."

He wrinkled his brow.

"I do not understand . . ."

I shook my head.

"There is a misunderstanding between us. I could not reason with him and we fought. I knocked him unconscious and I tied him up. I cannot free him, or he would attack me again. Neither can I leave him as he is. He may come to some harm before he can free himself. So I summoned you. Please go to him, release him, and see him home."

"What will you be doing the while?"

"Getting the hell out of here, losing myself in Shadow. You will be doing both of us a favor to keep him from trying to follow me again. I do not want to have to fight him a second time."

"I see. Now will you tell me what happened?"

"I am not certain. He called me a murderer. I give you my word I slew no one the whole time I was in Avalon. Please tell him I said that. I have no reason to lie to you, and I swear that it is true. There is another matter which may have disturbed him somewhat. If he mentions it, tell him that he will have to rely on Dara's explanation."

"And what is it?"

I shrugged.

"You will know if he mentions it. If he does not, forget it."

"Dara, you say?"

"Yes."

"Very well, I shall do as you have asked. . . . Now, will you tell me how you managed your escape from Amber?"

I smiled.

"Academic interest? Or do you feel you might have need of the route yourself one day?"

He chuckled.

"It strikes me as a handy piece of information to have."

"I regret, dear brother, that the world is not yet ready for this knowledge. If I had to tell anyone, I would tell you—but there is no way it could benefit you, whereas its secrecy may serve me in the future."

"In other words, you have a private way into and out of Amber. What are you planning, Corwin?"

"What do you think?"

"The answer is obvious. But my feelings on the matter are mixed."

"Care to tell me about them?"

He gestured toward a section of the black road that was visible from where we stood.

"That thing," he said. "It runs to the foot of Kolvir now. A variety of menaces travel it to attack Amber. We defend, we are always victorious. But the attacks grow stronger and they come more frequently. Now would not be a good time for you to move, Corwin."

"Or it might be the perfect time," I said.

"For you then, but not necessarily for Amber."

"How has Eric been handling the situation?"

"Adequately. As I said, we are always victorious."

"I do not mean the attacks. I mean the entire problem—its cause."

"I have traveled the black road myself, going a great distance along it."

"And?"

"I was unable to go the entire distance. You know how the shadows grow wilder and stranger the farther you get from Amber?"

"Yes."

". . . Until the mind itself is twisted and turned toward madness?"

"Yes."

". . . And somewhere beyond this lie the Courts of Chaos. The road goes on, Corwin. I am convinced that it runs the entire distance."

"Then it is as I feared," I said.

"That is why, whether I sympathize with you or not, I do not recommend the present time for your efforts. The security of Amber must come before all else."

"I see. Then there is nothing more to be said just now."

"And your plans?"

"Since you do not know what they are, it is meaningless to tell you that they are unchanged. But they are unchanged."

"I do not know whether to wish you luck, but I wish you well. I am glad that you have your sight back." He clasped my hand. "I had best get on to Benedict now. I take it he is not badly hurt?"

"Not by me. I only hit him a few times. Do not forget to give him my message."

"I won't."

"And take him back to Avalon."

"I will try."

"Then good-by for now, Gérard."

"Good-by, Corwin."

He turned then and walked on down the road. I watched until he was out of sight before I returned to the wagon. Then I replaced his Trump in the deck and continued on my way to Antwerp.

VIII

I stood on the hilltop and looked down at the house. There was shrubbery all about me, so I was not especially obtrusive.

I do not really know what I expected to see. A burned-out shell? A car in the driveway? A family scattered about the redwood patio furniture? Armed guards?

I saw that the roof could use some new slate, that the lawn had long ago returned to a natural condition. I was surprised that I could see only one broken window there in the rear.

So the place was supposed to look deserted. I wondered.

I spread my jacket on the ground and seated myself on it. I lit a cigarette. There were no other houses for quite a distance.

I had gotten close to seven hundred thousand dollars for the diamonds. It had taken me a week and a half to make the deal. From Antwerp we had traveled to Brussels, spending several evenings at a club on the Rue de Char et Pain before the man I wanted found me.

Arthur was quite puzzled by the arrangement. A slight, white-haired man with a neat mustache, ex-RAF officer, Oxonian, he had begun shaking his head after the first two minutes and kept interrupting me with questions about delivery. While he was no Sir Basil Zaharoff, he became genuinely concerned when a client's ideas sounded too half-baked. It troubled him if something went sour too soon after delivery. He seemed to think it reflected back on him in some way. For this reason, he was often more helpful then the others when it came to shipment. He was concerned about my plans for transportation because I did not seem to have any.

What one generally requires in an arrangement of this sort is an end-use certificate. What it is, basically, is a document affirming that country X has ordered the weapons in question. You need the thing in order to get an export permit from the manufacturer's country. This keeps them looking honest, even if the shipment should be reconsigned to country Y once it has crossed their border. The customary thing to do is to buy the assistance of an ambassadorial representative of country X—preferably one with relatives or friends connected with the Defense Department back home—in order to get the papers. They come high, and I believe Arthur had a list of all the going rates in his head.

"But how are you going to ship them?" he had kept asking. "How will you get them where you want them?"

"That," I said, "will be my problem. Let me worry about it."

But he kept shaking his head.

"It is no good trying to cut corners that way, Colonel," he said. (I had been a colonel to him since we had first met, some dozen years before. Why, I am not certain.) "No good at all. Try to save a few dollars that way and you might lose the whole shipment and wind up in real trouble. Now I can fix you up through one of these young African nations quite reasonably—"

"No. Just fix me up with the weapons."

During our talk, Ganelon just sat there drinking beer, as red-bearded and sinister-looking as ever, and nodding to everything that I said. As he spoke no English, he had no idea as to the state of negotiations. Nor, for that matter, did he really care. He followed my instructions, though, and spoke to me periodically in Thari and we would chat briefly in that language about nothing in particular. Sheer perversity. Poor old Arthur was a good linguist and he wanted to know the destination of the pieces. I could feel him straining to identify the language each time that we spoke. Finally, he began nodding as though he had.

After some more discussion, he stuck his neck out and said, "I read the newspapers. I am certain his crowd can afford the insurance."

That was almost worth the price of admission to me.

But, "No," I said. "Believe me, when I take possession of those automatic rifles, they are going to vanish off the face of the Earth."

"Neat trick, that," he said, "considering I don't even know where we will be picking them up yet."

"It does not matter."

"Confidence is a fine thing. Then there is foolhardiness. . . ." He shrugged. "Have it as you say then—your problem."

Then I told him about the ammo and he must have been convinced as to my mental deterioration. He just stared at me for a long while, not even shaking his head this time. It was a good ten minutes before I could even get him to look at the specifications. It was then that he began shaking his head and mumbling about silver bullets and inert primers.

The ultimate arbiter, cash, convinced him we would do it my way, however. There was no trouble on the rifles or the trucks, but persuading an arms factory to produce my ammo was going to be expensive, he told me. He was not even certain he could find one that would be willing. When I told him that the cost was no object, it seemed to upset him even more. If I could afford to indulge in weird, experimental ammo, an end-use certificate would not come to that much—

No, I told him no. My way, I reminded him.

He sighed and tugged at the fringe of his mustache. Then he nodded. Very well, we would do it my way.

He overcharged me, of course. Since I was rational in all other matters, the alternative to psychosis would be that I was party to an expensive boondoggle. While the ramifications must have intrigued him, he apparently decided not to look too far into such a sticky-seeming enterprise. He was willing to seize every opportunity I extended for dissociating himself from the project. Once he found the ammo people—a Swiss outfit, as it turned out—he was quite willing to put me into contact with them and wash his hands of everything but the money.

Ganelon and I went to Switzerland on fake papers. He was a German and I was Portuguese. I did not especially care what my papers showed, so long as the forgery was of good quality, but I had settled on German as the best language for Ganelon to learn, since he had to learn one and German tourists have always seemed to be all over the place. He picked it up quite rapidly. I had told him to tell any real Germans and any Swiss who asked that he had been raised in Finland.

We spent three weeks in Switzerland before I was satisfied with the quality controls on my ammo. As I had suspected, the stuff was totally inert in this shadow. I had worked out the formula, though, which was all that really mattered at that point. The silver came high, of course. Perhaps I was being over-cautious. Still, there are some things about Amber that are best dispatched with that metal, and I could afford it. For that matter, what better bullet—short of gold—for a king? Should I wind up shooting Eric there would be no *lése-majesté* involved. Indulge me, brothers.

Then I left Ganelon to shift for himself for a time, since he had thrown himself into his tourist role in a true Stanislavskian fashion. I saw him off to Italy, camera about his neck and a faraway look in his eyes, and I flew back to the States.

Back? Yes. That run-down place on the hillside below me had been my home for the better part of a decade. I had been heading toward it when I was forced off the road and into the accident which led to everything which has since occurred.

I drew on my cigarette and regarded the place. It had not been run-down then. I had always kept it in good shape. The place had been completely paid for. Six rooms and an attached two-car garage. Around seven acres. The whole hillside, actually. I had lived there alone most of the time. I had liked it. I had spent much of my time in the den and in my workshop. I wondered whether the Mori woodcut still hung in my study. *Face to Face* it was called, and it depicted two warriors in mortal combat. It would be nice to have it back. It would be gone, though, I felt. Probably everything that had not been stolen had been sold for back taxes. I imagined that was what the State of New York would do. I was surprised that the house itself seemed not to have acquired new occupants. I kept watching, to make certain. Hell, I was in no hurry. There was no place else I had to be.

I had contacted Gérard shortly after my arrival in Belgium. I had decided against trying to talk with Benedict for the time being. I was afraid that he would simply try to attack me, one way or the other, if I did.

Gérard had studied me quite carefully. He was out somewhere in open country and he seemed to be alone.

"Corwin?" he had said, then, "Yes . . . "

"Right. What happened with Benedict?"

"I found him as you said he would be and I released him. He was set to pursue you once again, but I was able to persuade him that a considerable time had passed since I had seen you. Since you said you had left him unconscious, I figured that was the best line to take. Also, his horse was very tired. We went back to Avalon together. I remained with him through the funerals, then borrowed a horse. I am on my way back to Amber now."

"Funerals? What funerals?"

Again, that calculating look.

"You really do not know?" he said.

"If I knew, damn it, I would not ask!"

"His servants. They were murdered. He says you did it."

"No," I said. "No. That is ridiculous. Why should I want to murder his servants? I do not understand . . ."

"It was not long after his return that he went looking for them, as they were not on hand to welcome him. He found them murdered and you and your companion gone."

"Now I see how it looked," I said. "Where were the bodies?"

"Buried, but not too deeply, in the little wood behind the garden to the rear of the house."

Just so, just so . . . . Better not to mention I had known about the grave.

"But what possible reason does he think I could have for doing such a thing?" I protested.

"He is puzzled, Corwin. Very puzzled, now. He could not understand why you did not kill him when you had the chance, and why you sent for me when you could have just left him there."

"I see now why he kept calling me a murderer as we fought, but—Did you tell him what I said about not having slain anyone?"

"Yes. At first he shrugged it off as a self-serving statement. I told him you sounded sincere, and very puzzled yourself. I believe it bothered him a bit that you should be so insistent. He asked me several times whether I believed you."

"Do you?"

He dropped his eyes.

"Damn it, Corwin! What am I supposed to believe? I came into the middle of this. We have been apart for so long . . ."

He met my gaze.

"There is more to it," he said.

"What is that?"

"Why did you call me to help him? That was a complete deck you took. You could have called any of us."

"You must be joking," I said.

"No, I want an answer."

"Very well. You are the only other one I trust."

"Is that all?"

"No. Benedict does not want his whereabouts known back in Amber. You and Julian are the only two I know for certain to be aware of his location. I don't like Julian, I don't trust him. So I called you."

"How did you know that Julian and I knew about him?"

"He helped you both out when you ran into trouble on the black road awhile back, and he put you up while you recuperated. Dara told me about it."

"Dara? Who is this Dara anyway?"

"The orphaned daughter of a couple who once worked for Benedict," I said. "She was around when you and Julian were there."

"And you sent her a bracelet. You also mentioned her to me by the road, back when you summoned me."

"Correct. What is the matter?"

"Nothing. I do not really remember her, though. Tell me, why did you leave so suddenly? You have to admit, it seemed the act of a guilty man."

"Yes," I said, "I was guilty—but not of murder. I went to Avalon to obtain something that I wanted, I got it, and I cleared out. You saw that wagon, and you saw that I had a cargo in it. I got out before he returned to keep from answering questions Benedict might ask me about it. Hell! If I just wanted to run, I wouldn't go dragging a wagon along behind me! I'd have traveled on horseback, fast and light."

"What was in the wagon?"

"No," I said. "I did not want to tell Benedict and I do not want to tell you. Oh, he can find out, I suppose. But let him do it the hard way, if he must. It is immaterial, though. The fact I went there for something and really obtained it should be sufficient. It is not especially valuable there, but is in another place. Fair enough?"

"Yes," he said. "It does make a kind of sense."

"Then answer my question. Do you think I murdered them?"

"No," he said. "I believe you."

"What about Benedict, now? What does he think?"

"He would not attack you again without talking first. There is doubt in his mind, I know that."

"Good. That's something, anyway. Thank you, Gérard. I am going away now."

I moved to break the contact.

"Wait, Corwin! Wait!"

"What is it?"

"How did you cut the black road? You destroyed a section of it at the place you crossed over. How did you do it?"

"The Pattern," I said. "If you ever get in trouble with that thing, hit it with the Pattern. You know how you have to sometimes hold it in your mind if shadows begin to run away from you and things start going wild?"

"Yes. I tried that and it didn't work. All I got was a headache. It is not of Shadow."

"Yes and no," I said. "I know what it is. You did not try hard enough. I used the Pattern until my head felt as if it were being torn apart, until I was half blind from the pain and about ready to pass out. Then the road came apart about me instead. It was no fun, but it did work."

"I will remember," he said. "Are you going to talk to Benedict now?"

"No," I said. "He already has everything we've gone over. Now that he is cooling off, he will begin pushing the facts around some more. I would just as soon he do it on his own—and I do not want to risk another fight. When I close this time I will be silent for a long while. I will resist all efforts to communicate with me, also."

"What of Amber, Corwin? What of Amber?"

I dropped my eyes.

"Don't get in my way when I come back, Gérard. Believe me, it will be no contest."

"Corwin . . . Wait. I'd like to ask you to reconsider. Do not hit Amber now. She is weak in all the wrong ways."

"I am sorry, Gérard. But I am certain I have given the matter more thought during the past five years than all the rest of you put together."

"I am sorry, too, then."

"I guess I had better be going now."

He nodded.

"Good-by, Corwin."

"Good-by, Gérard."

After waiting several hours for the sun to disappear behind the hill, leaving the house in a premature twilight, I mashed a final cigarette, shook out my jacket and donned it, rose to my feet. There had been no signs of life about the place, no movement behind the dirty windows, the broken window. Slowly, I descended the hill.

Flora's place out in Westchester had been sold some years before, which came as no surprise to me. I had checked merely as a matter of curiosity, since I was back in town. Had even driven past the place once. There was no reason for her to remain on this shadow Earth. Her long wardenship having ended successfully, she was being rewarded in Amber the last time I had seen her. To have been so near for as long as I had without even realizing her presence was a thing I found somewhat galling.

I had debated contacting Random, decided against it. The only way he could possibly benefit me would be with information as to current affairs in Amber. While this would be nice to have, it was not absolutely essential. I was fairly certain that I could trust him. After all, he had been of some assistance to me in the past. Admitted, it was hardly altruism—but still, he had gone a bit further than he had had to. It was five years ago, though, and a lot had happened since. He was being tolerated around Amber again, and he had a wife now. He might be eager to gain a little standing. I just did not know. But weighing the possible benefits against the possible losses, I thought it better to wait and see him personally the next time I was in town.

I had kept my word and resisted all attempts to make contact with me. They had come almost daily during my first two weeks back on the shadow Earth. Several weeks had passed, though, and I had not been troubled since. Why should I give anyone a free shot at my thinking machinery? No thanks, brothers.

I advanced upon the rear of the house, sidled up to a window, wiped it with my elbow. I had been watching the place for three days, and it struck me as very unlikely that anyone was inside. Still . . .

I peered in.

It was a mess, of course, and a lot of my stuff was missing. But some of it was still there. I moved to my right and tried the door. Locked. I chuckled.

I walked around to the patio. Ninth brick in, fourth brick up. The key was still beneath it. I wiped it on my jacket as I walked back. I let myself in.

There was dust on everything, but it had been disturbed in some places. There were coffee containers, sandwich wrappers, and the remains of a petrified hamburger in the fireplace. A lot of weather had found its way down that chimney in my absence. I crossed over and closed the damper.

I saw that the front door had been broken about the lock. I tried it. It seemed to be nailed shut. There was an obscenity scrawled on the wall in the foyer. I walked on into the kitchen. It was a total mess. Anything that had survived plunder was on the floor. The stove and the refrigerator were gone, the floor scarred where they had been pushed along.

I backed away, went and checked my workshop. Yes, it had been stripped. Completely. Passing on, I was surprised to find my bed, still unmade, and two expensive chairs all intact in my bedroom.

My study was a more pleasant surprise. The big desk was covered with litter and muss, but then it always had been. Lighting a cigarette, I went and sat behind it. I guess it was just too heavy and bulky for anyone to make off with. My books were all on their shelves. Nobody steals books but your friends. And there—

I could not believe it. I got to my feet again and crossed the room to stare at close range.

Yoshitoshi Mori's beautiful woodcut hung right where it had always been, clean, stark, elegant, violent. To think that no one had made off with one of my most prized possessions. . . .

Clean?

I scrutinized it. I ran my finger along the frame.

Too clean. It bore none of the dust and grit which covered everything else in the house.

I checked it for trip wires, found none, removed it from its hook, lowered it.

No, the wall was no lighter behind it. It matched the rest of the wall perfectly.

I put Mori's work on the window seat and returned to my desk. I was troubled, as someone doubtless intended me to be. Someone had obviously removed it and taken good care of it—a thing for which I was not ungrateful—and then only just recently restored it. It was as if my return had been anticipated.

Which should be adequate reason for immediate flight, I suppose. But that was silly. If it was part of some trap, it had already been sprung. I jerked the automatic from my jacket pocket and tucked it behind my belt. I had not even known that I would be coming back

myself. It was just something I had decided to do since I had had
some time on my hands. I was not even certain as to why I had
wanted to see the place again.

So this was some sort of contingency arrangement. If I should
come by the old homestead, it might be to obtain the only thing in
the place worth having. So preserve it and display it so that I will
have to take notice. All right, I had. I had not been attacked yet, so
it did not seem a trap. What then?

A message. Some sort of a message.

What? How? And who?

The safest place in the house, had it remained unravaged, should
still be the safe. It was not beyond any of my siblings' skill. I moved
to the rear wall, pressed the panel loose, and swung it out. I spun the
dial through its combination, stepped back, opened the door with my
old swagger stick.

No explosion. Good. Not that I had expected any.

There had been nothing of any great value inside—a few hundred
dollars in cash, some bonds, receipts, correspondence.

An envelope. A fresh, white envelope lay in plain sight. I did not
remember it.

My name upon it, written in an elegant hand. Not with ballpoint
either.

It contained a letter and a card.

Brother Corwin, the letter said, *If you are reading this, then we
still think enough alike for me to be able to anticipate you somewhat.
I thank you for the loan of the woodcut—one of two possible
reasons, as I see it, for your returning to this squalid shadow. I am
loathe to relinquish it, as our tastes are also somewhat akin and it
has graced my chambers for several years now. There is something
to the subject that strikes a familiar chord. Its return is to be taken as
evidence of my good will and a bid for your attention. In that I must
be honest with you if I am to stand a chance of convincing you of
anything, I will not apologize for what has been done. My only
regret, actually, is that I did not kill you when I should have. Vanity
it was, that played me for a fool. While time may have healed your
eyes, I doubt it will ever significantly alter our feelings for one another. Your letter—"I'll be back"—lies upon my writing table at this
moment. Had I written it, I know that I would be back. Some things
being equal between us, I anticipate your return, and not without*

somewhat of apprehension. Knowing you for no fool, I contemplate your arriving in force. And here is where vanity is paid of present pride. I would have peace between us, Corwin, for the sake of the realm, not my own. Strong forces out of Shadow have come to beset Amber regularly, and I do not fully understand their nature. Against these forces, the most formidable in my memory ever to assail Amber, the family has united behind me. I would like to have your support in this struggle. Failing that, I request that you forbear invading me for a time. If you elect to assist, I will require no homage of you, simply acknowledgment of my leadership for the duration of the crisis. You will be accorded your normal honors. It is important that you contact me to see the truth of what I say. As I have failed to reach you by means of your Trump, I enclose my own for your use. While the possibility that I am lying to you is foremost in your mind, I give you my word that I am not.—Eric, Lord of Amber.

I reread it and chuckled. What did he think curses were for, anyway?

No good, my brother. It was kind of you to think of me in your moment of need—and I believe you, never doubt it, for we are all of us honorable men—but our meeting will come according to my schedule, not yours. As for Amber, I am not unmindful of her needs, and I will deal with them in my own time and fashion. You make the mistake, Eric, of considering yourself necessary. The graveyards are filled with men who thought they could not be replaced. I will wait though, to tell you this, face to face.

I tucked his letter and the Trump in my jacket pocket. I killed my cigarette in the dirty ashtray on my desk. Then I fetched some linen from the bedroom to wrap my combatants. They would wait for me in a safer place, this time.

As I passed through the house again, I wondered why I had come back, really. I thought of some of the people I had known when I had lived there, and wondered whether they ever thought of me, whether they wondered what had become of me. I would never know, of course.

Night had begun and the sky was clear and its first stars bright as I stepped outside and locked the door behind me. I went around to the side and returned the key to its place beneath the patio. Then I mounted the hill.

When I looked back from the top, the house seemed to have shrunken there in the darkness, to have become a piece of the desolation, like an empty beer can tossed beside the road. I crossed over and down, heading across a field toward the place where I had parked, wishing I had not looked back.

IX

Ganelon and I departed Switzerland in a pair of trucks. We had driven them there from Belgium, and I had taken the rifles in mine. Figuring ten pounds per piece, the three hundred had come to around a ton and a half, which was not bad. After we took on the ammo, we still had plenty of room for fuel and other supplies. We had taken a short cut through Shadow, of course, to avoid the people who wait around borders to delay traffic. We departed in the same fashion, with me in the lead to open the way, so to speak.

I led us through a land of dark hills and narrow villages, where the only vehicles we passed were horse-drawn. When the sky grew bright lemon, the beasts of burden were striped and feathered. We drove for hours, finally encountering the black road, paralleling it for a time, then heading off in another direction. The skies went through a dozen shiftings, and the contours of the land melted and merged from hill to plain and back again. We crept along poor roads and skidded on flats as smooth and hard as glass. We edged our way across a mountain's face and skirted a wine-dark sea. We passed through storms and fogs.

It took me half a day to find them again, or a shadow so close that it made no difference. Yes, those whom I had exploited once before. They were short fellows, very hairy, very dark, with long incisors and retractable claws. But they had trigger fingers, and they worshiped me. They were overjoyed at my return. It little mattered that five years earlier I had sent the cream of their manhood off to die in a strange land. The gods are not to be questioned, but loved, honored, and obeyed. They were quite disappointed that I only wanted a few hundred. I had to turn away thousands of volunteers. The morality of it did not especially trouble me this time. One way of looking at it might be that by employing this group I was seeing to it that the others had not died in vain. Of course I did not look at it that way, but I enjoy exercises in sophistry. I suppose I might also consider them mercenaries being paid in spiritual coin. What difference did it make whether they fought for money or for a belief? I was capable of supplying either one when I needed troops.

Actually, though, these would be pretty safe, being the only ones in the place with fire power. My ammo was still inert in their homeland, however, and it took several days of marching through Shadow to reach a land sufficiently like Amber for it to become functional. The only catch was that shadows follow a law of congruency of correspondences, so that the place actually was close to Amber. This kept me somewhat on edge throughout their training. It was unlikely that a brother would blunder through that shadow. Still, worse coincidences have occurred.

We drilled for close to three weeks before I decided we were ready. Then, on a bright, crisp morning, we broke camp and moved on into Shadow, the columns of troops following behind the trucks. The trucks would cease to function when we neared Amber—they were already giving us some trouble—but they might as well be used to haul the equipment as far along as possible.

This time, I intended to go over the top of Kolvir from the north, rather than essay its seaward face again. All of the men had an understanding of the layout, and the disposition of the rifle squads had already been determined and run through in practice.

We halted for lunch, ate well, and continued on, the shadows slowly slipping away about us. The sky became a dark but brilliant blue, the sky of Amber. The earth was black among rocks and the bright green of the grass. The trees and the shrubs had a moist lucency to their foliage. The air was sweet and clean.

By nightfall, we were passing among the massive trees at the fringes of Arden. We bivouacked there, posting a very heavy guard. Ganelon, now wearing khakis and a beret, sat with me long into the night, going over the maps I had drawn. We still had about forty miles to go before we hit the mountains.

The trucks gave out the following afternoon. They went through several transformations, stalled repeatedly, and finally refused to start at all. We pushed them into a ravine and cut branches to cover them over. We distributed the ammo and the rest of the rations and continued on.

We departed the hard, dirt roadway after that and worked our way through the woods themselves. As I still knew them well, it was less of a problem than it might have been. It slowed us, naturally, but lessened chances of surprise by one of Julian's patrols. The trees were quite large, as we were well into Arden proper, and the topography sprang back into mind as we moved.

We encountered nothing more menacing than foxes, deer, rabbits, and squirrels that day. The smells of the place and its green, gold, and brown brought back thoughts of happier times. Near sunset, I scaled a forest giant and was able to make out the range that held Kolvir. A storm was playing about its peaks just then and its clouds hid their highest portions.

The following noon we ran into one of Julian's patrols. I do not really know who surprised whom, or who was more surprised. The firing broke out almost immediately. I shouted myself hoarse stopping it, as everyone seemed anxious to try out his weapon on a live target. It was a small group—a dozen and a half men—and we got all of them. We suffered only one minor casualty, from one of our men wounding another—or perhaps the man had wounded himself. I never got the story straight. We moved on quickly then, because we had made a hell of a racket and I had no idea as to the disposition of other forces in the vicinity.

We gained considerable distance and altitude by nightfall, and the mountains were in sight whenever there was a clear line of vision. The storm clouds still clung to their peaks. My troops were excited over the day's slaughter and took a long while getting to sleep that night.

The next day we reached the foothills, successfully avoiding two patrols. I pushed us on and up well after nightfall, to reach a place of cover I had had in mind. We bedded down at an altitude perhaps half a mile higher than we had the previous night. We were under the cloud cover, but there was no rainfall, despite a constant atmospheric tension of the sort that precedes a storm. I did not sleep well that night. I dreamed of the burning cat head, and of Lorraine.

In the morning, we moved out under gray skies, and I pushed the troops remorselessly, heading steadily upward. We heard the sounds of distant thunder, and the air was alive and electric.

About mid-morning, as I led our file up a twisted, rocky route, I heard a shout from behind me, followed by several bursts of gunfire. I headed back immediately.

A small knot of men, Ganelon among them, stood staring down at something, talking in low voices. I pushed my way through.

I could not believe it. Never in my memory had one been seen this near to Amber. Perhaps twelve feet in length, bearing that terrible parody of a human face on the shoulders of a lion, eagle-like wings folded above its now bloody sides, a still-twitching tail like that of a scorpion, I had glimpsed the manticora once in isles far to the south, a frightful beast that had always held a spot near the top of my unclean list.

"It tore Rall in half, it tore Rall in half," one of the men kept repeating.

About twenty paces away, I saw what was left of Rall. We covered him over with a tarp and weighted it down with rocks. That was really about all that we could do. If nothing else, it served to restore a quality of wariness that had seemed to vanish after the previous day's easy victory. The men were silent and cautious as we continued on our way.

"Quite a thing, that," Ganelon said. "Has it the intelligence of a man?"

"I do not really know."

"I've a funny, nervous feeling, Corwin. As though something terrible is about to happen. I don't know how else to put it."

"I know."

"You feel it, too?"

"Yes."

He nodded.

"Maybe it's the weather," I said.

He nodded again, more slowly.

The sky continued to darken as we climbed, and the thunder never ceased. Flashes of heat lightning occurred in the west, and the winds grew stronger. Looking up, I could see great masses of clouds about the higher peaks. Black, bird-like shapes were constantly outlined against them.

We encountered another manticora later, but we dispatched it with no damage to ourselves. About an hour later, we were attacked by a flock of large, razor-beaked birds, the like of which I had never seen before. We succeeded in driving them off, but this, too, disturbed me.

We kept climbing, wondering when the storm was going to begin. The winds increased in velocity.

It grew quite dark, though I knew the sun had not yet set. The air took on a misty, hazy quality as we neared the cloud clusters. A feeling of dampness worked its way into everything. The rocks were more slippery. I was tempted to call a halt, but we were still a good distance from Kolvir and I did not want to strain the rations situation, which I had calculated quite carefully.

We achieved perhaps another four miles and several thousand feet in elevation before we were forced to stop. It was pitch black by then, the only illumination at all coming from the intermittent flashes of lightning. We camped in a large circle on a hard, bare slope, sentries all about the perimeter. The thunder came like long flourishes of martial music. The temperature plummeted. Even had I permitted fires, there was nothing burnable about. We settled down for a cold, clammy, dark time.

The manticoras attacked several hours later, sudden and silent. Seven men died and we killed sixteen of the beasts. I have no idea how many others fled. I cursed Eric as I bound my wounds and wondered from what shadow he had drawn the things.

During what passed for morning, we advanced perhaps five miles toward Kolvir before bearing off to the west. It was one of three possible routes we could follow, and I had always considered it the best for a possible attack. The birds came to plague us again, several times, with greater numbers and persistency. Shooting a few of them, though, was all it took to rout the entire flock.

Finally, we rounded the base of a huge escarpment, our way taking us outward and upward through thunder and mist, until we were afforded a sudden vista, sweeping down and out for dozens of miles across the Valley of Garnath that lay to our right.

I called a halt and moved forward to observe.

When last I had seen that once lovely valley, it had been a twisted wilderness. Now, things were even worse. The black road cut through it, running to the base of Kolvir itself, where it halted. A battle was raging within the valley. Mounted forces swirled together, engaged, wheeled away. Lines of foot soldiers advanced, met, fell back. The lightning kept flashing and striking among them. The dark birds swept about them like ashes on the wind.

The dampness lay like a cold blanket. The echoes of the thunder bounced about the peaks. I stared, puzzling, at the conflict below.

The distance was too great for me to determine the combatants. At first it occurred to me that someone else might be about the same thing I was—that perhaps Bleys had survived and returned with a new army.

But no. These were coming in from the west, along the black road,

And I saw now that the birds accompanied them, and bounding forms that were neither horses nor men. The manticoras, perhaps.

The lightnings fell upon them as they came, scattering, burning, blasting. As I realized that they never struck near the defenders, I recalled that Eric had apparently gained some measure of control over that device known as the Jewel of Judgment, with which Dad had exercised his will upon the weather about Amber. Eric had employed it against us with considerable effect five years earlier.

So the forces from Shadow about which I had been hearing reports, were even stronger than I had thought. I had envisioned harassment, but not a pitched battle at the foot of Kolvir. I looked down at the movements within the blackness. The road seemed almost to writhe from the activity about it.

Ganelon came and stood beside me. He was silent for a long while.

I did not want him to ask me, but I felt powerless to say it except as answer to a question.

"What now, Corwin?"

"We must increase the pace," I said. "I want to be in Amber tonight."

We moved again. The going was better for a time, and that helped. The storm without rain continued, its lightnings and thunders increasing in brilliance and volume. We moved through a constant twilight.

When we came to a safe-seeming place later that afternoon—a place within five miles of the northern skirts of Amber—I halted us again, for rest and a final meal. We had to scream at one another in order to be heard, so I could not address the men. I simply passed the word along concerning our proximity and the need for readiness.

I took my rations with me and scouted on ahead while the others rested. About a mile farther along, I mounted a steep upturn, pausing when I achieved its crest. There was a battle of some sort in progress on the slopes ahead.

I kept out of sight and observed. A force out of Amber was engaged with a larger body of attackers which must have either preceded us up the slope or arrived by different means. I suspected the latter, inasmuch as we had seen no signs of recent passage. The engagement explained our own good fortune in not encountering defensive patrols on the way up.

I moved nearer. While the attackers could have come up by one of the two other routes, I saw additional evidence that this need not have been the case. They swept in from the west like great gusts of wind-blown leaves. The aerial movement I had witnessed from the distance had been of greater variety than the belligerent bird life. The attackers came in on winged, two-legged, dragon-like creatures, the closest parallel with which I was familiar being a heraldic beast, the wyvern. I had never seen a non-decorative wyvern before, but then I had never felt any great desire to go looking for one.

Among the defenders were numerous archers, who took a deadly toll of those in flight. Sheets of pure hell erupted among them also, as the lightnings flashed and flared, sending them like cinders toward the ground. But still they came on, landing, so that both man and beast could attack those entrenched. I looked for and located the pulsating glow given off by the Jewel of Judgment when it has been tuned to operate. It came from the midst of the largest body of defenders, dug in near the base of a high cliff.

I stared and studied, focusing on the wearer of the gem. Yes, there could be no doubt. It was Eric.

On my belly now, I crawled even farther. I saw the leader of the nearest party of defenders behead a landing wyvern with a single sword stroke. With his left hand, he seized the harness of its rider and hurled him over thirty feet, out beyond the lip-like brink of the place. As he turned then to shout an order, I saw that it was Gérard. He appeared to be leading a flanking assault on a mass of the attackers who were assailing the forces at the foot of the cliff. On its far side, a similar body of troops was doing likewise. Another of my brothers?

I wondered how long the battle had been in progress, both in the valley and here above. Quite a while, I guess, considering the duration of the unnatural storm.

I moved to the right, turning my attention to the west. The battle in the valley continued unabated. From this distance, it was impossible to tell who was who, let alone who was winning. I could see, though, that no new forces were arriving from out of the west to supplement the attackers.

I was perplexed as to my own best course of action. Clearly, I could not attack Eric when he was engaged in anything this crucial to the defense of Amber herself. Waiting to pick up the pieces afterward might be wisest. However, I could already feel the rat teeth of doubt at work on that idea.

Even without reinforcements for the attackers, the outcome of the encounter was by no means clear-cut. The invaders were strong, numerous. I had no idea as to what Eric might have in reserve. At that moment, it was impossible for me to gauge whether war bonds for Amber would be a good investment. If Eric lost, it would then be necessary for me to take on the invaders myself, after much of Amber's manpower had been wasted.

If I were to move in now with automatic weapons, there was little doubt in my mind that we would crush the wyvern-riders quickly. For that matter, one or more of my brothers had to be down in the valley. A gateway for some of my troops could be set up by means of the Trumps. It would surprise whatever was down there for Amber suddenly to come up with riflemen.

I returned my attention to the conflict nearer at hand. No, it was not going well. I speculated as to the results of my intervening. Eric would certainly be in no position to turn on me. Besides any sympathy that might be mine for what he had put me through, I would be responsible for pulling his nuts out of the fire. While he would be grateful for the relief, he would not be too happy over the general sentiment this would arouse. No, indeed. I would be back in Amber with a very deadly personal bodyguard and a lot of good will going for me. An intriguing thought. It would provide a far smoother route to my objective than the brutal frontal assault culminating in regicide that I had had in mind.

Yes.

I felt myself smiling. I was about to become a hero.

I must grant myself a small measure of grace, however. Given the choice only between Amber with Eric on the throne and Amber fallen, there is no question but that my decision would have been the same, to attack. Things were not going well enough to be certain, and while it would work to my advantage to save the day, my own advantage was not, ultimately, essential. I could not hate thee, Eric, so much, loved I not Amber more.

I withdrew and hurried back down the slope, flashes of lightning hurling my shadow in every which direction.

I halted at the periphery of my encampment. At its farther edge, Ganelon stood in shouting converse with a lone horseman, and I recognized the horse.

I advanced, and at a sign from its rider the horse moved forward, winding its way among the troops, heading in my direction. Ganelon shook his head and followed.

The rider was Dara. As soon as she was within earshot, I shouted at her.

"What the hell are you doing here?"

She dismounted, smiling, and stood before me.

"I wanted to come to Amber," she said. "So I did."

"How did you get here?"

"I followed Grandpa," she said. "It is easier to follow someone through Shadow, I discovered, than to do it yourself."

"Benedict is here?"

She nodded.

"Down below. He is directing the forces in the valley. Julian is there, too."

Ganelon came up and stood near.

"She said that she followed us up here," he shouted. "She has been behind us for a couple days."

"Is that true?" I asked.

She nodded again, still smiling.

"It was not hard to do."

"But why did you do it?"

"To get into Amber, of course! I want to walk the Pattern! That is where you are going, isn't it?"

"Of course it is. But there happens to be a war in the way!"

"What are you going to do about it?"

"Win it, of course!"

"Good. I'll wait."

I cursed for a few moments to give myself time to think, then, "Where were you when Benedict returned?" I asked.

The smile went away.

"I do not know," she said. "I went out riding after you left, and I stayed away the entire day. I wanted to be alone to think. When I returned in the evening, he was not there. I rode again the following day. I traveled quite a distance, and when it grew dark I decided to camp out. I do that often. The next afternoon, as I was returning home, I came to the top of a hill and saw him passing below, heading to the east. I decided to follow him. The way led through Shadow, I understand that now—and you were right about it being easier to follow. I do not know how long it took. Time got all mixed up. He came here, and I recognized it from the picture on one of the cards.

He met with Julian in a wood to the north, and they returned together to that battle below." She gestured toward the valley. "I remained in the forest for several days, not knowing what to do. I was afraid of getting lost if I tried to backtrack. Then I saw your force climbing the mountains. I saw you and I saw Ganelon at their head. I knew that Amber lay that way, and I followed. I waited until now to approach, because I wanted you to be too near to Amber to send me back when I did."

"I don't believe you are telling me the whole truth," I said, "but I haven't the time to care. We are going ahead now, and there will be fighting. The safest thing for you will be to remain here. I will assign you a couple of bodyguards."

"I do not want them!"

"I don't care what you want. You are going to have them. When the fighting is over I will send for you."

I turned then and selected two men at random, ordering them to remain behind and guard her. They did not seem overjoyed at the prospect.

"What are those weapons your men bear?" Dara asked.

"Later," I said. "I'm busy."

I relayed a sketchy briefing and ordered my squads.

"You seem to have a very small number of men," she said.

"They are sufficient," I replied. "I will see you later."

I left her there with her guards.

We moved back along the route I had taken. The thunder ceased as we advanced, and the silence became less a thing of relief than of suspense to me. The twilight resettled about us, and I perspired within the damp blanket of the air.

I called a halt before we reached the first point from which I had observed the action. I returned to it then, accompanied by Ganelon.

The wyvern-riders were all over the place and their beasts fought along with them. They were pressing the defenders back against the cliff face. I sought for but could not locate Eric or the glow of his jewel.

"Which ones are the enemy?" Ganelon asked me.

"The beast-riders."

They were all of them landing now that heaven's artillery had let up. As soon as they struck the solid surface, they charged forward. I searched among the defenders, but Gérard was no longer in sight.

"Bring up the troops," I said, raising my rifle. "Tell them to get the beasts and the riders both."

Ganelon withdrew, and I took aim at a descending wyvern, fired, and watched its swoop turn into a sudden flurry of pinions. It struck against the slope and began to flop about. I fired again.

The beast began to burn as it died. Soon I had three bonfires going. I crawled up to my second previous position. Secure, I took aim and fired once more.

I got another, but by then some of them were turning in my direction. I fired the rest of my ammo and hastened to reload. Several of them had begun moving toward me by then. They were quite fast.

I managed to stop them and was reloading again when the first rifle squad arrived. We put down a heavier fire, and began to advance as the others came up.

It was all over within ten minutes. Within the first five they had apparently realized that they hadn't a chance, and they began to flee back toward the ledge, launching themselves into space, becoming airborne again. We shot them down as they ran, and burning flesh and smoldering bones lay everywhere about us.

The moist rock rose sheer to our left, its summit lost in the clouds, so that it seemed as if it might tower endlessly above us. The winds still whipped the smoke and the mist, and the rocks were smeared and splotched with blood. As we had advanced, firing, the forces of Amber quickly realized that we represented assistance and began to push forward from their position at the base of the cliff. I saw that they were being led by my brother Caine. For a moment our eyes locked together across the distance, then he plunged ahead into the fray.

Scattered groups of Amberites united into a second force as the attackers fell back. Actually, they limited our field of fire when they attacked the far flank of the wizened beast-men and their wyverns, but I had no way of getting word of this to them. We drew closer, and our firing was accurate.

A small knot of men remained at the base of the cliff. I had a feeling they were guarding Eric, and that he had possibly been wounded, since the storm effects had ceased abruptly. I worked my own way off in that direction.

The firing was already beginning to die down as I drew near the group, and I was hardly aware of what happened next until it was too late.

Something big came rushing up from behind and was by me in an instant. I hit the ground and rolled, bringing my rifle to bear automatically. My finger did not tighten on the trigger, however. It was Dara, who had just plunged past me on horseback. She turned and laughed as I screamed at her.

"Get back down there! Damn you! You'll be killed!"

"I'll see you in Amber!" she cried, and she shot on across the grisly rock and made it up the trail that lay beyond.

I was furious. But there was nothing I could do about it just then. Snarling, I got back to my feet and continued on.

As I advanced upon the group, I heard my name spoken several times. Heads turned in my direction. People moved aside to let me pass. I recognized many of them, but I paid them no heed.

I think that I saw Gérard at about the same time that he saw me. He had been kneeling in their midst, and he rose to his feet and waited. His face was expressionless.

As I drew nearer, I saw that it was as I had suspected. He had been kneeling to tend an injured man who rested upon the ground. It was Eric.

I nodded to Gérard as I came up beside him, and I looked down at Eric. My feelings were quite mixed. The blood from his several chest wounds was very bright and there was a lot of it. The Jewel of Judgment, which still hung on a chain about his neck, was covered with it. Eerily, it continued its faint, glowing pulsation, heart-like beneath the gore. Eric's eyes were closed, his head resting upon a rolled-up cloak. His breathing was labored.

I knelt, unable to take my eyes off that ashen face. I tried to push my hate aside just a little, since he was obviously dying, so that I might have a better chance to understand this man who was my brother for the moments that remained to him. I found that I could muster up something of sympathy by considering all that he was losing along with his life and wondering whether it would have been me lying there if I had come out on top five years earlier. I tried to think of something in his favor, and all I could come up with were the epitaph-like words, *He died fighting for Amber.* That was something, though. The phrase kept running through my mind.

His eyes tightened, flickered, opened. His face remained without expression as his eyes focused on mine. I wondered whether he even recognized me.

But he said my name, and then, "I knew that it would be you." He paused for a couple of breaths and went on, "They saved you some trouble, didn't they?"

I did not reply. He already knew the answer.

"Your turn will come one day," he continued. "Then we will be peers." He chuckled and realized too late that he should not have. He went into an unpleasant spasm of moist coughing. When it passed he glared at me.

"I could feel your curse," he said. "All around me. The whole time. You didn't even have to die to make it stick."

Then, as if reading my thoughts, he smiled faintly and said, "No, I'm not going to give you my death curse. I've reserved that for the enemies of Amber—out there." He gestured with his eyes. He pronounced it then, in a whisper, and I shuddered to overhear it.

He returned his gaze to my face and stared for a moment. Then he plucked at the chain about his neck.

"The Jewel . . ." he said. "You take it with you to the center of the Pattern. Hold it up. Very close—to an eye. Stare into it—and consider it a place. Try to project yourself—inside. You don't go. But there is—experience. . . . Afterward, you know how to use it. . . ."

"How—?" I began, but stopped. He had already told me how to attune to it. Why ask him to waste his breath on how he had figured it out?

But he caught it and managed, "Dworkin's notes . . . under fireplace . . . my—"

Then he was taken with another coughing spell and the blood came out of his nose and his mouth. He sucked in a deep breath and heaved himself into a sitting position, eyes rolling wildly.

"Acquit yourself as well as I have—bastard!" he said, then fell into my arms and heaved out his final, bloody breath.

I held him for several moments, then lowered him into his former position. His eyes were still open, and I reached out and closed them. Almost automatically, I put his hands together atop the now lifeless gem. I had no stomach to take it from him at that moment. I stood then, removed my cloak, and covered him with it.

Turning, I saw that all of them were staring at me. Familiar faces, many of them. Some strange ones mixed in. So many who had been there that night when I had come to dinner in chains. . . .

No. It was not the time to think of that. I pushed it from my mind. The shooting had stopped, and Ganelon was calling the troops back and ordering some sort of formation.

I walked forward.

I passed among the Amberites. I passed among the dead. I walked by my own troops and moved to the edge of the cliff.

In the valley below me, the fighting continued, the cavalry flowing like turbulent waters, merging, eddying, receding, the infantry still swarming like insects.

I drew forth the cards I had taken from Benedict. I removed his own from the deck. It shimmered before me, and after a time there was contact.

He was mounted on the same red and black horse on which he had pursued me. He was in motion and there was fighting all about him. Seeing that he confronted another horseman, I remained still. He spoke but a single word.

"Bide," he said.

He dispatched his opponent with two quick movements of his blade. Then he wheeled his mount and began to withdraw from the fray. I saw that his horse's reins had been lengthened and were looped and tied loosely about the remainder of his right arm. It took him over ten minutes to remove himself to a place of relative calm. When he had, he regarded me, and I could tell that he was also studying the prospect that lay at my back.

"Yes, I am on the heights," I told him. "We have won. Eric died in the battle."

He continued to stare, waiting for me to go on. His face betrayed no emotion.

"We won because I brought riflemen," I said. "I finally found an explosive agent that functions here."

His eyes narrowed and he nodded. I felt that he realized immediately what the stuff was and where it had come from.

"While there are many things I want to discuss with you," I continued, "I want to take care of the enemy first. If you will hold the contact, I will send you several hundred riflemen."

He smiled.

"Hurry," he said.

I shouted for Ganelon, and he answered me from only a few paces away. I told him to line the troops up, single file. He nodded and went off, shouting orders.

As we waited, I said, "Benedict, Dara is here. She was able to follow you through Shadow when you rode in from Avalon. I want—"

He bared his teeth and shouted: "Who the hell is this Dara you keep talking about? I never heard of her till you came along! Please tell me! I would really like to know!"

I smiled faintly.

"It's no good," I said, shaking my head. "I know all about her, though I have told no one else that you've a great granddaughter."

His lips parted involuntarily and his eyes were suddenly wide.

"Corwin," he said, "you are either mad or deceived. I've no such descendant that I know of. As for anyone following me here through Shadow, I came in on Julian's Trump."

Of course. My only excuse for not tripping her up immediately was my preoccupation with the conflict. Benedict would have been notified of the battle by means of the Trumps. Why should he waste time traveling when an instant means of transport was at hand?

"Damn!" I said. "She is in Amber by now! Listen, Benedict! I am going to get Gérard or Caine over here to handle the transfer of the troops to you. Ganelon will come through, also. Give them their orders through him."

I looked around, saw Gérard talking with several of the nobles. I shouted for him with a desperate urgency. His head turned quickly. Then he began running in my direction.

"Corwin! What is it?" Benedict was shouting.

"I don't know! But something is very wrong!"

I thrust the Trump at Gérard as he came up.

"See that the troops get through to Benedict!" I said. "Is Random in the palace?"

"Yes."

"Free or confined?"

"Free—more or less. There will be some guards about. Eric still doesn't—didn't trust him."

I turned.

"Ganelon," I called out. "Do what Gérard here tells you. He is going to send you to Benedict—down there." I gestured. "See that the men follow Benedict's orders. I have to get into Amber now."

"All right," he called back.

Gérard headed in his direction, and I fanned the Trumps once more. I located Random's and began to concentrate. At that moment, it finally began to rain.

I made contact almost immediately.

"Hello, Random," I said, as soon as his image came to life. "Remember me?"

"Where are you?" he asked.

"In the mountains," I told him. "We just won this part of the battle, and I am sending Benedict the help he needs to clean up in the valley. Now, though, I need your help. Bring me across."

"I don't know, Corwin. Eric—"

"Eric is dead."

"Then who is in charge?"

"Who do you think? Bring me across!"

He nodded quickly and extended his hand. I reached out and clasped it. I stepped forward. I stood beside him on a balcony overlooking one of the courtyards. The railing was of white marble, and not much was blooming down below. We were two stories up.

I swayed and he seized my arm.

"You're hurt!" he said.

I shook my head, only just then realizing how tired I was. I had not slept very much the past few nights. That, and everything else . . .

"No," I said, glancing down at the gory mess that was my shirt front. "Just tired. The blood is Eric's."

He ran a hand through his straw-colored hair and pursed his lips.

"So you *did* finally nail him . . ." he said softly.

I shook my head again.

"No. He was already dying when I got to him. Come with me now! Hurry! It is important!"

"Where to? What is the matter?"

"To the Pattern," I said. "Why? I am not certain, but I know that it is important. Come on!"

We entered the palace, moving toward the nearest stairwell. There were two guards at its head, but they came to attention as we approached and did not attempt to interfere with our passage.

"I'm glad it's true about your eyes," Random said as we headed down. "Do you see all right?"

"Yes. I hear that you are still married."

"Yes. I am."

When we reached the ground floor, we hurried to the right. There had been another pair of guards at the foot of the stair, but they did not move to stop us.

"Yes," he repeated, as we headed toward the center of the palace. "You are surprised, aren't you?"

"Yes. I thought you were going to get the year over with and be done with it."

"So did I," he said. "But I fell in love with her. I really did."

"Stranger things have happened."

We crossed the marble dining hall and entered the long, narrow corridor that led far back through shadows and dust. I suppressed a shudder as I thought of my condition the last time I had come this way.

"She really cares for me," he said. "Like nobody else ever has before."

"I'm glad for you," I said.

We reached the door that opened onto the platform heading the long, spiral stairway down. It was open. We passed through and began the descent.

"I'm not," he said, as we hurried around and around. "I didn't want to fall in love. Not then. We've been prisoners the whole time, you know. How can she be proud of that?"

"That is over now," I said. "You became a prisoner because you followed me and tried to kill Eric, didn't you?"

"Yes. Then she joined me here."

"I will not forget," I said.

We rushed on. I was a great distance down, and there were only lanterns every forty feet or so. It was a huge, natural cavern. I wondered whether anyone knew how many tunnels and corridors it contained. I suddenly felt myself overwhelmed with pity for any poor wretches rotting in its dungeons, for whatever reasons. I resolved to release them all or find something better to do with them.

Long minutes passed. I could see the flickering of the torches and the lanterns below.

"There is a girl," I said, "and her name is Dara. She told me she was Benedict's great-granddaughter and gave me reason to believe it. I told her somewhat concerning Shadow, reality, and the Pattern. She does possess some power over Shadow, and she was anxious to walk the Pattern. When last I saw her, she was headed this way. Now Benedict swears she is not his. Suddenly I am fearful. I want to keep her from the Pattern. I want to question her."

"Strange," he said. "Very. I agree with you. Do you think she might be there now?"

"If she is not, then I feel she will be along soon."

We finally reached the floor, and I began to raise through the shadows toward the proper tunnel.

"Wait!" Random cried.

I halted and turned. It took me a moment to locate him, as he was back behind the stairs. I returned.

My question did not reach my lips. I saw that he knelt beside a large, bearded man.

"Dead," he said. "A very thin blade. Good thrust. Just recently."

"Come on!"

We both ran to the tunnel and turned up it. Its seventh side passage was the one we wanted. I drew Grayswandir as we neared it, for that great, dark, metal-bound door was standing ajar.

I sprang through. Random was right behind me. The floor of that enormous room is black and looks to be smooth as glass, although it is not slippery. The Pattern burns upon it, within it, an intricate, shimmering maze of curved lines, perhaps a hundred and fifty yards long. We halted at its edge, staring.

Something was out there, walking it. I felt that old, tingling chill the thing always gives me as I watched. Was it Dara? It was difficult for me to make out the figure within the fountains of sparks that spewed constantly about it. Whoever it was had to be of the blood royal, for it was common knowledge that anyone else would be destroyed by the Pattern, and this individual had already made it past the Grand Curve and was negotiating the complicated series of arcs that led toward the Final Veil.

The firefly form seemed to change shape as it moved. For a time, my senses kept rejecting the tiny subliminal glimpses that I knew must be coming through to me. I heard Random gasp beside me, and it seemed to breach my subconscious dam. A horde of impressions flooded my mind.

It seemed to tower hugely in that always unsubstantial-seeming chamber. Then shrink, die down, almost to nothing. It seemed a slim woman for a moment—possibly Dara, her hair lightened by the glow, streaming, crackling with static electricity. Then it was not hair, but great, curved horns from some wide, uncertain brow, whose crooklegged owner struggled to shuffle hoofs along the blazing way. Then something else . . . An enormous cat . . . A faceless woman

. . . A bright-winged thing of indescribable beauty . . . A tower of ashes . . .

"Dara!" I cried out. "Is that you?"

My voice echoed back, and that was all. Whoever/whatever it was struggled now with the Final Veil. My muscles strained forward in unwilling sympathy with the effort.

Finally, it burst through.

Yes, it was Dara! Tall and magnificent now. Both beautiful and somehow horrible at the same time. The sight of her tore at the fabric of my mind. Her arms were upraised in exultation and an inhuman laughter flowed from her lips. I wanted to look away, yet I could not move. Had I truely held, caressed, made move to—*that?* I was mightily repelled and simultaneously attracted as I had never been before. I could not understand this overwhelming ambivalence.

Then she looked at me.

The laughter ceased. Her altered voice rang out.

"Lord Corwin, are you liege of Amber now?"

From somewhere, I managed a reply.

"For all practical purposes," I said.

"Good! Then behold your nemesis!"

"Who are you? *What* are you?"

"You will never know," she said. "It is just exactly too late now."

"I do not understand. What do you mean?"

"Amber," she said, "will be destroyed."

And she vanished.

"What the hell," said Random then, "was that?"

I shook my head.

"I do not know. I really do not know. And I feel that it is the most important thing in the world that we find out."

He gripped my arm.

"Corwin," he said. "She—it—meant it. And it may be possible, you know."

I nodded.

"I know."

"What are we going to do now?"

I resheathed Grayswandir and turned back toward the door.

"Pick up the pieces," I said. "I have what I thought I always wanted within my grasp now, and I must secure it. And I cannot wait for what is to come. I must seek it out and stop it before it ever reaches Amber."

"Do you know where to seek it?" he asked.

We turned up the tunnel.

"I believe it lies at the other end of the black road," I said.

We moved on through the cavern to the stairs where the dead man lay and went round and round above him in the dark.